c. 1

the UNSEEN
ELEANOR

book 1

Copyright © 2014 by Johnny Worthen

First Trade Paperback Edition: July 2014

For information on subsidiary rights, please contact the publisher at rights@jollyfishpress.com. For a complete list of our wholesalers and distributors, please visit our website at www.jollyfishpress.com.

For information, address Jolly Fish Press, PO Box 1773, Provo, UT 84603-1773.

Printed in the United States of America

THIS TITLE IS ALSO AVAILABLE AS AN EBOOK.

Library of Congress Cataloging-in-Publication Data

Worthen, Johnny, 1966-
Eleanor / Johnny Worthen.
    pages cm. -- (The unseen)
Summary: "Shapeshifter Eleanor lives the life of a teenager in rural Wyoming until the only person who knows her secret shows up and challenges her existence and everything she hopes to be"-- Provided by publisher.
ISBN 978-1-939967-34-3 (paperback)
[1. Shapeshifting--Fiction. 2. Wyoming--Fiction.] I. Title.
PZ7.W887876El 2014
[Fic]--dc23

2014011699

10 9 8 7 6 5 4 3 2 1

For my mother.

the UNSEEN
E L E A N O R
book 1

a novel by
johnny worthen

JOLLY
FISH
PRESS
Provo, Utah

CHAPTER ONE

The coyote circled the campsite in ever tightening spirals. There were three people there; a man, a woman, and a child. The child was out of the box. The big ones, the adults, were still inside talking and clattering, making smells of bacon, milk, and pepper. The coyote discerned each distinct odor over the lingering sulfurous steam.

The child was female, seven summers at most. By size, she was at the upper end of what the coyote could bring down. It could kill the girl because the girl was a child. But that was dumb thinking. The big ones inside would not abandon the girl. Even dead.

It was not so hungry or foolish to actually attack the girl, not so hungry at all. A poacher had shot a moose from his car and the animal had died not far from here. There was meat there for a week at least. Enough to fatten up.

The coyote had been a coyote for so long that it hardly remembered not being a coyote. It did not want to forget its family. It was losing its history, its identity. It wanted to be safe, needed to survive, but it was time to take to a chance.

The coyote watched the girl skip through the morning

summer sunlight chanting a song it had heard before but couldn't remember.

It watched the girl wander out of the camp, collecting pinecones in her arms until they overflowed and she knelt to gather them again.

From the white camper drifted the smell of frying eggs. Camper. Yes. The thing was called a camper. The coyote remembered.

The little girl grew still and peered into the trees.

The coyote froze, letting its fur hide it in the undergrowth. It was tan, tawny, and copper-streaked. The blend made it nearly invisible against the forest background.

"Hello?" said the little girl.

The coyote remained motionless. It watched the girl with glassy, unblinking eyes and waited.

She had auburn hair, not wholly unlike the coyote's coat. Clean skin. Healthy size and weight. The child shrugged, giggled at something only she knew, and trotted off after more pinecones.

"Celeste," came a voice from the camper. "Don't go far. It's almost breakfast."

"'Kay," she called back.

When her back was toward it, the coyote padded closer. The girl turned around.

The coyote was out in the open but froze nonetheless.

"Doggy!" she cried. The coyote held still.

The girl took a tentative step forward. Her attention diverted, the pinecones spilled out over the ground again. The clatter sent the coyote bolting for cover.

"Doggy!" called the girl. "Doggy come back."

She loped to the bush where the coyote had run, but it was already gone.

It circled the campsite, head low, and watched the girl from a distance.

"Celeste, come on back," said a woman in the camper.

Shading her eyes with her hands, the girl searched for the coyote, turning all the way around. Finally, she shrugged her shoulders in an exaggerated gesture, a mimic of something she must have seen and hadn't yet perfected. Then she skipped back to the campsite.

Once out of the trees and in the clearing by the picnic table, she caught sight of the coyote behind an iron barbecue stand. She squatted down and held out her hand as if offering food.

Unmoving, the coyote watched her.

The girl shuffled forward in a squat, her hand outstretched.

Taking in every movement, studying every feature, remembering how it was done, the coyote studied the little girl. It smelled the air, listened for danger, and then took a cautious step toward Celeste.

The girl giggled, and instead of scaring the coyote, the sound cheered it.

The coyote was out of cover, ten feet from the camper. It knew it was in pistol range if a gun was at hand, and there was always a gun at hand.

"Doggy, come here. I won't hurt you."

It was not trust that moved the coyote closer to the girl—it did not even remember what that was. It was not hunger or fear, the only motivations that had moved it for over forty years. No, it was something unique and unnatural that stirred it. It was a yearning to take a chance at rejoining a world it had left nearly half a century before, a world that had taken everything from it. It was crazy madness, and the coyote felt every bit of that insanity as it defied its instincts, and crept closer to the squatting girl.

"Nice doggy," she cooed. "I'm just going to pet you. I'll be real careful."

Tense as a spring, its weight shifted for a sudden dash, the coyote stretched its neck and sniffed the girl's fingers.

The girl shuffled closer.

The coyote twitched where its animal instinct to run wrestled with the ludicrous longing to stay.

The girl touched the coyote's head and scratched between its ears. Though the coyote held her gaze in its cold unblinking stare, she was not afraid.

"You're nice," she said. "You don't bark or anything."

The coyote moved closer.

Celeste laughed.

The coyote lifted its muzzle up to her face and sniffed.

Celeste sniffed back. She rubbed her nose against the coyote's and giggled again.

The coyote inhaled the girl's breath, tasting her lungs, her heat, her blood.

Celeste threw her arms around the coyote and pulled it toward her in an ardent embrace. The sudden capture surprised the coyote and it yipped.

"Oh, I'm sorry," Celeste said, letting it go. "Sometimes I hug too hard. I know. I'm sorry."

"Celeste dear, what was that?" called the woman. "Come in now. It's breakfast."

Celeste looked over her shoulder to the camper and stood up.

"I've got to go now," she said. "I'll bring you some bacon after brunch, okay?" She started to go.

The coyote yipped again, and she stopped.

Celeste turned to face the coyote, her hands on her hips in a severe gesture of mimicked impatience.

The coyote sprung on her. It slammed her to the ground and pinned her beneath its spindly legs.

Celeste shrieked.

The coyote bent over her face, showed its teeth, and growled.

The camper fell silent for an instant, then burst into noise —plates clattering, doors flung open.

The coyote lowered its head over Celeste's face. The girl stared terrified at the animal. For a long moment they regarded each other in the depths of each other's eyes. Fear and wonder, despair and hope mingling in the potential of the moment.

Then the coyote opened its mouth and shot out its tongue. It licked Celeste from her chin to her forehead in a rough, dry kiss.

Celeste squealed in delight and surprise.

"Celeste!" said a man in panicked voice. "Don't move, honey."

The man had a gun. The coyote heard it, smelled it, saw it.

He sidestepped out of the camper and circled the pair on the ground. He was looking for a clear shot. Celeste squirmed out from under the animal. The woman cried, the man raised his gun.

"No, Daddy!" cried Celeste.

"It'll bite you, sweetie."

"No, it's nice."

Celeste ran to the coyote and threw her arms around its neck. "See?" she said.

The man half-lowered the gun.

The coyote tensed and kept its eyes on the man and the shining steel in his hand. Celeste stroked the animal's fur. The coyote watched the man.

The man pursed his lips and glanced at his wife.

That was all it could hope for. The coyote bolted. It ran low and fast under the picnic table, across the campsite, and disappeared into the forest. Sprinting for its life, it listened for the gun, expecting to feel the burning bullet in its haunches, but it did not come. The man did not shoot.

Two hours and two circuitous miles later, the coyote approached the dead moose. It could still taste the little girl in its mouth, smell her breath, remember her hair, her laugh, and her eyes.

It rushed at the vultures, snapped at them and snarled until they all fled. Then it ravenously set upon the moose meat. It needed to put on weight. Celeste had been at least forty pounds heavier than the coyote.

CHAPTER TWO

Eleanor Anders sat in her seat at the back of the class. She always sat away from the other students. She was shy to the point of being unfriendly, but didn't mind. Couldn't mind.

The school held grades kindergarten through twelfth. It had a total student body of less than three hundred fifty students. Most of them were bused to town, drawn from over a thousand square miles of Wyoming wilderness. Eleanor had visited every classroom since she joined the school in the first grade. She knew everyone, and everyone in the school knew of her.

The Wyoming summer was still bright and verdant through the window, and Eleanor watched birds move through the sky and listened to distant passing traffic while Mrs. Hart droned on about American expansionism and the destruction of the Noble Indian.

The lunchroom was preparing chicken-fried steak with cream gravy. It was still three hours away, but they'd opened the cases to thaw it out. The smell was unpleasant because Eleanor despised that meal. The meat was inconsistent; sometimes mostly beef, sometimes mostly pork or chicken or kangaroo, but always the parts of the animal that were usually thrown away.

"American Indians lived off the land, taking only what they needed," Mrs. Hart said. "They didn't hunt for sport or waste what they killed. They were peaceful stewards of the land. They used every part of every animal."

Something was happening in the principal's office. Eleanor didn't know what it was, but it was different than the usual sounds of conversation, phone calls, and paper shuffling she'd memorized over the last half month. The office was in the middle of the building, servicing the three nominal schools of Jamesford Elementary in the west wing, Jamesford Middle in the north, and Jamesford High in the east.

"The Indians lived in peace with their neighboring tribes," Mrs. Hart went on. "They came together to fight the invading whites as a unified nation, much like the European powers did in the first and second World Wars."

Eleanor wondered where Mrs. Hart got her information or if she'd even gone beyond her own imaginings for this lecture. Mrs. Hart's idea of the Noble Savage was drawn from a Kevin Costner movie and childhood fantasies. Eleanor knew what the Indians were, and they were not noble.

Eleanor thought that Mrs. Hart was playing on the proximity of the Shoshone reservation which lay only twenty miles down the road. They had their own schools, and occasionally the Jamesford Cowboys and the Wild River Shoshone Braves would square off for a football or baseball game, or, most importantly, a rodeo. These meetings were friendly and good natured. The teachers always made sure of it.

From the principal's office, Eleanor thought she heard a

name. Her heart stuttered, and she felt her face blush. She put her head down in her arms to hide it. She concentrated on the office, pushing out the smells and Mrs. Hart's ignorant speech.

Had she heard that? Had she heard the name David? David Venn?

"Eleanor," Mrs. Hart said. "Am I boring you?"

She ignored her teacher and strained to hear outside the room.

"Eleanor Anders," Mrs. Hart said sharply. "I'm talking to you."

She listened to approaching steps in the hallway.

Eleanor kept her face down. Mrs. Hart should ignore her as she usually did. Why now, now of all times, was she so interested in calling attention to her? Eleanor remained still, a rabbit in the open—tense as taught sinew, still as a stone.

She heard Mrs. Hart step out from behind her lectern and move toward her seat. The class fell into a sudden anticipatory silence; papers were stilled, texting was paused.

The classroom door swung open.

"Mrs. Hart?" said a man at the door.

Two steps from Eleanor she stopped.

"Yes, Principal Curtz?" she said warmly. The class turned to the door. Eleanor felt their eyes pull off her like a weight from her back.

"I have a new student for you," he said. "Or rather, an old student."

Mutterings in the class.

"David Venn is back with us," he said. "You remember him, don't you?"

"Of course, I do," she lied. Mrs. Hart was not here when

David last attended the school. She'd arrived when Eleanor was in seventh grade. David had left in third. But what was truth to this woman?

"Welcome, David," Mrs. Hart said. "Find a seat. We're just discussing the western expansion, and the role of the American Indian."

Eleanor sensed him take the seat closest to the door. His breathing was short and shallow, but even without looking, she knew he sat up straight and met the eyes of Jamesford High's sophomore class with cool regard as they no doubt sized him up.

Eleanor turned her head and, still resting it on her arms, stole a glance at David.

He hadn't seen her, or if he had, he'd already moved on to the more active stares.

He'd grown of course. Nearly six feet tall now. Big shoulders. His mop of brown hair over his pale complexion was as untamed and thick as she remembered. He had a new scar under his eye, small and well healed, but Eleanor noticed it. He had stubble and a scratch on his lip from where he'd shaved that morning.

Eleanor's hands were shaking. She realized she'd been holding her breath. She forced an exhale.

"Miss Anders," Mrs. Hart said. "I was asking you if you were paying attention."

The class released David from their stares and turned them at her.

Eleanor raised her head and let her long auburn hair frame her face like a half drawn mask. She knew her face was red, ashamed and excited. She looked at Mrs. Hart and prepared her usual, "I was just dozing off, sorry. Not enough sleep" excuse, the usual one, when in the corner of her eye she perceived a smile on David's face. It was not a malicious one like the others wore, smelling blood in the water, but a sincere and friendly one, a natural greeting to an old friend.

"You say the Indians were noble and united against the whites?" she heard herself say. "How then do you explain the Shoshone joining General Crook's army against the Lakota? They fought alongside the army at the Battle of the Rosebud which was after the Bear Creek Massacre where the army killed 500 Shoshone."

"W-what?" Mrs. Hart stammered, obviously surprised Eleanor had spoken at all let alone contradicted her.

"Before, during, and after the whites got here, these Noble Indians of yours were slaughtering each other in constant warfare. Life means little to them," Eleanor said.

She felt the collective gasp from the entire room. She knew then that she was the only one who'd bothered with the extending reading list. It was decoration on the syllabus, meant to make the class look better than it was in an attempt to garner Mrs. Hart a raise and bring in desperately needed funding for the school.

Eleanor let her hair fall further over her face, obscuring her right side. She looked through her long bangs at her teacher like a wolf in tall grass watching prey.

"Are you being insubordinate, Miss Anders?" said the teacher.

"No, ma'am," she said. "I just don't think your view of the Indians is entirely accurate." She couldn't believe she was still speaking. This was crazy, this was attention, this was danger.

Why was she doing this? Who cared what Mrs. Hart thought? Who cared what the others learned, or failed to learn in this class? Who was she to say anything? Who was she?

It was David.

An hour before, she'd have groggily nodded and accepted a low B in the class, never adding a syllable to a discussion that wasn't short, whispered, agreeable, and forced out of her under duress. But then David walked in, and she was a different person.

"I don't think you're right about your facts," Mrs. Hart said, retreating to her lectern. "And you're definitely wrong about their respect for life and all nature."

The class turned to follow Mrs. Hart, unsure what they'd witnessed. Robby Guide, the lone Shoshone-born student in the class, kept his gaze on Eleanor longer than the others. His eyes bored maliciously into her and she retreated behind her mask of her hair.

Mrs. Hart drew a timeline on the board and began adding dates showing the Manifest Destiny of the American Whites across the continent. Eleanor put her head down and listened. She would not be called on again today. She turned her senses to the boy by the door.

She smelled David's sweat, deodorant, and cheap shampoo. She drank it like water and allowed herself to hope he had not changed much. But did he even remember her? And why was he back? She thought she'd never see him again, had never allowed herself to even hope to see him again.

She felt he was afraid, like her. No, not like her. He sat up straight and proud and met the eyes of the others with cool control and detachment. She would dissolve if able.

After a short break where Eleanor did not leave her seat, the class fell into English lessons, and again Mrs. Hart, enamored with her own voice, lectured the class. Eleanor kept her head on her desk and listened to the birds and the cars and David's heartbeat, and when she could not avoid it, to Mrs. Hart's interpretation of *1984*.

"I'm sorry. David, is it?" Mrs. Hart said.

"Yes, ma'am," he said, his voice breaking not from emotion but from lack of use.

"Yes, David, the class was assigned to read this book over the summer. You'll have to catch up."

"I've read it," he said.

"You have?" she said.

"Yes, last year. In school," he said.

"Where was that?" she asked.

"Augusta, Georgia. Fort Gordon," he said.

"Your father is in the army?"

"Yes, ma'am. A signalman. He's overseas now."

"Well, you might be a little ahead of us then," she said. "Feel free to contribute."

"It was an advanced class," he said, and Eleanor knew he instantly regretted saying it. "I mean, an A.P. class." It was too late. The class decided at that moment to dislike David Venn.

"Very good," Mrs. Hart said and continued with her lecture until the bell rang sending the class to Mr. Graham for chemistry.

David presented Mr. Graham with a note from Principal Curtz and the aging teacher added his name to the roll and bade him take a seat. David found a tattered copy of the chemistry textbook on the shelf beside the college algebra and trigonometry books he'd need later that day. He took a seat in the back, behind the other students, but still not close to Eleanor, who sat even further back and isolated.

Mr. Graham plodded ahead as he had for years, wearing the same wide ties he'd owned for decades. His situation was not a secret. He should retire and wanted to, but the school district had been unable to lure another science and math teacher to northeastern Wyoming. They'd convinced Mr. Graham to stay on another year, promising to double recruitment efforts and accepting his ultimatum that no matter what, he'd hang up his chalk in June. Jamesford was a small town and what Eleanor had not learned listening to the sounds of the school, she had overheard in parking lots and at the grocery.

She liked Mr. Graham. He'd taught her the previous year and if he stayed, would teach her again next. He did not care for personality or words. He never put her on the spot, embarrassed her, or regarded her at all. He let her be as unnoticed as she wanted to be and surely wished her classmates would be as obligingly invisible as she was. He graded with numbers and percentages. Science and math were no place for opinion and so there was not even the suggestion of discussion. Lecture, demonstration, work time, test. That was chemistry, science, and math with Mr. Graham. He was beyond caring for his fourth decade of students and didn't even make an effort to learn names. If you did not ask for help, you did not receive it.

The class was so small that everyone could work alone, though only Eleanor did. The others cliqued up in groups, shared notes, and copied answers while Mr. Graham read fishing magazines and ignored the noise by turning down his hearing aid.

Last year, science was the only class in which Eleanor scored above a B on her report card. She'd made a promise to herself to correct that this year.

His back to the class, Mr. Graham began his lecture. The other students began whispering and passing notes. They could talk if they dared, hoping Mr. Graham's hearing aid was turned down as it often was. But if they got caught, he'd send them to Mr. Curtz directly. Three trips to the principal's office were an automatic one week suspension. Less than three weeks into the new school year, Mr. Graham had already sent two students, Barbara Pennon and Russell Liddle to the office once.

She watched as David listened to Mr. Graham and studied his book, trying to locate text to match the lecture. At the end of the class, he looked lost and frustrated. The lunch bell rang.

Eleanor avoided the chicken-fried steak and used her state voucher lunch coupon for a wilted salad and warm carton of milk. She sat at her usual table, alone in the shadows.

David had remained after class to speak with Mr. Graham, but Eleanor couldn't hear them over the rush of students in the cafeteria. When he finally appeared, the cafeteria had emptied outside to enjoy the warm late summer day. David found a table near the front and ate without noticing Eleanor watching him from the corner. He had just enough time to get his meal and eat it with a soldier's speed before math began.

After math was physical education with Mr. Blake. Eleanor moved through the locker room like a ghost, unnoticed by the other girls. She found her locker and took her clothes to a dressing room for modesty. Most of the other girls had dispensed with that and changed like the boys did, in front of the others. Only Eleanor, Midge, the fat girl, and Aubrey, the girl with scars on her back, changed in the dressing rooms.

The skinny girl, Penelope, changed with the others, but Eleanor thought her sickly skeletal body was more shameful by far than Midge's plump rolls. She did it to herself. Eleanor could smell bile on Penelope's breath after lunch and knew she purged in the middle-school restroom when those students were in class. She carried herself like royalty and regarded Midge with an outward contempt that frequently slipped into outright cruelty and bullying. Barbara Pennon and the other girls frequently joined in. The school was full of bullies. The town was full of bullies.

Outside, Mr. Blake had everyone run once around the track as a warm up. Eleanor was last. David had not brought gym clothes and so was excused. He sat on the bleachers with Mr. Blake's clipboard in the sunshine and Eleanor smiled for him, though no one could see it.

They split up into two co-ed soccer teams and played a game. Mr. Blake stayed in the center with his whistle, blowing frequent fouls and raising yellow cards like a World Cup referee.

It was a dumb game. No one was good at soccer. The boys wanted to play football or basketball or be let out to the stables for rodeo training, and the girls just didn't want to be there at all. Mr. Blake was from Nicaragua where soccer was king. He taught Spanish and sports and made the kids learn the offside rule the first day of class.

Eleanor found it easy to melt away from the game and find a calm corner near the weaker goal to wait out the hour. When a ball would accidentally find its way to her, she trotted to it with grace and deftly passed it to a teammate. Mr. Blake had taken her aside once and asked her where she learned to play.

"Nowhere," she said. "I saw it on TV once."

"No kidding," he said. "If we ever get a team going, you're on it."

The next time a ball came to her, she flubbed the kick and sent the ball sailing over the fence into the parking lot.

After sports, only some of the girls showered. Penelope did, using it as another opportunity to display her deathly frame. Barbara did as well, showing off her voluptuous chest and cleaning off any perspiration before re-coating herself in perfumes. Eleanor never sweated enough to need a shower but wouldn't have showered if she did. She was an aggressively private person.

Mr. Blake was still sweaty for their Spanish class but carried on with the kind of new teacher enthusiasm Mr. Graham had jettisoned before Mr. Blake was born.

David was waiting in the classroom with Mr. Blake before the others arrived, sitting in a seat that had been empty all year.

"That's my seat," said Russell Liddle to David. "That's where I sit."

"Oh, I'm sorry," said David standing up. David was several inches taller than the freckled boy challenging him for the seat. "Mr. Blake said it was available."

"Not today," Russell said, loud enough for his friends to hear.

David took another empty seat. There were many.

The lesson was robust and mostly in Spanish. No one was very good at the language, and there was always grumbling about its usefulness. With patience, Mr. Blake would listen to the complaints and try to explain the value of a broad education, then smile, shrug, and finish the lesson anyway.

When the bell rang to end the day, the seats emptied before the sound had died. Eleanor waited for everyone to go. She watched David get up and follow the others through the door and out into the sunny afternoon. Only when he was gone, when she heard his footsteps cross the threshold out of the building did she sigh, gather her books, and leave.

CHAPTER THREE

The school was tucked away from Highway 26, the only paved artery in or out of the town leading to other places. There was a bus Eleanor could take home but, unlike many of her classmates, she could walk home and preferred to. Many she knew, like Barbara Pennon and Robby Guide, lived nearly twenty miles away on secluded ranches in the tree cut hills. Eleanor could walk the two miles to her home faster than they could be driven in one of the town's three aging school buses.

Crossing Highway 26, Eleanor saw the usual speed trap at the town limits. Trucks and tourists slowed to admire the aggressively rustic wooden façades of a town grabbing at tourist dollars. Jamesford billed itself as the Cowboy Playground. For decades, in a hundred outdoors magazines, the chamber of commerce advertised the area's scenic wonders, spectacular fishing, abundant hunting, and authentic western experience. It had worked somewhat. Jamesford became a modest destination of its own and not just a rest stop along a lonely stretch of wild highway between Yellowstone and Cheyenne. Rich city people eager for a true western experience filled the county's eight dude ranches every summer to pay luxury prices for boiled beans, a wool blanket in a wooden shack, and the right to be woken up at dawn by a steel triangle.

Eleanor crossed the highway and made her way between two motels and a sportsman shop that promised every trout fishing device known to man. She noted the many out-of-state license plates and the smell of over-sweet barbecue from the Buffalo Cafe.

Beyond the highway, behind the façades, just a block away, Jamesford immediately transformed into just another rural Wyoming town where there were more aluminum trailer homes than actual wooden houses. Eleanor walked parallel to the highway behind the line of wood-veneered shops and hotels to avoid the traffic, and snaked her way to the bank.

The bank occupied a prime corner in town near the better artist galleries. In anticipation of the coming boom, Jamesford had attracted a certain artist class who embraced the wilderness and nature but scorned the locals. There was always an uneasy truce between the "actual residents" and the "transplants" or "hicks and civilized" depending upon which side you talked to. Many of the artists had lived in Jamesford longer than Eleanor and some of the "hicks" had just arrived last year when Chevron sank a test well up Pony Creek Canyon.

Eleanor waited outside until the lobby was empty and then pushed her way through the glass doors. There were two tellers on duty, a man and a woman. She knew them both. Of the two, she disliked the girl less, and so approached her window.

"Hello, Miss Eleanor," the woman said. She was in her late thirties and wore too much eyeshadow. She had a belly, but she kept it hidden below the counter, and smacked gum when her manager forgot to order her to spit it out.

"I just want to know if we got our deposit," Eleanor said.

"Speak up, honey," the teller said. "I can't hear you. Don't talk to the floor. I'm right here."

Eleanor knew the teller had heard her even though Eleanor had spoken low and to her feet. Eleanor had never made a different request of anyone in this bank. Always she came to see if the deposit was made. Did the bank people suddenly expect her to start a mortgage or exchange Italian money? They knew her name, recognized her on sight, and yet they somehow always forgot why she came in.

It was a mild cruelty, insignificant and automatic—a small, unnecessary meanness typical of the species.

Eleanor turned her face up, careful to keep her hair draped over her eyes.

"Did our deposit come in?" she said loudly.

"I'll just check," the teller said, popping her gum behind a broad insincere grin.

Eleanor passed a credit card through the window, pre-empting an unnecessary request to see it. The teller glanced at it and then typed her account number into her computer by memory.

The male teller, a boy barely out of high school, spun circles in his chair. The manager was out.

"Well, looks like it cleared this morning," Eleanor's teller said. "Eighteen hundred ninety-two dollars," she said.

"Thanks," mumbled Eleanor and turned away.

"See you next month," called the teller.

The groceries could wait, but Tabitha needed her pills. Eleanor traced her path back behind the businesses where fewer people would notice her and entered the drugstore through the back door.

She drew in smells and split the scents into threat and

non-threat without thinking. She noticed the changes in the shelves. The vitamins had been restocked. The candy aisle had been rearranged for the season's first orange and black Halloween treats. Too early. They always celebrated too early.

A tourist with an accent—California or southern Oregon—looked at post cards and described them to a man with a similar accent trying on no-label cowboy hats in a mirror.

"There's the traditional jackalope," she said. "Do you think she'd like that?"

"This is every bit as good as the Stetson in the other shop. What do you think?" replied the man.

"You don't look good in black," she said. "How about this guy holding this huge fish?"

Eleanor passed the toys and paused only for a second to look at coats. The drugstore had some clothes. They were cheaper than anywhere else in town except the Goodwill. Eleanor would go there for a new coat. She was bigger now than last year.

She stepped behind an excited tourist in line at the pharmacy counter who was anxious to buy a snake bite kit before he began a four-day trek in the mountains.

"We don't have one," said the pharmacist. "There's just no call for them."

"I need one," explained the man. "I had a dream I was snakebit. I need one."

"You know, I don't even know if they exist. I know the hospital has anti-venom but I can't honestly remember anyone ever needing it."

"Well then, give me a first aid kit," he said.

"Aisle five, next to the bug spray."

Eleanor stepped up and slid the credit card and insurance ID across the counter.

"I need my mom's pills," she said softly.

The pharmacist scooped up the cards and looked into a computer screen Eleanor couldn't see. She watched his hands and saw he typed her mother's name, misspelling Anders, hitting the "w" for the "e." She stopped herself from pointing it out and waited instead for the computer to error.

"Got them right here," he said after the correction. He disappeared behind a curtain.

The front door chimed and across the store Eleanor heard familiar voices. Alexi Kerr and Barbara Pennon burst in talking and laughing. Barbara had missed the bus. Alexi's family had money. She had her own car. She was probably giving Barbara a ride home.

"I don't remember him at all," Eleanor heard Alexi say.

"I do," said Barbara. "Just an ugly kid back then. He's filled out a lot."

"Something new to look at, I guess," said Alexi.

"And play with," giggled Barbara.

Eleanor went cold.

They ordered diet sodas from the counter and sat down at the small luncheonette table by the window. The drugstore tried to be all things to all people, a trait that had kept it open for half a century and now threatened its death in the wake of tourist-centric specialty shops along main street.

"Here you go, Miss Anders," said the pharmacist. He'd cut his hair this week and his dye was fading at the roots. His eyes were warm and caring, which always made Eleanor suspicious.

"How's Tabitha doing?" he asked.

"Better," she lied, then corrected herself. "She says she's getting better."

"Does she need a laxative? That's the most common side effect."

"I don't know."

"You should buy some just in case. It can be very painful."

"Aren't the blue ones for pain?"

"Yes, but this is a different kind of pain than the cancer. More of a chronic uncomfortableness."

Eleanor glanced at the receipt. Half their monthly budget in one bag of five bottles. "We probably have some," she said. If Tabitha needed them, she'd come back for them, but Eleanor wouldn't spend money just because someone wanted to sell her something.

"Wait a minute," the pharmacist said and disappeared behind the curtain. Eleanor looked in the bag and counted the four orange plastic bottles and one glass elixir with a name she didn't even try to pronounce.

Barbara and Alexi were leaving. Their conversation had turned to "the handsome Mr. Blake," as Alexi had called him.

"He's all foreign," said Barbara. "What's attractive about that?"

"It's just something new to look at."

"He's married, I think."

"So?" said Alexi, and the two giggled and left.

The pharmacist returned with a handful of cardboard envelopes.

"These are trial size," he said. "You can have them. Make sure you read the instructions before your mother takes them."

"No, I couldn't," said Eleanor.

"They were free to me. Take them. Don't be proud."

She should have just taken them. Now she was "proud."

"Thanks," she said meekly.

He dropped the samples into her bag, and Eleanor left the store through the back door.

Outside, a group of riders from one of the ranches walked their horses through town toward the bars where hitching posts were not only part of the decoration, but a required accessory. They talked boisterously and tipped their hats to Eleanor who instinctively ducked as if they were throwing rocks.

From far south, Eleanor smelled diesel fuel from Cowboy Bob's Truck Stop, the biggest single structure in town besides the school. Technically, it was outside of town. Some city ordinance or town regulation kept it away for the betterment of the cowboy town ambiance. It hadn't hurt the business. In fact, it had helped it by guaranteeing that it would be the first gas pump northbound travelers would encounter. The other local gas stations cursed it daily and, like the drugstore, sold trinkets, souvenirs, and greasy food to make up for the losses, all of which the Cowboy Bob did and did better. At least that's what Eleanor had gathered from countless overheard conversations.

In the off-season, after the snow fell and only snowmobilers were interested in booking rooms, Cowboy Bob's Truck Stop became the only nightlife in all of Jamesford. Everything else closed down sharp at nine o'clock and on Sundays did not open at all. With only the hardcore bars to compete with, Cowboy Bob, open twenty-four hours a day, outside the city limits, picked up a sketchy reputation and the lion share of Jamesford's winter after-hours spending.

A stray tabby and her late litter of kittens watched Eleanor from beneath a car across the street. One of the kittens had lost an eye. She paused and bent down to see which one. The mother hissed, the kittens retreated. A dusty pickup passed between them.

Eleanor made a sound and the cats came forward, curious and calm. Eleanor crossed the street and met the litter on the sidewalk. The little ones mewed as the mother rubbed her chin on Eleanor's hand. Eleanor mewed back, a perfect mimic of a contented cat, feline and inhuman.

She scratched the mother and felt welts underlying her matted fur. She pinched one and the cat hissed and jumped away. Eleanor examined the bloody steel pellet she'd pulled from the animals back.

She collected the injured kitten. It mewed and complained and wriggled. Mother watched closely but didn't take action. It was the half-black one, she saw, the brave one. It had been shot by a BB gun or an air rifle. The wound was bad and festering. It would likely die.

She put it down and straightened herself. The cats scattered. Hurriedly, the mother led her offspring under a rusted tractor and around the house. Suddenly, Eleanor became aware of a figure in a house watching her through curtains behind a cracked, facing window. She crossed to the other side of the street and saw a nine-year-old boy watching her with uncertain eyes.

Half a mile away, Eleanor relaxed. The houses thinned and the air was scented with grass, pine, and barns. They were different smells, not better, just different than the town's. The faces that watched her now were horses' and foxes' and birds'. They were not as threatening as people, but they were not her friends. She'd had precious few of those, one in fact, and she thought she'd lost him.

Quiet and alone, a shadow in the bright Wyoming sun, Eleanor made her way through the deserted mid-afternoon roads to her mother's house as she did every day. But this day, behind her curtain of hair, she chanced a smile.

CHAPTER FOUR

The Anders lived in a house, not a trailer. It was a small house with a narrow porch. A white weathered fence surrounded the little lot at the edge of town with a knee-high gate. In the back, the fence was six feet high but still white. Parking was on the street, but they had no car. It had originally been a guest house for another, grander structure that had not weathered the blizzard of '48. The debris from "the big house" had been cleared and the land sold, but no one had yet bothered to build anything on the old place. They were waiting for the coming boom which never came.

The Anders had a single tree on the corner of their lot, a pine planted by a previous owner. It had matured into a tall, majestic green cone, a pillar landmark Eleanor could see across town over the low buildings even in the deepest snow. It beaconed her home.

The house stood alone on the street, the land on either side and behind and across the road were weed-choked and ignored. The Anders' house, however, had a kept lawn and single, vibrant flower bed, opposite the tree, just under the window where Tabitha could see it from her chair in the living room. It bloomed with red and pink tulips in the spring, scarlet poppies, then yellow daffodils, purple petunias, and gold gazanias in the later summer. It was hard to coax them all to grow in the cold windy Wyoming weather, but Eleanor tended the plants like loved children and spent precious money to make them live.

In the back of the house, away from the pine's shadow, Eleanor grew tomatoes in buckets in the sunny spots. She had ten plants as tall as she was and as cared for as the flowers. She'd planted them in old five-gallon plastic pales she'd found discarded in a dump heap. To support them, she made frames from whatever she could find. She used wood from fallen aspen trees and splintered posts, wire from a cast-off chain-link fence, and, for delicate string, threads of trimmed telephone wire she'd found under a green switch box behind the post office. The tomatoes themselves had been nursed from seed in the winter in the back window of the kitchen.

The plants thrived and gave the little family plenty of cherry tomato treats, which they munched like candy in front of the television. They ate succulent slabs of the rich delicious fruit with a little salt and pepper like pancakes all summer long.

A flimsy aluminum shed stood in the back corner of the lot and kept the yard tools that had come with the house. Some were older than two world wars, but the family kept them working with glue, tape, and the occasional scavenged bit or pole.

Each year, Eleanor planned to put some tomatoes away in jars for the winter, but each year there were none left, Tabitha and Eleanor having savored them all. They had talked seriously about putting in a vegetable bed this year to increase their harvest.

The magpies in the pine chirped in alarm as Eleanor approached the house. She could see the nest from her upper window. The house didn't really have two stories. But the attic had a window and they'd made it into a bedroom loft for Eleanor. Even with her new height, she could stand upright in the center of the room where the slanted eaves met at the top. Toward either side, she had to crouch to reach her bed, bureau, or trunk. It was fine. She only slept and dressed there. It was a retreat if she needed one. But she seldom did.

The house would need painting next year, Eleanor thought. The creamy eggshell of five years past was peeling. The gloss white trim and maroon door and window frames were also showing the wear of five Wyoming winters. Eleanor would need to keep an eye open for unwanted paint. Like last time, she'd prowl the new constructions up the canyons where the transplants overbuilt mansions they'd see once a year. If any of them weren't log cabins, she might be able "borrow" some extra paint.

Suddenly, Eleanor realized that she'd noticed the paint because she was looking at her home as another person might. And that other, she knew, was David Venn. She cared little for what others thought of her, her home, and her mother, as long as they left them alone. But Eleanor wanted David to approve of her home when he saw it. If he saw it.

She shook her head, feeling foolish, and went inside.

"Mom, I'm home," she said quietly. She saw Tabitha sleeping in her chair, the television muted, a blanket over her legs.

The house was cool thanks to the shady pine, and Eleanor opened a window in the alcove to freshen the air in the room. Perhaps it would bring in some warm summer breezes across the flower bed.

Eleanor's keen senses had learned to tolerate the heavy scents of medicine and decay which filled the house more and more each week. It was impossible for her not to associate these smells with strong emotions. There was love, always love for Tabitha, but now, growing by the day, there was also fear.

She surveyed the room for changes, plotting the places her mother had moved that day. The couch—old, secondhand, threadbare, and mismatched—had been sat upon; a cushion jostled and a pillow moved. The coffee table, scratched and marred from the previous owner's cigarette burns, showed that Tabitha had read only a few pages of her book before laying it back down beside the box of tissue. The TV remote control, of course, had been moved, and Eleanor noticed the window curtains drawn closed where the afternoon sun would glare off the television screen.

Tabitha snored softly but slept deeply.

From farther in the house, Eleanor smelled the soup her mother had made in the kitchen only to be thrown up later in the bathroom. She sighed and felt some of her good mood fade away.

She kissed her mother on the cheek and tasted dry narcotic sweat on her skin. Eleanor adjusted her mother's headband where it had slipped up to expose an unnaturally bare patch of scalp above her ear, then Eleanor stepped quietly into the bathroom.

Leaving her backpack in the hall, she found the paper sack from the drugstore and slid the accordion door closed behind her. She was careful to be quiet, but knew it wouldn't matter. Tabitha would sleep all afternoon. She'd had a bad night. She'd woken late in the night, staggered to the bathroom, took a pill, and wept softly for half an hour. Eleanor had heard her, but stayed upstairs knowing she'd only embarrass her mother by offering to help. Eventually, Tabitha had returned to her room and fallen asleep. Only then had Eleanor done the same.

When Eleanor had woken up the next morning, Tabitha was already in the kitchen stirring a cup of cold tea.

"Morning, Mom," Eleanor had said.

"Morning, cupcake," Tabitha had said and smiled. Eleanor couldn't help herself and had smiled back, forgetting the terrible sounds of her mother's nocturnal weeping.

Eleanor put these thoughts aside and replaced the empty pill bottles on the shelf with the new ones from the drugstore and arranged the others so Tabitha would use the remnants of the old before starting the new. Efficiency was important when you didn't have much to begin with.

Checking that the door was sealed for silence, she knelt down and scrubbed around the toilet where Tabitha had missed. She'd thrown up twice today, Eleanor saw. She'd tried so hard to hide it. The odor of bleach was strong, but Eleanor could still sense the underlying smell. It must have hurt Tabitha to kneel so long with a brush and bucket. Eleanor tidied up and opened the window.

In the kitchen, Eleanor cleaned the pots and bowls and threw away the wrappers from the ramen Tabitha had failed to keep down. Again she opened a window and smelled the warm air.

It was not like her to want the windows open. She much preferred to keep them closed and locked, the curtains drawn. Today was so different. She couldn't wait to tell Tabitha about David. She'd know what to do. She'd explain to Eleanor why she was so excited to see a boy who hadn't seen her in half his lifetime and probably didn't even remember who she was.

Still, it had brightened her day and she inhaled deep and sighed long before starting her homework at the table.

It was past dark when Tabitha finally stirred. Eleanor put down her English book and said, "Evening, Mom. How you feeling?"

"Like a new woman," she said. She stretched her arms out wide and rolled her neck. The TV remote slid off her lap and clattered on the floor. "Did I leave the TV on?"

"You turned the sound down, but, yeah, it was on when I got home."

"Waste of electricity," she chided herself. "Sorry."

"We got money today," Eleanor said brightly. "I got your pills and stuff. Oh, and the pharmacist said you may need a laxative. He gave me some. For free."

"I won't confirm or deny his assessment," Tabitha said. "Just tell me where they are."

"On the shelf by the aspirin," Eleanor said.

"Have you eaten?" Tabitha got up and went past Eleanor into the bathroom.

"No, but I'm not hungry."

"You ate at school?"

"I had a salad."

"Is that enough?"

"I didn't do much today," she said. "I'm good. I'll have a tomato in a bit. How about you? Some soup?"

"My stomach's been a little edgy today," she said from the bathroom. "I should be okay after one of the green ones. An hour?"

"Sure," said Eleanor. "We'll eat something in an hour."

Tabitha put a kettle on for tea. Eleanor heard her fumbling with the tea jars, ginseng, chamomile, and green, all supposed to help the immune system and create calm. After the antique kettle whistled, Eleanor heard the infusing spoon snap closed and the water pour over it. Today there was a tinge of lemon in the mixture.

"Why'd you open all the windows?" Tabitha asked tentatively. "Do I smell?"

"It was a beautiful day today, and I thought I'd let some inside."

Tabitha carried her cup and saucer to the table and pulled out a vinyl chair next to Eleanor. She ran her fingers through the girl's hair and tucked her bangs behind her ear.

"So what made it such a beautiful day?" she asked.

Eleanor looked at the gaunt, pale face and into her mother's grey eyes. Eleanor's were usually hazel and she wondered, not for the first time, if she could change them to match the deep, wise dusk-pools her mother used to frame the world. She wanted to see as her mother did. She admired the fine web of lines around those grey eyes, and the deep smile creases in her cheeks. Her lips weren't the lush things she wore when they'd met, but they were still warm and beautiful. Age and sickness had thinned them along with the rest of her body. Eleanor kissed them.

"David came back," she said.

"David? You mean the Venn boy? He's back in Jamesford?"

"Yes. He came in during first period."

"Did you say hi?"

Eleanor shook her head. Tabitha didn't press.

"What does he look like?"

"He's grown of course. He has a new scar under his eye, and I think he sprained an ankle recently. He favors his left step."

"Is he tall and handsome?"

Eleanor blushed. "Mom," she said.

"Does he still have that mop of black hair?"

"Oh yes. That's how I knew it was him. Unmistakable."

Tabitha sipped her tea and regarded Eleanor until she turned away to fetch something from her backpack.

"He might have changed you know. You mustn't hold it against him if he has. People change every day. You might not be friends anymore."

"I know," Eleanor said.

"How was Mrs. Hart?" asked Tabitha changing the subject.

"I upset her," said Eleanor.

"How?"

"She called on me. She wouldn't let me alone. She went after me just when David was brought in."

Tabitha looked at her with concern. "What did you do?"

"I told her that Indians are not the Noble Savages she made them out to be. She was going off on how American Indians were somehow saints. I shouldn't have said anything, but I did."

"Because David was there?" Tabitha asked.

"No. Well, maybe a little," said Eleanor. "But she was wrong. Just wrong. Indians were not noble shepherds or peaceful neighbors."

"No, they weren't," agreed Tabitha, again stroking Eleanor's hair. Eleanor leaned into her mother's hand, relishing the contact. Her hands were cold, but her fingers felt like love itself caressed her head and neck.

"People change. Attitudes change. Don't be prejudiced," Tabitha said.

"Okay, but it's flat out ignorant to say the Indians were all rain dances and peace-pipes."

"Still, they're your people," began Tabitha and then stopped herself when Eleanor tensed. Tabitha dropped her hand down Eleanor's back and scratched it through her shirt.

"So did you get in trouble?"

"No. She just went on talking."

"She probably won't call on you again for a while, huh?" offered Tabitha.

"I was thinking the same thing. So it's not all bad."

"None of it is bad, cupcake. I'm proud of you."

Tabitha leaned forward and kissed her daughter on her forehead. On her mother's breath, Eleanor could smell green tea and lemon, strong and hot, mingling with the nausea pill dissolving in her stomach. The medley of odors nearly covered the wretched underlying stink of the murdering cancer eating her away.

CHAPTER FIVE

Robby Guide, the half-blood Shoshone, was the first boy to extend David friendship. Robby was the first to join David at lunch, and they talked about old times in the woods. Eleanor listened and watched, ashamed that she hadn't been the first to speak to him. She'd wanted to, but hadn't.

"Mr. Blake is new this year," Robby told David, "if you haven't figured that out yet. We haven't had a foreign language teacher since that German chick left a couple of years back."

Eleanor watched David with Robby. David was happy for the company. She knew he'd suffered under the silent-treatment. He'd reached out to several people, but in varied shades of rudeness from "quiet, here comes the teacher" to "bug off loser," each had put him off; none had welcomed him.

Once, in chemistry, when David was ruining an experiment, Eleanor had actually taken a step toward his table to help, but she held back. If she was the first to welcome David, she might well be the only one. Eleanor's reputation for non-existence was not something David needed. He needed to belong as much as Eleanor needed to hide. His survival might depend on it.

"There's no negotiating with Mr. Graham," said Robby. "If you're lucky and catch him on a full moon or something, he might let you do some extra credit, but once he enters a score in his book, that's it. It's over."

Robby was one of the "nice boys." There were basically two groups of boys in Jamesford. One, the nice ones, was a loose affiliation of kids who were behaved and decent and minded their own business. Then there were the bad boys. Tabitha had called them that back in elementary school when Eleanor told her about them kicking a dog at recess and pulling her hair when she cried about it. That group was a tighter circle of six or seven kids who were responsible, Eleanor knew, for all the vandalism and juvenile crime in Jamesford. The leader was Russell Liddle. He wasn't the biggest or the fastest or even the meanest, but he was cleverer than the others, and since every pack of wolves needed a leader, he'd stepped up to be it.

On the girls' side, there were ever-shifting circles of friends among the "regular girls" as Eleanor thought of them, and the "misfits." Eleanor was a misfit. Midge, who'd fought weight issues as long as Eleanor had known her, was a misfit. So was Aubrey, who was only slightly less shy than Eleanor and wore a web of scars on her back no one had ever dared ask her about. Everyone else in the class was accepted and rejected regularly into teenage society circles and got along well enough for teenage girls.

"Barbara's a fox, but Alexi is the catch," said Robby to David. "She wasn't here when you were before. Her father is some kind of millionaire. She has a car already, a red Range Rover, custom painted. She's snobby sometimes."

David nodded agreeably and chewed his pizza. Eleanor saw that the rest of the cafeteria watched Robby and David. She could feel the sea change. Robby's acceptance of David Venn was the cue to end their hazing.

"What's with Russell?" asked David. "He keeps giving me the stink-eye."

"He's the class bully," Robby said. "Best to just keep clear of him."

"Did he have a broken arm once back in second or third grade?"

"I don't remember," said Robby.

Eleanor did. Russell's father had broken it in a drunken fit.

"If that's the same guy I remember, he was a real jerk."

"Sounds like the same guy," said Robby. "So what do you do for fun?"

"Video games," said David. "But we don't have internet right now. Next month."

"Do you ride?"

"Bikes?"

"Horses."

"No. Not much call for it on an army base. I'm not really a cowboy."

"Shame. There's a rodeo coming up," Robby said. "County High School Rodeo. The Wild River Shoshone are coming up, along with the Dubois kids. It's not too late to enter."

"Except I can't ride a horse," said David. "Well, I guess I can maybe. The right stirrup is for 'go' and the left is 'stop.' Am I right?"

Robby laughed.

"Horseshoes," said Robby. "If you can throw horseshoes you can get out of class to practice for the rodeo with the rest of us. The school will empty out next week with everyone practicing for Jamesford pride."

"Seriously? Horseshoes?"

"They're trying to make it a broader competition. The Rez has better horsemen so they wanted more competition to give other schools a chance."

"I can shoot," David said.

"Perfect," said Robby. "There's like five different events around guns."

"Okay. Sounds like fun. Who do I talk to?"

Robby told him to talk to Principal Curtz after lunch. "Don't be fooled when he says there'll be try-outs and all that. We've never had a full team of anything as long as I've been here. If you want in, you're in."

"Thanks."

"No problem."

When they'd finished lunch, Brian Weaver invited them outside for a game of two-on-two basketball with Eric Collins. Eleanor watched them slip out the door into the sunlight.

The teachers sensed the change in attitude toward David and began to include the newcomer. They'd avoided calling on him out of courtesy, but now that the embargo was lifted, they made use of David's different educational experience.

"Did they not teach you science in Georgia?" asked Mr. Graham in a rare moment of student involvement.

"No, sir," David said. "Not chemistry."

"Nothing? Well, you're only a few weeks behind. Take a book home and study," he said and went on lecturing. David would have to find his own answer about chemistry.

September slipped away in yellowing aspen leaves, and October heralded "rodeo practice release" time, but Eleanor didn't go for anything. The other girls donned their leather chaps and sequined cowboy hats and joined with the boys in barrel racing and roping competitions, but the misfits just watched. Because the school had scored so poorly the year before in the state's mandated testing, school excused rodeo practice was only twice a week and then only one class was skipped. The schedule was juggled around so classes would be skipped evenly. Serious participants were expected to practice after school and on weekends depending on their events.

With the exception of shooting, cooking, quilting, and horseshoes, new additions all, the students practiced for the upcoming tournament at the indoor city arena, where the rodeo would be held. David, Russell, and Tanner Nelson, another of the bad boys, were taken by Mr. Blake to the gun range east of town. The others got their own rides. Eleanor very much wanted to join, them but couldn't figure an unobtrusive way to do so. Instead, she watched the girls rope horned posts and dart around steel barrels from the highest bleacher and listened for the gunshots that told her David was nearby.

Early in October, Eleanor was at school when Mr. Blake brought the shooters back. They were late and the buses had gone already. Russell and Tanner trotted away together toward the truck stop. From her view inside the building, she saw Mr. Blake offer to drive David home, but he waved him off and headed north. Eleanor collected her bag and followed him.

She fell into the familiar muscle memory of silent pursuit. She padded softly behind David, keeping to shadows and running parallel when she could. She stopped and listened and watched, and kept a perfect distance, though she had to force herself not to close when she could.

David did not live far from school. Just a mile or so to the north, he disappeared into a trailer park which was the cheapest rental housing in town. She smelled dogs and pigeons, rabbits and cats. She stopped behind a dumpster across from the street and glanced down the gravel road and saw where David disappeared into an aluminum mobile home.

She waited for traffic to pass, got up, and loped across the street. She went behind the trailer homes, between them and a white plastic fence that kept the winds from filling the place with tumbleweeds and allowed the owners to up the rent for aesthetic reasons.

When Eleanor reached the trailer, she stopped to listen. The next trailer had a blaring television spewing an angry talk show. The neighbor on the other side was quiet and dark.

Eleanor was too short to look in the windows. The trailer was raised on blocks and a cedar porch extended in front of the door. Wires reached from a pole by the fence to the trailer's corner and an ancient metal television antennae stuck up at the other end. A full-size propane tank rested on a pad behind the trailer with black hoses connecting it to the house. Eleanor squeezed behind it and listened.

"What's for dinner?" she heard David say.

"How about a pizza," a woman replied.

"Frozen or take out?"

"Frozen," said the woman.

"Ah," said David.

"Yes," said a little voice. "Pizza!"

It was a girl. A little girl. Five or six years old.

"It's easy, and I have to go," the woman said.

"Where you going?" asked David.

"I got a job," the woman said proudly. "I'm starting at the grocery tonight. I'll be in the back for a week, but then I'll be a checker. It's easy work and steady."

"That's cool, Mom," said David.

"Bring home cookies," said the youngster.

Eleanor placed the voice then and remembered David's mother from before. In startling half-forgotten detail, Eleanor recalled her height and weight, teeth, eyes, and hands, the part in her hair, the lilt in her speech when she called David in from play. Her voice had changed, grown weaker, tttwearier, but Eleanor was sure it was David's mother.

"We'll see," she said. "Things going better at school?"

"Great!" said the little girl.

"Yeah, it's all right," said David with less enthusiasm.

"It just takes some time," the mother said.

"Yeah, but I have nothing in common with anyone. Really."

"There's the shooting."

"Big deal," he said. "They don't know video games or movies or good music or anything. They're all a bunch of hicks. Russell talks about nothing but shooting animals and hoping someone tries to mess with him so he can gun him down with his dad's forty-five."

"He's just one kid."

"Yeah, he's the worst, but he's just an exaggeration of the others. Really, this is total Hicksville. I don't know how I ever lived here."

"Don't be so dramatic."

"I don't know who I am here," he said.

"You'll adapt," she said.

"You mean change," he said bitterly. "What if I don't want

to change? What if I want to stay who and what I was before? I liked who I was. I don't want to be a beer-swilling shit-kicker from Jamesford."

"David!" his mother chided.

"Davie said a bad word," chanted the little girl.

"David?" his mother said, a threat in her voice.

He hesitated and then said, "I'm sorry."

"Adapting is not changing," his mother said.

"That's not true. I either lie or I change, or they do, and they won't."

"Everyone's different in every situation," his mother said softly. Eleanor heard a moving chair and imagined her sitting beside him. "For example, at home, when dad's not here, I'm the boss—and don't forget it. But at work, I'm not. I'm an employee, and I take orders. I can be both people. I'm not changing. I'm adapting."

"So I'm supposed to be one person at home and another in public?" he said.

"Aren't you?"

"I don't want to become a sh—turd-kicker."

"Then don't," she said and kissed him. "Inside you are who you are. Just get by. Survival is adaptation."

"Glad you're getting something out of your biology degree, Mom."

"A buck above minimum wage at Sherman's Grocery," she said. "Everything's working out."

They laughed.

"The shooting's fun though, isn't it?"

"It's all right. Yeah, it's fun. I'm good at it. Thanks to Dad."

There followed a pause that made Eleanor uneasy.

"Do you have homework?" asked the mother.

"Of course," said David.

"Take the garbage out before you start. I should make a sandwich for work."

Eleanor saw that the garbage cans were in a nook next to the tank, and she jumped with fright. Keeping her head low as if dodging bullets, she scurried away behind the trailers, out the gate, and across the street.

Once clear, she made her way home carefully. Though she knew where she was with the familiarity of a long-time inhabitant, she looked for new secret places and paths between her house and David's. She knew she would make this journey again in the day and in the dark, and, as was always her precaution, she did not want to be seen.

CHAPTER SIX

"Your house is neat and clean," said Stephanie Pearce in her soothing and condescending manner. She sat on the sofa in the Anders' little house because she might not fit in a chair. She was in her late twenties of indeterminate European descent. Her rosacea was pronounced, made worse by her constant sweating. She was of middle height and upper weight. Eleanor figured her for two-seventy without her eyeliner. She was the town's only full-time social worker and she was overworked, underpaid, and dangerous.

Eleanor had spent two days dusting and vacuuming, cleaning every corner, lamp shade, and drawer in anticipation of her inspection. Stephanie Pearce was not subtle about her check-ups. She'd draw her finger across a window sill and slide open silverware drawers without as much as a "May I?" Eleanor usually kept the house clean, but on scheduled visits, she made double sure not to give the social worker anything to use against them.

Tabitha had cleaned up for the appointment. She'd put on

her wig and a clean dress. She used makeup to conceal the shallows of her cheeks, shadows under her eyes, and pallor of her skin. Before Pearce arrived, she'd walked through a mist of perfume and sucked on a dollop of toothpaste. Eleanor had helped Tabitha with her nails the night before, but she had chipped one this morning opening a pill bottle and now kept her hands together to hide it.

Naturally, Eleanor dressed up as well. She had only four sets of clothes that fit her larger body. She'd carefully chosen them from among the racks of secondhand clothes in a Nebraska Goodwill. She could arrange the shirts and pants and single dress into a variety of looks that all said, "Please don't look at me. I'm uninteresting." She'd wanted to buy more clothes in Jamesford, but she was deathly afraid to pick something that one of her classmates might have cast off and have it recognized. In a week or two, her mother would go down to the clinic in Riverton. Eleanor would look for clothes there.

These quarterly meetings with the social worker were routine, but each had been more threatening than the last. Stephanie Pearce was the eyes and ears of some bureaucratic machine Eleanor didn't understand. It sent them money and arranged for services like the van to Riverton and the expensive but failed medical care Tabitha had already undergone. These things (Eleanor knew because Stephanie Pearce had told her time and time again) could be stopped, and the beneficent force that had let them get by happily in poverty could also force Tabitha into a care center and Eleanor into a foster home.

"A clean house is a good indicator of how you're getting

on," Pearce said. "Of course, you had notice that I was coming. I might drop by unannounced some time just to make sure things are as they seem."

"We're getting by," said Tabitha. "Eleanor had a vacation, and she came back a new girl."

Eleanor smiled politely.

"She did spring up didn't she," Pearce said, eyeing Eleanor critically. Eleanor was careful to remain seated for this visit, as she had the previous one before her trip.

"How did you get on while Eleanor was away?" asked the social worker.

"Oh, I did just fine," said Tabitha easily. "It was actually kind of nice to have a little time alone. Eleanor is always fussing. I didn't throw any parties or anything, but it was nice to have some quiet. Teenagers, you know."

"Did you do the shopping? Go out?"

"I don't remember," Tabitha lied. "Eleanor left me stocked up. I don't think I had to leave the property."

Pearce made an ominous note in her file.

"No, wait. I did run out of cream for my coffee. I walked down to the 7-Eleven and got myself a chocolate donut and a quart of half-and-half."

"How was that walk?"

"It was a beautiful day," she said. Stephanie raised an eyebrow when Tabitha ducked the question.

"I took my time," she said as if confessing. "When the heat got bad or the dust too thick, I sat down under a tree and watched the clouds for a minute. It was delightful, but not something I'd do every morning."

The admission of physical limitations satisfied the social worker. How she didn't know it was a lie was beyond Eleanor.

"And how are you doing in school, Eleanor?" Stephanie asked, marking a check-list in her file.

"Fine. I'm getting B's."

"No C's? No F's?"

"Heavens no," said Tabitha. "I'd skin her bottom if she did so poorly."

"Any A's?"

"It's the start of school," Eleanor explained quietly. "We've only had a few assignments."

"And your citizenship grades?"

Citizenship grade meant behavior. It was a patriotic label that teachers used to grade students' attitudes and flattery skills.

"No problems," she said.

"I understand you had a quarrel with Mrs. Hart, your history teacher."

"Who told you about that?" asked Tabitha.

"I speak with all the teachers at the school. It's my job," she sighed. All this talking made her short of breath.

"No. It wasn't a quarrel. I just voiced my opinion and brought up some facts."

"Well, she said you might have authority issues."

Eleanor stared at the floor.

"She wasn't disciplined at the time," said Tabitha. "It couldn't have been that big of a deal."

"Probably not, but it was out of character, and Mrs. Hart brought it to my attention." She paused to catch her breath. "I'm just trying to be thorough."

"We understand."

She glanced at her watch. "Well, I've got to head up the canyon," she said. "This was a nice visit. I'll see you next month."

"Next month?" asked Tabitha.

"Yes, I think we should have more frequent visits. Eleanor's behavior could be a symptom of other issues."

"It was one time," Eleanor objected.

"We like the visits," Tabitha said, casting a silencing glance at Eleanor. "We'll see you next month."

She struggled off the couch and presented her hand to Tabitha, who, to Eleanor's relief, shook it instead of kissing the ring on it.

When Stephanie Pearce was outside squeezing herself into her white and rust Volkswagen beetle, Eleanor stood up and went to her mother.

"What if she'd noticed we don't have coffee?" she asked.

"I'd have said we ran out. Or I gave it up because it was making me jittery."

Eleanor knelt down and put her head on her mother's lap. "I'm sorry I had to leave you."

"Nonsense," she said caressing her hair. "I was fine. You think too much of yourself," she teased. "Cupcake, I was fine. You had to go. Let's not be careless now. Maybe you should go more often."

"We'll see," she said. She stayed on her lap for long moment, breathing in perfume and clean clothes.

"I'll make dinner," she said and got up for the kitchen. "Chili?"

"I'm game if you are," Tabitha said. "I don't have your sensitive nose."

"And tomatoes," Eleanor said.

"Yes, and tomatoes." Tabitha smiled.

On the last Monday of October, Mr. Graham asked David to stay after class. Like usual, Eleanor had remained in her seat until the classroom emptied. Mr. Graham began talking while she was still there, unnoticed or ignored. She shrunk back, waited, and listened.

"Mr. Venn," the chemistry teacher said. "You're doing alright in math, but your chemistry score is below par."

"I'll work on it, Mr. Graham," said David. "I'm getting the hang of it."

"No you're not. Each test score has been worse than the previous one."

David said nothing to this.

"Mr. Venn," he said. "You are failing this course."

David remained mute, but didn't take his eyes off the teacher.

"Chemistry is required for graduation," the teacher went on. "You will not graduate high school without a passing grade here. You will be required to re-take the course in summer school if you fail to pass."

"I didn't know Jamesford had summer school," David said.

"We don't. You'll have to bus to Riverton."

David snorted.

"Further, Mr. Venn, I have to report this to Principal Curtz. You'll be ineligible to compete in the rodeo next month if you're still failing."

David's mouth made to protest, but nothing came out. His shoulders sagged.

"I'll try harder," he finally said. The despondency in his voice was too much for Eleanor.

"I can tutor him," she heard herself say.

The two turned around suddenly, obviously thinking they were alone.

"Is that you, Miss Anders? What did you say?"

"I said I can tutor David. I'm good at chemistry."

David looked at her guardedly. She couldn't read him.

"I don't care what help you get, Mr. Venn, but you definitely need some. I am unavailable for private tutoring. Miss Anders wouldn't be my first choice for a tutor, but if she—"

"Okay," David said. "Yes, if she's serious. I'll have Eleanor help me."

"The next test is on Friday," he said. "If you don't get at least a B- on that, there'll be no statistical way for you to raise your grade above failing before the rodeo. Do you understand?"

"Yes," said David, but he was looking at Eleanor. The slightest smile lifted the corner of his mouth and Eleanor blushed.

David waited for Eleanor in the hall and walked with her to the gym.

"Will you really help me with chemistry?" he said as the bell rang, making them both late to P. E.

"I said I would," she said. "Does that surprise you?"

"I thought you were mad at me," he said. "You've ignored me since I got here."

Shame swirled in her spinning mind. She felt herself blush again.

"I didn't think you remembered me," she said.

David laughed. "Are you kidding me? We're engaged! How could I forget you?"

She smiled but hid it behind her bangs. "I'm not the same person," she said. "We were just kids then. Just playing make-believe."

"I'm not the same person either," he said, and then, as if hearing his own words for the first time, grew sullen and wistful.

"I'm really good at chemistry," Eleanor said. "It's my best class."

"Perfect," he said. "When should we start?"

"Today? After school?" she offered.

"Great, where should we study? Do you still live in that dollhouse on Cedar Street?"

"Yes," she said. "It needs painting."

"I'll tell you what," David said. "I'll paint your house if you can get me to compete against these yokels at the rodeo." David stopped short. He shook his head.

"I'm sorry," he said. "I didn't mean that. There are nice people here. It's just, just that they're not what I'm used to. You know? I was living in a big city. Culture and civilization."

Eleanor smiled.

"Oh no," he said. "I've done it again. You must think I've become a real snob."

"No," she said. "You're right. They are hicks. They know nothing of the world. Jamesford is a backwater. They don't know anything, and worse, they don't know they don't know anything."

"They've never been starving coyotes," he said, freezing Eleanor.

"No," she said. "They have little imagination."

"Their loss," he said as they came to the gym door. "My place?"

"Let's start in the library," Eleanor offered. "Less awkward that way."

"Yes, of course. What was I thinking?"

Eleanor shrugged.

"I know what I was thinking," he said. "I was thinking

I'd like to show you off to my mother and introduce you to Wendy, my little sister. Maybe you can come over after?"

"Not tonight," she said. "I've got to get home."

"It's not far. If you don't want to walk, we could take a bus and my mom can give you a ride home."

"I know it's not far. But I can't tonight," she said.

"You know where I live?"

Eleanor looked at her shoes, her hair closing around her face like a shroud.

David laughed. "This is becoming a pretty good day," he said. "I'll meet you after school in the library, okay?"

"Okay," said Eleanor.

Outside on the play field, Mr. Blake blew his whistle to assemble the class. David disappeared into the boy's dressing room. Eleanor stood in the hall a long time, collecting her thoughts and arranging her feelings, and utterly failing to do either.

CHAPTER SEVEN

In first and second grades, Eleanor was an exemplary student. She was polite and energetic and learned faster than the rest of her class. She was something of a prodigy. Her teacher sent home notes praising her and offering to have her tested to skip a grade. Eleanor and Tabitha talked about it at some length and decided that it would be best for Eleanor to slow down and not draw too much attention to herself.

"We don't want anyone looking too closely at us, cupcake, do we?"

"No, Momma, we don't."

In a sudden change, Eleanor became a quintessential, average second-grade student. She didn't like it, but she understood it and did it. She stopped playing with the other kids for fear of excelling. She'd been a beast at tag—no one could ever catch her and no one was safe. She moved with a predator's grace and sometimes made the other kids cry when she howled at them as she chased them down. But she stopped all that in second grade.

Eleanor took to the swings then as her primary recess

activity. Taking her turn and then getting back in line to take another.

"You like the swings as much as me," David had said to her. "Are you being an airplane or a bird?"

She'd known David since she came to the school. He was one of the "nice boys," a group of kids who didn't tease her or make her feel bad. In the last months of second grade, that list was shrinking quickly.

"What are you?" she asked.

"I used to be a plane. One of those old ones with lots of wings. Then I was a Spitfire because my dad said they won Britain. But now, you know, I think I'm just a bird."

"Birds are cool," Eleanor said, taking her turn. David took the swing next to her.

"Yeah," he said. "If I could be any animal, I think I'd be a bird. A big eagle maybe, or a pterodactyl. What would you be?'

"I've never been a bird," she said. "I think I could be a good one."

"I bet you could," he said.

They pumped their legs and swung higher and higher. David fell into rhythm with Eleanor and kept talking.

"You're really smart," he said. "And you can run really fast."

"So?" she said, trying to break their synchronicity.

"So it's cool, that's all."

"Why are you being nice to me?" she asked.

"Aren't you 'spicous," he said.

"What's 'spicous?" she asked.

"Means you don't trust nobody."

Eleanor pumped higher until butterflies mixed in her stomach.

"I guess I'm 'spicous then," she said.

"You can trust me," David said. "Let's be friends."

"Why should I trust you?"

"'Cause I'm your friend, silly," he'd reasoned.

"Oh," she said, not wholly convinced. "I guess we can be friends," she said. "Even if I'm 'spicous."

"That's awesome!" David said. "When we're birds, we can fly around together and see everything and go anywhere."

When recess was over, the class split into groups for a project, and David appeared next to Eleanor before she had a chance to object.

That was it. From that day on, David and Eleanor were friends. They'd eat lunch together and play together and always managed to be on the same team during games. At first she tolerated him, but then looked forward to seeing him. Once, when David didn't come to school for a dentist appointment, Eleanor started to cry before morning snacks and wouldn't stop. She was inconsolable. Finally, Tabitha had to come take her home.

Eleanor never told her mother why she'd broken down, she hadn't understood it herself, but the next day, when David was back with two new silver fillings, she ran up and hugged him.

He hugged her back and that led to a summer of terrible teasing from the other kids.

"Dave and Eleanor sitting in a tree, K-I-S-S-I-N-G!"

Eleanor couldn't stand it. She avoided David for weeks and stayed at home helping her mother on sunny days. David would come by, and most days she wouldn't even answer the door for him. Finally, he convinced her to go play with him in the park to swing as birds. There, Russell Liddle and his friends teased the two again.

"You guys going to make out?" he said. "Gross."

"You're just jealous," David said. Eleanor wanted to run. She'd already spotted a bush she could dart through and a path that would take her to a hiding place by the river.

"Jealous of what? You?"

"Yeah, because you're too ugly to even have a girlfriend, let alone one as cute as Eleanor."

Russell flustered. His friends waited for the reply. It took a while to come, when it did, he said, "She's as ugly as a horse's ass."

The swear word impressed his friends and got David's attention. He jumped off the swing, landing in the sand like an Olympic gymnast, and walked directly over to Russell. Russell was taller than David then, and Russell arched his back for his full height. David didn't slow down; he walked up to him, doubled up his fist, and smashed it into his gut. Russell fell over gasping.

"Anyone else want some?" he challenged the two wide-eyed friends.

They backed away.

"Say sorry or I'll make you eat grass," David ordered Russell.

He squirmed and moaned and kicked the ground. David flopped on top of him and turned him over. He pushed a fistful of grass into Russell's crying face until he shouted, "I'm sorry!"

The other boys were gone. It was just Russell, David, and Eleanor. Russell cried, Eleanor gawked, and David stood up.

"Good," he said. "'Bout time you learned some manners."

Afterward, the two of them went for ice cream.

"Ah, don't be upset," David told her. "He had it coming."

"I just hate to see fighting. It's so scary."

"My dad says to never start a fight, but always finish it."

"What does that mean?"

"I think it means don't run away."

"Did you hurt him?"

"Russell? Heck no," he said. "Well, maybe a little bit. When I punched him. But he'll be fine."

"You're going to get in trouble now, aren't you?"

"I doubt it," he said. "Russell is a lot of things, but tattletale ain't one of them."

"Why'd you do it?" Eleanor asked. She hadn't touched her ice cream. It melted down her fingers.

"Because he was being mean to you," he said. "You eat less than a mouse. I paid a dollar for that ice cream. You better eat it. Don't be wasteful."

"Oh, no. That wouldn't do," she said and took bite. "It's good."

"Yep, our first date."

"What?"

"My dad said he used to take my mom out for ice cream on dates. So we're on a date."

She didn't understand.

"We're going steady now," he said. "You're my girl and I'm your boy. We'll get married one day."

"You have to be in love to get married, don't you?"

"I love you," he said plainly. "Don't you love me?"

Eleanor thought about it.

"How do I know?" she asked.

"You like me?"

"Yes," she said.

"We're friends aren't we?"

"Sure."

"You'd do nice things for me, wouldn't you?"

"Yes, of course. I would if I could."

"Well, me too. Like today. That showed I love you."

"I'd be afraid to hit Russell," she said.

"No, silly. That's what I did. You could do something like make me cookies sometimes or read to me when I'm sick. That's like love."

"Oh, I could do that for you," she said.

"So we're in love," he said smartly. "And when a girl and a boy love each other, eventually they get married. That's how things work. Ask your mom."

Eleanor ate her ice cream thinking about what he had said.

"I could tell you a secret," she said. "To show you I love you."

"Yes, that would be good. That's how it works. I'm sure of it."

"I've never told anybody but Tabitha before," she said. "I'm not supposed to tell anyone. Do you promise to keep it secret?"

"Cross my heart and hope to die," he said.

She looked at him hard, using her years of experience to read his intent. She was good at that. She could sense moods like a seasoned predator, but she could not tell the endurance of those moods. She had not been around people long enough to develop that kind of empathy, and wondered if she ever would. She could sense fear, and joy, see lies in the way a person glanced away, and truth in the way their eyes melted, but people were fickle. One day they were your friends bringing you corn and beans, and the next day they had guns.

She looked hard at David who was down to the stick of his fudgesicle.

"It's okay, Eleanor," he said. "You don't have to tell me if it's too secret. That's also what friends do."

She opened her mouth to speak, but caution stopped the sound in her throat.

"If you want to tell me, you can trust me," he said. "I won't tell."

There it was. Trust. Tabitha had cautioned her about trusting too easily and too openly. She had secrets. They had secrets. Secrets that would rend the family to pieces and worse.

"I'm afraid you won't like me if I tell you," she said finally.

"Oh, that kind of secret," he said.

She nodded.

"I'll tell you what," he said. "I'll think of a secret first and tell you, and then you can tell me. Then we'll be even."

"Okay," she said.

David couldn't think of one that day, so they went back to the park and pretended to be crows on the swings until the sun set, and they had to go home.

Later that month, the week before school was to begin their third grade, David rushed to Eleanor's one morning and knocked on the door. Tabitha was having one of her better days. She had more good days than bad back then, and fed him and Eleanor toast with jam and a glass of juice.

"You guys sure have a nice place," he said very politely.

"Where did you learn your manners, David?" Tabitha asked.

"My father, ma'am. He's in the army. That's what I came to tell Eleanor. It's my secret."

Eleanor blanched. Tabitha glanced at her suspiciously.

"Secrets?"

"Sorry, Mrs. Walker," he said. "I can't talk about it with you. It's a secret for Eleanor."

After breakfast, the two kids went down by the stream to catch frogs.

"Where's your dad?" David asked.

"I don't have one. It's just Tabitha and me."

"Oh. Does it make you sad?"

"No," she said. "I don't think of it much. I used to have a dad and a mom and a little brother. But they died. Now it's just Tabitha and me."

"Was that your secret?" David said. "I haven't told you mine yet."

"Yeah, it's kinda one," she said.

"Well, I promise not to tell," he said and crossed his chest.

Eleanor caught a frog.

"My dad's going to war," David said. "That's my secret. He's going on a secret mission to Iraq. You can't tell nobody or it'll sink ships. It's a secret and no one knows but you and my mom and dad and me."

"Wow," she said. "That's a good one."

"Yeah, it is. We just found out this morning, and I had to run over and tell you."

She showed David the frog. It jumped out of her hand and they chased it across the bank until they lost it in the reeds.

"You ever eaten a frog?" David said. "My mom says they do that in France."

"Yes," Eleanor said. "I've eaten hundreds."

"You lie," he said.

"No," she said. "I have. I was so hungry. I was hungry all the time. Frogs were good and I got good at catching them. I could bite them and swallow them all at once."

"Eleanor, friends don't tell fibs, unless you're telling a tall tale."

"It's not a fib," she said.

"Then it's a tale," he said. "Go on. Tell me when you ate all them frogs."

"After my family died, I was not to be seen. I became a coyote and stayed that way for a long, long time. That's when I ate all the frogs."

CHAPTER EIGHT

David met Eleanor in the library after school and she looked over his recent quizzes and saw how he was in trouble. She took the oldest and worked each problem out with him and then gave him problems of her own fabrication to practice on. They worked for ninety minutes before the janitor chased them out.

"Thanks, Eleanor," David said, packing up his book bag. "I think I'm catching on. A little. I mean, I got that one right."

"It's not just the math, you've got to visualize electrons and atoms and molecules. See how they interact, attract, and repulse."

David groaned.

"Also, the stoichiometry gets harder. Those today were from a couple weeks ago."

"I've got to pass the test this week," he said. "I'm doomed."

"No, you can do it," she said. "You only need a B-; that's not hard."

"Easy for you to say," he said. "I'm never going to be a chemist. I'm going to be a writer. Why do I need to know about acids and bases?"

"I'll help you every day," she promised.

"You will?"

Eleanor nodded. "Re-read the earlier chapters again if you can."

"Okay," he said. "Thanks."

Eleanor collected her things, and they left the library together.

"Wait, I'll walk you home," he said.

"Maybe next time," she said and slipped away before he stopped her cold.

She ducked behind the side of a building with a deft leap and a sprint. When David opened the door a moment later and surveyed the grounds, she was nowhere to be seen.

"I'll never figure you, Eleanor Anders," she heard him say under his breath.

Eleanor had neglected to call Tabitha about staying late after school. She knew her mother would be worried. But buoyed on happy legs, she hurriedly skipped home, breaking into a run when she thought no one was watching.

"Where have you been, young lady?" her mother said when she came in.

"I stayed after school with David Venn," she shouted and hopped on her toes. Tabitha's anger melted, and she patted the sofa next to her.

"Tell me all about it, cupcake."

Tabitha listened carefully to Eleanor's detailed description of Mr. Graham's meeting and her daughter's dialogue with the boy in the hall. Eleanor's excitement was contagious, but she could feel her mother's cautiousness.

"He always struck me as a bright kid. Why is he struggling in chemistry?"

"He's never had it before. Chemistry is like math that works wrong. A lot of kids struggle with it."

"It's good of you to help him."

"It's what friends do," she said. "They help each other."

"Yes, they do," agreed Tabitha.

"And we love each other," Eleanor added.

"That was a long time ago, cupcake," her mother warned. "And love means something different to grown-ups than it does to kids."

"I'm not a kid," she said.

Tabitha looked in her daughter's eyes. "No, you're not. But you don't know everything yet. Time doesn't make you wise; experience does. Be careful. This is new territory."

"I will," she said.

"You know he might just want the chemistry help and not a girlfriend."

"We can be friends."

"Of course you can. I just don't want you getting hurt."

"I said I'll be careful."

"Okay," said Tabitha. "Let's eat something. And call me next time, understand?"

"Yes, I do."

That week, every day after school, the two met in the library and studied for Friday's test. By the third day, they fell into a comfortable routine of studying for fifty minutes, then taking a ten minute break before another half hour of problems.

"You're going to get that B. I'm sure," she said.

They were drinking cokes in the cafeteria, David's treat. Mrs. Church, the lunch lady, regarded them suspiciously before locking the kitchen and leaving the school.

"It is making loads more sense," he said. "You're a great teacher."

"How goes the rodeo practice?"

"I'll skip it this week," he said. "But it's going well. Mr. Blake says I'm the best in the school."

"Isn't Russell Liddle in the shooting competition, too?"

"Yeah. Pistols. Same as me."

"Is he still being a jerk to you?" Eleanor already knew the answer. She'd overheard Russell talking about David behind his back for weeks. He hadn't forgotten the mouthful of grass that summer.

"He's okay to me on the range," David said. "I mean, what can he say? The targets speak for themselves."

Eleanor nodded.

"Since when does the Fall School Rodeo have shooting and cooking contests?"

"We had a wheelchair kid a while ago. He's gone now, moved away, but the school thought it would be good for our image to include him. He could shoot so they added shooting. The cooking, that's just so the Home-Ec kids can burn bread."

"You never talk like this in school," David said.

Eleanor blushed. "What do you mean?"

"I mean you're like a totally different person with me than you are in school. You hardly ever say a word in class. The most I've heard you say since I got here was the first day when you told Mrs. Hart to check her Shoshone history."

"I don't know," Eleanor said softly.

"Now don't go into your shell," David said. "I like who you are with me. And not with me. You're genuine, Eleanor. That's what I've always admired in you. Nothing fake."

Eleanor felt her lip tremble.

"What did I say?" David said. "Are you okay?"

"You don't know me," she said. "Not at all."

"Yes, I do. You're Eleanor Anders, my oldest friend in the world. The best person in this entire God-awful state. The only reason I don't mind coming to school."

"I'm sorry I'm a different person sometimes."

"Don't apologize, silly," he said. "And please don't cry. My mom says everyone is different with everyone."

Eleanor glanced at the wall. "We have to get back. I promised you a B by Friday."

She walked away. She could feel his confused eyes follow her into the library before he came in after.

When they were done, David again offered to walk Eleanor home.

"It's cold," he said, like that made company a requirement.

"I've been cold before. I know cold. I'll be fine."

"Are you mad at me?" he asked. "You are. You're mad at me."

"No," she said. "I'm just being weird. Like usual. Ask anyone. Eleanor Anders is weird."

"I have heard rumors," he said and then froze.

"What?" demanded Eleanor. "What have you heard?"

"Just stupid stuff," he said. "When people in Wyoming don't understand someone, they make up stories."

"Tall tales?" Eleanor said.

"Exactly."

"What was it? Who was it?" Eleanor demanded. Her intensity made David's eyes grow wide. Suddenly, she felt the feral urge of fight or flight. Her muscles twitched, her mouth grew dry. She turned away and made herself breathe calmly.

"I'm sorry," David said. "I'm dumb for telling you. It was

Robby Guide. He said something about you being a witch or a ghost or something. It was all crap and I told him so."

He put his arm on her shoulder and turned her around. "It's crap. I told him if he said anything like that again, I'd sock him."

"What did he say I did?"

"We don't want to talk about this, do we?"

"Just tell me. I need to know."

"He said—this is so stupid—that in eighth grade, you were knocked out by a softball and when you came to, your eyes were different colors. Only for a minute or two. He said one of your brown eyes turned blue, and the other white. He must have been smoking dope."

"I didn't see the ball coming. It was a foul. If I'd seen the ball coming, if anyone had warned me, it'd have never touched me."

"I used to live here, and I still don't understand the kids in this school."

"It doesn't bother you that you're seen with me?"

"No," he said firmly. "Who's looking anyway? Who cares?"

Eleanor pointed across the parking lot. David squinted and held his hand over his eyes. "Who's that?"

"Russell Liddle, Tanner Nelson, and their friends. And over there"—Eleanor pointed to a car driving slowly away—"is Alexi Kerr and Crystal Tate. Barbara Pennon was there earlier."

"So the whole class then," he said. "No, I don't care. I didn't even notice them. With your eyesight, you should be on the shooting team."

"Never," she said.

David passed the Friday test with a solid B, beating his required B- by six points. He was thrilled. He could do the math because Eleanor had showed him the tricks, but he didn't understand the theory behind it. Mr. Graham was quick to remind him that he still had much to do to reverse his previous scores and theory would be a major part of it. Still, he got to stay on the shooting team, and Eleanor and David cut their tutoring sessions down to twice a week so he could practice.

David had skipped lunches the week before the test to rework his failed labs—a concession Mr. Graham had made only after Mr. Blake had made a personal appeal to him "on behalf of the school." The week after the test, David sat with Eleanor at lunch. When she wouldn't join him at his usual table he made a big show of carrying his tray through the cafeteria to her and sat down. Today he was waiting for her when she came in, and held her chair out for her when she sat down. Hidden behind her hair, she heard the unmistakable hush of all her classmates noticing the act.

"You're embarrassing me," she whispered and sat down in the offered chair.

"They're going to talk no matter what. Might as well give them something to talk about."

"I don't like people looking at me. I don't like them noticing me."

"Even me?"

She sipped her milk through a straw. "You're not people."

"Thanks," he said. "Do you remember when you made that moose call, and that big moose walked right up to your door?

"You wanted to ride him."

"I think I could have. You practically speak moose."

She laughed unexpectedly, spitting milk over her lunch.

"I'd think ketchup would have been a better choice for

fries, but milk works, too," said David. He mopped up the spill, chortling under his breath.

"Remember when you imitated my mom and did that whole Daffy Duck thing? I spat milk out my nose that day. You did her perfectly."

After lunch, Barbara Pennon cornered Eleanor in the hall. Crystal Tate was with her and Penelope, fresh from a middle-school bathroom. Crystal stank of horses and leather; Barbara of cheap perfume and cigarettes; Penelope of vomit. They were color coordinated in Barbie doll pink. It worked on Barbara with the blond hair and slim figure and big bust, but it was a wreck on Crystal with her rugged frame and short chestnut hair. Nothing would look good on Penelope but a straw hat and crows, thought Eleanor.

"What's the deal, Eleanor?" asked Crystal.

"Come on. Fess up. What's going on with you and David Venn?" said Penelope with an edge in her voice that made Eleanor uneasy, more uneasy.

"Leave me alone," she said.

"Don't be that way," said Barbara. "The whole school's talking about it. We just want to know."

"It's none of your business."

"You giving it to him?" said Barbara. "Is that what he sees in you? He can do better. Someone should tell him that."

It came on Eleanor instinctively; a muscle memory, a sudden recollection. Her throat tensed. Her vocal chords contorted. Her jaw jutted out. From her mouth came a sudden sharp bark before her teeth snapped in Barbara's face.

The girls staggered back. Barbara tripped over her backpack and fell on her boney butt. The others stared slack-jawed and wide-eyed. The canine yap had silenced the chatter in the hall. Everyone searched for an animal loose in the school. Unbelieving eyes fell on Eleanor and then looked elsewhere.

She ducked her head and walked away. She took a deep breath and got a hold of herself. She relaxed, but her throat was too taut with adrenalin, and she dared not speak.

She walked to the office and scribbled a note claiming laryngitis and wanting to go home. After a call to Tabitha, Eleanor was checked out. She walked home crying.

CHAPTER NINE

Tabitha insisted that Eleanor return to school the next day. "Act like everything's fine," she said. "Those girls will leave you alone and if they don't, just walk away."

Eleanor shook her head. "Why now?"

"You weren't ready for it. You're taking chances with David. You're stepping out of the shadows. Maybe you should let it rest for a while."

"No," she said. "He needs my help."

"Okay," Tabitha said heavily. "But you've got to be more careful, cupcake."

Tabitha rocked the shaking girl in her arms for a long time.

When she'd calmed down, Tabitha said, "I bet you're hungry."

Eleanor nodded.

"Get those steaks out," she said. "You need protein."

The steaks were old, left over from her Nebraska trip. She thawed two, knowing that Tabitha wouldn't have any. Lately her stomach rebelled against anything but the blandest food.

After dinner, the two played cards on the kitchen table.

Eleanor could see that Tabitha was tired, but she insisted on the game.

"You know, sweetie, I'm not always going to be here," said Tabitha, putting down a two.

"Don't talk that way," Eleanor said, drawing a card.

"Even without cancer, parents go before their kids. It's okay."

Eleanor put down a jack. Tabitha took it.

"We've got to think about it, cupcake. You still have three years of school."

"I don't need school," she said.

"Yes, you do," she said. "I've been thinking that it's a good thing for you to stretch out a little and interact more with the other kids. I know you're scared and suspicious, and you should be. But you need to learn about them so you can be among them the rest of your life."

Eleanor drew another card. She pretended to concentrate on her options and then finally laid down a seven.

"You're a fine girl," Tabitha said. "You'll be a fine woman. You can be anything you want to be."

Eleanor shot her mother a look. When it dawned on Tabitha, they both broke out laughing.

"Do you want the seven?" asked Eleanor.

"No." Tabitha drew a card.

"Momma, I don't want to think about it. We're okay now. That's all that matters. When things change, we'll see where we are then, okay? Plans just lead to disappointment."

"That's not true, Eleanor," said Tabitha. "We should have a plan. Just in case."

"Not tonight, Momma," Eleanor said.

"Okay, cupcake. Gin."

The school was abuzz with Eleanor's yap. If there was any doubt where the sound had come from before, Barbara, Crystal, and Penelope had made sure everyone knew that Eleanor had gone feral after being teased. She heard the talk in the halls before she was even in the school. She felt the stares and noted how the others stepped out of her way when she moved to her locker.

Her mother had told her to act like nothing had happened, and if that wasn't possible, to act like she'd been in a fight and won it. "Wear it like a trophy," she'd told her.

She was trying. In English class she stared down Barbara and Penelope by retreating deep into her own skull, imagining her eyes to be medieval arrow slits in a fortress wall. Safe behind yards of stone, she froze her expression with an unnatural stillness that finally made all the gawkers look away.

David tried to communicate sympathy and curiosity in a single look that Eleanor acknowledged with only a twitch of her lip, a brief chink in the wall, a smile of thanks.

"Friday there will be no school, as you know," said Mrs. Hart. "It's the Fall School Rodeo at the Center and I expect everyone to be there to support our Cowboys. I won't be taking roll, but I will notice if anyone isn't there."

Mrs. Hart looked quizzically at the class, perhaps sensing something she didn't know.

"Let's discuss Room 101," she said picking up her copy of *1984.* She'd promised to be done with the book by Halloween next week.

"Russell Liddle," Mrs. Hart said, making the boy jerk up from his doodling. "What does Room 101 say about the state's omniscience?"

"Um," he said. "That it wants some?"

A couple of students laughed, including David. Russell spun to face him.

"What are you laughing at, dick-weed?" he said.

"Mr. Liddle," warned Mrs. Hart.

David looked right at Russell. The class fell silent. Even Mrs. Hart paused.

"It's just hilarious that Mrs. Hart would ask *you* about omni-science," he said. "Talk about a trick question."

Snickers and titters broke the stillness.

Russell struggled for a comeback. He finally said, "What do you know?"

"Much more than you," David said. "But of course I have an advantage. I can read."

"That's enough, you two," Mrs. Hart broke in before it got ugly. Russell was fuming. David ignored Russell's hate-filled stares and spoke instead to Mrs. Hart.

"It's one of the most frightening things about the state," he said. "Through its spies and tricks, the state knows every secret. It can turn its knowledge against anyone by discovering their deepest fear and making them face it."

"Omniscience means 'all-knowing,'" Mrs. Hart said as a way of confirming David's remark and bringing the rest of the class, Russell specifically, along with the discussion.

Mrs. Hart lectured about the book for the remainder of the period, answering her own questions rather than throwing them to the class and risking another altercation.

Russell stalked David for the rest of the day. Eleanor held back from everyone as usual. The school's earlier interest in her bizarre coyote outbreak was lost in the pageant of David and Russell's growing feud. Within an hour, the entire tenth grade knew about it, and by the end of the school day, it had seeped into the gossip of the other grades as well.

David skipped lunch that day to complete a final lab assignment ensuring his ability to compete the next day at the rodeo shooting tournament. Eleanor sat alone at her usual table and listened to the talk.

"I'm going to get that son of a bitch," Russell bragged to his knot of friends huddled around their table. Eleanor looked up when she heard the telltale snick of an automatic knife. Russell covertly lifted it above the table to show the others. "This will get his attention, the jackass," he said. The others snickered. Eleanor felt the animal stir in her again.

"Just beat him tomorrow," said Tanner. "He's always going on about how good a shot he is thanks to his father. Beat him tomorrow and tell him you know why his Dad's still in the army—he hasn't passed basic marksmanship yet."

The others laughed.

"And don't forget to mention the cheap ammo—it's all his white trash family can afford," added another. "Living in that run-down, rat-bait trailer."

"I live in a trailer," said Russell.

"I mean," stammered the boy. "You've got land around yours. It's property. They live in a slum."

"I'm going to get him," Russell said. "Maybe today. Break his fingers so he can't shoot tomorrow."

"Okay," said Tanner enthusiastically.

"He'll tell."

"The hell he will," said Russell. "I'll warn him what'll happen if he does."

Eleanor made it to the bathroom before she threw up.

After classes, Eleanor waited for David outside the school.

"Eleanor," said David. "What are you doing here? Today isn't a study day."

"I thought I'd like to meet Wendy finally," she said quietly.

"Oh, okay. Yeah, that'd be great."

"We missed the bus," she said. "Let's get going."

Autumn had come to Jamesford. The air was cold and dry. There'd been one half-hearted snowstorm but the sun had driven it away in a day. Eleanor smelled the fall scents blowing from the farms up the canyon, mingling with the earthen fleshy tang of freshly carved pumpkins put out a few days early for the trick-or-treaters. As they crossed into town, the smell of passing traffic and cheeseburgers replaced the rural smells of final cut hay and falling leaves.

"Let's go this way," Eleanor said by the Wood Carver's Gallery. "I want to show you something."

David followed her behind the studio. Eleanor had heard the bullies following them. She hoped to draw them behind the stores through the maze of hidden paths and ways that Eleanor used to remain unseen, and where she could shepherd David home safely. She'd let them see the detour behind the art gallery, but once out of sight, she grabbed David's hand and sprinted away through a torn fence and across a vacant lot.

"What are we doing?" David said, laughing. "Slow down. I can hardly keep up."

She took David behind a rusting car on cinderblocks and pointed the way they'd come.

Russell and his gang came out of the alley they'd just left.

"Oh," he said.

Crouching low, Eleanor led David around the car and into a half-fenced yard. Careful to avoid the unpicked pumpkins in an unattended vegetable garden, they came out onto a paved street, and then quickly made the last leg to David's house.

"How did you know they were there?" David asked.

"How did you not know?" said Eleanor.

"I guess I should have expected it," David said.

"Davie!" called a little girl from the trailer door. She had dark black hair like David but hers fell straight and was tamed. She shared his pale complexion and wide eyes. She smiled with a missing tooth and then retreated behind the threshold when she saw Eleanor.

"Eleanor, this is Wendy," David said. "Wendy, this is Eleanor."

"Hi," she said. "My friends call me Wens sometimes."

"Hello, Wens," said Eleanor, making Wendy giggle.

"So this is Eleanor," said a woman opening the door wide.

"Hello, Mrs. Venn," said Eleanor. More than years had aged David's mother. Eleanor remembered the young housewife, still in the glow of a new marriage. Now there was a mother, worried and weary, fastening the last button on her super-market checker uniform.

"Come in, you two," she said. "It's too cold."

Eleanor followed David up the wooden steps and into the trailer's front room. The kitchen area was to the right. To the left behind a couch was a narrow hallway that had to lead to the bedrooms

"Wendy is five years old," David said. "She's going to be a pony when she grows up."

"A pony?" asked Eleanor.

"Maybe a unicorn," she said. "I haven't decided."

"She's a big fan of My Little Pony," David explained.

"Eleanor, you've grown up to be a beauty," said Mrs. Venn, stirring a pot of pasta on the stove. "How's your mother?"

"Tabitha is still ill," said Eleanor. "But she says she's getting better."

"Tell her hello, for us," she said.

"I will, Mrs. Venn," said Eleanor.

"Call me Karen," she said.

Eleanor nodded and let her hair fall. She glanced at some hanging pictures. David's father was pictured in many of them.

"My dad's still overseas," David said. "He's in Afghanistan now. Another tour. He might come home for Christmas."

"Maybe," corrected his mother.

"Maybe," said David. There was something in his voice that made Eleanor look at him.

"I made some spaghetti," Karen said. "As soon as the bread's out of the oven, we can eat."

"We eat early so mom can get to work on time," David said. Whatever Eleanor was looking for was gone as he offered Eleanor a glass of milk.

"You work at Sherman's Grocery?"

"Yes, I'm a checker. It's kind of fun. I get to meet everyone in town. It's like a high school reunion every day."

"I should call my mom," Eleanor said.

"Oh, there's an extension in my bedroom," said Mrs. Venn. "Last door down the hall."

Mrs. Venn's bedroom was sparse. The entire house was. It was neat, clean of dirt and dust, but there was no mistaking the poverty of its furnishings. She noted David's room, the bathroom, and a small room cluttered with stuffed animals that had to be Wendy's. She memorized their positions so she could find them in the dark. Then Eleanor called home.

"Be careful," Tabitha said.

"Always, Mom," said Eleanor. "Always."

Eleanor was quiet at dinner. She took the least amount of food she could and then only nibbled at it. She felt like she was stealing from them.

"You never eat much," David said. "Don't you get hungry?"

"Sometimes," Eleanor said. "Sometimes I eat a lot. It depends on what I've been doing."

"Our house burned down," said Wendy suddenly.

"She means our house burned down in Georgia," David said.

"That's why you came back?" asked Eleanor.

"'Surance won't pay," said Wendy. "Assholes."

"Wendy!" said Mrs. Venn. "Mind your mouth, young lady."

Wendy twisted her forehead rethinking what she said. "Oh, sorry," she said.

"Yeah, they're being real dicks about it," David said. His mother shot him a look.

"How'd it happen?" Eleanor asked.

"Something in the garage," he said. "They're still investigating."

"Oh," Eleanor said, but she had no idea what it all meant.

"It gave us an opportunity to come back to the country," Mrs. Venn said. "Fresh air, no traffic jams."

David rolled his eyes. His mother didn't see it, but Eleanor did. She spun noodles on her fork.

"I'm glad you're back," she said.

Eleanor caught a slight smile cross Mrs. Venn's lips before she hid it in a piece of garlic bread. "Yeah, well, it's not all bad," she said.

"You're going to win a trophy tomorrow," Wendy said.

"We'll see," said David.

"We'll all be there and I'll send photos to your dad," Karen said.

"Great, Mom. No pressure."

"You'll do great," she said and then, glancing at her watch, stood up. "I've got to go. Eleanor, do you need a ride home?"

"No, ma'am."

"I said call me Karen."

"Oh, sorry. I don't need a ride, Karen."

"Okay. Don't forget your homework," she said, collecting her coat and purse.

"Thanks for dinner," Eleanor said.

"Any time," she said and blew kisses at her kids before disappearing through the door.

"Let's play games!" said Wendy. "Do you like Hungry Hungry Hippos?"

"I should go," said Eleanor. "My mom's expecting me."

"You should have had Mom drive you," said David. "It's dark now."

"I see well in the dark," she said. "I'll be fine."

"I'll walk you home," he said. "Grab your coat, Wendy. We're going for a walk."

"No," said Eleanor. "I'll be fine."

David argued with her for five minutes, but she would not be moved. Wendy found a cartoon on TV and finally yelled, "Quit it! Can't you see I'm watching TV?"

"I'll see you tomorrow," Eleanor said. "I'll be rooting for you."

Before he could argue again, Eleanor slipped out the door and disappeared into the night.

In the darkness, she circled the trailer park three times before she was convinced that Russell and his friends weren't lurking about.

CHAPTER TEN

This year, schools from all over the county and the Wild River Reservation sent their riders to Jamesford. Jamesford had many rodeos. They couldn't compete with Cody, but Jamesford kept the Wyoming sport as alive and active as anywhere in the state.

Since the event expanded from being just a rodeo to a western skills competition with shooting and authentic pioneer cooking, the event took the entire day and was viewed as a country fair. The less popular events, the ones without horses, were done during the morning while the livestock was delivered. In the evening, when parents could more likely attend, the four-hour event would take place in the warmed, covered arena.

The students arrived early, having been bused before daybreak to arrive in time for a hearty meal of buffalo bacon, prairie hen eggs, and yes, burned bread. The shooters were driven to the range at nine o'clock in a Jamesford school bus. Many onlookers and those who didn't need the extra time to practice throwing a rope followed in another bus. Naturally, Eleanor was there.

The competition was pistol and rifle at different ranges. Simple target practice, no quick draw, ear and eye protection. The range wasn't equipped for spectators, so the crowd huddled behind the fence and peeked around the shooters from a good distance away. When Mr. Blake set up a video screen in a gazebo and trained a camera with a telephoto lens on the targets, most gathered there to watch.

At first Eleanor stayed by the fence. Unlike the others, she could see the targets down range. What she hadn't expected was the tremendous sound of the little guns and the instinctive terror that overcame her when she heard it.

When the first pistol fired into the paper target, she screamed.

A range master in an orange vest, raced up to her. The shooting stopped.

"Are you alright?" he asked and fell to one knee. He looked Eleanor over for bullet holes.

"It just startled me," she said. "I'm okay. It's so loud."

"You should hear it close up," he said. "Here take these. They might help." He offered her a pair of sponge earplugs and showed her how to put them in. She thanked him, and he waved for the competition to resume.

She'd disrupted the competition and felt the pathetic stares from her classmates. She cringed at the attention. She stole a look at the gazebo and saw Robby Guide holding his stare on her for a long time after the others went back to the screen, and the shots began again. His stare made her uneasy as only his could. He was half Shoshone, he said, but he looked pureblood. Eleanor knew he had family on the reservation and wondered if they knew of her. She couldn't look at the dark features of the boy and not think of her own family and its destruction. Finally, Robby turned to watch the screen, and Eleanor withdrew behind a pillar.

When the visiting shooters had had their six shots each, the home team, Jamesford, was called up. David and Russell were the two pistol marksmen for the school. Russell went first. He shot a silver revolver that boomed and bucked in his hand like a captured weasel. He shot well, though, and Eleanor saw a four-inch grouping around the center.

David was next and had a black pistol. He fired off his six with sharp, sure plinks. David shot better. His holes were smaller but the grouping was tighter and more central. They put targets out at a further distance and repeated the exercise. Then again. And finally, they put the targets out at the farthest distance the pistol range had, seventy-five yards.

With a charge of elation, Eleanor saw that at each range, David's shots were the best. Even out at seventy-five yards when some of the boys failed to hit the target altogether, David had put the majority in the colored sections.

With each round, Russell grew more and more vexed. Eleanor heard him complain first to Mr. Blake and then to the judges that David was using an illegal gun.

"The handgun tournament is for large calibers," he complained. "It's not even an American gun."

Finally, to stop his grumbling the tournament officials examined David's pistol.

"See? It's just a little .22."

The judge examined a bullet. It was long and pointed and reminded Eleanor of an arrow where the others made her think of rocks and clubs.

"It's made in Kentucky," said David. "It's a 5.7 x 28 mm.

NATO." David offered a box of shells, and the judge read the statistics and whistled. He glanced at a rulebook and then shrugged.

"This was written before these existed," he said. "Based on the box, though, there's no way in the world this could be confused with a little .22 unless it was a hot load shot out of a rifle. I'll allow it. Good shooting."

"That's bullshit!" said Russell. "He's cheating!"

"Way to support your team," said the judge.

Robby and several other kids had come up to the fence to see what was going on. They hissed and booed at Russell's tantrum, and he flipped them the bird.

"Gotta count you down, Mr. Blake. Bad sportsmanship," said the judge.

Mr. Blake glared at Russell, who finally stormed away.

Even with Russell's penalty, Jamesford won the handgun competition going away, thanks to David's shooting. The judges and instructors stood in line to take shots with his gun when it was over.

David didn't compete in the rifle competition, but went to cheer on the team anyway. Bryce Sudman was the man to beat from Jamesford and only the Dubois shooters did. He placed third, well enough to give Jamesford the overall shooting championship with their showing in the pistols, and of course David won best personal score of the match.

Eleanor was pleased, but stayed away from David as he was mobbed and congratulated by sophomores and upper classmen. Mr. Blake pointed out David had scored the single highest score in the shooting competition's history. He neglected to add it had only been going on for three years.

Still, everyone was pleased and "Sharpshooter David Venn" was the man of the day, at least until the riding events that afternoon.

Several times, Eleanor caught David looking around, and she flattered herself into thinking that he was looking for her. Later, during the men's roping contest, she finally worked up enough courage to go to him.

From across the arena, she saw him sitting in a knot of kids. Barbara Pennon was at his side, giggling. She reached over, took a soda cup from David's hand, and helped herself to a big drink from it. Giggling, she pressed it to David's lips.

Barbara's jeans were so tight, Eleanor wondered how she'd gotten into them. Her shirt, a western affair with beads and sequins, nearly burst its buttons it was so stretched. Eleanor thought she looked like a prostitute in those tight clothes. Did she not know what size she was? Then, David glanced at Barbara's chest, and Eleanor froze. Barbara noticed the look, too. She smiled and giggled, then took another long sip from David's drink and arched her back just a bit more. Alexi and Crystal were doing the same, falling over each other to be witty and interesting for the new boy in school. At one point, Crystal turned halfway around as if looking for someone behind her. When she turned back to David, another button on her shirt had been opened.

Bryce Sudman, Eric Collins, and Brian Weaver sat with David and basked in the girls' overflowing attentions. Eleanor couldn't help but notice Alexi's silver-banded blue cowboy hat and matching vest, and tried to imagine how much it cost. She'd caught the scent of a floral perfume she'd only encountered at Macy's when she'd visited Riverton. Over the cheers and whoops of the crowd, Eleanor caught snippets of giggles and laughter from the group and gritted her teeth. Eleanor stomped her foot and kicked a pebble into the fence. She marched outside.

In the parking lot, a bench under a broken lamppost offered her a place to sit unnoticed. She fumed. Again she stomped her foot. Then again. And then she started to cry. This was becoming a bad habit, she thought. She hadn't cried in years, and lately she was acting like a colicky infant. She was too old for this. Among the sagebrush and juniper, buffalo grass and thistle, she had not felt self-pity or jealousy. Had she learned nothing from that time? If not that, what?

It infuriated her that she felt this now. She grew angrier by the second. Her head swam in a spinning vortex of self-loathing that made her want to cast off her secondhand clothes, her hair, and her skin, and run into the woods where life and death were the only variables, and expensive perfumes could only get you killed. She could be a scavenger again, an honest creature, a righteous thief, a survivalist who took what she needed, and didn't covet nice clothes or need the attention of a boy who'd once been kind to her.

She leaned her head back to howl, felt her vocal chords shift and tighten, but stopped herself. She was being foolish. She was a human being. It was her classmates who were beasts, rutting around David like a new stud. She couldn't allow herself that kind of luxury. Eleanor, had to survive, and David, and all her feelings for him, mixed up and disarming as they were, were more dangerous to her than anything she'd ever faced.

She calmed herself. Her shallow breaths froze into puffs of icy clouds and were carried away in the cold Wyoming night. She watched them go like leaves down a stream. She listened to the darkness, heard mice in the grass and bats in the sky. From within the arena, she heard the shouts of the crowd and the announcer's calls. From the other side, she heard a car door open, a shuffle of boots on gravel, and a distant TV tuned to a popular game-show that Tabitha liked. The constant sound of large trailer trucks passing through town was a familiar and soothing background. She smelled fried food and clandestine beers. She saw stars and clouds and picked out several unhurried satellites arcing across the horizon. She breathed it all in and calmed herself. She was not in danger now. That was all that mattered. The rest was imaginary.

In the gloom, Eleanor made out Greg Finlay's blue stretch-bed Dodge. Greg Finlay had graduated the year before from Jamesford High. Just barely. He was to his class what Russell Liddle was to the sophomores, only worse. He'd spent months in juvenile detention and was one of Stephanie Pearce's monthly visits on behalf of the court and Family Services. Eleanor wasn't surprised to see him. The school rodeo had brought out the entire town. What bothered her was that he had hooked up with Russell and his gang shortly after the riding began and hadn't been seen since.

Leaving her bench and creeping softly on her toes, she slid between the cars to the far end of the lot where she could see the boys standing around the truck.

She could make out Greg and Russell and Tanner and two boys who went in and out of Russell's little gang with regular frequency.

"So Halloween?" said Tanner.

"Easy," said Greg, drinking whisky from a paper sack. Eleanor could smell it. "Even if he rats us out, we can claim Halloween trick-or-treat."

"But we're going to hurt him?" said one of the boys.

"Oh, hell yeah, he'll be hurt," said Russell.

"He'll rat us out for sure."

"His word against ours. And we'll have masks on," said Russell.

"Halloween, remember?" said Greg to the others. "I'll drive, but I can't do nuthin', you know. Gotta keep clean for a while."

"Not a problem," said Russell. "Pass the bottle."

The boys passed the bottle around until it ran out and Greg smashed it on the street. Then he offered them beers from the cab of his truck. While he passed them out, Russell flicked his knife open and closed with the regularity of a dying heartbeat.

CHAPTER ELEVEN

Halloween was on Wednesday, half a week away. Eleanor spent the weekend playing cards with her mother, cleaning the house, doing homework, and worrying herself sick thinking about what Russell would do to David. Of course it had been David they were talking about. David they'd ambush on Halloween. David they'd hurt.

She could warn him, but that would only postpone things. She couldn't walk him home every night. Even if she did, she couldn't protect him, only use her senses to steer him along a safer path. "Safe" was relative with people like Russell Liddle and Greg Finlay. Eventually they'd catch David and let loose their fury on him. The longer it went unspent, the greater it would be. It didn't matter if David never actually did anything to any of them. That never mattered. They'd blame him for things he couldn't imagine, strike out at him for their fears, their delusions, their own misfortunes and shortcomings. It would be wicked and brutal and savage, and even if he survived it, David would never be the same, and the attackers would never be made to account.

Tabitha sensed Eleanor's mood and tried to draw her out,

but Tabitha went in and out of focus under the pain pills and was easily deflected. That weekend was a particularly bad one for her, and Eleanor put her mother to bed early each night after she fell asleep in her chair, cards cupped in her fingers. Eleanor told her mother that she was still upset about the incident in the hall with Barbara, but she suspected her mother was not so easily deceived and knew something else was troubling her daughter.

By Monday, Eleanor had a plan. It was foolish, dangerous, expensive, and it probably wouldn't work, but she could think of nothing better. The only other plan that rivaled her crazy one was a confession to the police about what she'd overheard. But in so small a town, as precarious as she felt her existence in Jamesford to be, she dispelled it.

The school was abuzz about the rodeo's outcome. Jamesford High had won overall first place with individual trophies coming for marksmanship, female barrels, and male calf roping. It was the best Jamesford had done in a decade, and Principal Curtz arranged for a special cake at lunch in celebration.

Mrs. Hart made a point of congratulating David in her class and made him stand up. Eleanor felt Russell's hatred across the room as the other students gave David another round of applause. He'd been the only sophomore to trophy. Eleanor heard Russell grumbling about his cheating, but he said it low enough that only his closest neighbors, part of his gang, could hear it.

Eleanor made herself sit with David at lunch. Her usual table was filled with David's friends, and she had trouble getting a chair. When she did, she had to force herself to remain calm. Barbara was practically sitting in the same seat as David, rubbing against his shoulder like an animal marking territory.

Eleanor choked back an urge to scream and patiently waited for the group to thin. She ignored Barbara's inane prattle when David tried to tell a story about his dad giving him the gun when he shipped out last spring. She was interested in the story of David's father and wanted to strangle Barbara with her color-coordinated shoe laces.

While she waited, Eleanor ate heartily. Eleanor took seconds on her lunch and thirds on the cake. Miss Church, the cafeteria leader, was surprised to see her eat so much and made only a half-joking comment about Eleanor's skinny legs needing some girth before her hips filled out. Eleanor ignored her.

Back at the table, David finally had a chance to eat his own lunch. The conversation had kept him occupied, and his chicken was cold. He counted Eleanor's empty plates.

"I haven't seen you eat this much since, well, since ever," said David.

"Growth spurt," she said, relaxing now that Barbara had gone to smoke or puke or drop off the planet somewhere. "You going to eat your cookie?"

He gave it to her.

"So you can come trick-or-treating with Wendy and me if you want," he said. Eleanor had questioned him as subtly as she could about his Halloween plans. David had promised his mother to take Wendy out that night. He was worried about the cold front that had moved in and the argument he was sure to have with Wendy when he tried to have her put a coat over her princess costume.

"No, I've got to stay home and answer the door," she said. "Tabitha isn't feeling well."

"Maybe we'll drop by," he said.

"That's a long way to go for a piece of taffy," she said. "Wendy will hate the walk."

David shrugged.

Tuesday, Eleanor checked the balance on her government food card. Tabitha's military pension money covered the expensive medicine and paid the rent, the electrical, and the heating. By signing a paper that absolved the military for her cancer, Tabitha received a generous pension, but for food, they relied on regular government assistance.

There was not enough money on the card for all she needed, so Eleanor examined their bank account and budgeted out forty-five real dollars to her cause. It might not be enough, but it was all she could comfortably take.

Eleanor put her mother to bed early that night and retired to her loft to try on clothes.

She hadn't any that would suit the occasion. They were all too plain and serviceable. Nothing would make anyone take a second look at her. Tonight, Eleanor needed to get attention. She turned to makeup.

Eleanor had never used makeup before, but Tabitha had, and she'd seen her mother spend an hour in front of a mirror with brushes and pencils and transform herself into a healthy middle-aged woman from a pain-wracked skeleton.

Tabitha lay still in her bed, the pharmaceuticals giving her hours of untainted peace before slowly wearing off in the small hours to wake her in search of another pill. From her mother's dresser, Eleanor collected the things she thought she'd need, eyeliner, lipstick, foundation, and blush, and took them to the bathroom.

After an hour in front of the mirror, Eleanor realized she did not have the slightest idea what she was doing. Tabitha's coloring was different that hers, and unless she made some physical change, the colors in her available pallet would only make her look like a clown. She washed everything off and settled for mascara, eyeliner and the reddest lipstick she could find. Then she wiped off the lipstick.

Half past one, she left the house in a falling snow in her clean dress, warmest coat, and shoes that made walking hard. Her school backpack had been emptied of books and hung loose over her shoulder.

Cowboy Bob's Truck Stop was a beacon at the end of town. Following the flashing neon-light of its ever-burning sign, Eleanor plodded along empty side streets as far as she could, and then joined the highway when she had no other choice but that or a frozen snow-covered field.

Cowboy Bob's at night transformed from a humble mega-store gas station into a night club. Music poured from the restaurant and couples in boots and greasy baseball caps danced with thumbs in their belt loops and whooped to the juke-box. The parking lot was filled like a stable of resting trucks, their orange driving lights outlining their shapes, their diesel engines idling to warm the sleeping drivers inside.

Eleanor burst through the glass doors and past the airlock, snow in her hair, her bare legs red and shivering.

A woman Eleanor recognized from town sat behind the register, watching a small television under the counter. Seeing Eleanor, she raised an eyebrow. Eleanor nodded a greeting and ducked behind an aisle. When the clerk returned to her show, Eleanor walked into the café.

She slipped into a booth at the back and surveyed the room. She recognized more local faces. A woman of easy reputation danced with two truckers. She spun in circles to face each in turn, her hair swirling loops around her head. She was drunk. Another woman sat with a young man at a booth. They shared the bench, along with a pitcher of beer and a plate of French fries.

Eleanor watched the single men in the café as they ate cheeseburgers, drank beer, or stole sips from a secret silver flask. Soon Eleanor focused on one of them. He was a large man, six foot two or more. He had a round belly, stubble on his chin, and arms made large from wrestling steering wheels. He had a kind face and a wedding ring on his left hand. He sipped a cheap beer while watching the dancers. Soon she saw his eyes stare into the distance as fatigue crept into him.

When he refused another beer, Eleanor got up and took the long way around to his table, as unnoticed as possible in the dimmed lights.

Eleanor had thought to make herself look older, but when the makeup had failed to do anything more than make her look stupid, she'd changed her plan. She shuffled up to the table and into the man's vision. His eyes fell on her, focused, and he jumped. His mind had been a million miles away.

"Hello," Eleanor said softly.

"Hello," said the man cautiously. Eleanor could smell soap and shampoo on the man. He'd just showered, and his hair in the back had not yet dried. "Can I help you?" he said.

"Um," began Eleanor. It was easy for her to act vulnerable and awkward. Too easy in fact. She re-thought her plan and then said, "Um, maybe."

"You got problems?" he asked. Eleanor nodded.

"Sit down," said the trucker. "You want something?"

Eleanor sat down and shook her head hesitantly. The trucker signaled the waitress.

"You like cheeseburgers?" he asked Eleanor. "That's pretty much all you can get for a meal right now." Eleanor shrugged.

"Bring us a cheeseburger," he told the waitress. "And a hot chocolate."

Eleanor stared at the floor. "Thanks, mister," she said.

"My name's Dwight Lomas. What's yours?"

She'd planned to be Marilyn Flowers, but it no longer fit for her character. "Susie Parker," she said and instantly regretted it. It was a dumb name, but once she said it, what could she do?

"How old are you, Susie?"

"Thirteen," she said counting on his knowing that girls mature faster than boys. She'd have said eleven if she thought he'd have believed it.

"Are you lost?"

"No, I live in Jamesford," she said. "I just needed a place to go. You know, just for tonight. Until my dad sobers up."

"Oh," he said. Eleanor let the moment hang. The jukebox switched to a slow tune and the booth couple got up together to dance.

The waitress appeared with Eleanor's food. She was about to say something, when Eleanor cast her a look that stopped her, and she went away without a sound.

"Eat up, Susie," Dwight said. "I'm full."

"I can't pay you for this," she said.

"Did I ask you to? Just eat. I have a girl almost your age. If she ever needed a cheeseburger, I hope there'd be someone there to buy her one. I'm paying it forward."

Eleanor bit into the sandwich ferociously, half forgetting to chew.

"Slow down there," said Dwight.

"I didn't get dinner," Eleanor said, her mouth full of food. "Or lunch or breakfast. Daddy's been in a state."

"Does he know where you are?"

"No," she said. "I ran out when he got the belt. I didn't break nothing. He did." She stuffed fries into her mouth and drained her chocolate. "He gets this way sometimes. Melancholy. He'll be better after he sleeps."

"He gets melancholy a lot?" he asked.

"No. This time each year. It's when Mommy died." She was putting it on a little thick, basing herself on Shirley Temple and Tiny Tim without the optimism. She had to keep herself from lisping.

Eleanor finished the food and looked up at Dwight. He had a scar on his neck and wrinkles in the corners of his eyes that didn't go away, a receding hairline dyed brown over occasional grey roots. Eleanor smiled her warmest, most thankful grin, and studied him carefully. As they chatted, Eleanor took in every detail she could see, the calluses on his hands, the freckles and blemishes, scratches and scabs. She counted fillings when he talked and noticed the slight discoloration of an incisor.

It was three a.m., and the café was emptying out. Dwight stifled a yawn.

"Thanks, Dwight," Eleanor said. "Thanks for the burger, and I hope you have a good safe trip back to Portland. You better get some sleep. I'll just wait here awhile, and when the sun comes up, I'll head home. Daddy should be good and sleepy by then."

"You could stay in my cab," he said. He blushed and looked around the café, terrified that someone would have heard him. "I mean, I have a bed . . ." He groaned.

"I've slept in a truck before," Eleanor said. "It's nice."

"I don't want you thinking I want to take advantage of you or anything," Dwight said. "I can sleep in the passenger seat. It's plenty comfy."

"I've slept in one of those, too," she said. "I'll take that. If you're sure, I'd like that. They threw me out last time and called the police on my daddy. I had to make my own macaroni and cheese for a week while he was in jail."

Dwight shook his head. "No problem at all," he said.

Eleanor smiled. She was afraid to go, but she sensed no guile in him, only an embarrassed kindness that could land him in jail. She'd be safe with him if she was careful.

"Which truck is yours?" she asked. "I'll go out first and meet you there."

Dwight raised a suspicious eyebrow and Eleanor knew she'd been too worldly just then. Her schoolgirl demeanor had cracked as she showed too much interest in getting to his truck. Dwight's suspicions were aroused.

"I don't want nobody telling my daddy I was here. And I don't want to get you in trouble. You're being so nice to me. I always find nice people here. Truckers are the kindest folks I know. I wish my dad was a trucker. I'm going to marry one."

She'd gone too far again.

"Would you let your daughter marry a trucker?" she asked.

"What? I, ah, I really haven't thought of it. It's a good job, but not great for families. As long as he wasn't a long-haul trucker, I guess it'd be okay."

Eleanor nodded and yawned.

"Mine's the white Peterbilt pulling a green trailer. It's got Texas plates."

"I saw it coming in," she said.

Elf-like, she hopped off the chair and skipped away.

The snow fell steadily, and three inches lay undisturbed on the parked trucks. Eleanor didn't relish the idea of going home in that weather. Then she remembered she had another stop to make before home. She sighed and remembered Russell's switchblade and stood in the leeward side of the truck.

A few minutes later she heard Dwight's footsteps crunching in the snow. He threw the door open, and Eleanor scurried inside. He followed in and pulled the door shut. The cab was warm. He switched on a light and pulled curtains across the back.

"Just push my stuff to one side," Dwight said. "Just my dirties."

Eleanor glanced at the clothes and made her selections; a flannel shirt, down vest, jeans, and new running shoes. She hoped they weren't expensive.

Eleanor climbed under the blanket as Dwight took a spare and draped it over himself in the front seat. He reclined the chair until it was nearly horizontal.

"Good night, Susie," he said. "Tomorrow's Halloween. I'm sure you'll get lots of candy."

"Thanks, Dwight, for everything. You've been so nice. Yes, tomorrow will be a great day."

She waited silently, still as a tharn rabbit on the back bunk, until she heard Dwight snoring. Carefully, quietly, guiltily, she poked her head out from behind the curtain and surveyed the sleeping driver.

Trucks passed on the quiet wet roads, and their rumble shook the truck with a soothing vibration. She found Dwight's wallet tucked in a compartment between the seats. She carefully opened it and counted the cash. He had four-hundred-eighty dollars. She took three twenties, paused, then put one back and the others in her pocket. Then she replaced the wallet where she'd found it.

She collected her things and bundled them in her backpack. Then she crawled into the cab and knelt over Dwight. She hovered there a moment breathing in slow even breaths and imagining his family down in Texas without a father.

She leaned her face down to his and lowered her lips onto his forehead. Half asleep, he stirred. She held there for a moment, tasting his skin until she knew she had him.

His eyes opened in groggy surprise.

"Thanks, Dwight. For everything. But I gotta go. Be safe."

"What? Who?" He rubbed his eyes in the gloom.

"You can have the bed now," she said. He rubbed his face.

"Maybe I can help you more," he said. "If you're in trouble. I can be handy."

Halfway out the door, she stopped and leaned forward. She kissed Dwight again, this time for him.

CHAPTER TWELVE

The grocery store was deserted. The chain had required twenty-four-hour operation for a national publicity push and regretted it during these cold rural Wyoming nights. The store was decked out in orange and black streamers, pumpkins and straw scarecrows at the heads of the aisles. Bags of picked-over candy lay atop cardboard tables advertising bite-size Snickers and M&M's.

Eleanor wished she'd gone to the grocery store first, but until she had tasted the man, she wasn't sure she could go ahead, and she didn't want to waste the money if she failed.

With eighty-five dollars in her pocket, forty freshly stolen, Eleanor pushed a cart through Sherman's Grocery at four o'clock in the morning. She was the only customer. She thought there was only one employee. She'd smelled her when she came in. Karen Venn's Georgia perfume was a unique scent in Jamesford. It reminded Eleanor of cloves and daffodils. She almost left when she smelled it, but she was too far now to turn around.

She hadn't seen Karen Venn but feared she would. She paused and listened, and smelled and watched, and saw no sign of anyone else in the front. Someone drove a forklift in the back of the store in sudden spurts and hiccups. The smell of grease reached her nose, and she couldn't be sure who it was, but she suspected it was the manager.

Eleanor stared into the meat case for a long time. She gauged the caloric intake of each piece, its fat and muscle against its cost. She went with several hams. They were already cooked and on sale. She put four in her basket and worked out the cost. She'd have bought a fifth, but she hadn't enough. With the rest of the money, she bought cans of beans and SPAM. She'd have to heat those, but they'd work. Finally, she bought a cheap bottle of children's chewable vitamins. It was a trick she'd figured out last time in Nebraska.

She pushed her cart to the front of the store and went as quietly as she could to the self-check-out lane. She had a sudden hope of not actually seeing anyone in the store. It crossed her mind to just push the cart unpaid-for through the electric doors and disappear into the swirling snow. If she were somebody else, she might have risked that. There were cameras in the grocery store and tape recording machines tucked away in some corner she didn't know about. She'd seen enough TV to know that. She'd already done crimes today to a kind man, no need to risk herself unnecessarily doing more.

She passed the first ham over the scanner and it beeped in recognition. Eleanor thought the sound echoed off every wall in the store, past the bread aisle through the hanging plastic panels that led to the back, and out across Jamesford like a shot. She looked around to see if anyone was coming. She heard steps behind a side door and quickly passed two more hams across the glass before Karen Venn appeared.

She wore her grocery clerk outfit, complete with a button promising "Good Family Service & Good Family Prices."

Eleanor rang up the last ham, stuffed them all into bags, and put them in her cart. A friendly, though mechanical, voice warned her that items had been taken from the bagging area and she should wait for assistance.

"Eleanor? Eleanor what are you doing here this late?" said David's mother, leaning across her cart and punching touch-screen buttons.

"Hi, Mrs. Venn, I mean Karen. I'm just doing a little shopping," she said. She glanced into her cart. She'd concealed the hams in plastic bags. If Karen hadn't seen them before, she wouldn't see them now.

"It's pretty late, isn't it? Past curfew, or don't they have curfew in Jamesford anymore?"

"Oh, they do," she said. "It's just that my mother's not feeling well. I had to wait until she fell asleep before I could go shopping. I gotta get home before she wakes up."

"Oh," she said. "I understand."

Eleanor didn't know if she did, but she let the matter drop. Karen Venn finished ringing up the cans while Eleanor bagged them.

"You could work here in the summer," Mrs. Venn said. "I bet they'd hire you as a bagger."

"Maybe," Eleanor said, handing her the two twenties from her pocket, "if my mother can spare me."

Mrs. Venn slid the bills into a slot, and the machine gobbled them up. Another forty-three dollars remained. Eleanor took out her government assistance card and handed it to Karen. She took it, recognizing instantly what it was. Eleanor hadn't watched Mrs. Venn enough to tell if her small sigh was from surprise or disappointment. Either way, Eleanor felt a sudden stupid shame and couldn't look David's mother in the face. She'd been poor forever; why did it matter now?

"I gotta go," Eleanor said, pushing the cart away. "I have a long way to walk."

She knew she'd blown it the second she spoke. She was full of stupid things today. She was tired or scared or crazy, but all night she'd been pulling her foot out of her mouth.

"You're not walking home? In this weather?"

"It's not far," Eleanor said, not stopping.

"Yes, it is," Karen said. "Hold up."

She uncradled a white telephone and punched in a number. After a dozen rings, the other end picked up in the back of the store. "Mr. Woods, I'm taking my break now. I'll be out of the store for fifteen minutes."

Grudgingly the manager walked up to the counters. He was a large man, nearly three hundred pounds and not even six feet. His face was red from the exertion of the hike and he looked none-too-happy to be letting Karen Venn leave the store.

"Fifteen minutes," he said. "If you get stuck in the snow and come back late, you've lost your job."

Eleanor protested, but Karen walked with her to her car and opened the trunk for the groceries. Eleanor wouldn't let her touch them and loaded them all herself.

Karen drove the familiar roads to Eleanor's little house without directions. It meant something to her that David's mother remembered where she lived.

"That house is a treasure," Karen said, squinting in the headlights. "I'm glad you still have it."

"Just barely," Eleanor said. "They raise the taxes every year. We can barely keep up."

The house was unlit under a thick layer of snow. Eleanor jumped out of the car and opened the trunk. She took three hams at once to the front door. Karen followed behind with the last ham and the sack of canned goods.

"Thanks, Mrs. Venn," she said.

"Karen," she corrected her.

"Yes, Karen. You've been very kind. You go back to work now. Don't lose your job. Oh, and if you see him, will you tell David that my mom's really sick, and I'll be staying home with her tomorrow? Don't bother coming by either. I mean for trick-or-treating."

"Okay," she said and got back into her car. She waited until Eleanor had opened the door, brought in the groceries, and flashed the porch light before she drove away.

When she was gone, Eleanor went to the kitchen and set the coffee maker to automatically start brewing at seven o'clock. She wrote a note to Tabitha explaining that she had to go to school early today and not to wait up. "Don't turn on the porch light," she added. "We don't have any candy to give out."

She propped the note on the little table then quietly carried her groceries behind the house and into the flimsy aluminum shed. She would want for heat, but privacy was critical. She could let Tabitha know. She knew she'd have to tell her eventually, when it was done. But if her mother knew now, today, before it was done, she wouldn't allow it. And Eleanor had a plan.

She pulled the shed door shut, smacking her tongue against the roof of her mouth and tasting the trucker's flesh.

Halloween was cold but sunny. The storm that had dropped three inches of snow followed the highway east and across the plains. The sun broke out and, wherever it touched, melted the snow by afternoon. By evening, the sky was clear, the air cold, but the snow was only in the shadows.

An hour before dusk, the first trick-or-treaters left their houses. The later the hours went, the older the kids who'd be out. It was a school night, but kids would be kids and everyone knew the police would be busy chasing away toilet paperers and doorbell ditchers. Someone would fire a pistol at some point, a house would be egged, a trashcan set on fire. It happened every Halloween. If it was a good night, the shot would be in the air. If a bad one, the shot would be more level.

Dwight Lomas huddled under a streetlight by the mobile home park where the Venn's lived. He wore sneakers without socks, dirty pants, and an orange hunting vest over a flannel shirt. He stomped his feet and blew into his hands as if waiting for a ride. He watched the blue Dodge slowly pass the entrance gate three times.

At eight o'clock, the sun was long gone but the candy-hungry children were far from satisfied. Kids who lived far off in the county were driven to town to trick-or-treat, and the town swelled to twice its normal size with greedy children. The tighter the houses stood together, the thicker the mobs of kids. The mobile homes were popular but didn't provide the candy haul the new Jacob's Ranch subdivision promised.

David and Wendy skipped out of the trailer park heading toward Jacob's Ranch. Dwight fell in behind them at a distance, keeping to the shadows, as quiet as his massive form could be.

They crossed the highway and followed First Street toward the throng of parked cars a mile down the road. Dwight pretended to admire some sculptures in a gallery window and let them get some distance on him. His long legs carried him swiftly, and David could only walk as fast as little Wendy would go, which was painfully slow.

Behind Dwight, the blue Dodge turned off the highway and toward Jacob's Ranch. Dwight followed.

He'd let them get too far ahead. The truck had passed the Venn's and stopped twenty yards up the road. Kids in masks spilled out of the truck like startled flies off roadkill. They rushed David and Wendy at a run. David herded his sister behind him and began a slow backward retreat.

Four kids in rubber horror masks caught up to him and blocked the road. David, shielding his sister, backed away the only direction now open to him, into the ditch between the gravel road and a barbed wire fence. The group closed on him. Wendy began to cry.

"Let's make this quick," said one of them.

"Quick enough," said another.

Dwight skidded into the throng between David and the masked boys.

Out of breath, Dwight said, "What the heck do you think you're doing?"

"Mind your own business, mister," said Russell. He was behind a mummy mask with crudely enlarged eyeholes.

"Who the hell are you?" said Tanner Nelson, his stout frame unmistakable under the werewolf mask.

"I'm the guy who's going to teach you a lesson about fair play," said Dwight calmly. He was strong and able. Adrenaline warmed his muscles, readied him for a fight.

"I don't know about this," said Frankenstein.

"Stay out of this, mister," said Russell. "That kid's got a lesson coming."

"I know you, cowards," Dwight said. "If you lay a hand on him, you'll regret it. In fact, you're going to regret even trying. Tonight. Who wants to be first?"

Dwight balled up his massive fists.

"You're a grown-up, and we're just kids," said Tanner. "You're breaking the law."

"Call a cop," he said.

Russell defiantly walked up to Dwight, straight and tall, and stood inches from the man's chin.

"Screw you," he said.

Dwight swatted him upside the head. It was a weak little slap, no kind of punch, but Dwight's weight and strength put the boy on the ground.

"David take Wens and go home," ordered Dwight. "Now. Run!" They did. Dwight watched them reach the end of the road and turn around the corner toward home. When they were safe, he relaxed and balled up his fists again. He was strong. This was going to be easy.

Suddenly, Russell dove for Dwight's legs, but couldn't pull him down. Dwight kicked him in the belly, and the boy flew across the gravel on his face.

Frankenstein inched toward Finlay at the truck. Finlay watched but didn't move. He'd done his part providing the wheels. He wasn't up for another trip to the Honor Farm in Riverton.

Tanner pulled on Frankenstein's sleeve and stopped his withdrawal. Russell was back on his feet. He made a motion with his hand and the boys spread out around Dwight, circling him the way they had around David. Dwight tensed and waited.

"Get him!" yelled Russell.

The four boys leapt at Dwight like a pack of wolves on a bear. He spun and flailed his massive arms at the boys, sending one after another to the ground. He felt their fists pound on his back, reach for his face, even graze his chin once, but he was too large and too strong and too familiar with pack attacks to be caught so easily.

Finally, Russell got behind him and jumped on his back. He wrapped his arm around Dwight's neck and squeezed. If any of the other boys had been upright, it might have turned the battle, but they weren't. Dwight spun around and bucked. He caught Russell's arm, whipping him off him like a limp snake and throwing him across the road.

Behind a rubber hockey mask, one boy cried, "You got no call beating up kids."

Dwight laughed. "I know all about you, you bullies. I've been told. I've been watching. I'll be here if you ever try anything again. Now you brats go home or I swear you'll regret it."

Russell was on his feet again, crouched and ready to attack. He pulled off his mask to see better, and Dwight saw his twisted angry face. As the other boys took steps toward the waiting truck, Russell made a final dash at Dwight.

The big man sidestepped and made to trip the boy, planning on launching him into the ditch with a kick to the pants as he went by—good and hard. But he was caught short. Before he knew what had happened, Russell was behind him. The boy hadn't barreled into him as he'd expected. Instead he'd swerved at a tangent, reached out, and touched his side like an Indian counting coup. For a moment, Dwight had a new respect for Russell, but then he heard him shouting.

"I knifed the sucker!" he yelled. "Let's get out of here. I killed him."

Dwight dropped his hand to his side and felt the end of the knife sticking out under his ribs. There was no blood, and the sensation was more curious than painful. One of the kids pulled out a flashlight and shone it on Dwight. The black handle looked like a firm shadow poking out of his orange vest. Dwight could not see the silver blade. If any of it was not in his body, it was hidden in the coat.

The boys stampeded for the truck. Dwight watched them clamber onboard. The truck engine coughed awake and filled the lane with cold red lights.

With his left hand, Dwight reached around his body, wrapped his fingers around the knife handle, and pulled. He felt the blade fight to stay in, a sucking magnetic-like resistance, like the head of a deer tick. Then all at once it released with a sloppy gasp. Immediately the spot where it had been turned red and wet with blood. Dwight watched it spread and run down his pants. The strangeness of the thing confused him and his legs threatened to buckle under him.

The blue Dodge spun around, spat gravel, and raced past Dwight in a cloud of freezing dust before turning down the highway and disappearing. Holding the blood soaked knife limply in his hand, Dwight watched it go.

CHAPTER THIRTEEN

The school office called Eleanor's home the day after Halloween to report her absence. Tabitha explained that Eleanor was home with the flu.

When David came by the house on Saturday, Tabitha answered the door while Eleanor hid in the loft.

"She's just not feeling well, David," she said. She didn't offer to let him in. The house was in disarray, Eleanor being sick and all.

"Is it bad?"

"She spends half the day on the toilet," Tabitha said. Up in her loft, Eleanor's jaw dropped. She hid her head under a pillow and grunted from embarrassment.

"Oh," said David. "If there's anything I can do."

"Thanks, dear, but no," Tabitha said. "I hope you had a good Halloween."

"It was—interesting," he said.

Eleanor watched him walk up the street from behind the blinds in her room.

"Mom!" she yelled when she was sure he was gone. "How could you?"

johnny worthen

"It's the truth, isn't it?" she called back.

Monday, Eleanor was back in school. She arrived nearly an hour early, having given herself plenty of time to make the walk. Though she was feeling better, she wasn't entirely her old self and didn't want to be late. Winter had come to Jamesford and the snow that had fallen over the weekend promised to hang around until spring.

Eleanor dropped a note at the office, a signed letter from Tabitha explaining her absence due to sickness, and wandered toward Mrs. Hart's class.

She was wary. She didn't know what to expect but knew things would be different somehow. She longed to talk to David, to learn what she'd missed, but she had to be careful.

The door was locked. She'd never known it to be locked before. The window into the classroom was covered with a motivational poster on the other side encouraging her to "read for a lifetime of delight." She heard whispers inside. She pressed her ear to the door and listened. There were low voices, a sliding chair, and papers rustling, and then a book moved. A zip. More whispers. Steps. Then she smelled them. It was a mingling of scents, perfume, cologne, sweat, and chalk dust. Over the strange mix of scents she heard the sound of feeding, a frenzied lapping, heavy breathing. Kissing. It confused her for a moment, but only for a moment before her imagination fitted the pieces and she looked for a place to hide.

She'd taken two steps toward the next classroom when the door opened behind her, and a flushed Mr. Curtz walked out of Mrs. Hart's classroom. He adjusted his tie with both hands, saw Eleanor, and walked swiftly away. Eleanor peeked into the room as Mrs. Hart straightened her blouse. Her look of surprise confirmed Eleanor's suspicions. That look disappeared and turned to anger.

"What are you doing here?" she snapped. "School doesn't start for another hour."

"Um," Eleanor said. "I thought maybe I'd pick up my homework."

"I'll give it to you after class," she said. "Close the door. It's drafty."

"Can I come in?" she asked.

"If you must," Mrs. Hart said. "I've got some grading to do. Sit down and be quiet."

Eleanor shuffled to her usual seat back in the corner. She grabbed the first book she touched in her backpack and read over a math chapter.

Mrs. Hart snorted and shuffled papers. She cast sidelong accusatory gazes at Eleanor for twenty minutes before finally snatching her purse and storming out of the room as if she were late for a plane.

The smell of the Mr. Curtz's cologne hung heavy in the room. Mrs. Hart's smeared lipstick and tossed hair was a clear indictment that she had been making out with the school's principal. Eleanor knew both were married. Mr. Curtz had kids. Mrs. Hart's husband, a long-distance trucker, was a large man who chewed tobacco and used so much casual profanity that he was no longer allowed to visit his wife at school.

Eleanor couldn't think of anything that linked the principal and her humanities teacher together before that morning. Either it was a new thing between the two of them, or they'd been very careful. She suspected the former; she was observant and would have picked up on something as emotionally charged as an affair. Mr. Curtz was a poor deceiver. The guilty face he wore in the hall was an unmistakable broadcast of shame.

It was none of Eleanor's business. She knew many secrets. This was just another. She put it out of her mind.

Fifteen minutes later, Mrs. Hart returned with fresh makeup. After a quick survey of the room, she went to her desk. She stacked, moved, and shuffled papers with her right hand while nervously clicking a pen in her left. Once, Eleanor glanced up and caught her teacher staring at her with unabashed loathing. When their eyes met, Mrs. Hart flashed a mirthless grin and then went back to her papers and pen.

A few more minutes passed where Eleanor would not look up. She heard the telltale hiss of an aerosol air freshener. The smell of lilacs wafted by a moment later. She stifled a cough.

The rest of the students finally wandered in and flopped noisily into their seats. Eleanor kept her nose in her book and didn't notice David's approach.

"There you are, Eleanor. You okay?"

"I'm good," she said, startled.

"Wow, you missed a lot. I've got to tell you about Halloween."

"Take your seats, everyone," said Mrs. Hart directly to David. "Now. The bell will ring and anyone not in their seats will be marked tardy."

Mrs. Hart wasn't usually such a hard-case and several kids raised their eyebrows at the new rule. But she was the teacher and could make their lives hard, so everyone found their seats and waited the last three minutes for the bell to ring.

Mrs. Hart lectured for the hour, stumbling through a poor reading of a Jack London short story. Halfway through it, she set the class to silent reading and graded papers.

When the bell rang ending English, there was an exodus to the hall. They all had history next in the same room with Mrs. Hart, but a change of scenery was always welcome if only for ten minutes. Eleanor didn't usually get up during the break, but today she was the first one out of the room.

David caught up to her at the drinking fountain.

"What's up with Mrs. Hart?" he said. "She might as well as hummed it for all I got out of her reading."

"I don't know," she said.

"Hey, anyway. Russell hasn't been to school since Halloween. Neither has Tanner Nelson."

"Weird," said Eleanor.

"Yeah, I think a trucker beat them up by Jacob's Ranch. I gotta tell you what happened." David slipped his arm around Eleanor's midriff and led her away.

"Ouch," she said.

"Did I hurt you?"

"I'm fine," she said. "Tender."

He opened his locker door and used it as a screen against curious eyes.

"So, I took Wendy trick-or-treating by Jacob's Ranch, only we never got there. A bunch of guys in masks jumped out of a truck and came at us. I'm not sure, but I swear it was Russell Liddle and his gang."

"Did they hurt you?" Though he'd pulled it away, Eleanor could still feel David's hand on her side. She was sore, but she wished David's arm was still around her.

"No, but they were going to. I was scared. Wendy is still scared. It was terrible. It's good you didn't come."

"So what happened?"

"A good samaritan saved us. No joke. They exist. This big

dude came out of nowhere and told us to leave. He said, 'Take Wens and go.' And I did." He faltered for a moment and bit his lip. "You know," he said. "That was kind of weird actually. He said Wens. He called us by name."

"Probably heard it from the boys," said Eleanor. "So what happened? Who was the guy?"

"Yeah, maybe," he said. "Well, I don't know what happened to him. He was big. I think he knocked them around, and that's why Russell and Tanner haven't been to school. I bet they're covered in black eyes."

"Seven or eight each," Eleanor teased.

"Ha ha," he said. "Anyway, isn't that weird?"

"What's weird?" asked Barbara. She leaned around David's locker and looked inside as if hunting for the answer in his stuff. She held her hands behind her back and pointed her chest at David. Without another word, Eleanor went back to class.

"Hey, where're you going?" David called, chasing after her.

"Miss Anders," said Mrs. Hart. "I'd like you to stay after class today. It's about your report."

She nodded and let her hair fall over her face.

"I didn't hear you, Miss Anders." The malice in her voice was clear and hard.

"Yes, ma'am," she said and sat down. David watched her go and then looked hard at Mrs. Hart. She ignored him. The class returned.

When history class began, Mrs. Hart prefaced the lesson by saying, "I've been grading your history papers. I shouldn't have to remind you that history is not a subjective subject. It's about facts. Opinions have no place in your reports."

The class waited uneasily for their teacher to come to a point. She didn't. Instead, she began her lesson.

"Lewis and Clark would have starved had it not been for the help they received from Native Americans along their way," she said, reading from notes.

When the class ended, the other students left as fast as their bored bodies would carry them. Eleanor remained behind. David signaled that he'd wait for her outside.

"You wanted to see me, Mrs. Hart?" Eleanor noticed a picture of Mr. Hart on her desk. It hadn't been there that morning.

"I'm concerned about your history report," she said.

"What about it?"

"It's not a report as much as it is an editorial," she said. "What I wanted from you is evidence that you've paid attention in my class and learned something. What you handed in was an op-ed. Did you listen to any of my lectures? Did you read any of the material?"

"Yes, I did," she said.

"Then how did you come away with such a negative view of the American Indians? Is your family prejudiced?"

Eleanor held her tongue.

"If you'd have stayed within the assigned reading, that would have helped."

"I read the material and the optional stuff, too," Eleanor said. "My facts are correct."

"Don't talk back to me, young lady," Mrs. Hart said sharply. "Your facts may or may not be accurate. I personally don't think they are, but I don't have the time or interest to check them. The problem is your attitude, Miss Anders."

A year ago, Eleanor would never have dared turn in any assignment that would draw attention to herself, let alone be controversial. She'd studied mediocrity and learned to match her work with what the teachers wanted to see. Teachers taught to the test, and the students learned to the teachers. However, for this report, something had moved her to lay out a different view of American Indians than the happy, peaceful fantasy Mrs. Hart so heartily espoused. The selected readings backed Mrs. Hart's view of the noble savage, or at least didn't outright challenge it the way Eleanor had. She took the facts as she saw them, without the white-guilt, and painted a portrait of superstitious savage and opportunistic natives.

She wrote it over the weekend. It was cathartic to proclaim something about the Indians, her people, that didn't make them out to be saints. She knew them and hated them as Mrs. Hart or any of the revisionist historians could never do. They might have been a noble people, a people as good and bad as any other, but they had lanced her brother with a spear and shot her mother in the head with a rifle before cutting her father's bullet ridden body apart with bowie knives. And that was how she saw them.

Even so, Eleanor chastised herself for not just burning her pages and handing in what she knew Mrs. Hart wanted. Tabitha said that all teenagers grow rebellious, but Eleanor was no teenager. She was old, though she didn't look it. She was world-weary and wounded, though her face hid it. Maybe it was hormones driving her to recklessness. Or maybe it was David.

"Your interpretation of the material shows that you obviously didn't absorb it as I presented it," she said. "You get a zero on the report."

"That's a little harsh," said David.

"Mr. Venn, eavesdropping is not tolerated. Go to Principal Curtz this instant."

"At least give her a chance to rewrite it," he said.

"I'll see you in detention, Mr. Venn, after you see Principal Curtz."

"Think of the class levels, Mrs. Hart. We might fall below standard and then the school won't get its funding."

"Two detentions, Mr. Venn," she said. Eleanor looked at David, beseeching him to leave it alone.

"I'd like to look at her paper," he said. "I'd like to send it to my old school and see if my honors teachers would grade it as you have."

"At four detentions, Mr. Venn, it's a week's suspension. You have three now."

David looked at Eleanor at last. Scowling, he withdrew into the hall.

"Don't punish David, Mrs. Hart," begged Eleanor. "I'll take the detentions. It was my paper."

"I don't want to appear to be unfair," she said. Having spent some anger on David, she appeared calmer now. She even made eye contact with Eleanor. "I will let you rewrite the paper. You have been sick, after all. Have a new one to me by Wednesday."

"Thank you, Mrs. Hart," said Eleanor, sensing she'd been dismissed. "And the detentions?"

"You and Mr. Venn will both have detention."

CHAPTER FOURTEEN

In the years between third grade and tenth grade, Eleanor had no friends. She was not invited to parties. She did not throw any of her own. She spent many afternoons in the counselor's office defending her right to be shy. When the school counselor reminded her that she'd had a friend before, that nice bushy-haired boy, David Venn, she'd say only that he was gone.

She'd tried other friends before David and some after, but everyone turned on her eventually. David's constancy was unique. The others were shallow and cruel and didn't love her, so she did not love them. It wasn't some magical unconditional love that she wanted, just a sincerity that Tabitha had once told her was either an innate gift or the product of profound experience. Her mother told her to seek out the good people, but to be careful. She was a special little girl, and she had secrets to keep.

In her years of searching the Jamesford school halls for friends, she'd found no one worthy of her trust besides David. She had shared some of her secrets with him, and he had listened and not judged, even when she would have liked him to. He said he believed her. That was the thing. He said he believed her and she believed him. "Even if they're tall tales, if you believe them, they're real," he'd said.

"So you think I'm telling tales and not truth?"

"They're true," he said. "I believe them. I believe them as much as I believe in China—no more than that. I've never met anyone who's been to China but you've been a coyote and I think that's cool."

Their friendship survived against petty social stresses. David endured the teasing of having a girl best friend until everyone finally just left them alone. David went out for games with other kids, and he was invited to parties Eleanor didn't attend, but always he was there for her. He began calling her his best friend and kept it up until she believed it. He said that made him happy because "it was the best tale he ever told and as true as north and television."

David once asked Eleanor to show him the coyote.

"I can't," she said. "I'm not good at it. It hurts and it's ugly, and I don't want you to think of me like that." Then she started to cry.

"Ah, don't cry," he'd said. "It's okay. I'll never make you do nuthin' you don't wanna do." And he never had.

David was kept at the principal's office until lunch. He was sullen and visibly irritated when he sat his lunch tray next to Eleanor's.

"I'm sorry," Eleanor said immediately. "I didn't mean to get you into trouble."

"You didn't," he said. "I did. Or rather, that witch Mrs. Hart did. I thought I liked her. What got into her? Last week I could do no wrong; today she gives me three detentions."

Eleanor shrugged. "I got detention, too."

"Why? For your paper? Let me read it; I bet she's up in the night."

"Maybe. But I asked to take yours instead."

"You did? Why?"

"So you wouldn't get in trouble."

"And she gave you one for trying to help me? Typical." He shook his head and ate some spaghetti.

"Tonight after school. Chemistry homework?" he asked.

"Okay, sure," she said. They ate in silence for a while. The food improved his mood.

"Ah, wait a minute," he said. "I've got detention. We can't."

"I've got it, too," Eleanor said.

"You think they'll let us work on it together?"

"We'll find out," she said hopefully. This might not be so bad after all.

"Man, that sucks you have detention. Mrs. Hart made an enemy today," he said, and Eleanor knew he was right, and not only in the way he meant it.

Eleanor stayed after school for the next three days. Though her detention was only for one, David's was three, and so Eleanor arranged to tutor him in the library. The library staff didn't mind. They'd been surprised to see them but didn't ask questions. They allowed them to sit together and do their homework away from the chronic detention-sitters who spent the hour with their heads down on their desks, asking to use the lavatory every ten minutes

On the following Thursday, Russell and Tanner reappeared in school. Eleanor studied them carefully. They carried themselves arrogantly like they always did, but she sensed their confidence had been shaken, their boisterousness muted ever so much. Besides a patch of rough scabs on Russell's hands, Eleanor saw no other physical change from when she'd seen them last. She carefully listened to them all day, watched them whenever she could, and was caught looking at them several times. They were tight-lipped. When asked where they'd been, they avoided the question, mumbled something about "hanging out at home and stuff," and then changed the subject. Eleanor waited for David's name to cross their lips, but it didn't. Even when surrounded by the gang in a tightly formed knot at lunch, no one spoke of David or where the boys had been. Neither did they mention Halloween at all. Eleanor wanted to hear their explanations, their interpretations, and their plans for David, but she heard only timid silence. She had to be satisfied with that.

Friday, when Mr. Graham identified David as the student who'd improved the most in science that quarter, and handed out final grade notices, Russell didn't even blink. She'd expected some under-his-breath remark about cheating or sucking up, but none came. David's success didn't merit his attention. Eleanor smiled.

David had caught on and didn't need more tutoring in science, but the two friends continued to study together twice a week after school. If their assignments were done, they'd just talk. David helped Eleanor rewrite her report for Mrs. Hart, adding direct quotes from the teacher's lectures he'd written down and used himself.

"That's what teachers want to hear," he said. "Their own voices."

Her paper received a flat C, which incensed David.

"It's better than mine," he said. "And I got extra points—one hundred and ten percent. She's got it in for you."

Eleanor hated to think he was right, but as the November shadows stretched across the little Wyoming town, she became more and more convinced that was indeed the case. No more did she leave Eleanor alone in the back to stare out the window and slide by without notice. Daily, or at least so it seemed, she'd flash on some question and put it to her directly, the harder the better. She seemed to relish Eleanor's discomfort and wouldn't let up until she gave an answer she could ridicule in front of the class.

Mrs. Hart was subtle. Not overtly cruel. She did nothing that would show obvious malice, no direct insults or petty teasing, but there was still such a change in her attitude toward Eleanor that the entire class soon realized something was going on. Eleanor, the class wallflower for so many years, was now a target. Most of the kids shook their heads, grateful it wasn't them; others joined in the fun and took the opportunity to build up their own egos at her expense, often reciting her mumbling answers back to her in the hallway.

"Food, huh?" said Alexi one time. "That's the entire motivation of Jack London's character. 'Food?' Now there's a deep reading."

Eleanor had said survival, but Mrs. Hart had heard "food" and ran with it as an example of how shallow interpretations hinder deeper understanding of a text. "It's existential," she'd said.

David, for his part, fumed. He raised his hand to back her up, but Mrs. Hart seldom called on him anymore and hadn't then.

In English and history, Eleanor was a marked woman, but in her other classes, she was left alone as usual.

Late in November, Mr. Blake paused the class to draw

special attention to Eleanor's accent and pronunciation of Spanish vocabulary. The next time he called on her, she deliberately failed to trill a double R. It was so obviously an intentional mistake that David asked her about it after school.

"I just forgot," she said.

"Eleanor, you just lied to me. Friends don't lie to each other."

"Can we talk about this tomorrow? I gotta get home."

"You walking again?"

"Yes."

"I'll come with you."

She didn't object. They walked easily together along the cold, windblown Jamesford roads to Eleanor's outlying house.

"So why'd you do it?"

"So he'd stop calling on me," she said.

"Why? You're super good with languages—animal and human. Why hide it?"

"I don't like being noticed."

David thought about that for a while.

"Yeah, I can see that," he said. "But you gotta take a few chances now and again."

"I take plenty," she said.

"You are so different when you're with me than with anyone else, aren't you?"

"My mom," she said, then added, "No, you're right. I'm different with you."

"Me too," he said. "With you, I mean. I really hate this town sometimes. Sometimes I wish we hadn't moved back."

"Why did you come back?" she asked. She'd waited months for him to tell her, but he had never brought up the subject. He deflected it from everyone, other friends, teachers, even her when she'd made a half-hearted query in October. He hesitated this time, too.

"I told you about Spanish," she said.

"Yeah, you did," he said. "We had to leave Georgia. There was a fire right before my father shipped out. It burned up our house and most of two neighbors'. Everyone was pretty sore at us, blamed us for it. With Dad gone, it became too much for Mom. The off-base rent was horribly high and without Dad, there was really no reason to stay. Mom just decided to move us back here."

"You don't have people here anymore, do you?" she asked. She knew David's mother had grown up around Jamesford and brought his father there after David was born, but she didn't think Karen's family was still around. And Eleanor knew there were no Venns in the county phone book. She knew because she looked every year.

"No, they're all gone. But Mom figures this place will be good for Dad if he comes back."

"He might not come back?" Eleanor said, then felt stupid and insensitive. "I'm sorry. Is it really dangerous where he is?"

"Maybe. But that's not it. Dad's having some issues," he said. "He's in a combat zone and all that. It's got to be pretty nerve-wracking."

"Look there, David," Eleanor said, pointing under a car. "What is it?"

"There, that black and white cat. Do you see it?"

David squinted and bent down as Eleanor pointed.

"No. I don't," he said.

Eleanor knelt down on her haunches and mewed. It was

a perfect mimic. David was surprised at the pitch. The cat answered immediately, left the shadow, and trotted across the street to Eleanor's hands.

"How could you see that under the car?"

Eleanor was ready for the question. "I was looking," she said.

The cat rubbed itself on David's ankle. He bent down and picked it up.

"It's missing an eye," he said.

"Yes, I think the boy that lives in that house shot him with a BB gun. His mother too. I haven't seen her in a while. She had a litter. I see only this one and one other. The other lives in the neighbor's garage."

"You think the kid killed the mother cat?"

"Yes, I do. And three kittens. People are mean, David. Most people. The vast majority of them are selfish and cruel. This cat was the best and bravest of them all and what did it get? A BB in the eye."

"It's still alive," he said. Eleanor shrugged her shoulders noncommittally.

David petted the cat who purred like it had found paradise.

"I keep thinking of that big trucker who saved Wens and me," he said. "Not everyone is mean and selfish."

Eleanor shrugged again.

David put the cat down, and they walked on. The cat followed them for half a block and then ran back under the car.

"You saved my butt in science," he said after a while. "You're a good person. I want you to know that, Miss Eleanor the invisible."

"What are friends for," she said.

"The others have accepted me again, more or less. I could start introducing you around, you know? Meet the others again."

"You assume I don't know them," she said.

"Maybe you only think you do. They're not all bad. Well, some are kinda lousy, I'll grant you, but not all. Don't hold grudges, if that's what you're doing. People change. They learn. They improve."

"Change is usually superficial. People are only nice to get something from you. They don't really want to be nice. They pretend."

David stopped. He took Eleanor's hands and turned her to see her face.

"Is that what you think I'm doing? Do you think I was nice to you just so you'd help me study?"

"No, of course not," she said. "You're different. The exception that proves the rule."

"What rule?"

"The rule that people are mean, base, and cruel."

"That sounded rehearsed," he said.

"I've thought it for a long time."

"But I'm not? What makes me different?"

"I don't know," she said, turning to continue the walk. David kept one of her mittened hands and walked beside her. "I don't know why you're special. I'd like to know why you and Tabitha are good when all the rest are so bad."

"Love," he said. "We love you."

"That doesn't mean what it used to when we were young," she said. "Maybe you and my mom have a mutated gland that emits a certain protein which makes you different. I don't know."

"So it's got to be chemical? Physical? What about spiritual?"

She shook her head. "Don't bring in the supernatural," she said. "That just plays on fear and ignorance. And those play to violence and murder."

"Murder? You're getting pretty dramatic," he said.

"They used to burn witches," she said. "Still do."

"Not in this country," he said. "Things change, Eleanor. For the better in this case. We don't kill witches any more. That was hundreds of years ago."

"Sulfur Springs, Arizona, 1962. A group of Navajo led by a medicine man attacked and murdered a family in their home because they said they were witches."

"Is that what you put in your paper that pissed off Mrs. Hart?" he asked.

She shrugged and pulled her hat down over her ears. The cold didn't bother her, but she felt her ears glow red with rage from the topic, and didn't want David to see it.

"Well," David said after a minute. "I'm not that way."

"No, you're not," conceded Eleanor.

Still holding hands, they walked quietly. Eleanor relaxed and squeezed David's hand through her mitten. He squeezed back. She liked that.

"You know," he said at her gate. "I got an A- on the chemistry final. I saw yours. You got a B."

"The student becomes the teacher," she said.

"The teacher tanked the test," he said.

She shrugged. "Better a B on the test than a BB in the eye," she said.

CHAPTER FIFTEEN

Eleanor and Tabitha spent a quiet Thanksgiving at home. Tabitha's sickness diminished her by the day, but she kept up her morale by rereading her favorite books and just watching Eleanor carry on with the daily chores.

Eleanor roasted a chicken, and made stuffing and the instant mashed potatoes with cheese they both liked. She opened a can of jellied cranberries and left it standing upright like a monolith on the saucer.

Seated around their little table, their games put aside, Tabitha said a prayer before Eleanor cut into the chicken.

"Thank you, God, for all you've done for me and my lovely little girl. Thanks for making her kind. Watch over her when I'm gone. Amen."

"Aren't you supposed to say something about the food?" Eleanor asked.

"Nah, the food's got a great and certain future. It's you I worry about."

At times, Tabitha would glance at Eleanor, and she would catch the look, the sad forlorn helplessness of a mother knowing she won't be there when she's needed. Tabitha would look away instantly. The future was a sad subject for her mother. Though she'd often be the one to bring it up, Tabitha would get misty at even a discussion of next summer's trip, let alone plans for graduation or jobs or colleges. It frightened Eleanor. She smelled the death inside her mother, tasted it in the air she breathed, knew it grew stronger, that wicked thing inside of her, and, like her mother, often fell into sullen hopelessness.

"Is Mrs. Hart still riding you?" Tabitha asked.

"I don't know," Eleanor said. "She only called on me once yesterday."

"That's once more than she used to. What was the question?"

"Something about the metaphor of snow in *To Build a Fire.*"

"It's cold and puts out fires," her mother said.

"You'd think so, but apparently it has something to do with industrial dehumanization."

"That's a stretch," Tabitha said, moving her chicken around her plate.

"I thought so, but didn't say it."

"Don't let her get to you. She's just focusing her guilt for a while. It'll pass."

"Yeah, it's getting better already," Eleanor lied.

After dinner, Eleanor put the leftovers away and served pumpkin pie with whipped cream.

"This is too much," Tabitha said.

"They were on sale," Eleanor bragged. "I picked it up this morning. They were way over-baked. They were only two dollars."

"Still so much more than I can eat. I'm so full." She'd only had a spoonful of mashed potatoes, a taste of cranberries, and a sliver of chicken Eleanor had cut for her and later scraped into the bin.

"We'll have it later," Eleanor said. "Let our food settle first."

The two curled up together on the sofa and watched three hours of commercials interrupted occasionally with a James Bond movie. Tabitha was tired by nine. Between the food and her pills, she fought to stay awake.

"Have you heard anything more about Halloween?" she asked, blinking her eyes after stifling a yawn.

It was just a conversation piece, one that Tabitha had thrown out every day after that night. At first her tone was concerned and scared, but over the weeks, her interest had softened to curiosity and gossip. She'd been furious at Eleanor for what she'd done, but couldn't stay mad at her. Eleanor had been in a terrible state, and the frail woman put aside the cause for the cure with the trained efficacy of a seasoned nurse. They'd worked through the time together and now only feared the aftermath.

"You know," Eleanor answered evasively.

"What is it, Eleanor? You're holding something back. I can tell. What happened?"

"It's nothing. Gossipy people. Small town."

"Eleanor what did you hear?"

She snuggled closer to her mother, smelling the fresh-scented dryer sheet in her clothes, her clean skin, and the death lurking beneath it.

"There was a waitress at Cowboy Bob's," Eleanor said. "She was at the grocery. She recognized me. I heard her talking to her friends about seeing me at the truck stop that night."

"What were they saying?" Tabitha lowered the volume on a swerving SUV commercial. Eleanor was grateful she hadn't muted it.

"She was speculating why I was there, with Dwight."

"And what did she conclude?"

"That I needed money," Eleanor said quietly.

"Oh, dear," Tabitha said.

"It's okay, Mom. It's just talk," she said. But Eleanor knew the danger. When she'd heard the talk in the grocery store, she'd frozen and ducked behind her cart. She was alone in the aisle—the gossipers were three aisles over with the bread—but she could hear them, and they were talking about her. They suspected—no, accused—her of promiscuity and low morals.

"Poverty," one of them had said. "It was only a matter of time. I bet her mother put her up to it. You know, I hear she's a heroin addict. That's why she never leaves the house anymore."

"It's always the quiet ones you have to worry about. My little Penelope would never sink so low. She's saving herself. She's never even kissed a boy."

That was a lie. Eleanor knew Penelope. When she wasn't throwing up her lunch in the bathroom, she promenaded through the halls in tube tops and traded spit with a senior named Trent in the parking lot.

"Why don't they take that girl out of that household and into a foster home or an orphanage?"

"It's too late," said another. "I think it'll have to be prison now. No reforming that kind."

"Shameful. Two in the morning you say?"

"She practically sat in his lap. He bought her food. I saw him let her into his truck."

"Why didn't you call the police or something?" asked Penelope's mother.

"Not my business. I'm not a busybody."

"Are you sure it was her?" asked the other.

"Ninety-nine percent," answered the waitress.

"Well, someone should be told. I think I'll write a letter."

Once out of the store, halfway across the parking lot, Eleanor threw up. She hadn't eaten much. The morning's toast, jam, tea, and sugar spewed out of her quickly until black bile choked in her neck.

Tabitha looked like she was about to throw up herself.

"Don't worry, Momma. She wasn't a hundred percent sure it was me."

Eleanor didn't speak of it again. She checked out *Anne of Green Gables* from the library and read it to her mother in the winter afternoons while snow blew in circles outside. It was a nice weekend. Eleanor cleaned the house, made food, answered the mail—bills and junk mail—and doted on her mother like she was a queen. Late Sunday night when Tabitha got out of bed and stumbled into the bathroom for her pills, Eleanor was there with a cup of water and the tablets. Her mother thanked her and let her help her back to bed. Eleanor went up to her room and listened as Tabitha tossed herself into a fitful sleep.

The next week, Eleanor sensed something had changed. Voices hushed when she appeared. She caught glances and stares and felt a thickening and twisting rope in her stomach. She hid behind her hair, slumped, and hurriedly moved between classrooms.

Late in the week, Mrs. Hart was taken sick, so a substitute set them to quiet reading. Eleanor caught snippets of whispered conversation.

"What a whore," someone said.

"Always the quiet ones," said another.

"Poor David," said someone else.

The looks and whispers didn't stop. If David heard them, he showed no signs of it affecting him. He sat with her as usual at lunch.

"So you know what tonight is?" he asked her. They sat together alone. David's friends had chosen other seats that week.

"Friday night fights on HBO?" Eleanor suggested.

"Yes, exactly," he teased. "But strangely enough, it is also the first day you can ask someone out to prom."

The winter prom was two weeks away. Eleanor had noticed the posters and banners all over school but hadn't thought twice about them. Now she did.

"What are you saying?"

"I'm saying no one can ask anyone else out to the prom before midnight tonight. According to the rules, twelve-oh-one is the first minute someone can be asked out. Not a second before, or it doesn't count."

Eleanor blinked at him.

"Kind of interesting don't you think?" he said.

"Yeah, sure," she said. "Stampede to Barbara's house then?" She'd overheard Barbara whisper about David to her friends. Barbara knew he was going to ask her to prom but didn't know how to respond.

David laughed. "I guess there might be."

"Advantage to have a car," Eleanor said. "Juniors and seniors get first pick."

"I hadn't thought of that," David said.

"Hurmph," snorted Eleanor. "How's Wens?"

"She's good," he said.

"What's wrong?" Eleanor said, sensing a lie.

"What?" said David. He shook his head. "You can see through me that easily?"

Eleanor nodded. He smiled.

"She's having a hard time. Mom got moved to days. There's no one to watch her. Mom had to put her in Percy's Preschool. She hates it."

Percy's Preschool was a house with faded plastic play equipment in the backyard and a hand-painted sign out front. Mrs. Percy lived in a back room of the house and paid two girls to help her look after fifteen or so kids for ten hours a day.

"Isn't she making friends?" Eleanor asked.

"Not yet. She's sulking. The extra money Mom's getting barely covers the cost. But at least she's getting some sleep now."

"She works hard," Eleanor said.

"And worries about Wendy all the time," he said. "If she worried about me half as much as she does her . . ." He trailed off.

"What?"

"I don't know," he said. "It's like I could go missing for a week, and she wouldn't notice I was gone until she needed a babysitter for Wendy. She's my mother, too, you know. I mean, I love Wendy; it's not her fault. It's Mom's."

"Maybe she doesn't worry about you because she doesn't have to," Eleanor said.

"She doesn't have to worry about Wendy either, but she does."

Eleanor sipped her milk and tried to read David's expression.

"Do you want to talk about it?"

"No," he said. "You do—you brought it up."

"I'm sorry," she said.

"No, no. I'm sorry," he said. "Mom got a letter from Dad. He's being moved forward to some tiny town. Mom looked it up. It's pretty dangerous. She's just tense."

"She yelled at you?"

"She's just tense," he said.

With the soccer field frozen, Mr. Blake's P.E. class turned to basketball. He divided up the class into four teams and went over some basics before setting them to play. Eleanor was too short to be very helpful, but she could dribble where few others could. She was made a guard and ran up and down the court with the ball. She'd throw it to whoever yelled the loudest. No one, except the in-bounder, ever passed it to her.

After class, Eleanor changed out of her gym clothes and waited for the others to leave. The snippets of conversations she caught were not about her. She wondered if the novelty of her slander had finally worn off.

Midge was waiting for Eleanor when she stepped out of the changing booth. Eleanor was surprised to see her. She hadn't sensed the girl's presence. Midge sat on the bench, her book bag on her lap. Over the fragrances of industrial soap and designer shampoo from the shower, Eleanor smelled an open bag of Cheetos hidden in Midge's bag.

Midge and Eleanor had never been friends. Neither really had any. Midge was ostracized because of her weight. Even when she lost a few pounds, she was always referred to as "the fat girl" behind her back. Eventually, she'd stopped trying to be anything else and accepted her lonely position. She snuck food from the cafeteria and stole mouthfuls between classes. For years Eleanor and Midge passed each other in the halls like distant sailboats on the same lonely voyage with a wave and a hello and a parting of the ways until next time.

"Hi, Eleanor," Midge said.

"Hi, Midge. You okay?"

The big girl nodded. "Yeah, I'm okay."

"Good," said Eleanor.

"I heard something, though. I thought I should tell you."

Eleanor tensed. "What?"

"I heard some talk. Some ugly talk about you, and I thought you should know what everyone's saying."

"What are they saying?"

Midge looked around to make sure they were alone. Eleanor listened and smelled and knew they were.

"I don't usually tattle on people you know. People sometimes talk in front of me like I wasn't there. I usually don't care or even think about anything, but I thought you should know about this."

"What?"

"Some girls are saying," she said slowly, picking her words like Bingo numbers, "that you slept with a guy at the truck stop so he'd beat up Russell Liddle and his friends on Halloween."

"Who said that?" Eleanor said.

"Penelope and Barbara," she said. "And Alexi was there, too."

"And everyone believes this?" Eleanor asked. The knot in her stomach had moved up her ribcage and threatened to choke off the blood to her heart.

"They're just talking," she said. "It's just mean talk, and I wouldn't have even said anything to you except . . ."

"Except what?"

"Except that Russell Liddle and Tanner Nelson confirmed it. They said they were attacked on Halloween but got away. They said the guy's still out there, and they're going to find him and get him before he gets them."

"They're going to get the guy that beat them up?" Eleanor said.

"Yeah, they're going to get him," said Midge. "The way Penelope talked, Russell said it was him or them."

Eleanor sighed.

"Why are you telling me this?" Eleanor asked and felt stupid before the words were out of her mouth.

"You'd do the same for me," Midge said. "If I had a beau."

Eleanor thought for a long moment. "I will," she said. "I promise."

"You got to warn your friend, Eleanor," said Midge. "I think they intend to kill him."

CHAPTER SIXTEEN

Eleanor walked home from school with Midge's words ringing in her ears. They made her scared and confused. It was a terribly familiar combination of emotions. For her whole long, miserable life she'd been scared, and whenever she interacted with people, she'd been confused. She was not accustomed to kindness. She did not seek it, and when it found her, she didn't know how to react. Stumbling through diesel exhaust clouds on frozen gravel roads, snow freezing to her face, Eleanor wondered what trick Midge was trying to play on her.

She tried to think which of the girls had put her up to it. Was it Barbara or Alexi? Penelope? Crystal? Midge was friends with none of them. Had they promised to be her friend if she played this trick? But what was the trick? Eleanor attacked the problem from every devious angle she could think of, invented conspiracies including teachers, waitresses, and even the FBI. She fitted each, regardless of how unlikely, to Midge's warning. Finally, she racked her brain for something she had done to Midge to make her hate her, and, failing that, to like her.

The wind drove freezing rain against her face and she

pulled her hood as tight as it would close and soldiered on the deserted roads toward home.

Eleanor had never done anything to Midge but leave her alone. Was that all the kindness needed to earn her a favor today? Midge had said that Eleanor would do the same for her. Sure she'd gone on a limb for David, but would she warn an acquaintance like Midge if something were heading her way, or her "beau's?" Eleanor didn't think so. And yet something had made her promise the big girl that she would do it now. Had she been lying? Had it been an emotional response? An instinctive reaction? She valued instinctive reactions much higher than logical ones. Instinct keeps one alive; logic is uncertain. What was she to believe about herself?

By the time she crossed into her yard, Eleanor was sure that something momentous had happened today. A kindred spirit had reached out of the storm and offered her shelter. She gave Midge, the round faced girl, butt of all the fat jokes she had ever heard, a little place in that special room in her heart inhabited only by Tabitha, David, and her dead family.

Eleanor shed her wet coat and shoes at the door but kept her sweater. The house was cold. To save money, they wore sweaters and long johns indoors. Eleanor heard Tabitha hang up the phone in the kitchen, then she came out to greet her daughter.

"Is everything okay, Mom?"

"Fine, dear," Tabitha said, sitting down. Eleanor waited expectantly for her mother to tell her about the phone call. They got so few calls, and none ever with good news, so she was naturally curious about it. Tabitha didn't mention it.

"We should have a fire tonight," she said. "I'd like a fire tonight."

"Okay," said Eleanor. Her mother didn't seem worried. In fact, Eleanor thought she detected a wry smile curl her upper lip.

"Go change clothes, cupcake," Tabitha said. "Looks like you've been walking in a snowstorm."

"I have."

"Well, there you go then."

After changing, Eleanor attacked the mail. The electric bill was down, but the gas bill was higher. A fire was a good idea, she thought. She'd look for more wood to heat the house. Construction sites would be unguarded this time of year. Two by fours burned well. She'd sneak out later and look for scraps.

After dinner, they played cards in silence. Eleanor had moved beyond wondering about the warning to the warning itself. Even if it was a trick, which Eleanor no longer believed, it demonstrated a dangerous mindset. Dwight was in no danger. He was long gone, probably in Texas with his little girl right now, watching college football on his widescreen. No, the danger was to Eleanor. The gossip was not far from the truth, but uglier. Eleanor knew that it would never completely go away. The talk would be passed around like a bottle in a brown bag. In the retellings, in the base minds of the people of Jamesford, it would become verified fact, and Eleanor would be forever branded with a sordid reputation. If she was lucky, it would keep people away. If she was unlucky, it would bring trouble.

As if reading her mind, Tabitha said, "Stephanie Pearce called today. We're all set to go to Riverton in the morning. A car will be here at eight."

"She's not going with us, is she?" The thought of three hours in a car with the social worker made Eleanor want to heave.

"No. But I've arranged to do a little shopping after my appointment. You need new clothes. What's left in the budget?"

"We have some, provided the doctor doesn't change your pills to something redonculous."

"Do we have enough for new clothes?"

"Sure, maybe even a pair of socks—one for each of us," Eleanor kidded. "Why? Do you need something?"

"Just thinking out loud," said her mother. She placed her last card on the table. "Fifteen for two, and the next crib is yours."

It was past ten when they stopped playing.

"We got a big day tomorrow, Mom," Eleanor said. "You should get to bed."

"I'm not sleepy," she said. "I'm going to watch some TV. Keep me company."

Now Eleanor knew something was wrong. Tabitha was tired, she knew it. The pills were knocking her mother out. But she didn't press for answers. She felt her mother's reluctance in talking to her about it. Tabitha would tell her when she was ready, Eleanor decided.

"Okay, Mom," she said. "So what's on?"

Eleanor cuddled with Tabitha on the couch. They watched an old movie with martinis, murder, a cute dog, and long evening dresses. Eleanor felt her mother drift in and out, and then fall asleep outright before the second act. Eleanor watched until the final moment, never guessing who it was until the killer was revealed at a dinner party.

The next movie was a "B" horror film from the eighties about a scampering pack of puppets terrorizing a small town. Eleanor switched it off and watched the dying embers in the fireplace. In just a few minutes, she fell asleep still wrapped in Tabitha's arms.

She dreamt poorly. Old memories mixed with new fear; blades, bullets, lies. Murder in the desert, her house on fire, a knife in her side.

She dreamt there was a car outside her house. People furtively got out of it and snuck up to her porch. She imagined their footsteps on the path, crunching the windblown snow leading to her door.

All of a sudden, Eleanor snapped awake. Her heart raced. Sleep evaporated like alcohol on a summer sidewalk. Adrenaline slowed the world. She lay still and listened. She could hear her mother's breathing, smell smoke from the dying wood fire, and see only shadows on the wall.

Carefully, she pulled herself away from Tabitha and looked toward the door. The streetlight glow was interrupted by a figure as someone crossed in front of the window outside.

Russell Liddle, she thought. *He's out there with his friends. Greg Finlay drove them here. They're going to kill us, burn our house down. It's happening again.*

She saw a flash of light and then the unmistakable piquant smell of sulfur from a burning flare. Could she smell gasoline?

"Momma," she whispered. "Momma, get up. There are people here. They're going to kill us, Momma. We have to run."

Tabitha blinked her eyes. She saw the flickering red lights dancing on the curtain. And asked, "What time is it, cupcake?"

"I don't know," she said. "It's late. We've got to go. Take the blanket."

Crouching and silent, Eleanor hurried to the back of the house to see if it was guarded.

"It's midnight," her mother said, standing up, stretching, and wrapping herself with the blanket, but making no move to follow Eleanor out the back door.

"Come on, Momma," Eleanor pleaded, her voice panicked and breaking. "We have to go now."

The doorbell rang.

"Eleanor. Get the door."

"Momma," beseeched Eleanor. "Tabitha. Come now!"

Real terror gripped her. She could only gape as her mother just stood there waiting, expecting Eleanor to get the door.

Instinct. Life. Survival. She took a step back into the kitchen. This was it. It was over. She would run. She would figure out this mystery somewhere else, somewhere safe, and she would mourn, but she would live. She would miss Tabitha. Miss David. Miss it all. But she had to run.

She looked again at her mother in a sad horrible farewell. Tabitha grinned. She was mad. She didn't know what was coming. How could she? Eleanor crept farther away.

Tabitha's grin melted into concern. Was she beginning to understand? Did she finally recognize the danger they were in? Why did she not run while she still could?

"Come, Momma!" Eleanor said, shifting her weight for a leap. She turned to flee. She could wait no longer.

"Eleanor, no," her mother said. "It's alright."

Ready to spring, knowing she could use the window over the sink if she had to, she paused.

"Trust me," her mother said.

The words felled her like a shot. She stumbled. The bell rang again. The red flaming lights cast bloody shadows through the drapes. She was scared. She was confused. Instinct said run. Tabitha, her living mother, asked her to trust her and stay. She froze, her body as taught as a coiled snake.

"Eleanor, cupcake," her mother said. "Trust me and get the door."

Disoriented and angry, confused by her own insane movement, Eleanor found herself easing back inside. She stepped
toward her mother, who welcomed the step with a smile and
a nod. "Come on, child," she said. "Answer the door."

Against everything she felt, everything she knew that was
happening, against her own survival instinct, Eleanor walked
to the door as if hypnotized.

At the door, she smelled hell. Outside was cordite, gun-
powder, sulfur, and paper—all burning outside the house.
Why was she doing this?

She would die now. Die because she had trusted Tabitha
instead of her instincts. For love she would die. She was insane.

She opened the door.

The air erupted in fiery light and smoke. Explosions deafened her hearing, her eyes were useless, blinded by magnesium
flashes. She gasped for breath to scream, choking on chemical
smoke. Before she could let loose and wail her final sound,
Wendy Venn stepped onto the porch. She held a piece of notebook paper. Her mother held a flashlight over her shoulder
so she could read the text.

"Fireworks are such a sight," she recited.

"They make the darkness all the bright.

"If you will, if you might,

"Come with me to prom that night.

"I would be your noble knight.

"You would be my shining light."

Eleanor's jaw fell slack as she gawked at little Wendy Venn.

"The second *knight* was a *k,*" she said. "You know the kind
that slays dragons and stuff?"

When Eleanor didn't say anything, Wendy cocked her
head to the side and said, "It's David. He's inviting you to go

dancing. You don't need to decide right now. Tomorrow's okay. Or the next day even. But I hope you say yes. He really wants to go with you. It'll be so much fun."

Just then the sky burst into a chrysanthemum blossom of blue and yellow sparks. Roman candles set on the road in front of her house shot blazing whistling fireballs overhead. Eleanor saw David kneeling beside a tube. He touched a red road flare to a fuse, and it hissed to life. A fountain of silver and gold glitter burned away the darkness. David stepped away and squinted in the light. He shaded his eyes with his hand and peered at the house. He caught sight of Eleanor in the doorway, and ducked behind his mother's parked car.

"Won't you come in?" offered Tabitha.

"No, thanks," said Mrs. Venn. "We just came to deliver the message." Wendy had turned around to watch the pyrotechnics. She squealed and hopped on her toes with each burst of light.

Tabitha stepped outside, and the four stood on the porch and watched the fireworks together. Neighbors wandered into the street to see the last of the show. Eleanor glanced around, expecting a lynch mob to form, but everyone just watched the lights. Eleanor caught sight of one woman pointing her out to her husband. They both waved at her. She waved back without thinking. She knew then that David had told them all what he was going to do. They expected this. They were all part of it. Tabitha, too.

Eleanor's head buzzed with excitement. Her knees threatened to drop her. Her hands shook like autumn aspen leaves. She was scared and confused again, and, when she felt her mother's arm lovingly wrap around her, she also felt ashamed.

She rubbed her cheek on the old woman's hand and looked

up at her mother. Tabitha shivered under the blanket. Her cheeks were sunken, her color sallow and made unreal in the firelight, but she grinned. It was the proudest smile Eleanor had ever seen her wear.

CHAPTER SEVENTEEN

They were tired the next day. Tabitha had promised Eleanor that she could sleep in the car, but she couldn't. Her mother dozed for half the drive, but Eleanor hadn't closed her eyes since she heard the footsteps in the snow the night before.

After the Venns left and Eleanor recovered her senses, she collapsed into a hysterical fit of laughing and crying. Tabitha made some warm milk and sat with her until she couldn't stay awake any longer and fell asleep on the couch. Eleanor watched her mother sleep and envisioned the far off Canadian tundra she had almost fled to that night.

In the morning, she cleaned up and made herself some breakfast, then helped prepare Tabitha for the long drive and the doctor's visit. At eight fifteen, a state van pulled up in front of their house, crunching the spent fireworks tubes under its tires. The driver honked, and Eleanor led her mother outside and into the back seat.

The driver tried to make small talk. He offered to stop for a drive-thru coffee or a breakfast sandwich, but Eleanor responded with such terse monosyllables that he shut up and drove in silence, leaving her to her thoughts and her mother to sleep.

Riverton was not a large town. Eleanor had read about large towns, cities, actual cities with millions of people. Riverton was the largest human habitation she'd ever actually entered. She had skirted around larger ones, Denver in fact, but she'd kept to the fringes and gone a long way around.

She was of two minds now about cities. There was the old distrust of people, the concentrated danger for her and her kind that cities represented. But now she imagined also a marvelous melting pot where she could hide unnoticed among the throngs of city dwellers. Cities promised an anonymity not shared by small towns like Jamesford or Riverton, where everyone knew and watched and judged everyone else.

The Riverton Oncology Clinic was a modern glass-and-steel construction that tried to conjure feelings of modern miracles and capable technology. None who visited it more than once kept that feeling long. To Eleanor it was a glistening tombstone. It smelled of lingering death and the wicked thing inside her mother that teased and tortured, and now, growing tired of the game, had set itself to her final destruction.

Tabitha told Eleanor that the day they met, she'd meant to die. She'd checked herself out of a Salt Lake City hospital by simply walking out the door. No one stopped her. She drove home, changed clothes, let her dog out, and never went back to her apartment. She drove north at speed. She'd crossed into Idaho before she knew where she was going and why.

Turning toward Yellowstone, the most wonderful place she'd ever been, she conjured happy childhood memories of bears and fishing with her father, her mother sweeping out a rented camper with a borrowed broom. That was where she'd die.

She knew the diagnosis was fatal. She was a nurse. She knew the odds, and no one pretended there was a chance of recovery. She might stay alive a year or ten, but the cancer would kill her as certainly as night followed day. Her doctor told her bluntly that the only way it wouldn't kill her was if she died sooner by another, less horrific means. She'd worked as floor nurse long enough to know what was ahead of her and to despair.

She knew a place by the lake on a beach—a special spot where she had seen the rabbits so many years ago when her parents were still alive. There she would eat her pills. She'd wash the entire bottle down with cheap whisky she bought in West Yellowstone. And then, when her head grew dizzy, she would swim out into the cold mountain water and never look back. She would cross the lake or she would die. She would die.

It had been a bright beautiful day as Eleanor remembered. She'd watched Tabitha from behind a thick pile of deadfall past the parking lot. Eleanor had felt exposed. She glowed like a fish's underbelly in the light, and felt a need to hide, but something about the woman in the little car interested her.

Tabitha tossed her keys onto the seat, and, carrying only a purse, left it with a certain finality Eleanor found alarming. She'd followed the woman to the lake, hurting her feet, still woefully soft and inadequate for the forest.

She watched her sit down and stare out over the lake for a long time.

Tabitha did not know Eleanor was there until the girl called out. Eleanor was sure she'd heard her clumsy footsteps in the pine needles, but Tabitha later swore she hadn't.

When she was right behind Tabitha, Eleanor said, "Asdzaan."

Tabitha was surprised to see the naked girl standing so close behind her. She was covered in dust and dried mud, briars and twigs in her hair, cuts on her legs, mosquito bites everywhere.

"Asdzaan," she repeated.

"I'm sorry, dear," Tabitha had said. "I don't understand."

"Woman," she translated.

"Yes," Tabitha said.

"Bidin," she'd said then shook her head. "Need," she said. "Alone me."

"Oh, baby girl," said Tabitha standing up and opening her arms. "Come to me."

And Eleanor had.

When she retold this shared story the many times over the many years, Tabitha would often say that at that moment, when the little girl had run into her arms, Eleanor had saved her and given her the strength to live.

She had fought ever since to stay alive. "To repay the favor, if for nothing else," she'd say.

The van dropped them off and they arranged for a short shopping trip before heading back to Jamesford. The driver was in no hurry. He was there for the duration with nothing waiting for him at home. Tabitha thanked him and wished him a good lunch.

The waiting room was bright and cheerful. Arrangements of fresh flowers masked the scent of desperation. A professional decorator, fond of yellows and pinks, had tried to conjure feelings of spring mornings, healthful breezes, and enduring life with swirling colors and wavy lines. He had done the best he could, but the atmosphere in the office still weighed heavy with misery.

The staff busied themselves and avoided direct eye contact with the patients. Under orders, they forced pleasant, hopeful expressions onto their weary, spent faces. Eleanor knew they had seen death a thousand times and were tired of it. They did not want to know Tabitha. They refused to even remember her name and had to look it up each time even though she'd come here every other month for over seven years. By their calculations, surely Tabitha was a miracle, a long-time cancer survivor beating the odds if only by one day, one month, one year. But it was only delay, and they couldn't allow an emotional investment in her or her daughter. It would only lead to sorrow when the inevitable happened.

Eleanor waited on a bench and tried to ignore the neutered, upbeat music filtering down from hidden speakers. She waited while Tabitha was radiated, scanned, probed, and stabbed. She'd be strapped to a gurney for an hour while one-eyed robots stared through her skin, determining the cancer's advance. They'd promised to bring her back to sit with her mother when the tests were done—about an hour. Of course they lied. She knew it was two at least, likely three.

Eleanor also knew what the doctors would tell her. They'd say it in their most compassionate voices, using their carefully chosen vocabulary that kept hope alive when none should. The cancer had spread. Eleanor had smelled it on her mother's breath, heard it in her stiffening bones, seen it her mother's weak steps and uneaten food. She'd seen it in her mother's eyes and knew that Tabitha also knew.

"The goal will be to get some meat on your bones," the doctor said. "Bread, chocolate, ice cream, and high fats. Go for it," he said like he was letting a child out for recess. "Get a few pounds on you and we'll try more 'aggressive' therapy."

He handed Eleanor a stack of prescriptions. "Take these to the pharmacist for your mother," he told her.

"Are these the same as before?" she asked him.

"I increased the pain medicine and added something to perk up her appetite," he said. And then he looked at Tabitha. "If you know anyone who knows anyone, you could also try that other thing," he said and winked.

Tabitha nodded. "Are these expensive?" she asked.

"They should be the same," said the doctor. "Are they too expensive?"

"No, just curious," said Tabitha.

The doctor opened a drawer and took out a box of pills individually packaged. He checked the expiration date. "Perfect. Okay, when you run out of these, fill the prescription," he said. "I'll see if I can get you some more."

"Are you sure?" asked Tabitha.

"They expire at your next visit. It's perfect. I won't have to send any back."

"What about your other patients?"

"I'll call the drug rep. He'll be here in an hour with more samples. Trust me. He will."

Eleanor helped her mother dress. When they were done, the doctor came in with two more boxes. "There," he said. "This should tide you over until next time."

Eleanor took the boxes.

"That'll save us a bunch of money," Tabitha said when they were in the van. "We have enough for a prom dress now."

"What?" Eleanor said. She'd entirely forgotten about the dance. She'd focused entirely on her ailing mother. "No," she said. "We can't afford a new dress."

"Okay, then let's see what's at the secondhand."

When they stopped, the driver offered to unfold a wheel chair from the back for Tabitha, but she refused it. She leaned on Eleanor for support, and together they shopped for a dress.

"Of course I'm assuming you'll go with David," said Tabitha.

"Do you think I should?" she asked.

"Of course I do," her mother said.

"But you're sick."

"I've been sick for a long time."

"What if you—"

"Then I do," she cut in. "Live, Eleanor. Live. This is life. Grab it. Dance. I'll be fine for one night. I survived without you for a week, didn't I?"

"I'll be noticed," she said, thinking she should tell her mother about the new gossip. Tabitha had forgiven her for what she'd done, helped her recovery, and even, finally, when Eleanor was still in pain, barely able to move, but finally herself again, her mother had kissed her forehead ever so tenderly and told her she was proud of her. She called her "the bravest little girl she'd ever known with a heart as big as a bear." It was something her real mother had once said to her, or something like it. She couldn't remember telling Tabitha about it, but it made her happy, and she recovered faster for it.

"Eleanor, you're a beautiful girl no matter what you look like. People are going to see that, the good people especially. You're going to be noticed. Let's stretch a little bit, come out from under our rock and live a little."

Eleanor wasn't sure. Survival instinct told her to remain in the shadows, dart out, scavenge, and run for cover. It was that instinct that had kept her alive. It was the same instinct that had nearly driven her from this woman's side the night before into a frozen wasteland, never to meet again. She realized then that she had made this decision last night. By taking that step into the house instead of out the back door, she had given herself up to trusting Tabitha. She had overridden a millennium of instinct, decades of practice, and her own personal fear, for trust in Tabitha, the dying woman she'd met at the lake.

"I think I'd like something in blue," she said to her mother. "Maybe something with puffy sleeves, you know, like Anne of Green Gables wore?"

Tabitha laughed. "Do you even know what that looks like?"

"No," Eleanor admitted.

"We'll just see what they have."

CHAPTER EIGHTEEN

Tabitha made the driver stop at a fireworks store on the way home. They'd found a dress, shoes, and even a shawl so she wouldn't have to cover up with her old cloth coat. Some mending and tailoring would be needed, but Tabitha thought she could handle it.

"You have to answer in kind," she told Eleanor. "It's tradition."

They couldn't afford a show like David had made. Eleanor was startled to see how much such things cost and quietly calculated what David had literally blown asking her out.

"We can't afford any of these," she said to her mother.

"When money's low, your imagination should be high," she said and pointed to a box of sparklers. "I have an idea."

When they got home, Eleanor fetched a piece of salvaged plywood from the shed. Using a rusted saw left over from a previous owner, they cut off the chipped edges. With a handle-less file, they smoothed off the splinters. They worked into the night with crayons and a hair dryer. They melted the wax crayons in psychedelic designs around the simple message: "Yes." The next day, Eleanor punched holes into the letters with a hammer and nail. She threaded the sparklers through the holes, bent and taped the ends on the reverse side.

"What are we going to light it with?" wondered Tabitha.

"A match?" suggested Eleanor.

"We have to get all the sparklers going at once," she said. "A match won't do it. We need a road flare."

"How about another sparkler?"

"That might work," she said. "If we work together."

"You're coming?" said Eleanor, surprised.

"Of course. I wouldn't miss it."

And so that night after dark, Eleanor and Tabitha, bundled up in layers of coats and socks, carried the board between them to the trailer park. They made their way slowly. The weather was mild. They saw their way by low clouds reflecting flashing neon light from main street diners.

Tabitha had arranged with Mrs. Venn to be home with David at ten o'clock, but they didn't arrive until closer to half past.

They propped the board against a barbecue grill by the door. Eleanor heard sounds inside the house. They'd made so much noise setting up the board that she wasn't surprised when the house fell silent. But they hadn't opened the door yet, so she lit two sparklers from a wooden stick match and handed one to her mother.

The big three-letter word had forty six sparklers in it. They started together at E and moved out from the center, Eleanor to the Y, Tabitha to the S. As fast as they could, they lit the sign. Eleanor finished first and sprinted to the door and rang the bell, then she jumped off the porch and ran across the road.

Tabitha had just lit the last sparkler when David appeared in the doorway. Eleanor saw him in the brilliant white light.

His expression lit up as he scanned the darkness for Eleanor but couldn't find her. He settled on Tabitha and grinned.

"How'd you get those colors?" he asked her.

"Imagination," she said. She waved to Mrs. Venn and Wendy, who peeked out around David's shoulders and legs. Then Tabitha left and found Eleanor waiting down the road. Eleanor threw her arms around her mother and hugged her a long time.

David had done a miracle. The following days, Eleanor was still talked about in the halls of Jamesford High, but not as she had been. David's pyrotechnic dance invitation was the talk of the school. There'd been creative invitations in the past—a car filled with balloons, cookies baked and delivered, a singing telegram, but nothing as spectacular and memorable as David's firework display.

It was a hard act to follow. When David described Eleanor's answer, the girls were also put on notice. She thought she had done a good job with her mother's idea, but David embellished it until that old piece of plywood could be hung in the Louvre. Eleanor heard their names mentioned as potential prom royalty. She was gobsmacked.

Girls whom Eleanor had never talked to sought her out to ask what she was going to wear. Girls who'd tried to talk to her in years past, maybe even tried to be her friend but were unsuccessful, approached her again like they were bosom buddies.

Eleanor's suspicion kept them at a distance, but after the third day, she relented at her mother's urging and took part in discussion of hair styles and makeup. Eleanor's sudden popularity was contagious, even to Eleanor.

Jennifer Hutton laughed at Eleanor's ignorance of lip-gloss, but it wasn't mean-spirited, at least she didn't think so. She patiently told Eleanor about the benefits of lip-gloss over lipstick. "It makes your lips look wet," she said.

Jennifer was a popular girl who floated in and out of different cliques without social consequences. She was something of a barometer of school popularity. She orbited new stars like a roaming comet, and Eleanor felt both privileged and frightened to have her attention.

News of David's fireworks also reached the teachers, and Mr. Graham commented on it in one of his lectures, saying that David Venn knew about exothermic reactions better than anyone. Russell Liddle stopped ignoring David and began to actively dislike him again. He guffawed at Mr. Graham's comment, possibly thinking there was a double entendre there somewhere, but he was alone. Eleanor remained wary and watched his comings and goings carefully during the days leading up to the dance.

Five days before the dance, she watched him leave his friends and walk to Barbara Pennon's table. Barbara sat with Alexi and Crystal. Eleanor knew that Alexi was going to the dance with Robby Guide and suspected Bryce Sudman had asked Crystal, but she didn't know if Barbara was going. She couldn't imagine her not going.

At Eleanor's table, David and Brian Weaver were in a conversation while Eleanor, Jennifer, and Midge, who'd become a silent regular at her table, listened to Aubrey, also a new addition, describe her cat's acrobatics on the drapes. Eleanor had known her for years and never heard more than a sentence wrung out of her mouth, but at Eleanor's lunch table, she had become a little chatterbox.

"My dad was so mad," she said. "The whole thing was ruined—tears and rips, floor to ceiling. But it was so cute seeing her climb up. I couldn't stop her."

"Shhhh," said Eleanor. "Look."

The group followed Eleanor's gaze across the lunchroom. She'd been watching Russell, trying to pick out snippets of his conversation with his friends when he got up and approached Barbara's table. The entire lunchroom noticed his awkward advance and fell silent. Eleanor perked up her ears.

"So, we're going right?" said Russell.

"What?" Barbara said.

"The dance, you know," he said, his hands in his pockets. He glanced over his shoulder to his friends who also watched with interest. "The guys, well Tanner, thought that I should, you know, make sure we're still on."

"He's asking Barbara to the dance," said Eleanor.

"No way!" said Jennifer.

"Here? At lunch? A week before?" said Aubrey. "She's not going to like that."

"She doesn't," said Eleanor.

"What's she saying?" asked David.

"That's the best you got?" Eleanor translated. "You're a punk, Russell. A classless punk."

"She really said that?" Jennifer said.

"Yeah, I got that, too," said David, though Eleanor doubted he had.

Barbara lowered her voice. "That stupid David Venn made that wallflower Eleanor Anders the queen of the prom, and this is all you got for me?" Eleanor didn't relay this to the table.

"Well, you know," Russell stumbled, his flushed face visible clearly to the entire sophomore class who all watched the drama now. "You know, we're already going together, so I assumed that, you know, we were already on for the dance."

"Looks like he's getting eaten alive," said Brian. "Oh man, serious girl foul."

Barbara suddenly became aware of the entire room looking at them. Even the upper classmen sensed something and followed the stares of the tenth graders to her table. She leaned in to him and whispered.

"Okay, you lout," she said. "I'll go with you, but only because no one else has asked me yet." Whispers carry farther than people think. Eleanor had no problem picking her out of the quiet crowd. "You better pull out the stops at the dance," she said. "Actually, you better start pulling them out now. Flowers every day until the dance." She glared at him. He nodded.

"She's going with him," Eleanor said. "But he has to bring her flowers every day."

"It's your fault, David," said Brian. "You made it hard for all of us. You cut Russell off at the knees."

"Yeah, I have a knack for that," he said and laughed. Eleanor didn't share his mirth. She watched Russell walk back to his table. By the time he rejoined Tanner and the others, he was all bravado and confidence again, but Eleanor knew he'd be at the florist's after school.

The next day, Russell delivered a bouquet of flowers to Barbara's table. She accepted them like a ballerina on opening night and then dismissed him like an autograph seeker.

"So here's the plan," David said. "We'll double with Brian and Jennifer. We'll go to Chang's for dinner and then the dance."

"What about Aubrey and Midge?" she said.

"Oh, um," David said looking at the girls. "It's kinda up to the guys. Their dates haven't talked to me."

"Is there room?" asked Aubrey.

"Yeah, I think so," said David. "We have a van."

"Are you sure it's okay?" asked Aubrey. David nodded. "Then I'll see if he has plans."

"Who's taking you?"

"Eric Collins," she said.

"Oh, okay. Yeah, I get along with him. Tell him to call me if he wants in. We're starting at five."

"I have a ride," said Midge. No one hid their surprise.

"Who asked you?" said Jennifer in a way that did not wholly insult Midge but only a little.

"You don't know him," she said.

"So we'll get to meet him at the dance?" said Aubrey.

She nodded.

"Great. We'll all sit around and drink punch and hope no one sees us dance," said Brian.

"Speak for yourself," said David. "I know how to boogie."

"I can line dance," said Aubrey.

"Arghh," said David. "Tell me it's not all going to be all country and western. I hadn't even thought of that."

"I've never been," said Jennifer, "but we are in Wyoming."

"We don't have to dance," said Eleanor.

"Oh, we'll dance," he said. "I'll burn a couple songs to a disc that we can dance to without spurs."

"Okay," she said. Eleanor had begun wearing a headband to keep her hair off her face and she was not used to it. She'd put it on in the morning when she was anxious to go to school and see her new friends and talk to David. Halfway on her walk, she'd take it off and stuff it in her backpack feeling stupid and self-absorbed. Before the bell rang, however, she forced herself into the bathroom and put it back on before David saw her. Typical boy, he hadn't noticed the accessory, but had commented frequently and earnestly on how pretty she was.

David glanced at her and smiled. She felt suddenly exposed and bobbed her head to summon her shield of hair out of habit. When it failed to cover her, she looked away and hoped her cheeks didn't blush.

"It's going to be a great dance," David said.

"It'll be the best I've ever been to," said Jennifer.

"You've never gone to one before," said Brian.

"Then you have a chance to set a high bar," she giggled.

"He's from the res," Midge said suddenly.

"What?" said Aubrey.

"My date," said Midge to her lunch tray. "He's lives on the reservation."

"Oh," said Jennifer.

"That's fine," said David. "As long as he likes warm punch, he'll fit right in."

Midge relaxed and finished her lunch. Aubrey talked about dancing and wanted to know what everyone did with their arms during a two-step.

Eleanor listened to her friends talk, but her mood had darkened. Like Jennifer, she was unsure about an Indian joining their group.

She mulled it over with Tabitha that night as they fitted the dress. Without a sewing machine, Tabitha had done all the stitching by hand. "I got nothing better to do," she said through a mouthful of pins. She understood Eleanor's trepidation with Midge's date, but told her to ignore it.

"You're going to run into people," she said. "You can't hold what others did against them. That's just wrong."

"I'm scared," she said.

"You're always scared, cupcake," she said. "And that's healthy, especially for you. But they're just people. People do dumb things, ignorant things, all the time. But even the ones who are stupid are not without value. They can learn. People can change. I've often thought that even those Indians back then lived to regret what they did. I don't mean they were punished, or put on trial or anything. I'm not that optimistic. But I bet it weighed on their souls."

Eleanor didn't think so. But Tabitha was right. She was being prejudiced. She'd gotten along well enough with Robby Guide. True, he'd not moved to their lunch table, but maybe he had a better offer. Or maybe he'd sensed Eleanor's unease with him and stayed away out of courtesy. And then she wondered, as she always did around Native Americans, if he hadn't sensed what Eleanor really was and kept away because of it.

"You're going to be the prettiest girl there," Tabitha said, standing to admire her work. Eleanor turned around and looked at herself in the mirror. She didn't recognize herself. It took her breath away. She was beautiful.

CHAPTER NINETEEN

Aubrey and Eric didn't join David's carpool, though they did eat at the same restaurant. The night of the dance, Chang's was filled with formally attired teenagers. It was one of the more unusual places to eat within easy commuting distance from the Masonic Hall, where the dance was held.

Karen had driven David to Eleanor's house at five o'clock. She followed him to the door with a camera. Eleanor opened it while Tabitha hovered behind her with a camera herself.

Before they were allowed to leave to pick up Brian and Jennifer, the mothers posed the couple against the fireplace wall for a hundred pictures. David remarked on Eleanor's stunning dress. At her mother's insistence, Eleanor had forgone the big puffy sleeves that had been popular in Canada a century earlier for spaghetti straps and a tight waist. Instead of the hoop skirt which she'd imagined, her mother had talked her into a long, flowing, slender gown that sparkled in the light. There'd been two of them at the secondhand shop, obvious wedding party castoffs, but they were nice, and one was nearly Eleanor's size, so Tabitha had little difficulty fitting it to her. The blue paisley-patterned shawl could be taken off to expose

Eleanor's pale, satiny shoulders or worn delicately around them, showing off her slender neck without detracting from her gown. Eleanor was hard put to remove the shawl, even in her front room for pictures. She felt nearly naked in the tight dress, and barely recognized herself in the mirror after her hair was curled and styled, and Tabitha had done her eyes. She'd stared at her face, memorizing it like it was a new shape and then deciding she liked it.

She was pleased, more pleased than she'd imagined she'd be, that David liked it, too. He could barely contain his excitement and frustrated his mother, who demanded he look dignified and mature for the photos. Tabitha wasn't as concerned and snapped candids of him gawking proudly at Eleanor's outfit.

Jennifer had gone with lavender, a shade not dissimilar from Eleanor's. The boys of course were in black tuxes, a boutonniere on each lapel labeling them to their dates. The wrist corsage on Eleanor's arm was strange and heavy, but she loved it and tried to leave it at home where it wouldn't get ruined dancing. One look from her mother killed that idea instantly. All night, she held her arm close to protect it. She'd never seen rosebuds so small and so delicate; they looked like playmates to the baby's-breath.

The waiters at Chang's had fallen into formal character, and the entire restaurant had transformed from an upscale ethnic bistro for visiting moneyed tourists, to a dimly lit, romantic getaway for the town's children. Waiters presented the long menus with a flourish and stood by to answer any questions the diners might have. Naturally no one drank wine or spirits, but the waiter counted off a list of other beverages the kids might want and, without writing down a word, took their orders and disappeared.

"I've never seen this place like this," said Brian.

"I've never seen inside this place, period," said David.

"I have," said Jennifer. "My mom took us here when my uncle visited. It's really good. We have to do it family style— that's what that big lazy Susan is for." She pointed to a disk in the center of the table. "We order all kinds of different food, put them there, and then share, picking at them with our chopsticks."

Eleanor had never used chopsticks before. The others all had, and David was best with them. After their hors d'oeuvre arrived—pot-stickers, whatever they were—David scooted his chair over and showed Eleanor how to hold the sticks.

His hands were warm and strong, and as he positioned the sticks in her fingers, he lingered a moment longer than required, cradling her hand like a gem. His touch, so gentle, so alive, was powerful and electric. Eleanor felt lightheaded.

"Well?" he said.

"Well, what?" she said. She hadn't heard a thing he'd said.

"Give it a try?" he said. When she hesitated, trying to recall his instructions, David reached out again, took her one hand in both of his and led it over the plate. He manipulated her hand, his soft fingertips suggesting movement, not forcing it, until the sticks clasped a dumpling.

"Now dip it in this sauce," he said. "It's crap without it."

She did.

"Now eat it, silly," he said, laughing.

She did. It was wonderful.

They ordered a family meal. The management had a "Christmas Prom Special," tonight only. The meal was hearty, tasty, and affordable. They drank hot tea. David encouraged his friends to drink it without sugar, but he was ignored by

Eric and Jennifer, who thought it was too bitter. Eleanor drank it without sugar and found it savory.

Jennifer scanned the restaurant for familiar faces and measured the success or failure of each couple's evening by the expressions on their faces while eating.

"It's a science," she said. "Hunger and kindness are linked."

"What are you talking about?" said David.

"It's scientific."

"Let me guess," said Brian, "You read this in *Vogue?*"

"*Elle,*" she said defensively. "It's still real."

By Jennifer's own logic and scowling brow, she and Brian were on shaky ground.

At six thirty, David's mother picked them up in front of the restaurant to take them to the dance.

Eleanor had eaten more than she'd have liked, but the novelty of the spices was intoxicating. Her usual fare seldom rose to grander culinary heights than macaroni and cheese casseroles or canned spaghetti sauce doctored with "Italian Spices," from a plastic shaker.

The entire town of Jamesford pitched in for the Winter Dance. That was a great thing about the small town. Local artists brought new pieces to the hall to show off. Restaurants competed to give away the grandest door prizes, and there was a music try-out before the band was booked. Women's clubs had taken on the decoration, and local businesses had donated streamers, balloons, punch, cake, confetti, and a twelve-foot Christmas tree for a festive photographic backdrop. There was no shortage of chaperones. They arrived as couples and grouped up with other adults to admire the youth, reminisce, and every so often, when the right song played, steal onto the dance floor.

To David's dismay, there was no DJ, only a live band in western shirts and cowboy hats. The familiar twang of a steel guitar was the first dark cloud of the evening for Eleanor as David asked about the possibility of playing songs from a CD he'd brought.

Mr. Blake, the tenth grade chaperone, shook his head. "Give the band a chance," he said.

The couples split up to explore the room, which was rapidly filling. Soon it would be a slow, civilized, and formal reenactment of the halls of Jamesford High in between classes, but with music and better clothes.

David found a seat for Eleanor then gallantly fetched two glasses of pink punch from a long table in the back. A thin slice of orange peel floated in her cup and Eleanor nearly picked it out before realizing that it was part of the beverage.

She took in the room. The dance floor was seniors and juniors only. No sophomore had found the courage to step onto it yet. The music was lively, but not sweat-inducing.

David pointed out people they knew as they came in, though of course, Eleanor had seen them first. She waved to Aubrey. Eric was wide-eyed and nervous, a cornered mouse looking for a sudden escape. When Russell and Barbara came in with Tanner and Crystal, David commented that Russell looked whipped.

She studied him. He wore his tux like it was a bear skin. He tugged at his collar and fumbled with his cummerbund. His patent leather shoes were slippery, and he slid and skidded on the tiles. He watched his feet and trailed two paces behind Barbara as they crossed the room to a table where Alexi sat drinking punch with her date.

"He's dangerous, you know," Eleanor said. "You shouldn't try to provoke him."

"I don't. He just takes it that way. Bad family or something, I suppose."

Eleanor was surprised with David. He knew it had been Russell who'd attacked him on Halloween, knew he'd intended to hurt him as much as possible, but here he was pardoning him. She didn't understand.

"You know what would really provoke him?" asked David.

"No, what?" she said tentatively.

"If we have a good time tonight," he said, brightening.

"So we shouldn't?" she said.

"Actually, in this case, I don't think there's a way in the world I can't provoke him."

A new song began, a wandering tune. David stood up. He took Eleanor by the hand, bowed ever so much, and invited her to dance.

Eleanor had never danced before, but she was a quick study. She'd watched the other dancers and instinctively memorized their movements and mannerisms. She didn't want to look stupid. She knew she was being watched. David and Eleanor were the first sophomores to dance that night.

David slid his arm around Eleanor's waist and held her left hand up. "Just twirl," he said. David took a step, Eleanor matched it. He turned a quarter and she followed. With each step he persuaded her body to follow. The music grew louder, and Eleanor realized they'd twirled across the entire expanse and were now under the bandstand. David chose to remain there, and together, they danced.

Eleanor blocked out the hundreds of eyes following her,

and focused instead upon David's face. He looked happy. He had looked happy for weeks, but now, with her, he looked profoundly content. Before she could stop herself, she mimicked his feeling and lost herself in the dance.

When the music stopped, David signaled one of the musicians. "Got something slow and swaying?" he asked.

The musician nodded and called the tune.

From wandering to moody, the music began again. It was not a country song, but a haunting lament.

"This is the Cure," he said to Eleanor. "These guys do a pretty good job with it."

Eleanor didn't know what he meant, but as he dropped her hand and reached around her waist with both arms, she tingled.

It wasn't as much a dance as a rocking embrace. Eleanor found that the only comfortable place for her head was on David's shoulder. He nuzzled her when she put it there. She listened to his breathing and his strong steady heartbeat. She checked them against her own and matched them perfectly. She breathed in his cologne, smelled his skin, and picked out the mint shaving lotion he'd used that afternoon. Before closing her eyes, she noticed the tiny parallel cuts on his neck where his razor had stumbled. A sudden urge to kiss him there was barely turned away.

When the song ended, neither David nor Eleanor let go. They continued to sway to music in their minds until the band played the dreaded line dance and called for everyone to separate into a cowboy side and a cowgirl side.

"Let's sit down," David said, clearing his throat.

He led her to a table where Midge and Jennifer sat alone. Eleanor felt as if the entire room watched her, though she didn't catch anyone staring except Mr. Blake, who wore a happy, but faraway expression.

"Where are your dates?" asked David.

"Bathroom," said Jennifer.

"This place is huge," Midge said.

They all agreed it was.

The dancers pranced forward and then back again, kicked up one heel and slapped the other with a palm before resetting to go again.

Barbara and Russell were in the line, though neither looked to be having fun. Several times Russell glanced at David, which made Eleanor's blood race. Barbara too stole looks at David, which made Eleanor's blood boil.

When the music ended, the dancers applauded. The missing boys rejoined their dates. Midge meekly introduced her date as Henry Creek. Henry was full-blood Shoshone, she said. His skin was the color of fine leather and his hair, longer than any girl's in the hall, was pulled in a tightly knotted braid. He didn't wear a tuxedo, but a studded western shirt and vest. His Levis were still creased, and his cowboy boots shone in the light. He wore a bola tie cinched with an arrowhead clasp carved from obsidian and surrounded by pebbles of turquoise. He shook hands with David, who introduced him to Eleanor.

"I saw you guys dancing," he said. "You were . . ." He trailed off.

"We were what?" said David.

Henry made circles with his thumb and fingers.

"Uh," he said staring into space as if the streamers overhead would tell him what to say. "You guys looked to be enjoying yourselves."

David wanted to know what had taken them so long in the

bathroom. Eleanor knew the answer. She could smell it on the boys' breath. Not too much for the average person to notice, not over the half can of breath mints they'd each eaten, but Eleanor knew they'd both had a drink of whiskey.

Another song began, and Midge took Henry to dance. Unable to hold off any longer, Brian too was led out onto the dance floor. David nibbled on an éclair. Eleanor watched the dancers.

She felt him put his arm around her.

"Why are you doing this?" she asked.

"Doing what?"

"Being so nice to me. You know I'm not exactly the most popular girl in school. At least I wasn't until you showed up."

"We're engaged," he said.

"Don't be silly," she said, happy he hadn't removed his arm. "You could have any girl in school you wanted. Even Alexi with all her money and Barbara with all her curves."

David laughed. "Don't get all insecure, Eleanor," he said. "There's not a person in town who'll remember either of them tomorrow, probably not even their dates. But you, you they'll remember."

"I hope not," she said.

"You're beautiful," he said, moving closer, his arm becoming a part of her, a warm comforting part.

"I don't think so," she said.

"Then you're wrong, Eleanor Anders," he said. "And it's not very often I get to tell you that."

"Isn't it all superficial? I look this way because, well, because my mother helped me pick out a dress I would never have considered, and made it fit me. She used makeup and paint and pencils on my face. She did my nails. I'm fake. What you see, David," she said earnestly, "is not who I am. It's not even what I look like. Not in real life."

"I didn't invite you to prom when you looked like this. I didn't look like I do now when I caught my shirt on fire in front of your house. Yeah, we're dressed up. Yeah, we're playing a game. We're in character, but it's fun. Neither one of us is the person we were this morning, but that doesn't mean what we are isn't us. This is a different side of us. A fun side. You're having fun aren't you?"

"More than I should," she said catching Barbara's glance at her and David. "But I don't know about all the attention."

"I'm sorry if it makes you feel uncomfortable," he said. "Truth is, I guess I am being selfish. I wanted the world, or at least the town, to know that they have a very special girl living amongst them and I was the lucky guy who got to take her out."

"You don't know the half of it," she said.

"What do you mean?" he said. "Are you talking about how everyone's talking about the fireworks?"

She wasn't but she nodded anyway.

"Eleanor, if you saw you the way I do," he said, shaking his head when words failed him. "There's something about you," he said. "Something wonderful, mysterious, and intoxicating. You shine tonight. For me, you shine every day."

Eleanor felt the mood change, and David took his hand away.

"I've had some tough times," he said. "I truly thought moving back to Jamesford would be the final nail in my coffin, but it hasn't been. Even with my mom ignoring me, my dad away, and Wens, well, being Wens, I can't remember being happier than I am now." He looked at her, and Eleanor let him. His gaze bore into her face, falling into her eyes and reading the depths there. It was the way she'd looked into Dwight's eyes, seeking truth behind the appearance.

"Listen to me," he said, exasperated. "I'm making it worse, aren't I?"

Eleanor didn't know what to say, didn't know what she felt. She felt so old sometimes, felt like she'd seen it all, lived it all, but this sensation baffled her. Her mother had said her hormones would kick in. "Fifteen-year-old girls burn like black powder," she'd said. But Eleanor had dismissed that. She wasn't a fifteen-year-old girl. She was over sixty, at least five years older than Tabitha. She was only a girl for now.

David leaned forward as if to whisper in her ear, and instead of telling her a secret, he shared one, when he lightly kissed her ear.

She felt chills from her toes to her scalp. Gooseflesh covered her body. Her fingers tingled. Her lips warmed.

"I can be anything you want me to be," she said.

"You are everything I want you to be," he said.

Aubrey and Eric arrived and fell into chairs. They were tired.

"Where'd you learn to kick like that?" asked David, drawing their attention.

"My mom loves square dancing," he said. "She competes. I'm her partner when Dad has to work."

David held Eleanor's hand beneath the table.

"You meet Henry?" asked Aubrey.

"Yes, he was just here," said Eleanor. She looked for him. He and Midge sat in a row of chairs against a wall across the room. Midge was talking, and Henry nodded as she spoke into his ear, but his eyes were fixed on Eleanor.

"Let's dance more," said Eleanor.

"Okay," said David. "I'll arrange for a song that doesn't require a guidebook."

Eleanor followed David to the bandstand, and the musicians obliged him with another slow number. The change of mood fit the late hour and the dimmed lights. The floor filled up. David had made them promise several slow dances and the guitarist had agreed with a wink.

With her arms around his neck and his around her waist, they swayed and moved in the thickening crowd. They bumped into neighbors, and neighbors bumped into them. They exchanged mumbled apologies without opening their eyes.

Eleanor's were closed, and she lost herself in the public anonymity of a crowded dance floor. She allowed her senses to take in all she could without judgment—feeling, smelling, being in the moment. She wanted to remember it.

Suddenly something crashed into them. They were nearly knocked down. They stumbled and saw Russell and Barbara standing beside them.

"Sorry there," Russell said, smirking. "Just trying for a little space."

David glared at him. Eleanor watched, afraid he was going to punch Russell then and there. He didn't. He said only, "No problem." He reached out to Eleanor and led her away.

But before they were out of sight of them, Eleanor caught David's glance fall onto Barbara Pennon's dress and chest.

She tried to tell herself that it was nothing, that boys always noticed that. It was instinct. She could understand that. She'd even glanced at them herself. You had to; her dress was cut so low and her bra so tight that it was a wonder they didn't spring out like a Jack-in-the-box.

David held Eleanor again as a third slow dance started, this one the slowest yet. Eleanor concentrated on David's touch, the tender way he pulled her just a little bit closer when they fell into step with one another. She was glad David held her; otherwise she might have melted on the spot. She felt drunk or drugged, the way she imagined Tabitha felt after getting a shot of morphine before a long scan.

Barbara crossed her mind again. Barbara was pretty in a model kind of way; narrow hips, big chest, perky, well-maintained face, blonde hair, and the finest clothes her fashion magazines could suggest. Eleanor knew those things were nothing. She could be all those things if she wanted to. If David wanted her to.

The change came upon her unconsciously. A deep primitive part of her mind commanded blood and muscle along a design laid out from her imaginings and memory. A simple modification; a variation on a theme. It wasn't much. But it was enough. It was change, and it hurt. Not as much as it could have, not as much as Dwight or Celeste, but enough to make her grit her teeth, tense, and moan.

Before she was wholly aware of what was happening to her own body, David released her.

"Are you alright?" he said. "Are you okay?" He took a step back to look at her; they'd practically been standing in the same shoes after all.

Eleanor blinked as if coming out of a dream and shuddered. David, frightened, looked at her. He searched her face and then his eyes fell to the front of her dress. Suddenly, possibly because the dress had become so tight she could no longer breath in it, she realized what was happening.

She looked down at herself and tried to stop it, but the die was cast, the change begun. Her body fought her attempts to stifle it with pain that made her regret ever trying.

Neighboring dancers stopped, looked at Eleanor, and fell silent.

Before her eyes, before the others' eyes, before David's eyes, her dress pulled and stretched, grew loose at her waist and threatened to tear at her shoulders until little Eleanor Anders stood stupid and afraid with curves the size and shape of Barbara Pennon's.

CHAPTER TWENTY

Eleanor bolted from the hall like a scared rabbit. She roughly pushed through the throngs of dancers and chaperones until she was at the door. She pulled it open and burst through it at a sprint. Behind her she heard David call her name, but she didn't look back. She ran into the night, into the cold December Wyoming night, with all the energy she had, and headed north. Her home was north.

When her shoes broke in the parking lot, she abandoned them without a thought, and ran on in her torn stockings. She did not feel the broken glass under her feet, did not feel their gashes and stabs, slashes and cuts, her feet ruined beneath her. She did not feel anything but panic even after she was out beyond the parking lot. When her dress caught her knee, she kicked through it, ripping the fabric, wrecking it forever. Her sense of direction pointed her through yards and across fields, around farmhouses, and away from roads. She never stopped. She ran as hard as she could, scaling fences, flopping over barbed wire, hardly noticing it tear at her flesh, her horrible betraying flesh.

Her breath was copper fire in her lungs as she rounded the

block leading to her porch. Her tears froze to ice on her face and clung to her eyelashes. They turned her porch light into a kaleidoscopic beacon.

She ran to the door and pushed it open. Only after she'd turned and locked it, did she collapse in front of the dying fire. Tabitha, startled awake, pulled herself up and rushed to her. "What's wrong, girl?" she demanded. "Oh, my God. Look at you. What happened? All these cuts. Oh, God. Your feet. Oh no. What happened? Eleanor? I'm calling a doctor."

"No!" Eleanor screamed. "No, no, no." She sobbed.

"What happened, Eleanor?" she said.

Eleanor couldn't answer if she wanted to. She wanted just to die, alone and unseen as all wise animals did. Where was a quiet clearing, a fallen log she could hide beneath and perish?

She turned over, gasping, hyperventilating, sobbing with each breath.

She blinked away her frozen tears, melted them with new ones, and regarded her anxious mother. One glance at Tabitha's alarmed face was all she could do. She rolled over and climbed to her feet, but slipped on the blood which ran freely from her soles. Tabitha tried to touch her, help her, calm her, but she shrugged it off. She regained her feet and ran to the ladder leading to her loft.

"Your feet," her mother cried. "Your arms. Your chest. What happened?" Her voice strained, but she didn't cry, didn't panic.

A car skidded to a stop outside their house. Eleanor, torn and cold, dove for her bed and coiled under her blankets in a ball. She stopped crying and held quiet.

"Mrs. Anders," came David's voice from the porch. "Mrs. Anders." He rapped on the door. Tabitha switched on a light.

"Mrs. Anders, is Eleanor here?" said David in the doorway.

"Yes, she's home," she said evenly. Eleanor could hear the strain in her voice but hoped David couldn't.

"David said there was some kind of incident at the dance, and Eleanor ran away," said Karen.

"She's home now," Tabitha said.

"Is she okay?" said David. "Is this her blood?"

"Yes, she cut her foot coming home," Tabitha said.

"She's barefoot?" said Karen.

"Yes," said Tabitha. "She must have lost her shoes. She's pretty upset."

"Have you called a doctor?" demanded David.

"We'll see to it," said Tabitha. "She's still upset. I haven't been able to get a word out of her. Maybe you can tell me what happened."

"Can we come in?" asked Karen.

"No," said Tabitha, and Eleanor loved her for it. "Not right now."

"There was a . . . She, uh . . ." stammered David. "I don't know exactly what happened."

"You didn't do anything to her, did you? Make any advances?" asked Tabitha.

"Mrs. Anders, my son is a perfect gentleman. I do not like what you're implying. Eleanor and David were dancing, and she turned and ran."

"Did you do anything or see anything that might have frightened her?" said Tabitha to David.

"No, I don't think so," said David.

"Well then it was probably all just a misunderstanding," said Tabitha. "I'll put Eleanor to bed, and we'll straighten this out in the morning. It's cold. You all go to bed."

"Mrs. Anders, I don't want you even thinking that David—"

"Just a misunderstanding," Tabitha cut in.

Eleanor heard Karen huff. David was gasping, almost as if he had run the five miles from the hall himself.

"All this blood," he said feebly. "Are you sure she's okay?"

"She'll be fine. She has a strong constitution. We'll tend to it."

There was an awkward silence. Eleanor crawled out from under her blanket and peeked through the window over her bed to the street. She could see Karen's van parked in front, the engine running, the lights still on. Inside she could see Brian and Jennifer's stunned faces staring out of fogged windows at her front porch. Their prom was ruined, along with David's, and how many others? Eleanor buried her face in a pillow and hoped to suffocate herself.

"Here's her shawl," David said. "She left it."

"Thank you, David. I'll give it to her," said Tabitha. "Good night. I'll call you in the morning."

She closed the door, and after a while, a long while Eleanor thought, she heard the car doors slam shut and the van pull away.

She cried until there wasn't a tear left to be shed. When they were spent, and she lay gasping and moaning, wishing for death and hating herself for being human, she heard her mother below.

"I'm coming up now, cupcake," Tabitha said at the base of the ladder. She hadn't been in the loft in years. The climb offered the danger of a slip, but on she came. Eleanor stared at the ceiling, only half aware when her mother sat down on her bed beside her.

"You're a complete mess," she said. "But you're alive. That's all that's important to me right now."

Eleanor was vaguely aware of her mother cutting off the tatters of her prom dress with a pair of scissors. She rolled over and hid her face in a pillow. From far away she felt echoes of pain from a thousand scrapes on her arms and legs. She felt her mother shift her skin, examining deep cuts from wires and trees. When her mother bent over her feet, a sudden intake of breath brought her back.

"Are they bad, Momma?" she said weakly, barely able to hear herself.

"You won't be dancing again for a while," she said. "But we've had worse, haven't we, cupcake? Nothing life threatening. Not for you anyway. The bleeding's nearly stopped already, but they aren't pretty."

"How bad?" said Eleanor. "They don't hurt much."

Tabitha took another deep breath and wiped a tear from her face. "I should lie to you, I know, but I won't. You're down to the bone, Cupcake. Lots of glass, dirt and gravel. Worst I've ever seen." Her voice broke. "I'm surprised you made it home. You'll be alright, though. It'd cripple a normal girl, but you'll be okay."

The words made Eleanor hiccup and cough. She wanted water, wanted to refill her eyes so she could drown herself in tears.

"Oh no, cupcake," Tabitha said. "I didn't mean it like that. Don't take it that way. I'm counting my blessings."

Eleanor filled the silent loft with labored panting. She wanted to stop breathing, but she was a slave to instinct and instinct told her, had always told her, to survive. Tabitha caressed her daughter's head, careful to avoid a deep cut over her eye. She kissed her forehead and got up.

"We've got to get you cleaned up," she said. "I need you to come downstairs."

Eleanor didn't stir.

"Eleanor," Tabitha said firmly. "I need you to come downstairs. I can't haul up water and bandages. I'm not that strong. You can come downstairs and lay on the couch. I won't let anyone in, I promise. I'll seal the house like Fort Knox. You're safe here. Just come down now."

She turned over and looked at Tabitha. Her mother's face was tear streaked and red, but also beamed reassuring confidence that lifted Eleanor's feelings like a balloon. Her mother had been a marine nurse and an officer. Her authority was compelling.

Eleanor tried to speak, but gave up. Instead, she nodded and flopped out onto the floor. Wearing a half-rag of a dress, Eleanor crawled to the ladder. The dull ache in her feet was profound and constant, a terrifying bass note throbbing up her legs that bespoke of severe damage. Dawn glowed behind the curtains.

She climbed down the ladder slowly on her knees. The movement broke open a scab and she heard a light patter of blood drip from her heel to the floor below like a steady, terrible rain.

Her mother directed her to the tub and fetched a first aid kit. Eleanor removed the last scraps of her beautiful dress and dropped them in a heap.

"Drink this milk," Tabitha said, offering her a big glass. The carton was on the floor beside her, an unopened one beside it. "Get your strength up so you can do your thing. I can only do so much and you don't want a doctor."

Eleanor drank the milk as Tabitha washed her. She used a silver forceps and hair tweezers to pull glass and pebbles from her feet for forty minutes. She ran a little warm water and used a sponge and pile of wash cloths to clean away the debris. The water ran muddy pink. The cold finally caught up to Eleanor, and she shivered.

Suddenly Tabitha noticed. Eleanor's wounds had distracted her, and even though she was naked, she'd not noticed the change.

"Oh, dear," she said looking at Eleanor's chest. "When did this happen?"

Eleanor covered herself with her arms and began to sob.

"At the dance," she cried. "I didn't mean for it to happen. I caught David looking at Barbara Pennon, and I was dizzy and didn't know."

"It's okay, cupcake," her mother cooed.

"Everyone saw," she sobbed.

"It's okay. It's okay," she said, but not as surely as before.

Eleanor cried in the bathtub, shivering, hurt, ashamed, and undone, she cried and cried. Tabitha cleaned and mended her, and let her cry. She cried for herself and her stupid pride. She cried for Tabitha, for the troubles she heaped on her. She cried for her friends whose dance she had ruined. She cried for David who had cared for her—a monster.

Finally, Tabitha said firmly, "Now you stop that. You stop that right now. What's done is done. We'll get through this. We always have. You're my cupcake and I won't let anything happen to you. If we have to move, we move. Don't you worry. Ain't nothing broken that can't be fixed. Now finish this carton of milk before we go to the living room and get you under a blanket."

Eleanor caught her breath and did as ordered. She allowed herself to go limp emotionally and gave herself over totally to her mother's will. She had none of her own left.

Her mother helped her get onto the sofa and wrapped a warm blanket around her. She threw a new log in the fire and stoked it until it blazed. Outside the sun was up, but it diffused through clouds. It might snow. Eleanor hoped it would. It would cover the bloody footprints leading to her door.

"I'm afraid we haven't restocked the kit since Halloween," Tabitha said. "But I can make do. Not half as bad as that. Not half as bad."

CHAPTER TWENTY-ONE

There were only three days of school between the prom and Christmas vacation. Eleanor stayed home for them all. She stayed on the couch drinking milk and chewing vitamins while Tabitha answered concerned phone calls from David, Karen, and the school.

David dropped off some homework on the last day of school and begged to be let in to see Eleanor, but Tabitha staunchly refused. He went away upset. He called to her window from the porch.

"Eleanor, call me," he yelled. "Please call me."

By Christmas, Eleanor was able to walk. She did not heal as quickly as she usually did. Her heart wasn't in it, Tabitha said. Still, the recovery amazed her nurse-mother, who never failed to comment on it with each dressing change. Her breasts had receded to their normal form before the sun set the day after the prom.

Tabitha kept close watch on her. Twice during that first weekend, she talked to Eleanor about possibly going to the hospital. "Your blood pressure is so low," she explained. "You're weak. So much blood lost." Eleanor had, of course, refused. She told her mother that she'd be fine and dispelled any suspicions she had, that she secretly wanted to die and refused treatment because of that. "I wouldn't have come home if that were my goal." Tabitha agreed to wait and see.

By Monday, it was academic. Against Eleanor's wishes, her body had replaced the blood, and her pressure was normal. She had no appetite, but her body hungrily absorbed every calorie her mother made her eat. Her mood was somber, bleak, and broken, but her body wanted to survive and knitted itself together against its master's wishes.

Eleanor finally forced herself off the couch and gingerly into the kitchen a week after the dance where an exhausted Tabitha had fallen asleep in her chair. Their stores were nearly spent. Eleanor had drunk every drop of condensed milk, eaten every piece of protein, and consumed all the bread, butter, and fat in the fridge. Tabitha had lived on Spaghetti O's, black coffee, and pain pills. She'd stayed at Eleanor's side like a loyal angel. Eleanor would wake up in the darkest hour of the night only to find Tabitha asleep beside her, a chair pulled to the couch, her hand holding Eleanor's. She held her all the time, as if by touching her she might channel hope into her daughter.

Eleanor searched the kitchen and checked their account balances. It was time to work the magic of changing invisible credit into food, a spell that required her to get to the store. Tabitha, for all her energized caregiving, was not up to so long a walk, not now, not in the snow. Eleanor heated a can of corn on the stove and watched the snow bury her tomato pots in a silent shroud of cold.

When Tabitha woke, she and Eleanor made a shopping list. It was the weekend before Christmas. The stores would be crowded. Eleanor didn't relish a public appearance, let alone

one in front of the whole town. They decided they could last a few more days. Late Sunday night, two days before the holiday, Eleanor would go to the store and bring back enough provisions to see them through the new year. That would give them time consider their options.

Eleanor used the time to mend her feet. She stayed off them as much as possible and, though it made her mother sad, she crawled around the house on her aching knees. By Sunday, she felt strong enough for the trip.

Jamesford rolled up the sidewalks on winter nights. Without tourists, in constant freeze, few went out after sunset. Eleanor saw not a soul and nary a light on her trek to the grocery store.

She waited outside the glass door and looked in to see if Karen Venn was working. She knew she'd been moved to days and didn't expect to see her, but if she did, Eleanor would turn around and head to Cowboy Bob's for supplies. She didn't see her. She didn't see anyone. She slipped in the automatic door, took a cart as quietly as she could, and like a burglar, gathered provisions.

It didn't take her long to find what she needed; canned stuff mostly, and a chicken for Christmas. She bought real potatoes and some cheap pork she could freeze for emergencies. The sales gave her a little extra spending money. She found a cute red and blue wool cap for her mother. Her old one was pretty tired. It served its purpose of warmth and vanity for a woman whose hair had not come back from years of chemotherapy, but a new one would not be unwelcome.

Eleanor surveyed her cart and realized she couldn't carry

all the groceries back to her house. She could manage two, maybe three bags, but this was five at least. She'd just have to take the cart.

She headed to the self-check-out lane when Mr. Woods appeared at the front and beckoned her over. They exchanged small talk which consisted of asking Eleanor if she'd found everything she needed and offering to sell her stamps and ice, a company script copied on every register. When he was done, he wished Eleanor a Merry Christmas and disappeared into the office. When he was out of sight, Eleanor pushed her cart out the doors and into the darkness

"You going to push that all the way home?"

Eleanor turned to see David waiting for her by the door.

"What are you doing here?" she asked.

"Waiting for you," he said. "You won't see me. You won't come to the door. You won't talk to me on the phone."

He looked awful. In the last vision she had of him, he was splendid in a tuxedo, rapt with dancing, flush with heat. He looked cold and broken and lost now.

"I can't," Eleanor said and pushed her cart forward.

David followed. Eleanor didn't stop.

"What about all the blood?" he said.

"I scraped my foot. No big deal."

"Your mother said it was more than a scrape."

"She worries. It was nothing."

"She told my mom that you got afraid at the dance, that Russell scared you."

Tabitha had come up with the story from the few details Eleanor had given her that night. When Karen Venn called early next morning, she spun it as a silly girl overreacting to a shove. It satisfied David's mother, who was clearly relieved to hear that David had not caused Eleanor's fright.

"What did you say to your mom?" Eleanor asked.

"I didn't say anything," he said. "I didn't know what to say."

"But you didn't tell her it wasn't Russell?"

"No."

"What about Brian and Jennifer?"

"They didn't see," David said. "I told them it was Russell."

"There was nothing to see," Eleanor said sharply. She pushed the cart out of the lot and along the icy sidewalk. Her feet were sore, but she could run if she had to.

"Eleanor, I want to understand," David said, trotting behind her. "Please, give me a chance."

"I can't," she said.

"What I saw—" he said.

Eleanor spun on him. "There was nothing to see. You imagine too much."

Even under the heavy coat, Eleanor could see his drooping shoulders and defeated chest.

"What you did was . . ."

"David, leave me alone."

"Yes it scared me—surprised me," he said, ignoring her protests. "Eleanor, nothing has changed with me."

"It has with me," she said.

David looked like he'd been slapped.

"Eleanor, don't," he begged. "Please, talk to me. Trust me."

"I'm sorry, David. It's no good. Go away."

"Eleanor, please."

"Don't make me run away. My feet haven't recovered, and we need this food."

"Let me—" He reached for the cart.

"David! I'm not who you think I am. Leave me alone. It's better for everybody." She wished she could have said it without her voice breaking, without her face flushing, without tears. But that was too much to ask.

"Eleanor . . ."

"Please, David. Please," she said and pushed the cart out of his hands. His fingers slipped from the bar and fell to his sides. She pushed past him. He didn't follow but stood in the cold dark and watched her go. She forced herself not to look back, but when she did, he was gone.

She took her time going home. Besides her feet, her heart ached like it'd been crushed, like it had slipped out of her chest and she herself had stepped on it. She let herself cry a little in the quiet darkness between street lamps, and by the time she arrived home, her eyes had mostly recovered.

Tabitha was asleep in a chair when she came in and roused herself to help with the groceries.

"You should have gone to bed," Eleanor told her mother. "You know I can manage."

"I know you can," she said. "That doesn't mean you should." She looked at Eleanor and brushed her cold cheeks. "You were crying again," she said. "Why?"

"David was at the store," she said as calmly as she could.

"At this hour? Whatever for?"

"He said he was waiting for me," Eleanor said.

"I always said he was a smart boy," Tabitha said. She clucked her tongue and pulled the wool hat out of a shopping bag. "What's this?"

"Oh, Mom, you weren't supposed to find that. It's for Christmas."

"I love it," she said. She slipped off her scarf, and Eleanor saw the bald scalp beneath. She puffed up the cap and slid it over her head.

"Finally, something warm," she said. "How do I look?"

"Like you're going skiing," Eleanor said, a little crestfallen.

"Perfect," Tabitha said. "I'm in disguise."

Eleanor smiled. "Do you really like it?"

"Oh, yes," she said. "Yes, I do."

"I'm glad."

"So, what happened with David," her mother pressed. "I won't be able to sleep if I don't know. I can't wait until morning."

"He backed up your story," she said.

"Smart boy," Tabitha said. "It gets him off the hook."

"Mom, he wasn't on the hook. It was me. All me."

"That's true, but you did it for him. It's the sad tale of women everywhere that we feel we have to change ourselves to please a man. You don't, cupcake. I hope you know that."

"I don't think you can say that about me," she said.

"You stop that, Eleanor Anders, right now," her mother said. "You are a woman. You can be many things, but you are a woman. Your people were people, you are a person. You're a different race, is all. So what? You are female. You have the body and mind of teenager, and you are becoming a woman."

"I'm older than a teenager," she said.

"Years don't mean anything. You have years, yes, lots of them. But they were lost years. You were twelve when you lost them and six when you got them back. Since then you've been progressing wonderfully as a young woman, displaying in your own way every silly idiosyncrasy of the species I know.

Don't think you're any worse than people, nor any better. You're perfect."

Eleanor sulked and nearly put the chicken in the freezer.

"Aren't we going to eat that?" Tabitha asked.

Eleanor put it in the fridge to thaw for Christmas dinner.

"Was he scared?" Tabitha said after a while. "What else did he say? What about your friends?"

"He said the others believed the Russell story. They didn't see me."

"That's good. Everything will blow over, you'll see."

"I told him I didn't want to see him," Eleanor said.

"I thought we were going to wait and see about that?"

"It's stupid to try, Tabitha. I'm going to slip up again, or get caught, or go to the doctor and then I'm going to have run or, or . . . or else. There's no future for me with David."

"Eleanor, cupcake, I won't tell you the future doesn't matter, that I don't think about it constantly. I do. I worry and cry and fear and plan. I tried to face my future once, take it all at one time, and it took me to that lake. I swallowed my entire future, and I was done. But then there was Eleanor, beautiful, mysterious, lovely Eleanor, and I was saved. I stopped thinking about my future when you gave me our present. I don't want to sound too philosophical, but all of us, even you, yes, even you with your regeneration, are going to die one day. Does that mean we shouldn't live while we're here?"

Eleanor didn't say anything.

"Of course not," Tabitha said. "We do the best we can. I want you to dance, Eleanor. You deserve a dance. I'm glad you got one. I want you to have more. I understand why you did what you did. You're in love."

"No, I'm not," she said. "I was confused."

"At your age, it's much the same thing," Tabitha said.

"I can't face him, Mom. I just can't."

"Okay, cupcake. We'll let it alone for a while. We'll see how things go. But, my lovely little girl, you know better than anyone that things change."

"Ha ha, Mom," said Eleanor with a smirk. It was the first real moment of mirth she'd had in weeks.

Christmas morning, Tabitha was too sick to leave to her bed. Eleanor served her butler style, and they read aloud while it snowed outside their windows. They fell asleep in each other's arms.

CHAPTER TWENTY-TWO

The new year started in a snowstorm. Eleanor hadn't left the house except to shovel the walk since Christmas, and she and Tabitha had hibernated happily in their little house at the edge of town, away from what dangers waited beyond the yard. Eleanor cared for her mother, and her mother cared for her, though there was little to do. She'd mended and looked every bit as healthy as she did when she returned from Nebraska. Every bit.

Tabitha's strength was sporadic, but there was no need to test it. Eleanor kept her company and did all the chores, played cards, and broke out board games when that grew tiring. The two grew closer than they'd ever been.

Eleanor dreaded going back to school and being seen again, but with Tabitha's help, they approached the problem theoretically and dispassionately, as if writing a script for someone else. When the curtain rose, the day school started back after the Christmas holiday, Eleanor donned her clothes and coat like a costume, fell into character, and trotted off to the fiction that was her life.

There hadn't been time to shovel the fresh snow before

school began and, of course, Eleanor refused to take the bus. She was late by ten minutes. She made it fifteen by pausing in the hall to gather her courage before facing her classmates. She'd be gone from Jamesford for good if it weren't for Tabitha. Her mother had soothed her fears and convinced her to return to school. It hadn't been easy. In a fit of denial and desperation, in a weak moment, Eleanor had lashed and blamed her mother for the mess she was in.

"Was it so terrible?" Tabitha asked her. "Was it not wonderful?" she said. "Think of the dancing. Before your little stunt. How was that?"

Eleanor had had to pause. "It was wonderful," she said.

"If you could go back, would you? Taking it all, or leaving it all, would you trade that away?"

"No," she said.

So in the end, Eleanor had to trust her mother that things would get better. She just had to bear them until they did.

Of course, the door squeaked. It screamed in Eleanor's ears like a siren in a bowling alley. It silenced the class, who looked up from their papers and watched her come in.

"Glad you could make it back," Mrs. Hart said with dripping sarcasm.

Eleanor kept her head down, her hair a wall. Her headbands, even the new ones her mother had given her for Christmas, were hidden away in a drawer in her loft for the foreseeable future. She found her seat and ignored the staring students. Mrs. Hart continued talking only after a long painful pause to give everyone time to gawk at Eleanor.

In between Mrs. Hart's classes, Eleanor remained at her desk and read papers her eyes would not focus on. She kept to herself, and no one approached her.

At lunch she found her usual table empty. She ate with her back to the cafeteria and pretended no one was looking at her. David brought his lunch tray to the table and set it down.

"Don't sit here," Eleanor said bitterly.

Without a word, he collected his tray and left.

No one said a word to her the entire day. She'd forgotten her gym clothes and so watched as the rest of her class did stretching calisthenics. In Spanish, Mr. Blake didn't call on her or offer her a reading. When the bell rang to go, Eleanor was the first outside and past the parking lot before the buses even arrived.

And so it went for January. Eleanor kept to herself, and no one bothered her. She forced herself to stop looking for her old lunch mates but she was unable to keep her back to the room at lunch. Too much Hitchcock in that. She'd wanted to see what was coming at her.

She caught snippets of gossip, and though her countenance was firm and expressionless, inside she swallowed her guts when they chewed at her bones.

"I heard David felt her up on the dance floor. Right in front of everyone."

"I heard that Russell Liddle grabbed her."

"No, I heard she took her top off—flashed her boobs to everyone. What a slut."

As troubling as these whispers were, it was from Robby Guide, the Shoshone, that Eleanor heard an old, familiar, and terrifying word, a word she'd last heard used to describe her dying family before she ran into the desert. Witch.

David was miserable. Eleanor could see it. She felt sorry for him, ached to be with him, but kept away nonetheless. Several times, he tried again to talk to her, but each time she told him to go away with increasing venom. The notes he slipped into her locker she threw away without reading. When his grades began to fall in chemistry, she ignored Mr. Graham's suggestion that she tutor him again.

"Your grades have slipped a bit, too, Eleanor," he said, "so I think it would be beneficial for everyone."

"No," was all she said.

Rumors swirled and boiled, became greater, became smaller, until what had actually happened was completely lost. Eleanor racked her brain to remember who had actually seen the transformation, but aside from David, she couldn't remember.

The one rumor that stayed alive, albeit in different forms, was Eleanor's promiscuity. Conflicting stories about the dance found purchase with the old rumors of her Halloween tryst when she was seen sharing a booth with Dwight at Cowboy Bob's. Though details were sketchy, the overall picture was one of a girl out of control. It wasn't long before the rumors reached the ears of teachers and then administration. Eleanor wasn't surprised when she was called to the counselor in early February.

Mr. Sullivan was the Jamesford High School counselor. Since the other counselor had quit in November, at the moment, he handled the school from kindergarten through graduation. Most of his time was spent with juniors and seniors helping them graduate and plan for college, but he also dealt with "troubled youth."

"Eleanor," he said. "Tell me what's happening at home."

"Not much," she said behind her bangs.

"I understand your mother is very ill," he said, reading a

file the origin of which Eleanor could only speculate. "I see you're on public assistance."

"So," she said. "Many kids are. This is Wyoming."

"That's not a constructive attitude," he said with an edge to his voice. "Why would you say that?"

"I know a lot of kids on public assistance."

"According to my records, you don't have any friends."

"You keep track of my friends? Who are you, Big Brother?"

"No, of course not," he said. Eleanor glared at him. This was not going well; her hackles were up. "I've just been asking around about you."

"Don't believe everything you hear," she said.

"No, of course not," he said, steepling his fingers. "But I have heard some disturbing things concerning you."

Eleanor tried to read the file under his elbows, but couldn't.

"I understand there was an issue at prom," he said. "Would you like to talk about it?"

"No."

Mr. Sullivan smiled a crocodilian grin, and Eleanor retreated as far back in her chair as she could. It wasn't a nice office. It was cluttered and smelled of aerosol room freshener and clandestine smoking.

"Why don't you want to talk about it?"

"Why do you?"

"I'm here to help," he said. "Did someone threaten you at the dance? Did someone touch you?"

"No," she said.

"Sometimes boys get a little aggressive. It's nothing to be ashamed of. It wasn't your fault. Was it?"

"Was what my fault?"

"What happened at the dance. You going topless on the dance floor."

"That didn't happen," she said.

"I heard otherwise," he said, leaning back in his chair.

Eleanor decided to ignore him.

"I've had a talk with David Venn," he said. Eleanor stared at a mug of pens. "He said you were upset about Russell Liddle. Is that what happened? Did Russell take your shirt off? You don't need to be afraid to tell me. I can protect you."

"That didn't happen," she said. "Russell was an ass, but my shirt stayed on. David didn't say that. Get your mind out of the gutter."

She instantly regretted insulting him. That kind of thing would only prolong this terrible interview and make things worse. But she felt she had to fight back, if not for her, then for David, the true innocent.

"Can I go?" she said.

"No," Mr. Sullivan said firmly. "I want to talk to you about Halloween. You were seen at Cowboy Bob's truck stop with a man late at night. Why were you there?"

Eleanor fell mute. Mr. Sullivan endured the silence for several minutes before pressing again.

"Eleanor," he said as soothingly as his wooden voice would go, "many girls have a hard time coming to terms with teen-age changes. They think that it will make them popular and thus make bad decisions. That doesn't mean that they're bad people or that they can't change. A reputation can be restored. Souls can be saved."

"I didn't do whatever it is you think I did," she said.

"What do you think I think you did?"

Eleanor stared at the desk. "Anything wrong," she said.

He sighed. "Your grades are slipping, Eleanor. What you do in your own time is ultimately your own business."

"Thanks," she put in.

"But," he went on. "If I think that it's affecting your academic career or general wellbeing, I have to step in. I'm stepping in. Mrs. Hart tells me that you've been a problem student for months. She says you've been disrespectful and show racist tendencies. I see you had detention for it. These are all signs of a student sliding into bad habits, bad habits that could lead you very far from where you are now."

"Where am I now?"

"In a nice safe place with people who want to help you."

"I just want to be left alone," she said.

"Did your father molest you, Eleanor? Did your mother?"

With that, Eleanor stood up and left the office without another word.

That night while she was telling Tabitha about Mr. Sullivan, Stephanie Pearce decided to drop by unannounced.

"I just wanted to see how you all came out of the holidays," she said, pushing her way through the door.

Eleanor was glad she'd cleaned up. Busying herself with chores kept her mind off of things. Their home was in good order. There was even a new cactus plant on the window Eleanor had bought from the drug store earlier that week.

The social worker glanced around the house, taking it in, looking for dust or other neglect.

"That smells great," she said. "What's for dinner?"

"Eleanor is making a casserole," Tabitha said. "We had a lovely Christmas. Thanks for the card, by the way."

"My pleasure," Stephanie said. She fell into the couch, and the springs heaved under her weight. "I understand you're going to Riverton again this month. Is Eleanor going with you?"

"She usually does," Tabitha said. "We make it a girls' trip."

"I understand she's been having trouble at school," she said. "Her grades have slipped, and she's fallen into some bad habits."

"What do you mean?"

"Mr. Sullivan called me today, Tabitha," she said. "Maybe Eleanor should leave."

"Yes, of course," said Tabitha. "Go do your homework in my room."

Eleanor picked up a paperback and strolled to her mother's room at the back of the house. Tabitha knew that Eleanor would be able to hear everything said in the house regardless of where she was.

"Eleanor has a reputation," Stephanie Pearce said.

"What kind of reputation?" asked Tabitha.

"A reputation," she said again with emphasis.

"Oh, that kind."

"Exactly," she said. "I'm afraid you've got to control your daughter better, Miss Anders. She's out of control."

"It's all rumors," Tabitha said. "Do you believe every rumor you hear?"

"When it comes from her counselor, and her teachers, and people I know personally, yes, I do."

"What about people who were there? Or how about Eleanor herself? Russell Liddle was rude to her at the dance, and she fled. You need to control that little brat."

"I heard there was something at the prom," she said.

"Well, good. You have a reference for the rumors. That's a start. Next you can verify them before threatening us."

"I'm not threatening you, Miss Anders. I'm here to help."

"You're here to meddle and slander. My Eleanor is not that kind of girl."

Eleanor heard a deep sigh escape the big woman.

"I'm not at liberty to discuss other clients," she said. "But I know Russell Liddle. He says that he did nothing to Eleanor at the dance."

"Are you kidding?" said Tabitha.

"Let me finish," Stephanie said. "He said he did nothing, but I'm inclined to disbelieve him."

"Okay," Tabitha said. "That's something."

"Do you know that Eleanor was seen at Cowboy Bob's in late October? With a man in the cafe? Very late at night?"

"I sent Eleanor to get some aspirin. She was cold and warmed up. I can't help it if someone talked to her."

"People say she stayed the night in his truck," she said.

"People say that Children's Protection is just out to break up loving families. We can't always believe what we hear, can we?"

Eleanor heard the social worker shift on the couch. She'd gotten bigger since she'd last seen her, holiday treats no doubt. She felt sorry for the sofa.

"Tabitha," she said.

"Mrs. Anders will be fine," said Tabitha curtly.

"Mrs. Anders," she said, patience stretched thin in her voice, "be that as they may, Eleanor is going through some hard times at school right now. I think you'll agree. Her grades are suffering. She's now barely passing several classes. She's in real danger of failing English and social studies."

"That would be Mrs. Hart," said Tabitha. "Am I right?"

"Yes."

"I'll have a word with her."

"That would be a good idea," she said. "As for the rest of it, well, the reports aren't good. Mr. Sullivan said she walked out of his office today. I've got to make a note of that in my files. It's not a good thing."

"Is that another threat?"

"I'm just trying to keep a wide picture of what's going on here. Your family is 'troubled.' The state wants to help. We want to do what's best for everyone. Eleanor and you."

"Did Mr. Sullivan tell you why Eleanor stormed out?"

"No, just that she was being uncooperative."

"He accused me of sexually abusing my daughter," Tabitha said flatly. Eleanor wanted to scream. How could this be helping? Her mother was making all the mistakes she'd made earlier that day. They needed to run, not fight; roll over and play dead until the danger got bored and left. This confrontation would only bring more trouble.

"I'm sure he didn't mean it like that," she said. "Mr. Sullivan is very good at what he does."

"I'm sure he is, but Eleanor doesn't need to be treated like a criminal by him or anyone else. Are you going to take away our food stamps if you keep hearing rumors? Are you going to stop driving me to Riverton? Or deny my insurance? What are you going to do?"

"Mrs. Anders," she said. "I have to report what's going on. We want your family to succeed. That's what we want. We want you to get better and Eleanor to have a wonderful life and fulfill her potential. If we see things going the wrong way, we try to steer them back. That's all I'm doing."

"We're doing fine," Tabitha said. "Stop listening to rumors. Eleanor's grades will improve. She's been sick. How other people think about her or us are none of our concern and out of our control. It's their problem. Not ours."

Another heavy sigh and a shift of the springs. "I should be going," Stephanie said. "I'll check back with you as scheduled. Say good-bye to Eleanor for me."

"Thanks for dropping by," said Tabitha with little warmth. "Come by any time."

Eleanor heard the door shut and listened to the heavy footfalls crunching away in the snow. When Stephanie's car puttered away, she came out.

"Looks like we're through it," said Tabitha happily.

"Are you kidding?" Eleanor said. "We're sunk."

"No, cupcake," she said. "This is good. No one's talking about what really happened at the dance or Halloween. They've just slapped you with a reputation every girl gets at some time in their life no matter what they do. Don't you see? You're going to be okay. It's blowing over."

"Could she really take away our insurance and food?"

"No," said Tabitha. "I said that to show her how weak she is. She can't dictate to me."

"So what's the worst she could do?"

Tabitha thought for a minute and some of her enthusiasm evaporated. "The worst she could do is split us up," she said.

It sounded to Eleanor as if Stephanie Pearce had a lot of power over them.

CHAPTER TWENTY-THREE

As February crept on, the talk about Eleanor subsided. New targets of gossip and scorn appeared with the regularity of piranha feeding frenzies. Eleanor didn't reach out to her old friends, and they didn't reach out to her. Her two weeks of social standing after David's fireworks invitation was too little to wipe away the years of disregard everyone remembered. Eleanor returned to obscurity, out of sight and out of mind for most people.

David was not among them. To his credit, he'd stayed away from Eleanor and even stopped slipping her notes. However, he stole glances at her when he could, and once each day, at some point in school, he'd hold her gaze for a long time, offering her an opportunity to talk if she wanted. She didn't.

A week ahead of Valentine's Day, David's locker was decorated with pink and red crepe paper hearts, candies, and streamers. Eleanor saw it before class. From down the hall, she watched him rush excitedly to it and fling open the door. Confetti spilled out and David found a card. He opened it and read. His excitement vanished. He closed the locker and went to class.

Before Mrs. Hart entered the classroom, Barbara sauntered up to his desk.

"So?" she said, bending over his desk.

"So?" said David.

"So, will you be my Valentine? Take me to the Valentine's Stomp on Friday?"

Valentine's Stomp was a girl's choice dance. Not a true dance like at Christmastime, just a Friday evening in the gym with music and balloons, but since it was the only girl's choice dance, it had a reputation of being one of the best events of the year.

"Don't tell me you've already been asked," she said and cast a sad look at Eleanor who turned away quickly, knowing she'd been caught watching.

"No, I haven't been asked yet," he said. "Let me answer you tomorrow."

Barbara giggled. "I can't wait," she said. "My locker is A202."

Mrs. Hart wafted into the classroom smelling of men's cologne, and Mr. Curtz's office chairs. Eleanor settled down behind her tome of short stories and tried not to cry.

She heard giggles and talk about Barbara and David all day. Crystal wanted to double date with them, and even Aubrey said that they made a cute couple.

Then came gym class. Mr. Blake was anxious to get the class back outside and accepted fifty degrees as warm enough for a jog around the track. Eleanor followed behind the bunch of complaining joggers. The temperature was closer to forty than fifty. She saw Russell jog up beside David, and she closed the distance.

"I hear you're taking Barb to Stomp," he said. "You better not."

"It's a girl's choice," David said. "And I haven't decided."

"She's my girl," he said in between gasps of cold air.

"She asked me," David said.

"Just to get me jealous."

"Are you?"

"Jealous of you? That's a laugh. Hell no."

"Then go away," David said.

"It's a joke, Venn. It's all a joke. Don't fall for it. Leave her or you'll pay."

"How?"

"You don't have your big friend here no more, Venn," he said, pulling him to a stop on the inner track. "I won't be scared away with a broken switchblade."

So he'd gotten it. She'd broken the knife with a vice in the shed and left the blood-stained parts on Russell's doorstep the day after the attack, as soon as she was able. She'd scratched the message, "lay low or I'll put you low" on the cement by the knife and ran home. She had listened for some clue that he'd gotten the message for months—that is, some clue besides him not going after David again. The dramatic gangster threat had worked. For a while.

"What are you talking about?" David said. "What happened? Tell me."

"Go back to your skunk, Eleanor," said Russell up in David's face. "Your cow with the udders."

He never saw the punch. David rounded on him with a doubled-up left haymaker and clocked Russell behind the ear. He stumbled back and then down on his rump. The class stopped to watch. Russell crab-walked backwards while David stomped after him. He was surprised more than hurt. The hurt would come later Eleanor knew. She'd heard the strike.

"You filthy little maggot," snarled David and leapt at him. Russell covered his face with his arms as David, in a frenzy, landed punches against his head and chest. Blood seeped between Russell's fingers where David pounded his nose through his blocking hands. He slapped his ears, and grabbed a tuft of hair just as Tanner and Brian pulled him off.

"Calm down, David," said Brian. "Break it up."

Russell got to his feet and rushed at David. Brian let go to allow David to dodge, but Tanner held fast and Russell's head butt caught David square in the gut. His lungs emptied and he flopped on the ground where Tanner dropped him. Russell got one kick into David's belly before Brian pushed him down. Then Tanner sprang into Brian and pulled him down. David rolled onto his knees and tried to catch his breath. Russell ran at him like he was lining up a field goal.

David rolled to the side and tripped Russell with a hard kick to the shins. Still gasping for air, David threw himself on top of Russell again, and pinned his arms beneath his knees.

He leaned his head in close over Russell's terrified face. In short gasps, he said, "If you ever . . . breathe an unkind word . . . about Eleanor Anders again," he gasped, "I'll tear your tongue out . . . and feed it to you!"

Mr. Blake grabbed David in a headlock. Two Seniors, P.E. aids, pulled Brian and Tanner apart. Mr. Curtz sprinted across the lawn to the commotion.

Everyone talked excitedly at once. Mr. Curtz cut the four boys out of the herd and, together with Mr. Blake, marched them to his office.

The period was over by then, and the remaining sophomores headed back to class comparing accounts of the dust-up and speculating on punishments.

Eleanor trailed behind them, feeling mixed-up and excited. She was aware of someone else behind her, walking quickly to catch up. She turned to see Robby Guide. She slowed to let him pass her. He stopped in front of her. The excitement had made her bold, and she met his eyes, read them deeply, studied his scars, his hair color, memorizing his shape, weight, handedness, pupils, teeth, everything. She felt his moods in his eyes, and if she could taste him, she had all she'd ever need to be him.

"Henry Creek says you're Nimirika," he told her.

"Who?"

"Henry Creek. Shoshone from the dance. Midge's date, remember?"

She nodded.

"He says you're Nimirika. It's a kind of ogre. A cannibal. A witch."

"That's a terrible thing to say," she said coldly but her head buzzed and her legs ached to carry her away.

"Is it true?"

"Get lost, Robby," she said, and, forcing herself to go slowly, she walked on.

"Leave him alone," he said. "David. Leave him alone."

Eleanor stopped. She turned to look at him. Her fear had turned to anger.

"I said leave David alone." Robby said, struggling to hold her gaze. He was shaking.

"I've left him alone," she said.

"Do it better."

"You don't know anything," she said.

The bell rang, announcing the start of Spanish. Mr. Blake

would be late, but the bell was the bell. Robby left her at a run and disappeared into the building.

Eleanor made her way slowly back to the dressing room.

The next day, the school was abuzz in talk about the fight. David wasn't allowed to go to the dance; he was suspended for a week. Russell, too. Though everyone said that it had been David who'd started the fight, Russell's part was not overlooked, and this being another in a string of disciplinary problems, he got the full week instead of a day that Tanner and Brian got for a first offense.

David's exclamation about Eleanor's honor also buzzed through the school that whole week. Eleanor felt eyes on her again, measuring her looks against David's attentions, speculating within the old rumors what she might have done to get them. She tried to ignore it, but it weakened her resolve and late that week she found herself short-tempered at the worst time.

"Miss Anders," Mrs. Hart said after class. "You've once again handed in a terrible paper. You show absolutely no knowledge of the subject matter."

"I wrote about the short story. I understood it," she said.

"Oh, you know the words, but not the meaning," she said. "Didn't you pay attention during lectures? The story was about hubris and the baseness of marriage."

"I thought it was about being stupid and losing your boat while senselessly killing ducks."

"See? You got nothing out of it. You've got to learn to be more observant. I'm giving you an F for the paper. You can re-write it over the weekend, but for only half points."

"I said hubris in my paper," she said.

"Not in the right context, dear," she said. She'd turned to her desk and wasn't even looking at Eleanor anymore. "You used it against nature. That's not there."

"It is. I saw it. I pointed it out. I'm right." Eleanor's voice grew in volume with each syllable, and the last word was practically screamed.

"Parent-teacher conference is coming up soon," Mrs. Hart said. "If it is at all possible, could you get your white-trash mother to attend? We have to discuss how this year's shaping up." She turned back to her papers. Eleanor was dismissed.

She stormed out of the room and sulked for the rest of the day. Her grades had improved across the board in every class but those Mrs. Hart taught. She was a solid B or B+ everywhere, an A in Spanish thanks to a generous bell-curve she couldn't defeat. But Mrs. Hart was determined to make her life miserable. Nothing she'd handed in had been good enough. She'd find spelling errors where there were none, disregard Eleanor's protest as disrespect, and throw out whole assignments when she didn't agree exactly with Mrs. Hart's interpretations. She knew that David had approached the short story from the same angle she had. She'd glimpsed it on her desk. He'd received an A; she got an F. It was useless to fight it. She had to conform, get by, and pray she would not have her again next year.

That Saturday, Eleanor found David sitting on her porch. She was going shopping. She considered waiting inside until he left, but Robby's words rang in her ears. She'd fretted all week about how she'd ruined David's life. Robby had been right. She had to do better.

She opened the door and walked past him as if he was

garbage. She held that image in her mind so she wouldn't betray herself and run to him.

"Eleanor," he said, getting up and trotting after her.

"Hello, David," she said as coldly as she could. "What are you doing trespassing on our property?"

"Eleanor, I know what you're trying to do," he said.

"You just don't know when you're not wanted," she said, not taking her eyes off the sidewalk.

"I know why you're doing this," he said. "You're trying to protect me."

"Get over yourself," she said, mimicking the girls in the halls.

"Eleanor, I'm going to find it myself. When I do, when I know, when I understand, you'll have to come back to me. I'll show you."

Eleanor kept walking.

"I love you, Eleanor," he said. "I love you."

She stopped and looked at him.

"You don't know anything," she said.

"No, I don't," said David. "Because you won't tell me. But I can see I've got to learn it anyway. That's why I came here today. To tell you I'm going to find out. I'm going to show you that you can trust me, Eleanor. You always could. I'm your friend."

"And we're engaged, right?" Eleanor teased. It was the most unkind thing she'd ever done, and she felt a part of herself die before the sound was out of her mouth. Unable to hide the pain, she turned away and sprinted up the street leaving David behind, watching her go.

CHAPTER TWENTY-FOUR

Eleanor accompanied Tabitha to Riverton. Tabitha told Eleanor that she didn't have to go with her, that she could do it herself, but Eleanor always went and so would go this time. There was something different about this time's protests, however, and Eleanor sensed a real effort by her mother to have her stay home. Tabitha had lost more weight since Christmas, and though her mother would never suggest it, Eleanor believed that her dramas were to blame for her mother's decline.

"It's President's Day," Eleanor reminded her. "No school today. No Mrs. Hart." Eleanor had told Tabitha about the "white-trash" comment, and her mother had laughed. "Just need a little talk with that woman," she'd said cheerfully. "She's got no place to talk, now does she, cupcake?"

They boarded the van together at eight o'clock and drove south to Riverton. Tabitha looked as good as she could, with makeup, a stylish wig, and nice clothes, but there was no denying her frailty. Though not yet fifty-six, she moved with the cautious steps of an octogenarian.

"Honey, this is going to be a long one," she said. "Go see a movie and pick up some books. Come back around four."

Tabitha kissed her forehead, and Eleanor had a sudden urge to cry.

"Momma, I'll stay," she said.

"They haven't changed out the magazines in that office since Clinton was president. Go see a movie. I'll be fine. You'll be back in time to talk to the doctor. You go. Have fun."

Reluctantly, Eleanor allowed the van to take her to town. There was an excellent bookstore in Riverton, Sam Bracker Bookstore. It carried new and used titles, took two stories of half a city block, and networked throughout the world to find whatever you needed. It was sometimes expensive, sometimes slow, but eventually, if it was in print, Bracker's Bookstore would get it for you. The original Sam's great-grandson ran it now with his two sons. Many times Eleanor and Tabitha had traded old books for new and haggled down torn paperback treasures from a dollar to a quarter.

Eleanor liked the smell of the store. She knew that particular smell was decay, cheap acid paper disintegrating the books it was made into, but for a reader, it was perfume. How short-sighted, she always thought. Still it was a welcoming smell, full of promise and adventure.

She went to her favorite sections, all on the secondhand floor. Children's literature, classics, paranormal romance (which was getting bigger by the day), history, and science. After ninety minutes of browsing, she found nothing interesting and wandered into the medical section. She'd combed this area with Tabitha, hunting for holistic cures and information. About a year ago, Tabitha had stopped searching these shelves and casually perused the romance sections instead. Today Eleanor caught herself browsing the end-of-life section. Her head was tilted sideways, and she was reading titles before she knew where she was. It made her sad. She left without touching a book and wandered deeper in the store.

First she smelled him. Then heard him. Then, peeking out behind a heavy pine bookcase, she saw him. David Venn. He was talking to a research clerk, sharing a piece of notebook paper.

"I haven't heard of most of these," the clerk said. "But these three I think we have. Check Western American, Indian Studies, Folklore." He pointed to a corner of the store Eleanor had visited many times. "European folklore is in the same area, a couple aisles over." David looked where he pointed.

"Werewolves would be in movies," the clerk said.

"No," David said. "Folklore, I think. Maybe history?"

"I'll look it up." He turned to his computer and typed. "Yeah, it's a science textbook. Anthropology. University of Arizona Press, Dr. Sikring. *Werewolves and the Case for Shapeshifters.* It's ninety-five dollars. I'll see if I can find it used, but I doubt it. It's pretty new. The other book of his on your list, *Skinwalkers,* I actually have. Someone ordered it and never picked it up. Here, I'll show you."

He led David downstairs to the new books. Eleanor knew that title, *Skinwalkers.* She had ordered it a year before and never picked it up. She hadn't been able to scrape together the forty-three dollars it cost and so had let it go onto the shelf, losing a five dollar deposit. She'd read it in snippets over the past year, ostensibly browsing the section, but ultimately saving the money and learning nothing she didn't already know.

When David had disappeared with the clerk, Eleanor stole

to the table and looked at his list. It shocked her. She recognized most of the titles. They'd been the ones she herself had sought out over the years. She'd found most of them and most had been useless. The only thing she'd gathered from her studies was that though there were many cultures with similar stories, no one believed them now, no one except superstitious American Indians and crack-pot satanists. Dr. Sikring had been energetic about the cultural "witnessing of ancestral magic," as he called it, but had attributed sworn accounts of skinwalker sightings to peyote use. He did mention an incident in 1962 though, but offered no details.

"Is there no way you could come down on the price?" David asked.

"I don't know," said the clerk. "University presses don't give us much of a wholesale. But I think we'd have sent it back if we could. I'll ask."

Eleanor ducked behind bookshelves and circled around to the stairs. She crept down the steps and then made a bee-line for the door. A clerk grabbed her from behind.

"What's the hurry," she said. "You forget to pay for something?"

Eleanor looked up at the woman holding her. She was in her thirties, black hair with grey roots, too much eyeliner, and a wad of chewing gum whose flavor was a distant memory.

"What?" Eleanor said.

"You look awfully suspicious," she said. "Whatchu got in that bag?"

Eleanor glanced up the stairs, grateful that David wasn't there to see this humiliation but sure he would appear at any moment.

"Leave me alone," she said. "I haven't stolen anything."

"Then you won't mind if I look in your purse." The woman snatched Eleanor's little handbag from her hands and opened it.

"You have no right," Eleanor protested. "Who do you think you are?"

"Just a quick peek," she said.

Eleanor's blood boiled. A low rumbling growl issued from behind Eleanor's clenched teeth. It started deep in her belly and ran up her back into her neck where she felt her vocal chords twist, turn, thicken, and stretch. The sound grew deep, louder, and more menacing by the second. The woman looked at Eleanor, her eyes wide.

With a sudden roar, Eleanor snatched he purse back from the woman's hands. The clerk jumped back and fell into a table display of Tony Flaner mysteries. Eleanor ran out the door.

A quarter mile around the block in front of a convenience store that smelled of beer and urine, Eleanor found a bench. She closed her eyes and willed her voice back. She grimaced as it returned to Eleanor's. It hurt.

She went in the store and bought a carton of milk and a candy bar. Eating on the bench, she tried to think what happened. What had that been? A coyote? A wolf? A bear? No. She recalled the noise perfectly, her memory being what it was, and picked out the subtle pitches of all three predators. She'd merged them all into a new sound. She knew coyote, she knew bear, but she'd only heard wolf. It had not been a copy—it became something new.

Her agitation over the incident gave way to excitement about her discovery. She remembered the terrible night at the Masonic Hall, when she'd picked a single attribute to copy, not the whole thing, as she was used to, but only a part. Hadn't she become something new then? And now she'd made a new voice.

Had her parents—her real parents—told her about this? They must have. Or maybe they hadn't since it wouldn't have been necessary had things proceeded naturally. But of course they hadn't.

She cast her mind back, but couldn't remember. She barely remembered her family's faces and then only in bloody flashes, the last instant before she fled to the desert. She had willingly let the years on all fours erode those times. Recalling the happy, daily memories, the water gathering, the cook fire, her brother's laugh, her mother's smile, her father's strong arms—these things caused her more heartache than even the memory of hungry winters, thirsty miles, or even the savage attack that had killed them. And so she'd buried them.

To the world, she was an average girl of fifteen, top of the bell curve; able, but not excelling, competent, and regular. But she knew she was old and ignorant. Tabitha and school had taught her to be a white American girl, but she had had no teacher to show her what she truly was, to explain the monster she was. Except for the impotent reading she'd done, chasing books written by fools more ignorant than she, she'd done little to explore what she was. She denied it. Before this year, she allowed herself only a single annual trip to Nebraska to use her weird talent. Part of the reason had been Tabitha. For all her love and caring, Eleanor saw that she scared her mother. For Tabitha, Eleanor had been only Eleanor and that had been enough. But now things were falling apart, and she felt woefully unprepared.

"Miss? You okay?" a man said. "You want to come inside where it's warm?"

It was the convenience store manager.

"What?" she said, feeling groggy.

"You've been sitting out here for over an hour. You must be frozen solid."

"I'm pretty tolerant to cold," she said.

"That may be, but it is cold, and so are you," he said. "I'll tell you what. I'll get you a hot cocoa if you won't come in." When Eleanor just stared at him, he left and returned in a few minutes with a foam-topped cup.

"Do you need me to call anyone?" he asked.

"No," she said. "I'm alright. Thanks for the drink. You're very kind. I'm just resting my feet."

He looked at her secondhand clothes and worn shoes. He tipped an imaginary hat and went back inside.

Eleanor glanced at her watch. It was late. She had been there a while. She stood up and stretched. Her muscles were cold and stiff. She'd been still too long. She shivered. She headed west toward the clinic at a pace she measured would get her there in an hour, when she agreed to meet her mother.

Tabitha was waiting for her when she walked in.

"You're early," her mother said warmly. "Good. Let's go. I'm tired of this place." She turned to the receptionist. "Could you call and see if our ride is available?"

"What'd the doctor say?" Eleanor asked.

"Same old, same old," Tabitha said.

"Where are the notes? The scripts and pills?"

"I got them in my purse. We'll talk about them later."

"Did you schedule another appointment?"

"No," she said brightly.

Eleanor knew then. There was no need to come back to the clinic because there was nothing more they could do. Tabitha's bag would be full of directories of hospice care centers, legal firms specializing in wills, and brochures for cut-rate burial plans. Eleanor had seen the literature before, seen it in the handbags of broken daughters and the pockets of weeping sons and husbands while they pushed a beloved skeleton in a wheelchair through the automatic glass doors for the last time.

"Pain pills?" she said quietly.

"Yes," she said. "We'll have to pick those up. Good ones this time. I'll have fun."

"Your ride is on his way," the receptionist said without looking at them.

Tabitha took Eleanor's hand and together they walked out of the clinic to a bench on the curb.

"Sun's going down," her mother said. "It'll be a beautiful sunset. We'll be driving right into it."

"Momma, I'm scared," Eleanor said so softly she was sure her mother couldn't hear her.

"I know, cupcake," she said. "But it'll be okay."

CHAPTER TWENTY-FIVE

Their budget was opened up. Tabitha's medicine was cut to only two prescriptions, and they ordered pizza twice that week. In an unspoken agreement, they had not talked about the doctor's prognosis or the future beyond that week. Eleanor knew that the conversation had to happen, had been coming for years. Their family had always been on a short timer.

Eleanor threw herself into her schoolwork and, just to show her mother she could, she aced two math quizzes and a Spanish midterm. Her homework came back with high marks and even Mrs. Hart commented on her improvement, though she'd only awarded Eleanor a low B for a lecture transcription she called an essay.

Tabitha spent her days opening the house. She prepared the tomato seedlings in the warm sunshine of the kitchen window, and finally had the energy to cook again. It was something of a renaissance for her. She only had to combat the illness now, she said, and not the cure.

The Friday after their last trip to Riverton, Eleanor saw Robby take David into the bathroom after math class. He cast a warning glance at Eleanor before disappearing behind the door. Unable to stop herself, she crept closer but then when she could find no excuse to go nearer, she went back to the math class and watched from the doorway. Five minutes later, the boys emerged. David came out first. He looked irritated and marched up the hall without a glance back at Robby, who followed a step behind and then ran to catch up.

"Don't take it personally," he said.

"How else should I take it?" said David.

"They answered your question," he said. "You just didn't like the answer."

"No, they didn't. I want to make my own decision." He stormed. The bell rang.

"I'll ask them again, Dave. Okay?" Robby said. "But seriously. She's not worth it."

"I'll make my own decisions," he spat back before disappearing down a side hall. Robby turned and looked back. He peered down the hall to where Eleanor hid, but she didn't think he saw her. He was, however, looking for her.

That weekend, Tabitha amazed Eleanor by accompanying her to the grocery store. They took it easy and stopped many times, taking advantage of every bench, stump, and lawn chair on the way. But finally, in good spirits, they arrived, and together they bought groceries. It had been over a year since Tabitha had last set foot in the store.

"We'll have apple pie tonight," Tabitha proclaimed, tossing a frozen dessert in the cart.

Eleanor hesitated. It was a spendy treat, but her mother insisted.

Tabitha filled the cart with everything Eleanor liked,

PopTarts, apples, chicken, artichokes, mushrooms, bacon, eggs, heavy dark bread that could sink a canoe, and real butter, lots of real butter.

That night they had a feast. Tabitha nibbled, and Eleanor ate like she had a reason to, but didn't. When the many leftovers were put away, and the dishes done, they sat together at their table playing cards while a radio played. Tabitha had chosen a modern station and listened with interest to songs Eleanor didn't know.

It was during their third game that Eleanor told her mother about the bookstore, about David's research, and her reaction. The time hadn't been right before.

"He's a smart one, cupcake," she said. "Glad he's on our side."

"Is he?"

"Of course."

"He might not be forever," she said.

"That is a lame word and a lamer sentiment," her mother scolded her, taking a crib full of sevens and eights. "You're slipping up," she said.

"I know. What's wrong with me?" sighed Eleanor.

"The book clerk had it coming. I hope she peed herself."

"What do you think it means?" Eleanor asked as off-handedly as she could. She thought that both she and her mother were going to pains to act as if this was just another night of pointless small talk and cards, but they knew that each word, each moment was precious. She fumbled the shuffle.

"You're growing up, cupcake," her mother said. "You're an artist who's done copying the masters and is now trying to find her own style. It's a good thing. Very good."

"You make it sound like a gift," she said, giving her mother too many cards.

"Of course it is," she said. "You're gifted beyond imagination."

"I don't feel gifted," she said.

"That's part of the gift."

Eleanor dropped two cards into her crib and slid them to the side. "Ten," she said opening with a king.

"Fifteen for two," said Tabitha and scored the peg. "People are good, Eleanor."

"Mrs. Hart?" she reminded her. "Twenty-five."

"Thirty-one for two," she scored again. Eleanor was losing badly. "Yes, there are bad people, the worst. But they're balanced by the good ones, the best ones. You'll have to find others to trust," Tabitha said. "When I'm gone."

"Don't say that, Momma."

"You will," Tabitha said, keeping her eyes on her cards. "I want you to. Maybe it'll be David. Maybe it'll be the kind man at the convenience store who gave you chocolate, but Eleanor, I want you to trust someone. I don't want the world to lose you again."

Eleanor stared at her cards, unable to focus.

"It's your turn, sweetie," Tabitha said.

"Yeah," she said. "I guess it is."

The following Thursday was parent-teacher conference, a meeting between educators and student guardians held three times a year to discuss performance. It was usually either a love fest for the good students or another long, drawn out lecture about parental responsibility for the bad kids. There wasn't much in between. The good students dragged their parents in to brag, the bad were required to attend, and the average kids ignored the whole event. Eleanor and Tabitha Anders had ignored them for years.

So it was something of a surprise when Tabitha, on

Eleanor's arm, walked into the gymnasium. Teachers had been planted along the walls at lunch tables bearing their names on landscaped school letterhead secured with blue painter's tape.

Since Jamesford was so small, the entire high school could have its conference simultaneously. Since most of the teachers taught all three upper grades it was easier for them to get it over with. There was a carnival atmosphere with free popcorn, college admissions barkers passing out flyers, and the anticipation of a three-day holiday. Friday classes were cancelled to allow the teachers to recover.

"There's Mrs. Hart," Tabitha whispered to Eleanor. "We'll do her last. Who's Mr. Curtz?"

"I don't see him," she said. "But he's got to be here somewhere."

"Keep an eye out for him."

Eleanor watched the room not only for the school principal but also for David. She knew his grades were better than hers. He was above average, but his grades had slipped after Christmas. His science courses particularly suffered, but he'd kept a passing grade.

As she scanned the crowd, she noticed her other classmates stealing glances at her and her mother. If Tabitha noticed them, she showed no signs of discomfort.

They stood in line for Mr. Graham. He was in no hurry and the line had stalled on a senior failing physics. Eleanor left the line and went to the kitchen. She found a folding chair leaning against a counter and took it without a word, while Miss Church, the lunch-lady, looked on, unpacking gigantic cans onto a steel shelf.

Back in line, Eleanor opened the chair and Tabitha sat down. She waited patiently, her hands neatly folded over her little handbag, her visage content. She looked as good as she had in years. Though her weight hadn't come back, her energy had, and her sharp eyes darted around the room in eager curiosity.

"Eleanor," said Mr. Graham when it was their turn. "Glad to see you."

"I'm Tabitha Anders. Eleanor's mother." Tabitha offered her hand. He shook it but didn't stand.

"Have a seat," he said. "I see you already have one."

"I've been ill," explained Tabitha.

They settled in while Mr. Graham searched his papers. "I'm glad you came, Mrs. Anders," he said. "I was hoping you would."

Eleanor felt a knot twine in her stomach.

"I thought Eleanor was doing well in your classes," she said.

"She is," he said. "Slightly above average. Unremarkable."

They both waited for the old man to continue. He placed two pieces of paper in front of Tabitha. Eleanor recognized one as a quiz and the other as a midterm exam. Both were scored at a solid B.

"These seem adequate," said Tabitha.

"Look at problem ten here," he said pointing to the quiz. "It's a complex use of the quadratic formula. Eleanor was one of only four students who got it right."

"Good for her," she said. Eleanor was numb.

"Here's the same problem on the midterm," he said pointing to the other paper. "The values are different, but it's essentially the same problem."

Tabitha examined it.

"She missed it," Mr. Graham said. "Ninety percent of the class got it."

"And?" asked Tabitha after a pause.

"I think she missed it on purpose," he said. He looked at Eleanor. Eleanor imagined her face a stone carving and stared back.

"What are you saying?"

"I think Eleanor is afraid of success," he said. "She's smarter than she's testing. She's holding back."

"Why would she do that?"

Mr. Graham shrugged. "I don't know."

They sat in silence for a moment, Eleanor an unreadable statue.

"Eleanor," Mr. Graham said finally, "Are you holding back?"

"Why would I do that?"

He sighed and turned to Tabitha.

"Anyway, Eleanor is doing fine in chemistry and math. I suspect she'll do fine in all her science classes."

Tabitha stood up. "Thanks, Mr. Graham," she said. "Eleanor speaks highly of you."

"I won't be here next year," he said almost as a warning.

"We'll miss you," Tabitha said and followed Eleanor away.

Mr. Blake was polite and went over their Spanish curriculum with eager new-teacher enthusiasm. "She's talented," he said. He could offer encouragement and make it sound fresh. Give him ten years, Eleanor thought.

"Mrs. Anders, how are you feeling?" It was Karen Venn.

"I'm feeling much better," she said.

"That is good news," she said.

"Where's David?" Tabitha asked. Eleanor looked for a good direction to flee.

"He took Wendy to the restroom," she said.

Eleanor gave Tabitha's hand a light pull.

"I've been meaning to ask you," Karen said. "Where do your people come from?"

"What do you mean?"

"Anders. Is that Danish or something more exotic?"

"English," she said.

"Oh," she said. "No American Indian?"

"No. Why would you think that?"

"David once said something," she said. "Years ago. Was Eleanor adopted?"

"Really, Mrs. Venn," Tabitha said.

"I'm sorry," she said. "Oh, look, there's David."

Wendy skipped ahead of David. He smiled when he saw Eleanor and hurried his pace.

"Mrs. Anders," he said. "It's great to see you out."

"Thank you, David," she said, but Eleanor could tell Karen had upset her.

"Eleanor," he said still smiling. "Good to see you. You got any plans this weekend?"

It was something any student would say to any other student, but it shocked her. He'd put her on the spot. She didn't want to talk to him, had gone well out of her way to avoid him, had given him no encouragement, and had actually been rude, unkind, mean even. But here he was, taking advantage of their parents as witnesses to speak to her.

"We're going to the park," she said.

"We're going to an Indian reservation on Sunday," Wendy said excitedly. "We're going to see where Indians live. See a real medicine man."

Eleanor shot David a look that she hoped didn't betray more than surprise. David's smile shrank and Eleanor could see he was forming apologies and explanations.

"There's Mr. Curtz," Eleanor said to her mother.

"Nice seeing you," Tabitha said to the Venns and followed Eleanor to the principal.

Tabitha straightened herself and said, "Mr. Curtz? I'm Tabitha Anders, Eleanor's mother. I'd like to speak with you."

"Yes, what can I do for you," he said.

"It's about Mrs. Hart," she said. "Maybe we should talk about this in private."

The principal hesitated then reluctantly agreed. He led her into a side office after opening it with a key.

"Stay here, sweetie," she said. "I won't be long."

Feeling abandoned, Eleanor watched them go. She saw the Venns in line for Mrs. Hart. David watched her from across the room. Eleanor turned her back and walked to the popcorn machine.

She knew her mother was laying out the case against Mrs. Hart's ill-treatment of her. She knew also that Tabitha would not hesitate to use the information Eleanor had given her about her teacher and the principal. They had no hard proof, but this was a small town and rumors ran wild like wolves, and when there was a hint of truth behind them, they bit like them, too.

Eleanor wandered back to the door and nonchalantly tried to listen through the din of the gymnasium to the conversation inside.

She focused on her mother's voice and caught only snippets of talk. She picked out phrases, "your wife," "school board," "scandal," and "career-ending" and had to smile at her mother's cold, calm blackmailing. Mr. Curtz spoke too softly for Eleanor to make out or else he responded with only grunts and sighs. Either case was good.

In truth, Eleanor didn't mind Mrs. Hart half as much as her mother did. Eleanor had accepted the teacher's ire and injustice as just another truth, but Tabitha had taken it personally, and had penned several unsent letters outlining more or less the conversation that was happening now. "There's injustice you have to take and there's injustice you can fight," she said. Eleanor was afraid that saying anything would only make things worse. She pleaded with her mother to let it be, but she wouldn't. "Trust me," she said. "I got this."

Tabitha emerged from the office followed by Mr. Curtz. He held the door open for her, but his face was anything but courteous. He averted his eyes from Eleanor and officiously strolled over to Mrs. Hart's table.

David, who'd been watching Eleanor, followed Mr. Curtz with interest. The principal whispered something into the teacher's ear. Mrs. Hart shook her head, but Mr. Curtz persisted. Mrs. Hart got up, excused herself, and followed Mr. Curtz to a quiet corner by the exit.

Eleanor watched Mr. Curtz explain whatever he had to say to Mrs. Hart in the briefest terms. He held his hand over his lips as he spoke like Eleanor had seen gangsters do on television. After a couple minutes of back-and-forth, Mr. Curtz caught the teacher in his gaze and held her there until she nodded in vigorous assent. Mrs. Hart's eyes searched the room and fell on Eleanor. She calculated her teacher's expression as equal parts contempt, anger, humiliation, and fear; a soup of unsettling emotions merging into a meek, submissive countenance that Eleanor found strangely satisfying.

David glanced from Mrs. Hart to Eleanor. He smiled to her as if understanding. Eleanor held his gaze a moment too long, and his smile widened even more.

"What now, Mom?" Eleanor said.

"Ice cream?" she said.

"Aren't we going to talk to Mrs. Hart?" she asked.

"I don't think we have to. Do you?"

"I know I don't want to," she said.

"Then, ice cream it is."

CHAPTER TWENTY-SIX

Sunday morning before dawn, Eleanor woke up and left the house while Tabitha slept quietly. An early spring rain threatened to cover the valley with clouds and stinging drizzle for the whole day.

Eleanor swiftly navigated her way through the foggy wet streets and, before the sun was up, she slipped past half a dozen sleeping dogs and into the Venn's trailer park.

Carefully and quietly, she pried up the skirting around the base of the mobile home and crawled under it. There wasn't much room, but it was dry and she could hear inside the house from there. She closed the skirting behind her and waited for the family to wake up.

Her plan was not wholly thought out. In one iteration, she considered sneaking into their van and stowing away with them on the trip to Wild River Reservation. A more sensible one, one that she finally settled on in the cold, freezing morning rain, was to get inside the house and see David's room.

It was an impulsive plan. She didn't know what she expected to find. She knew only that she had to know more about what was happening in David's life. It woke her up in the early hours of the night, and she hadn't been able to get back to sleep.

She cared about him. She thought about him daily, dreamed of him, remembered him warmly, and then inevitably, she'd flush with shame when remembering prom night. He was one in a million, and she was a monster. But that hadn't kept her from thinking about him or from missing him. Tabitha had accused her of being stubborn, but Eleanor knew better. She was being safe. Safe keeps you alive. Stubborn keeps you alive. But now she was also curious. Curiosity, well, that can get you killed. Just ask the cat.

She wished she could ignore David, pretend he wasn't stalking her like an owl after a field mouse. But she couldn't. She knew he was. He wasn't going away. He'd figure it out. He'd discover she was a monster and that would end it there. She only had to wait. But her curiosity wouldn't let her. She had to know what David was up to, and so she lay on the dirt under his house and waited.

Eleanor couldn't help but think that his trip to the reservation was about her. It was egocentric of her, she knew, to think that their family trip was about her, but that's where her paranoia took her.

Wendy was up first and watched cartoons for an hour before anyone else roused. Karen was next and woke David up with frying bacon. He stumbled into the kitchen.

"You'll still take me, won't you, Ma?" he asked over a yawn.

"Why do you keep asking me that? It'll be fun."

"And you're okay with letting me talk to Mr. Crow alone?"

Eleanor heard a spatula scrape on a pan.

"Mom, is it okay?" David said again.

Karen sighed. "Yeah, it's okay. Can you at least tell me what it's about?"

"I told you. It's personal," he said.

"Is it about Eleanor Anders?" she asked.

"I told you it's personal," he said.

"It was good to see Mrs. Anders out again at school, wasn't it? Glad she's getting better."

"Yeah, that was nice."

"Have you talked to Eleanor? What does she say about the cancer?"

"You know," he said. "Not much."

"She won't talk to him," Wendy said.

"Shut up, big mouth."

"David thinks she's cursed," she said. "He's going to get a witchdoctor to save her."

"I never said that, you little twerp. It's not what I said at all. Mind your own business."

"So this trip is about Eleanor," said David's mother. "You think she's cursed?"

"No. Don't be stupid."

"But she won't talk to you?"

"Can we change the subject?"

Eleanor heard David stomp out of the kitchen and into his room. A couple of minutes later she heard Karen's footsteps follow. She knocked and went in.

"Mom, I could have been naked."

"I've seen you naked plenty of times," she said. "I want to talk to you about Eleanor."

"Can't I have a personal life, Mom? What happened to privacy?"

"Of course you can, dear. I just want to say something."

"Say it," he said. "I have to get ready. We have to be there by ten."

"David, I know you like the Anders girl. It was great you took her to prom. I'm sure it did her a world of good. You're a nice guy, always looking out for underdogs. That was really nice of you."

"But?" David said.

"But, if she doesn't want to see you, maybe that's not such a bad thing. I've heard stories about her, and it might be for the best if you to keep your distance."

"What stories? That she can change her hair color at will? Or was it that she can smell fear? Hear whispers across a grandstand? That she heals too fast? What bunk have you heard?"

"No, honey, don't get upset," she said. "I haven't heard anything like that. There are just some people who say she's got a reputation. There was something about a trucker, and then there was whatever happened at prom."

"Were you there?" asked David. "You know how people get a reputation? Other people talk about them. It's all gossip and slander, Mom."

"Of course it is," she said. "I don't say I believe it. I'm only telling you what other people think."

"And that matters?"

"It might."

"I've got to get ready, Mom. Can we leave soon?"

"Sure, honey," she said and closed the door.

Eleanor listened under David's bedroom, barely able to breathe.

Half an hour later, the Venns piled into their van and drove away. Eleanor waited under the house for twenty more minutes before coming out. She looked up and down the trailers, smelled, and listened. She was alone. The rain kept everyone inside. The drizzle had changed to a downpour.

She found the key under the steps hanging on a nail. She took one more look down the rain-blown street and let herself in. She waited for her eyes to adjust to the dark. The kitchen hadn't been put away, and the smell of bacon hung heavy in the air. Wendy's toys were strewn about the couch and floor, and a half-finished glass of orange juice rested on the TV.

A black shape suddenly jumped out from behind a chair. She shrieked and stumbled backwards. A black and white cat mewed and leapt on her leg. It dug its claws into her pants and climbed up her thigh like it was a tree trunk. It complained when she plucked it off her. Then it purred as loud as an idling tractor and cried for attention. She knew this cat. It was the one-eyed cat from her neighborhood. She'd not seen it in weeks and assumed it'd died. But it hadn't. It was in David's trailer, saucy, fat, and playful. Knowing what to look for, she smelled the cat food, litter box, and dander in the air. She'd missed it for the bacon.

Carrying the purring cat, Eleanor threaded her way through the narrow trailer hall. She knew where everyone's rooms were and went into David's. She pushed the door open, and, seeing his curtains drawn, she switched on the light.

She'd never been in a boy's room before. She expected it to be wall-to-wall dirty clothes, pin-up posters, and dust, but David's room was neat and clean. It was small. His narrow bed was made and set under the window. On the opposite wall, David had a picture of himself standing beside his father in uniform in front of a military barracks. The picture was a few years old. In it, David beamed with pride, but there was something strange in his father's face. Eleanor couldn't make it out, but she thought that beneath the photo smile, there was something else. Something dark. She was paranoid, she reminded herself, and looked away.

David's school books were piled on a small desk beside a computer next to a narrow chest of drawers. David's shooting trophy stood on top of it beside the dried boutonniere he'd worn at the prom. Over the desk was a cork-board with a small printed map of Afghanistan. Eleanor identified the colored pins as showing places David's father had been or might be.

Eleanor opened David's closet and breathed in the scent. She'd not been this close to him since prom, and she drank in his smell excitedly. She poked around his shoes and looked in boxes of old toys and then came across a locked soft-sided suitcase under his bed. She pulled it out and felt the weight. It was heavy. She shook it and heard papers and books inside.

She examined the lock. It was a little three digit combination padlock on the zipper. Eleanor went to the desk, found a pen, and slipped it under the zipper where it attached at the hinge. She drew the pen along the zipper, opening the case in a few seconds. It was a trick she'd learned from her mother. Where she learned it, she never said.

Eleanor lifted the top and looked inside. She braced herself for a collection of skin magazines, but that's not what she found. She wished it was. What she found was David's research on her.

There was the forty-three dollar book by Dr. Sikring, *Skinwalkers,* that he'd bought at Bracker's Bookstore and several secondhand paperbacks about Indian legends. There were hundreds of printed web pages about werewolves, doppelgängers, witches, banshees, mimics, and chameleons—monsters all. She felt sick.

David had found old school photographs of Eleanor. She looked at herself in each of her yearly class pictures and then, to her horror, found a picture of her from the summer after eighth grade pinned next to the photo of her at the beginning of eighth grade. The pictures were identical. She hadn't grown a millimeter. Her hair was exactly as it'd been before, she'd no tan, no scratches, nothing to differentiate the one self from the girl pictured ten months earlier. David had noticed it. He'd blown them up and printed them side by side from his computer.

Eleanor put everything back, ran the zipper down the side, centered the lock as she'd found it, and left.

She locked the front door behind her and replaced the key. She walked home slowly, letting the rain soak her and beat her, and wishing it would melt her away. Wasn't water supposed to do that to things like her?

Tabitha was waiting for her on the porch when she got home.

"Where were you?" she asked. "You could have left a note."

"I was worried about David's trip to the reservation," she said frankly. "I went over there."

"You talked to him? You saw David?"

"No."

"What did you do?"

"I spied on them and when they left, I snuck into David's room."

"And you say you aren't in love," Tabitha giggled.

"Mom, it's serious," Eleanor said.

"At least you're not in jail," she said.

"He thinks I'm a monster. And he's right."

"I really hate it when you say stupid things," Tabitha said. "What did you find?"

Eleanor gave her mother an account of the suitcase she found under David's bed. "You still think he's on our side?" she asked miserably.

"I don't know," she said. "But he doesn't know anything yet. He's curious, that's all. He cares about you. Those books are crap, and you know it. It's all got to sound crazy, even to him."

"What if he believes them anyway?"

"Honey, there's not even a name for you. Shapeshifter, doppelgänger, skinwalker—they're all great names, but they don't describe you."

"They're not great names. They're evil names."

"People are afraid of what they don't understand. David is trying to understand. He's going to do what he's going to do, think what he's going to think. He's got a lot to work with. He's got rumors, lies, books, and computers. But mostly, he has stories he's heard about you from your own mouth. You trusted him a great deal once. You don't do that often or easily. I don't think you've trusted badly. I won't lie to you and say that I'm not concerned about what he's doing, but if someone had to get on our trail, I'd rather it was him than some others. We're here now, baby. We'll get through this, whatever it is."

"He's gone to the Indians, Mom."

"You haven't done anything to anyone, cupcake. You've got nothing to fear."

Though she smiled assuredly, Eleanor could see that her mother didn't believe it any more than she did.

"He has a cat," Eleanor said thoughtfully.

"There, you see," Tabitha said. "He can't be all bad."

CHAPTER TWENTY-SEVEN

The next week, Mrs. Hart was a reincarnation of her old self. She made a point of ignoring Eleanor, not even looking at her in two hours of lecture. When English essays were handed back, Eleanor saw she'd scored an A. It had been a C; she could see where the teacher had erased the previous grade for the one she thought she deserved. Eleanor sat back and enjoyed her renewed anonymity and did nothing to upset the teacher. Though Tabitha had momentarily quelled the problem, Eleanor knew it was not gone.

Tabitha tried to explain to her that Mrs. Hart had transferred her own guilt into Eleanor. She hated herself by hating Eleanor. She wasn't so sure about the diagnosis, but Tabitha knew something about psychology, so she didn't dismiss it. Eleanor saw the link between her knowing about the affair and the bad treatment, but she thought it was more mercenary than psychological. She thought Mrs. Hart wanted to discredit her now, so if Eleanor said anything later, no one would believe her. It all came down to the same thing, and for the moment, at least, she was leaving Eleanor alone. Tabitha had prevailed.

On Wednesday, the lunch was beef stew. It was one of the school's favorites and lauded as the kitchen's signature dish because it was "homemade from scratch." Eleanor never trusted it. She knew they used low grade ingredients and added pepper to cover it up. Eleanor smelled the pepper and onions and then, with a start, caught the acrid whiff of sickness. The meat had gone bad. She could detect the stench of rot and wondered why it didn't go away. All through morning classes, she traced the odor of the spoiled meat being cooked in heavy spices and then added to a pot of leeks and cabbage which were also suspect.

Before chemistry, she went to the lunchroom. She let herself in the kitchen and wandered over to the pot where the stew simmered. She lifted the heavy lid and smelled. She had to cover her nose for the fetor. She was surprised none of the cooks had noticed it. The place was bustling with half a dozen helpers, but no one had noticed it, or Eleanor for that matter. It was only when she dropped the lid on the floor trying to replace it on the pot that she drew anyone's attention.

"What are you doing here, child?" Miss Church demanded. She had been in charge of the kitchen for as long as Eleanor had been there. Eleanor couldn't remember ever seeing her without a hair net, even in the parking lot after school. She wore it home.

"Miss Church," Eleanor said softly. "The lunch smells bad."

"What are you on about, child?" she demanded.

"The stew. I think it's bad."

"Then you don't have to eat it," she said. "Go back to class."

"Miss Church, the meat is rotten. The food is spoiled. Don't serve it."

The lunch lady took a hard look at Eleanor. "I know you,"

she said. "You're the girl who takes her clothes off at dances. I've heard about you." The words came out surly and mean and silenced the other workers.

"You stay out of here," she said. "You've got no business being here. You'll spread disease. It's against health code rules. You want to be suspended?"

"No, Miss Church," she said trying to look her in the eye. "You can't serve the stew. It's bad."

"Out or I'll call Mr. Curtz," she said pointing to the door.

Eleanor looked for support from the other cooks, but seeing none, she turned and left. Outside the kitchen, she flopped her back against the brick wall and slid down to the floor. She sat there a while thinking. She listened to the staff talking in the kitchen.

"What was that about, Betty?" someone asked.

"She doesn't like the stew," Miss Church said. "Wants me to change the recipe I guess."

"No, it's perfect."

"I think so, too."

Eleanor got up and went to class wondering why she'd even tried. She needed to mind her own business. How could she explain how she'd known the meat was bad from halfway across the school? It was better she hadn't been believed.

At lunch, Eleanor bought a bag of chips and a coke from a machine. It wasn't much of a meal, but she'd have nothing from that kitchen today. She sat at her table watching students line up for hearty portions of stew and mounds of buttered bread.

Then she saw David carrying his tray. Coming out of the line, he glanced at Eleanor the way he did every day, silently asking permission to approach. Eleanor automatically looked away and David wandered over to his other friends and sat down.

Suddenly Eleanor sprang to her feet knocking her can of Coke over on the table. She ignored it and hurried to where David sat.

"Eleanor," David said warmly. "Hi. Sit down." He kicked a chair out for her. She looked at it but shook her head.

"I won't stay," she said. "Don't eat the stew. That's what I came to say. Don't eat the stew. It's bad. It's poisonous."

Brian smelled his lunch, as did Aubrey, Robby, and Barbara Pennon.

"Smells fine to me," Barbara said. She'd made a habit of sitting with David at least once a week. She bounced around the lunchroom with regular visits like traveling royalty. Today was David's turn. Today, she had her groupies, Crystal and Alexi, with her. The table was crowded.

"Then you go ahead and eat it," Eleanor said to Barbara before she could stop herself. "But David, you don't, okay? It's bad. Promise me. Promise me you won't touch it," she said.

Without hesitation, David said, "I promise."

Robby dropped his spoon, too. "I'm not touching it either," he said but kept a suspicious eye on Eleanor.

"Thanks," she said and turned to leave.

"Eleanor," David said, getting up and following her. Eleanor didn't stop, but neither did David. He caught her at her table and immediately set to cleaning up her spilled soda.

"Eleanor," he said.

"What?" she said.

"I miss you," he said.

Eleanor looked into his face and saw it change from forlorn

to hopeful when their eyes met. "Can we please be friends again?"

"We've always been friends," she said. "That's why I can't see you."

"Let me make that decision," he said.

"You don't know enough to make a good one."

"Eleanor, let me make it up to you."

"You haven't done anything," she said.

"I'll make it up anyway, whoever did it. I can do that. Whatever is missing, I'll replace. Whatever was broken, I can mend. Whatever was done, I can forgive. Let me, Eleanor. Please."

"You've been practicing that," she said unable to stifle a grin.

"Yes, I have," he said proudly.

Eleanor looked back at the table. Barbara had convinced her friends Eleanor was crazy and spooned huge spoonfuls of stew into her mouth and shot dirty looks at Eleanor.

"Your friends miss you," said Eleanor.

"They'll survive."

"Maybe not," she said, watching them eat.

"What do you say? Can I come by? Play some three-handed Cribbage?"

"I'll think about it," she said.

"Okay," he said. "This is progress. I'm good with that."

"I thought Aubrey was smarter than that," Eleanor said. David looked back at his table. She dipped bread into her bowl and ate it.

"I'll go convince them," he said. "I'll see you later." He walked back to his table like a man cured of gout. He took Aubrey's bowl right off her tray and together with his, dumped it all in a trash can.

The school was closed for a week. Eighty percent of the student body and ninety percent of the faculty were out with severe food poisoning. News crews descended onto the little town, tainting its wholesome summer vacation image under the headline "Worst School Food Poisoning Incident in History." The headline was misleading. They'd come to that conclusion by virtue of the percentages of students who got sick, but the school was so small it gave a false impression. Not that anyone noticed.

The town went crazy. Soon rumors were rampant, allegations were tossed around about suppliers, cooks, students, and faculty incompetence. Finally, a policeman arrived at Eleanor's door. Tabitha opened it.

"Hello, ma'am. I'm Sheriff Hannon," he said.

"I know," Tabitha said cautiously. "I voted for you."

"Thank you," he said, a little embarrassed. "Is it alright that Eleanor come with me to the school?" he asked. "We're taking statements about the food poisoning."

"Is she in trouble?"

"No, ma'am. We just want to talk to her."

"Then I'm coming along, too," she said. "Wait one minute, won't you?" She closed the door before he could respond.

When Eleanor and Tabitha came out of the house, David was talking to the sheriff.

"Hello, David," Tabitha said. "What are you doing here?"

"It's such a beautiful day, Mrs. Anders. I thought I'd invite Eleanor to the park."

"I can't," Eleanor said quickly.

"Yes, I see that," David said and got into the back of the police car.

When Sheriff Hannon did nothing to stop him, Eleanor slipped in beside him and Tabitha took the front seat.

The school was surrounded by twenty-four-hour news vehicles.

"Another slow news day," commented the Sheriff sarcastically. "You'd think they'd have something better to do."

"We're not going to be filmed are we?" asked Tabitha.

"No. Those vultures won't see you. We'll go in the back."

True to his word, Sheriff Hannon drove to the back of the school, past a cordon, and then escorted them into the gymnasium through a side door. Inside was a long table where half a dozen people sat, including Mr. Curtz and Miss Church.

They were placed in chairs facing the table. The sheriff joined the other officials. He whispered to a politician Eleanor thought she recognized in a tailored blue suit and strong exotic cologne.

"Hello, Mrs. Anders, Eleanor, and, David Venn is it? I'm Hank Gomez, from the State Division of Health and Public Safety. We're investigating the incident at Jamesford High last week. This is Mr. Poulson, Homeland Security, and his deputy, Miss Lamb. You already know the sheriff, Mr. Curtz, and Miss Church."

Tabitha nodded. Mr. Curtz wouldn't look at her.

"Eleanor, what happened Wednesday last week? We understand you were in the kitchen before lunch."

"Poisoning the stew," shrieked Miss Church. "Terrorism."

"Miss Church," chided Mr. Gomez. "Please."

There was no mistaking the panic in Miss Church's voice. She had removed her hairnet for a professionally done hair style. Her clothes were new and her makeup was startling.

Eleanor had never her seen her wear so much of it. Though she sat like a judge at the table, Eleanor couldn't help but think that she was the one on trial.

"I told Miss Church that I thought the stew smelled funny," Eleanor said meekly.

"Did you put anything in the pot, Miss Anders," Mr. Gomez said. "We have several eye witnesses saying you were tampering with it before Miss Church caught you."

Tabitha snorted.

"I wasn't sure, so I took the lid off to smell it," said Eleanor.

"You smelled bad meat in a pot of stew?" asked Miss Lamb. "You could smell it over the cayenne pepper?"

"A little, I guess," Eleanor said to the floor. "I'd smelled it before it was in the pot. It was easier then."

"Where were you when you smelled it the first time?" asked Mr. Gomez.

"In English class."

"She has English first period," said Mr. Curtz.

"And you smelled it then? Isn't your class far away from the kitchen?"

Eleanor looked at her mother. Tabitha was tense. She could sense her heartbeat racing, but she remained silent.

"I smelled it, too," said David. "I have English with Eleanor. I smelled something wrong, but I didn't know what it was."

The jury considered what David said for a moment.

"David, we understand that Eleanor found you at lunch and warned you not to eat the stew. Is that correct?"

"Yes, sir," he said.

"Why did you take the stew if you thought it was bad?"

"I wasn't sure."

"But you were after Eleanor warned you?"

"Yes."

"She never said it was dangerous," broke in Miss Church. "She only said she didn't like it. She wanted me to change the recipe."

"Is this true? Did you tell Miss Church you didn't like the stew? That she needed to change the recipe?"

"No, I told her the meat had gone bad," said Eleanor desperately.

"Liar," shrieked Miss Church. "She put something in the pot. I cooked that stew myself. It was fine until she broke into the kitchen. She has a reputation, you know."

"Miss Church," said Mr. Gomez. "Calm down."

"I told her it was bad, and she told me to mind my own business," said Eleanor.

"How do you explain that we have several witnesses saying that you claimed to have poisoned the stew?"

"I never said that," Eleanor said.

"Miss Barbara Pennon said you did. And Miss Crystal Tate."

"They misheard her," said David. "I was there. She told everyone at our table that the stew was bad. She said it was poisonous, not that she had poisoned it. I think she was right, don't you?"

"Miss Pennon said she thinks it was deliberate," said Mr. Poulson. "She thinks you have it in for the school. Were you being bullied?"

"I get along fine," Eleanor said.

Tabitha had had enough. "Seriously, gentlemen and ladies. You're throwing around some pretty heavy allegations here. Terrorism? The papers say it was e-coli. You think my daughter has a jar of e-coli in her handbag? That's what you think happened? Maybe she's a witch. You've got a theory from a fifteen year old accusing another fifteen year old of terrorism and you're buying it? Shame on you. Shame."

"I'm a witness, and I'll tell you that Barbara Pennon is flat out wrong," added David. "Eleanor tried to help, and this is how she's treated?"

"We're just making inquiries," said Miss Lamb.

"Why don't you talk to Robby Guide or Aubrey Ingram?" asked David. "No, better yet, how about we go talk to the news vans outside. We'll tell them the truth. That Eleanor Anders is an unsung hero who tried to save the town from an incompetent lunch lady and is now being made a scapegoat."

"Calm down, Mr. Venn," said Mr. Poulson.

"No, you calm down. This town is run on rumors, and it's about time someone put the record straight. Eleanor Anders is a shy girl who won't stick up for herself. She's an easy target for lies and repeated lies. Well, I'm sick of it. Take your damn rumors and put them to the test. We'll tell our side, and you tell yours. Let's get some fresh air in here."

The table fell silent.

"What do you say, Mr. Curtz?" asked Tabitha. "Should we let in some air?"

The principal cleared his throat. "Though his manners may be lacking, Mr. Venn has a point. Every school has someone the other students pick on and gossip about. I'm afraid to say that Miss Anders may be ours."

"That's why she poisoned the food," said Miss Church. "Because she was bullied. It proves my case."

"It proves nothing," said Mr. Curtz. "It only means that it's easy for people to blame her for their own mistakes and project their own failures on this timid girl."

"Why didn't you eat the stew, Miss Church?" asked Tabitha.

"I wasn't hungry," she said.

"It's your signature dish," said Tabitha.

"I wasn't hungry," said Miss Church bitterly. "I know what you're implying. Several of my cooks are out sick right now, I'll have you know."

"Should have listened to Eleanor," said David.

"Calm down, everyone," said Mr. Gomez pounding his fist on the table. "Come to order."

Everyone fell silent, but the air was thick with tension and dirty looks.

"Let's adjourn," he said. "Mrs. Anders, Eleanor, David, Sheriff Hannon will take you home."

"I think I'll walk," said David. "I feel an interview coming on."

Mr. Gomez smiled. "Let's not do anything hasty," he said. "Let's get all the facts before doing anything hasty."

"Are you telling us we can't talk to the press?" he asked.

"No, of course not. Do as you like," he said, glancing at his compatriots. "I'm asking you not to. Give the committee a chance to look at the facts first. No need to blacken anyone's eyes yet."

"How long will that take?"

"Not long," said Mr. Gomez. "I have to report to the governor tonight."

"If we hear our names spoken unflatteringly anywhere," Tabitha said, "we will sue."

"Are you threatening us?" asked Mr. Poulson.

"I'm asking you," said Tabitha.

Outside, the sheriff threaded through the reporters rushing

to point cameras into the car windows. The cruiser pushed through the throng and out onto the street with the lights flashing.

"Where do you live, David?" asked the sheriff once on the highway. "I'll drop you off."

"Maybe David can come to our place," said Eleanor. "Stay for lunch, maybe. There's still time for the park."

David beamed.

CHAPTER TWENTY-EIGHT

There was no mention of any of them in the final press release. The incident was blamed on bad meat and poor kitchen procedures. The entire kitchen staff was quietly fired and a retired health inspector was hired to replace Miss Church.

School resumed the next week, but the halls were all but empty. It was important to show that the problem had passed, so even with only a fraction of the students able to attend, school resumed. Mr. Blake was out on sick leave, in the hospital actually, and Mrs. Hart had to excuse herself at least once an hour to visit the lavatory. Mr. Graham soldiered on and never spoke a word about it. He lectured as if he had a full class but suspended labs. Eleanor knew that the faculty had been put on notice to adjust curriculum so ailing students could keep up at home. Mr. Curtz promised that "this unfortunate event would not endanger anyone's education or graduation." The school board had taken out a full page in the paper to say just that.

March became silent reading and worksheet month. In driver's education, Eleanor passed off her driving hours in a week since there was only one other student in the class. She'd get her temporary before her birthday and have her unrestricted license six months to the day afterward. She and Mr. McDonnell, the driver's ed teacher, and Carston Weeks spent every Tuesday and Thursday puttering around the streets of Jamesford looking for interesting places to turn. Finally, they'd drive to Cowboy Bob's and have coffee and a donut, Mr. McDonnell's treat. Mr. McDonnell would fix them up with snacks and then disappear into the adults-only section where he'd smoke cigarettes like they were going to be banned. The kids didn't mind. It was better than watching vehicular safety scare videos.

Carston was a smart boy, a kid who'd never bothered Eleanor. She knew he was an excellent student, particularly in art and mathematics. Before they were alone in driver's education, they'd never spoken a word to each other over their entire school careers. Out of boredom, they became acquaintances and shared pleasant small talk and did homework together in the hours at the truck stop. When they were done, Eleanor would often read and Carston would sketch.

One afternoon as they were climbing back into the school sedan, Eleanor noticed a sketch Carston had done of her at the table.

"May I see it?" she asked.

"It's not good," he said. "It's fanciful. Not a real portrait."

"I'd still like to look," she said. He handed her his pad.

He'd captured her face, the one she saw in the mirrors anyway. He'd put her face on a contorting cloud.

"What does it mean?"

"It's nothing," he said embarrassed. "I try to think what people remind me of. Like Russell Liddle, he reminds me of a dull spike. Mr. McDonnell reminds me of a road. You remind me of a cloud."

"Why?"

"I don't know," he said taking the pad back. "Kinda far away I guess."

The quiet, lazy, spring school days were made perfect since she and David were friends again. She hadn't gone to the park with David after the hearing, but instead they'd all stayed home and played cards, discussing the witch trial they'd all just endured. Eleanor found the time easy and familiar. She allowed herself to laugh and joke. David stayed for dinner and left only after dark when Tabitha had fallen asleep on the couch.

When back in school, David walked Eleanor home every night and went shopping with her on the weekends. He took her to a movie and on a hike. Eleanor braced herself for the conversation, for the questions and accusations, but they never came. He never broached any question that Eleanor feared, never even gave her a chance to open such a conversation.

Then one Saturday late in March, David took Eleanor on a long hike. They followed Carter Creek up the canyon and found a pond of newly hatched tadpoles. "You can eat those you know," Eleanor said, remembering a previous conversation about frogs. "If you're hungry enough."

"I hope we're never that hungry," he said. He rolled up his pants and waded in. He scooped up a handful of the wiggling things and showed them to Eleanor.

"They're neat," he said.

"I think so, too," said Eleanor.

Eleanor waded in beside him and it was only a matter of time before they got in a water fight. Eleanor took the worst of it, but David evened it out by diving in. Laughing and teasing, they climbed out of the pond dripping with spring runoff.

"I know a place," David said. He took Eleanor's hand and led her up the embankment. He followed a half-invisible trail through a tangle. Eleanor could smell deer and raccoon and house cat. Brave house cat.

Suddenly they broke through the brush and into a small round clearing. Tufts of grass were bent down where a deer had slept just the day before. Another trail led to the north, but otherwise it was like a little room with a ceiling open to the warm Wyoming sunshine. David took off his shirt and wrung it out. He hung it on a branch and then they lay on their backs in the grass to watch clouds.

"That one looks like a turtle," he said.

"A turtle eating a snake," she corrected him.

"No, it has a long tongue."

She watched it morph into a blob and then change into a fair approximation of a fish. She remembered Carston's drawing of her and felt uneasy.

"I've been dying to show you this place since I found it," David said.

"It's nice. How did you find it?"

"Honestly? I needed a place to think. I ran out of the house and along the river. I heard some fishermen and ducked into those bushes. Best shortcut I ever took."

"Why'd you need to think?" asked Eleanor, nibbling on a piece of grass shoot. They lay at a narrow angle to each other, their heads inches away, their faces turned to the sky.

"Stuff," he said.

"Okay," she said.

"No, I'll tell you," he said. "I was missing you. That's all."

She left it at that. They lay in the sunshine for an hour, picking out cloud shapes and drying off. Eleanor would identify the sounds in the forest. She didn't know the names of all the birds, but she could tell David what they looked like and some of their habits. David told her about how Wendy had become a real pill, and her mother was overcompensating. "If Dad were home, he'd do better," he said.

"When's he coming back?" Eleanor asked.

"We don't know," he said. "Mom thinks it good that he's gone."

"Why?"

"Money maybe. Maybe stress," he said. "He wasn't happy at home."

Eleanor could sense a melancholy in his voice. He'd tell her more if she asked, but she didn't. Everyone's allowed some secret pain.

"How's your cat?" Eleanor asked instead.

"Odin? How do you know about him?"

"I can smell him on you."

"Hard to keep anything from you," he laughed. "He's great. Do you remember that one-eyed kitten you showed me last fall? It's him. I went back and got him. Nobody seemed to mind."

"Why'd you take him?" Eleanor asked. "There were better kittens."

"No there weren't," he said.

"I mean kittens who have both eyes. Normal."

"Normal's overrated," he said. "I wanted Odin."

"You wanted to prove me wrong, didn't you? Because I said he wouldn't survive."

"Yup," he said without hesitation.

When they were dry, David walked Eleanor home. He took her hand, and Eleanor let him. They walked in comfortable silence, smelling spring blossoms and new grass on the mountain air. On her doorstep, in the failing sun, there was a wonderfully awkward moment when something could have happened but both chickened out.

"I'll see you later," he said. "Don't forget we have a test tomorrow."

"I won't forget," she said. "Bye."

She opened the door and floated inside. Her head swam with impossible possibilities, denials, and fantasies.

She glided into the kitchen looking for her mother. She had so much to tell.

She crashed to earth at the sight of Tabitha sprawled on the bathroom floor.

"Mom!"

Tabitha was unconscious beside the toilet. The bowl was full of blood. Streaks of it ran from the rim, down the floor, and led to her mother's chin. She'd vomited it up.

"Momma," Eleanor howled. "Momma! Wake up. Wake up."

She lifted her mother's shoulders and set her up against the wall. She ran a faucet and washed her face with a moist towel. She couldn't think of what else to do.

"I'm okay, sweetie," her mother rasped. "I just passed out. Never thrown up so much in my life. I must have had some of that stew."

"Momma," Eleanor cried. "Momma."

Eleanor collapsed in her mother's lap and sobbed.

Tabitha opened her eyes to slits and said, "I'm sorry I scared you, cupcake. I'll be okay."

"No, you won't," Eleanor bawled. "You're dying. You're going to die."

"We're all going to die." It was her patent response.

"Don't," she cried.

"It's okay, sweetie. I just passed out. I'm not going anywhere today. Get me to bed and make me some broth. Tell me all about your walk with David."

"I'm going to call the doctor."

"No," her mother said sharply. "You're going to get me to bed, make me some broth, and tell me about your walk with David. That is what you're going to do."

Eleanor watched her mother's face, read her eyes, and then nodded reluctantly. She finished washing Tabitha's face and helped her out of her stained clothes. She helped her into bed and put her under warm blankets.

"This is nice," Tabitha said. "Turn on some music while you're making dinner. Something modern and upbeat."

Eleanor made dinner and turned the music up loud enough to cover her mother's coughing.

Sunday, Eleanor didn't leave her mother's side. It was only with the most strident insistence that she returned to school Monday.

"Honey, if there was something you could do, I'd let you do it," she said. "Go to school. Be with your friends. I'll see you when you get home."

The student body was back. Three students and one teacher had spent time in the hospital, but luckily no one had died.

Eleanor felt her new uneasy status among the returning kids. Naturally, rumors spread like sickness, and soon everyone knew that Eleanor had somehow been involved in the food poisoning scandal.

With David back at her table, her other friends returned; Brian, Midge, and even Aubrey who'd suffered from the stew. Robby Guide stayed away. Barbara Pennon limited her royal visits to a smaller handful of tables, spending most of her time with Russell and his friends, leaving David and Eleanor alone.

As far as the stew incident went, David was an adamant champion of the truth and told everyone how Eleanor had tried to warn people about the bad food. Since Miss Church had been fired, his story was accepted. Even so, there were some who were still mad at Eleanor. They felt that she should have done more to warn them and not just saved her selected favorites from the horror they'd endured. It added to the lexicon of stories and bad rumors about Eleanor Anders.

One afternoon in gym after the other girls had dressed quickly and sped off to class, Eleanor found herself alone with Midge. Midge cleared her throat, once, then twice to get Eleanor's attention.

"Hey, Eleanor, um," she said. "There's this rumor going around that, ah, that ah, that you're a witch."

Eleanor sighed into her locker.

"I don't care about that," Midge said quickly. "I think it's cool. Really, I do. Henry says it's not, but I do. I think it's cool."

"Henry?"

"You met him. He took me to the dance."

Eleanor remembered the full-blood Shoshone, remembered Robby's weird warning, and remembered how he'd watched her dance. In remembering it now, it occurred to Eleanor that he'd been extraordinarily rude to Midge, practically ignoring his date while studying Eleanor.

"What did Henry say?"

"He's a little backwards," Midge said. "He believes all kinds of stuff."

"About witches?"

"Yeah, that's maybe how you can help me," Midge said.

"What? How?"

"Can you cast a love spell on him for me?" she said. "He's hardly talked to me since the dance, and then he only talks about you. You have David, and that's so cool. You don't need two boys. Could you help me? Could you make him love me? Or at least forget you?"

CHAPTER TWENTY-NINE

The plate of stuffed mushrooms was nearly gone. Stephanie Pearce had eaten most of them and started on the mozzarella sticks. She chewed them slowly after dipping them in the heated marinara sauce. The social worker had been there for fifteen minutes and hadn't opened her dossier yet. The food had been meant to placate her, and it appeared to work.

Eleanor sat on the armrest of her mother's chair, and they held hands in a tableau of contented domesticity.

"These are really good," said Stephanie. "Are they homemade?"

"The mushrooms are," said Tabitha. "The mozzarella sticks are from the store."

"Aren't you eating?" she asked.

Eleanor took a mushroom and nibbled it.

"The house looks good," she said. "I like all the light."

"Springtime," said Tabitha. "We're going to put tomatoes in."

"You always have tomatoes."

"This year we think we can put a row or to in the ground. We've been doing pots up until now."

The small talk went on too long. Either the civil servant was stretching the visit to eat more food, or she was gathering the courage to do something unpleasant.

She sipped her pink lemonade and wiped her mouth on a paper napkin.

"How are you feeling, Tabitha?" she asked finally. She clutched her papers and pushed herself back on the sofa. The springs moaned.

"I'm fine," she said.

"You don't look fine," she said without looking up.

It was true. She didn't. After the renaissance, Tabitha had declined swiftly and surely. Since Eleanor had found her on the bathroom floor ten days before, she'd hardly eaten a thing. Her already-thin features had turned skeletal and no amount of makeup could conceal her sunken set eyes, hollow cheeks, or pale gums. Though cheerful, she looked ghastly.

"I've had a cold," she said.

"Uh-huh," Pearce said again to her papers.

"I had it, too," said Eleanor.

"I got a report from Riverton," she said to a faxed document. "You've gone hospice?"

"No," said Tabitha. "I've been taken off the poisons they were giving me, but not hospice."

"The doctors say you won't recover," she said, finally meeting Tabitha's eyes. The social worker's eyes were dark, cold, and certain. They frightened Eleanor.

"No one ever recovers," Tabitha said. "The angel of death hovers over us all, Miss Pearce."

Stephanie glanced at Eleanor. "Maybe we should discuss this alone," she said.

"This concerns my daughter, Miss Pearce. I'll have her here."

"Okay," she said. "The report predicts you don't have much time. Maybe this summer. Probably not."

Eleanor tried to hide the surprise, but the bluntness had caught her off guard. She didn't know this. Summer? It was already April.

"And that's optimistic," she went on. "June probably. He prescribed hospice care and, according to his report, you agreed to it."

"I agreed to consider it," Tabitha said. "I never said I'd leave my house."

"Can you stand?" Pearce asked. "Can I see you walk around the room?"

"This is outrageous," shouted Eleanor. "Who do you think you are?"

"I can," said Tabitha and stood up. She moved slowly and cautiously but got to her feet unaided. She pulled herself erect and pranced around the room, imitating a runway model. Eleanor could sense the pain each step caused her, smell the cancer on her breath, hear it in her bones. Tabitha sat back down and glared at their guest.

"Satisfied?" she asked. Eleanor saw the beads of sweat form under her mother's wig and looked away.

"I'm not the bad guy here," Pearce said. "I'm trying to help."

"I'm fine. Eleanor's fine. Thanks for the visit. See you next month."

The big woman sighed.

"Tabitha, you've lost so much weight," she said.

"You could stand to lose some yourself," Eleanor said, unable to help herself.

"This must be some of that disrespect your English teacher told me about."

"I think you'll find things are fine with Mrs. Hart now," said Tabitha.

Pearce sighed. "It's time to face this," she said. "I'm going to recommend that you be admitted into a top-rate hospice facility. There's a very nice one in Riverton, Willow Canyon Care. It's very nice. Top rate."

Stunned and speechless, they stared at the woman on their sofa. Eleanor felt sick.

"Eleanor would naturally have to be moved to a foster family. Luckily, we have some in Riverton. There are people there who'd love to have her."

"Love to have the money for taking in a foster child, you mean," said Eleanor.

Pearce ignored her. "She could visit all the time."

"I don't want to live in Riverton," Eleanor said. "I don't want to leave my mother. Mom, say something. Tell her this is crap."

"We're doing fine, Miss Pearce. You've no cause to break up our family."

"Tabitha, you're ill. Very ill. Your house looks nice, the snacks are nice, but we both know this is all a façade. You need more care than your daughter can give you. You need full-time care. Even in this little house, I can see that it's a trial for you to move around."

"We're doing fine," said Eleanor. "Didn't you hear her?"

"No, dear, you're not. Tabitha needs care."

"I can give her that," Eleanor cried.

"No, you can't. She needs medical help and she needs a full-time custodian, and you can't leave school to do that, even if you were qualified."

Before Eleanor could protest again, her mother silenced her with a squeeze of her hand.

"It's going to get worse, much worse," Pearce said. "You know this Tabitha. You'll be unable to feed yourself, or dress yourself. Or clean yourself. Do you want to put Eleanor through that?"

"I can help her," Eleanor said softly. "I don't mind."

"Eleanor, I think you can, but it's affecting you. Your grades have steadied, but your school life is tumultuous, to say the least. I have to think that your life in this house has contributed to it."

"Mom, say something," Eleanor pleaded.

"We're doing alright," Tabitha said. "Don't break up our family."

"Is it fair to Eleanor, Tabitha? For as long as you've been here, Eleanor has been caring for you. Don't you think it's time for her to get some of that herself? Don't you think she deserves a chance to be a kid and not a nurse? You can spare her the worst of it now and make things easier for yourself as well. Your insurance and pension will cover the costs. A new start in another town might be just what Eleanor needs. It's time, Tabitha."

"No," whimpered Eleanor. "No. No, no."

After the last syllable trailed away, the three sat in silence a long time. Silent tears left thin trails of black mascara down Tabitha's cheeks.

"My report is due after Easter," Pearce said. "Take the week and discuss it."

"What can we do to change your mind?" Eleanor pleaded. "How can you make us do this?"

The woman sighed, lifted herself up, and collected her things. "Child endangerment," she said. "If we think a household is unfit or damaging for a child, the state can step in and take action."

"Police?"

"Police," she said.

No one walked her to the door.

"Thanks for the snacks," she said. "They were really good."

The silence stretched out long after the little Volkswagen drove away. Tabitha and Eleanor sat together holding hands as if it were the only thing keeping them from dissolving. The sunny room grew bleak and unforgiving to Eleanor. The smell of spices and death mingled into a stench of despair, and when it weighed too heavy, she threw herself into her mother's lap and sobbed.

"You know, cupcake, when I met you, you never cried. You had to learn to do it, remember? You practiced in front of a mirror. It was cute and sad. The first time I saw you really cry was when David missed school that day. It broke my heart. Still does to see it. Please don't cry now, Eleanor. I don't think I can take it."

"What are we going to do?" she said, wiping her face.

"If I were stronger, we'd move away. We'd find a new place with even fewer people to grow up with. But we can't do that. I've failed you, daughter. Stephanie's right. It's going to get bad now, and there's no need to make it worse than it has to be. I should have done more to prepare."

"No, Momma."

"It's happening just as the doctor said. I got better for a

while, then I got worse. It's happening fast, faster than he said it would. In truth, darling, I can barely stand. I hurt all the time. The pills don't work like they used to. I'd get better drugs if I were in a hospital."

"Is that what you want?"

"No. I don't mind the pain. I'd rather be with you. You're the only thing that's kept me alive for years. You save my life every morning. I could have died at the lake, but you saved me."

"You saved me," Eleanor howled.

"Okay, we saved each other, but I was always on borrowed time. I've lived six years longer than I was promised. You know the doctor in Riverton wrote an article about my miraculous longevity last year? He did. He called me a miracle survivor. But the miracle was you. You gave me the strength."

"How can I give you more?"

"You can't. My body betrays me. We gotta face this, cupcake. It's coming."

"I don't want to go to Riverton," she said. "David's here. Don't make me."

"I don't want to go to Riverton either, but maybe it's what's best."

"Do I have to lose both you and David?" she cried.

Tabitha sighed and stroked her daughter's head.

"Honey, I am a foster mother. We did alright."

"Don't make me," Eleanor whimpered. "Please don't make me."

"Okay, sweetie. Nothing's decided yet."

"Pearce said it was."

"Since when do we live as others tell us?"

That made Eleanor feel better. "I could become Midge, maybe. Or Alexi. She's rich," said Eleanor.

"They have people who love them," Tabitha said warily.

"They'd love me," Eleanor said softly.

"No. Please no. Promise me you won't do that," said Tabitha. "Promise me. Promise me, girl." She lifted Eleanor's face up to look in her eyes. "Promise me!"

"I won't," Eleanor said. "I didn't mean it. I'm sorry."

Tabitha pulled her close and hugged her. She rocked her back and forth like she used to when Eleanor was little.

"Okay, cupcake," she said. "Okay."

They rocked together a long while. It comforted both of them, but Eleanor had lied. She knew her promise was only as good as her ability to deny her nature. Survival would trump everything. It always had. She'd fall into the Old Ways. She was what she was, regardless of what Tabitha had taught her, wanted to be, or thought she was. It was simple instinct.

"Go see Celeste again," Tabitha said. "She's far away. Give yourself some time."

"Okay," Eleanor said.

"And if it happens, cupcake, go to Riverton. Survive."

"I will, Momma."

Tabitha's arms released her only when she fell asleep. Eleanor stayed on her lap, still as a lizard watching a hawk. She knew she would not let herself be taken to Riverton. She wouldn't lose both her mother and her friend. She'd lied to her mother, but that was the least of her troubles.

CHAPTER THIRTY

"Why do you keep staring at me? Buzz off, twerp."
Eleanor hadn't realized she was staring at Barbara Pennon, but wasn't surprised to see she was. She turned back to her locker and rearranged a box of tissue on the top shelf before scanning the hallway again.

Bryce was a little smaller than she. Eric was about her size. Becoming him would be quick and relatively painless. She dismissed the idea though. She liked being a girl.

She slammed her locker door and leaned her head against the cool steel. What was she doing? What was she thinking? Hadn't she been taught better than this? Didn't she promise?

She sized up everyone she met, compared their masses, calculated the calories she'd need, examined the details of their lives and situations, and then, horrifically, she'd catch herself planning their murder. She slapped herself hard across the face. Anyone else might have bruised, but Eleanor was left with only a red mark, and even that was gone in an hour. She stared at her face, her borrowed face, in her bathroom mirror and watched the finger lines disappear like high clouds in sunshine.

She couldn't concentrate. Sitting at her desk, she'd suddenly hear a bell, look up, and realize the class was done. She'd be unable to remember a single thing that had been done or said the entire hour. She'd gather her things, leave the room, and stop in the hall, not knowing where she had to go next.

At lunch she was such bad company that her friends took forkfuls of potatoes off her plate without her noticing.

"You going to eat all that?" asked David, giggling.

"What?" Eleanor said.

"Your potatoes. They're getting cold."

She looked down, saw they were gone, and said, "I already did."

The table broke into laughter that startled Eleanor. David finally had to let her in on the joke. He wasn't laughing.

Walking her home the day before Easter break, David finally said. "Eleanor, you don't have to tell me what's bugging you, but if you want to talk, I'll listen."

"It's that obvious," she said.

"Only to anyone with eyes," he said.

"You wouldn't understand," she said and regretted saying it immediately. "It's complicated."

"Is it about your mother?" he asked.

"Yes, part of it."

"I haven't seen her in weeks. Is she doing poorly?"

She nodded. They walked in silence for a while.

"The social worker told us that we should move to Riverton; Tabitha for hospice care and me to a foster family." Her words hit him like a rock.

"Oh," he said.

"I'm scared," said Eleanor. "I'm scared of what will happen to me. I'm scared of what I will do."

David forced a smile. He was about to say something, something comforting Eleanor was sure, when he suddenly stopped.

"What do you think you'll do?" he said.

"Does Odin love you?" she asked.

"Odin? My cat? Yeah, I think he loves me."

"Why does he love you?"

"Because I'm so lovable," he said with a grin.

"You take care of him, right? That's all. You give him something he needs and so he seems to love you. But do you know that if he were big enough, he'd eat you? That's what animals do."

David didn't answer. Eleanor listened to the crunching gravel beneath their feet and the passing trucks behind them on the highway. She'd thought many times about stowing away on one of those trucks. She could do it, disappear and become someone else, somewhere else. Maybe she'd have the sense to be an adult next time, not a stupid, hormone-wracked, teenage girl in the middle of nowhere. An adult who'd stopped growing.

"You're not an animal," David said.

"What do you think I am?"

The question hung in the air a long time. The gravel cracked, the trucks boomed, and Eleanor felt the weight of David's research weighing him down. Had he formulated a theory? Did he suspect? Did he know? Had he allowed himself to believe? Then why was he here with her?

"We're all animals," he said. "Maybe all love is based on need fulfillment. I don't know. Odin loves me because I feed him. He loves me more than Wendy because I don't pull his tail. He loves me for my soft pillow, ear scratches, and a clean litter-box. I don't think he'd eat me."

"You didn't answer my question," Eleanor said.

"You're complicated," he said after a pause. "You are many things. You're a girl, a friend, a daughter, a student, and a mystery. You can be many things, too. One day you're going to be a driver, a college graduate, wife, mother—whatever you want. Whatever you are right now, you won't be in a second. Everyone changes every second."

"If you took Odin to Riverton, do you think he'd find his way home to you, or do you think he'd find someone else to love?"

"I see what you're doing," he said. "We'd still be friends if you move. I never stopped being your friend when I was away. I hope you didn't."

"They'll put me in a foster home with people who'll only put up with me because they get paid every month to do it. They won't love me. Not like Tabitha."

"They'll learn to love you," he said, but his voice was unhappy.

"Do you think we could still be friends if I looked different?" she said. The question caused him to shorten his pace.

"Yeah, of course," he said. "I like you. I'd like you with blue hair or in a wheelchair. What kind of friend would I be if I let that get in the way?"

They walked a while.

"You know what I think?" David said. "I think most problems are really not worth worrying about. It sucks the life out of you. It's been my experience that most things, the vast majority of them, no matter how big and scary they may look, work themselves out."

"Good advice, but naïve."

"No. It just takes trust."

"I don't have a lot of that," she admitted.

"I know you don't, but you have enough," he said. "Once my dad told me that he never feels so alive as when he's in combat." David's voice sounded far away and lonely. "He said that knowing he could be dead at any moment makes everything clear. Puts things in perspective. That's when he knows he worries too much."

"That's survival instinct," Eleanor said sadly. "It transcends morals. Kill or be killed."

"I don't think that's what he meant," David said.

"It was."

Eleanor had hoped that talking to David would ease her mind, but it hadn't. She felt like an animal running up a blind canyon. She wasn't cornered yet, but she was about to be. What would she do then? What would she be then?

She felt like a fool letting herself be trapped. It was because she'd trusted Tabitha so long and so much. She saw a chain of events from the campground, and the moose, to Tabitha by the lake, Jamesford, and David. She asked herself why she'd done it.

Thanks to Tabitha, she'd learned math and Shakespeare, but what good were those things to her kind? Her mother, her real mother would have shown her how to survive. She'd have taught her how to hunt, how to mimic. How to kill. Kill or be killed, that was the rule. Her kind were parasites. She'd learned the word in science class and learned to despise it like any sensible human being. But she was not a human being. She was a monster parasite feeding off other people's lives.

Did David know the skinwalker legends? He must. He'd read Sirking's book. He knew the tales of the witch who took the shape of a dead human being. Had he figured out that the skinwalker was usually responsible for the death? Sikring hadn't said it outright in his book, but he had suggested it.

"This is not my real body," she remembered her mother telling her. The Navajo words were birdlike. "Yours too is not your own."

"Sure it is," she'd said.

"No, it's a copy. When you get older, you'll have to find another. This one came from me. Soon it will stop growing and you'll need to find another. I will show you how. You are skinwalker."

She never got the chance.

Wounded and sore, her hair singed from the burning hut, she happened upon a dead coyote by the road. She ate from it and copied it. She stayed the coyote for years. She never aged. Never scarred. Bullets were expelled from her skin. Her tail grew back when a wolf ripped it off. Given time and food, she could heal from anything, becoming, in the end, exactly what she'd been before. She was a living reset button.

She'd been six-year-old Celeste for two years until people started commenting on her lack of physical development. Tabitha and Eleanor had searched for the little girl she'd met in Yellowstone, and thanks to Eleanor's memory, they tracked the family through their license plates to a small Nebraska town. That summer Tabitha took Eleanor on vacation. They stalked the family for a week until eight-year-old Celeste was allowed to go into a bathroom alone. Eleanor, hood pulled over her head, followed her inside. When she came out of the stall, Eleanor took off the hood and faced the girl.

Celeste was bemused and not scared. She looked at the image of herself two years younger. Cautiously, like a cat moving to pounce on a bird, Eleanor moved close to the wide-eyed girl. Still slowly, but ready to strike like an adder if need be, she leaned forward and kissed Celeste on the cheek.

She pulled back and saw the girl was smiling. It was a wonderful game to her.

"Who are you?" she asked.

"I am you," said Eleanor. Then she bolted from the bathroom before she could speak another word.

That night Tabitha stayed up with Eleanor in their motel room. She ordered a half-dozen pizzas and still had to go out for more food. Eleanor wept from the pain as her body bent and buckled and stretched and morphed into its new shape. It took hours. She wasn't very good at it. She knew it could be done faster, better, with less pain, but every part of her resisted it, and she felt like she had to convince each and every cell in her body to release its hold and be reworked. It was laborious.

By morning, Eleanor had finished. From her toes to her head, she was Celeste Batton at eight years old. She'd even managed to exactly replicate the hair style she'd seen her wear and the scar on her hand she didn't even remember seeing.

Tabitha had bought Eleanor all new clothes and they stayed away from Jamesford for another month to complete the illusion of a sudden and dramatic growth spurt.

Since then Eleanor had gone to Nebraska every summer to find Celeste, the last one on her own, stowed away on eastbound trucks.

It had become routine. Like a vampire, she'd approach Celeste's farmhouse at night and steal up to her window. She'd find it unlocked. She'd enter silently on bare feet and stand over the sleeping girl. She'd lean over to kiss Celeste, to taste her, to draw the pattern from the girl. Inevitably, Celeste would wake up like a Disney Princess and kiss her back.

"You've come back," she'd say. "I knew you would."

"I've got to be a secret," Eleanor would say. "They wouldn't understand."

Celeste would nod, staring into her own face for a long time without saying a word. She'd hold Eleanor's hand and feel it rumble and shake, Eleanor already beginning the change.

"I have to go," she'd say. "Be well."

"You too, other me."

Regular visits to Celeste had allowed Eleanor to live in plain sight of people. Her kind usually lived on the outskirts of society, but Tabitha had planted her right in the middle of a town.

Eleanor Anders was an average girl in a high-risk family. Eleanor Anders would surely be moved to a foster home if her mother died, and probably even if she didn't. If Eleanor Anders were to vanish, there would be a search. She was known to everyone, liked by some, and loved by two. There would be a search, but it would not last long. After a month or so, she'd be forgotten like a passing cloud.

David would recover over time. He'd mourn unnecessarily for a monster. One day he'd meet her again, but she would look different. Maybe very different. She wondered if he could love her again if she did not look like the mirror of a Nebraska girl? Would he recognize her if she looked like Crystal, Aubrey, or Barbara? Would he understand? Could he forgive her? Would she want him to?

"I wish I didn't love you," she said under her breath. It stopped David cold.

"I love you, too, Eleanor," he said. "And I'm not sad about it at all."

"You may be," she said.

CHAPTER THIRTY-ONE

Eleanor sat with Tabitha all day on Good Friday and slept the night in her mother's bed. It was a tight fit, but Eleanor wouldn't think of leaving. Tabitha took pain tablets at twice the rate the doctor prescribed and was unable to get herself to the bathroom unaided. She mostly slept, waking up suddenly at times and looking around the room as if newborn and frightened. Eleanor would soothe her mother, put her arms around her until she found her bearings.

"It's such a nice day, cupcake. You should go outside and play," she'd say before falling asleep again.

Eleanor stayed in the bed so as not to jostle Tabitha out of her fitful sleep. Her muscles stiffened and ached. She listened to her mother's labored breathing, smelled the death in it, large and certain. Color faded from her mother's hands until Eleanor thought she could see bones beneath the skin like through wax paper.

Eleanor didn't cry. She thought and worried and waited. Mostly she waited. She didn't know what she waited for—for death most likely, but also she waited because she had trust in David. He had said problems work themselves out, and not to worry. So Eleanor tried not to worry and waited instead for things to work themselves out as promised.

At dawn on Easter Sunday, Tabitha shook Eleanor awake with her cold thin hands.

"Cupcake," she said. "Happy Easter." Tabitha looked joyful. It made Eleanor smile, and she kissed her mother good morning.

"Happy Easter, Mom," she said. "Should I make us some eggs?"

"No," she said. "Open the drapes, and let's watch the sun come up."

She got up and threw open the curtains. Tangerine light filled the room. The sky was clear and bright; azure heavens grew out of the darkness touched by the orange rays.

"It's beautiful," Tabitha said.

She sat up in her bed and pulled Eleanor beside her. Arm in arm, they watched the Easter sunrise together.

"I feel like some ice cream," Tabitha said. "How about you go get us some."

"What kind?" she asked.

"Cookie dough," she said. It was Eleanor's favorite.

"Okay," said Eleanor. "If the grocery is closed, I'll go to the truck stop."

"Take your time," she said, her voice cracking with emotion. "Enjoy the day. Enjoy every day."

Eleanor knew then.

Her insides turned inside out and emptied. The vacuum inside her gasped for air. She was suddenly cold. She stopped in the doorway and looked at her mother.

Tabitha pulled a melancholy smile across her tired lips. Her eyes glistened in the sunlight, moist and sorrowful.

"Momma?"

"Sorry, cupcake," her mother said softly. "Go," she said. "Get two spoons." Then she turned to face the light and closed her eyes. She lifted her chin to feel the warmth caress her face. She turned her head as if listening to music, a slow, wandering, silent waltz.

Eleanor watched for a while then found her jacket and left.

A block away she ducked into an abandoned lot and hid behind a pile of old mattresses and tires. She fell onto her knees and covered her face. She burst into tears and sobbed until she could not breathe. Gasping and dizzy, she fell over and curled herself up as small as she could be. She cried like it was prayer, as if she could buy a favor from the universe if only she could shed enough tears. She cried like she had not cried for fifty years. She cried as she had for her lost family and tasted the same tears today as she had then, when she had lost everything but her life. It was cold comfort then and also on this day.

She lay there and cried until she could cry no more. She felt her puffy face with her fingers and imagined she looked like a raspberry. She laughed despite herself. The sun was well high when she found her feet again and staggered home.

Tabitha was dead. She lay just as Eleanor had left her, her face toward the window, her hands on her lap. She knew what had happened. Death wanted solitude. She'd seen creatures leave their dens, abandon their families, herds, or packs and crawl away wounded and bloody to find a place to die alone. It was instinct.

Eleanor sat in her mother's room all Easter and watched

the sunshine move across the walls of the little room until she sat lost and alone in the darkness. She didn't cry anymore. She waited and watched the terrible stillness which had been her most cherished thing in the world. Her thoughts went to the woman who had brought her out of the wilderness, who had loved her like her own child, monster that she was.

It was not until the small hours of night, when the moonlight filled the room with blue memories of the morning's dawn, that Eleanor began to think of what to do next. She pondered the question until Monday morning when she heard the school bus pass by the house. It didn't even slow down to look for her.

At eleven o'clock, the phone rang. Eleanor knew who it would be. She answered it.

"Hello," she said in Tabitha's raspy voice.

"This is Jamesford High School. Eleanor Anders didn't arrive at school today."

"She's staying home," she said. "Possibly all week. Please make a note of it."

"Will do, Mrs. Anders. Good-bye."

Eleanor hung up and took a shower. She smelled of tire rubber, mouse droppings, and tears. She put on heavy work clothes, the ones she used for gardening. Out back, she found a pick and shovel from the shed and opened a grave in their tomato garden. By the time school let out and Eleanor heard the bus pass going the other way, she had laid the last spadeful of earth over her beloved Tabitha.

She'd wrapped her in her bed sheets, sewed her into them as sailors did. She was shocked at how light her mother's body was. She'd carried her into their backyard and carefully placed her in the hole, bending her knees into a fetal position, which Eleanor thought was right and proper. She took a long moment to look in the shallow hole, at the strange sheeted specter within it. Then she covered it in soil.

Nothing was just going to just work out. Why did she trust so much? It was stupid, and painful, and she was a fool to keep doing it. It had cost her parents their lives, cost her this agony and uncertainty. She was stupid, and she was lost, and she was afraid.

She went into the house, numb and tired. She collapsed in a chair and fell asleep.

When she woke, the room was lit in dusk-yellow sunshine. She woke knowing instantly where she was and what had happened. And also, what she was going to do.

She took off her clothes, and after checking that all the doors were locked and lights put out, she went into the bathroom and latched the door.

She had her mother's taste in her mouth. Up in the soft palate above her throat, in a pocket that she didn't think others possessed, was the taste of her mother, a memory, a map. She absorbed it from the pocket.

A sudden jolt, like an electric shock down her throat, sent her to the floor convulsing in tremors. She screamed from the pain. Her body was on fire, the change had begun. Tabitha was taller but much lighter than Eleanor. So much to rearrange. This would not be as painful as Dwight, she thought, but it was not going to be a summer Celeste visit either. Her bones extended, broke, healed, and snapped again. She threw herself in the bathtub and ran a cool shower to absorb the heat pouring out of her body like blood from an open wound.

She jumped out once, twice, three times to use the toilet as her body excluded unnecessary mass and reshaped the rest.

Her fresh young skin sloughed off in sheets like a shedding snake, and she broke it up with her toes until it could slide down the drain. The bath tub ran red and black with blood. She stifled her screams and gritted her teeth and tried to find something in her monstrous transformation to be happy about. She could not.

She tried to embrace the monster she was. She searched for someone who'd done this to her, who'd led her to believe she could be happy, lied to her, betrayed her, abandoned her. Someone she could strike out at. But she had only herself to blame. Tabitha had been nothing but love, and stupid Eleanor, stupid whatever-her-real-name-was, had let herself be seduced by it. And now Eleanor was dead, as surely as the withered husk buried in the garden, Eleanor Anders was dead. There was no going back.

By morning, it was over. Eleanor found herself asleep under a cold shower and moved to shut off the water. Reaching across her body caused an immediate shot of pain like a wall of hot needles. Her new shape was sore and stiff. When she finally turned the water off, she sat back and waited for the pain to cease. It didn't.

She rolled out of the bathtub and on to the floor. Pain stabbed at her from the inside. She screamed. It was Tabitha's scream. It was a sound she never heard because her mother had never faced this suffering without her pills as she did now. Eleanor-become-Tabitha writhed on the floor wracked in agony, every bone, every joint, every muscle, and every organ in her body dying in a hellish cancer. She could only scream and then she laughed, catching her breath between screams—she laughed.

She was Tabitha dying of cancer. It was a new hell. She

knew it would not kill her. Her cells, her monster cells, would not let it progress to that end. This could not kill her. Instead it would hold her in limbo at the very edge of destruction. It was constant, painful suffering, torment, forever teetering at the limits of endurance. Her body resetting the disease and then her healthy cells in perpetual battle every minute of her life. The only comfort she found was in thinking that this frail body would be easier to kill than her last one. Perhaps a cold could overcome her suddenly and finish her miserable life. Or maybe a terrible fall, so massive that her copy cells would not be able to save her.

She crawled to Tabitha's bedroom, her bedroom now, and found her mother's pill bottles on the nightstand. She pulled one down and looked at the label, but her eyes could not for the throbbing in her head and their long degeneration. At the end, Tabitha had been nearly blind and had kept it from Eleanor.

She concentrated. She felt her eyeballs pull and contort in her head until she could see enough to read the label and saw it was the right bottle. She took twice what was directed and pulled herself onto the bed to wait for them to work.

In thirty minutes, she could breathe normally. In an hour, she could stand. With effort, she might be able to learn to work around the illness. She'd made her eyes into something else. Tabitha couldn't see, but she'd been able to reform her eyes, if only for a while, and use them. The same thing might work on her legs. She began practicing and planning.

CHAPTER THIRTY-TWO

It didn't come easy. Without a direct need, her body was content to remain as it was. Sudden emergencies could make it happen, or stress, when survival depended upon it, or when that unknowable primitive part of her took control, like at the prom or the bookstore. Five days after Tabitha died, she'd made little progress. She could walk a half-dozen steps before the pain, even through the narcotic tablets, drove her to a chair. She visualized her muscles strengthening, found she could will blood to them, make them firm up, but when she lost focus, her body snapped back to its frail copy like a released rubber band.

David called every day. Tabitha answered and told him that Eleanor was busy, and she'd call him back. When she didn't, he grew more insistent.

"Mrs. Anders, I just want to know she's okay."

"She's fine, David. Just leave her alone."

"Can I just say hello? I might be able to help."

"No, David. She doesn't want to talk to anyone. Please leave her alone. You're making things worse."

"What things?"

"Good-bye, David."

What could she tell him? She didn't have answers. Eleanor couldn't come to the phone. It was as simple as that. Eleanor was gone.

She practiced applying makeup in the mirror until her arms shook from the strain. She was running out of pain killers and had cut back to make them stretch another week. No limit had been placed on the refills, but she didn't feel up to getting them.

On May Day, she walked to the mailbox and retrieved two weeks of bills, coupon flyers, and a pink enveloped addressed to Eleanor. She took the bills to the kitchen table and scribbled checks in her broken handwriting. The rest she threw in the garbage.

After missing two weeks of school, Mr. Curtz called personally about Eleanor.

"She's in danger of failing her classes," he explained.

"Eleanor is out of town visiting a sick aunt," Tabitha said. "I'm sure she can catch up."

"She left you alone?"

"I'm feeling much better," she said.

"That's good news." He spoke as if he knew more about her condition than he should. She immediately suspected Stephanie Pearce, the big mouthed social worker.

"She might not be back for a while," she said. "What are her options? Will she have to retake the grade?" It was something a mother would ask.

"No, but a semester of summer school might be needed."

"Will that be necessary?" she asked, putting a challenge into her voice.

Mr. Curtz hesitated then said, "We'll look at it when she gets back. When will that be?"

"Soon, I hope."

When David's calls grew more desperate, she used the same story on him. Hearing his voice upset her. She had to stay focused. So she lied to him to give herself a chance.

When Stephanie Pearce called on Monday, she did not have to lie. Pearce didn't ask about Eleanor or even about Tabitha's health. She was quick and to the point. "I'll be by on Thursday," she said. "See you then."

The house was neglected. Unable to move easily, she'd let it fall to pieces. It was dusty and dirty and she hadn't been up in the loft since Easter, not that there was any threat of Pearce looking up there. The kitchen smelled of canned tuna, rotten apples, and garbage. The garden was overgrown with uncut grass. The front flowerbed was untended and thick with weeds.

It was time. She was out of food anyway and nearly out of painkillers. If she didn't act now, she'd lose the opportunity. The day before Pearce's scheduled visit, Tabitha took triple pain medication, put on her best clothes and spent an hour finessing her makeup with unsteady hands. There were two driving services that operated in Jamesford during tourist season, and she called one for a ride.

She didn't know the driver, but was pleased that he knew the location of the social support building. She sat in the back seat, clutching her handbag and looking out a window. Jamesford was aglow in tulips and tree blossoms. Early vacationers rode rented horses down the dusty roads to the art galleries to show off their new Stetson hats and designer boots. The air was warm, fragrant, and clean.

She waited in the foyer of the former hardware store turned civil offices. Her visit was unscheduled. Stephanie was in the office but tied up on a conference call for another quarter hour. Tabitha told the receptionist she'd wait.

A Native American woman with a babe in her arms stared at her across the waiting room. Tabitha smiled in polite greeting, but the woman didn't react. The woman's other child, a four-year-old boy, played with blocks in the corner and ignored her.

"Mrs. Anders," Stephanie said. "I'm surprised to see you here."

Tabitha got up and offered Pearce her hand as she'd done countless times before. "I was in the neighborhood. I thought I could save you a visit tomorrow."

She led Tabitha to her office and shut the door.

"How'd you get here?" the social worker asked.

"I got a ride," she answered cheerfully. "I was out shopping."

"Where's Eleanor?" she asked.

Tabitha knew she had to be careful.

"She's moping at home," she said.

"Mr. Curtz said she was out of town."

"Only for a little while," she said. "She's back now, just not ready to go back to school. She wonders what's the point."

"She has to go to school," Pearce said.

"I know, but she thinks you're going to ship her off to a new one."

Pearce sighed. "Yes, I'm afraid that's true. I have a family in Riverton who're ready to take her. I was going to tell both of you tomorrow."

"When?"

She studied Tabitha appraisingly. "Actually, I thought you'd be anxious for the care center by now."

"As you can see, I'm not," she said and smiled, hoping her gums had some color in them.

"It's good to see you up and about, but we're past this," Pearce said. "Willow Canyon has a place opening up Monday. I've already made the arrangements."

She was shocked. "Five days?" she said.

"And the McNamara's are anxious to meet Eleanor. They have a boy just a little older than her. In fact they have three other kids. Eleanor will have a family of new siblings."

"Same day?"

"Naturally. It's all arranged."

"Couldn't she stay in Jamesford?" Tabitha asked. "She wants to stay here and be with her friends. She wants to attend school here. Can't she be here?"

"Honestly, Tabitha. I don't think that would be such a good idea. Eleanor needs a fresh start. She needs it emotionally and socially. This is a small town. She should get out and try new things."

"Did you even look in Jamesford?"

"There was no need. We have no foster families here," she said. "And if we did, I don't think they'd take Eleanor. I'm sorry, Tabitha, but Eleanor's troubled past haunts her."

"Rumors. We're damned by rumors." Her voice broke, and she was overcome with a coughing fit. The pills were wearing off, and she felt death in her body.

"But look at me. I'm getting around."

Pearce was unmoved. "It's all for the best," she said. "Don't be afraid of change."

Tabitha laughed, a dark meaningful laugh that made Stephanie pull back in her chair.

"Put your things in order," she said. "Don't make it harder on Eleanor. We don't need a scene."

Tabitha cleared her throat only to bring on another fit. Stephanie got up and fetched her a cup of water. Tabitha took the cup and sipped it. When she stopped coughing, she crushed the cup and let if fall to the floor.

"Mrs. Anders," Pearce said sympathetically.

Tabitha looked at her and shook her head. "I tried," she said. She got up as if in a trance and walked out of the office and into the street.

Every movement hurt. Every step shot pain up her back and into her skull like a flaming rocket. The water in her stomach threatened to come up. Her eyes were blurred and she was tired enough to die.

That was it then. The last hope for Eleanor. Gone.

She passed the drug store without going inside. Her pills were waiting there, but she didn't need them anymore. She had enough for the day. That's all she'd need.

At the grocery, she loaded a cart with milk, ice cream, pork roasts, steaks, Pop-Tarts, vitamins, and the dregs of the Easter candy. She bought three gallons of stove fuel and a stove she didn't need.

At the checkout, the cashier was unable to give Tabitha the three hundred dollars she wanted to withdraw using her debit card. A sweaty manager was summoned to deal with the situation. Tabitha produced her bank card and identification. She stared them down while the manager compared the healthy face in the picture to the dreadful visage before them asking for money.

"Don't be a fool, Mr. Woods. You know that's Tabitha Anders." It was Karen Venn. She walked from behind the customer service desk and took the cards from the manager's hands. "Sorry, Tabitha," she said, handing them back to her.

"We don't usually allow this much," Mr. Woods said. "Fifty is usually as high as we go."

"I need three hundred," Tabitha said coldly.

"I guess we can oblige," he said. "Miss Venn, can you see to it?"

Tabitha paid for her groceries with her state food card and then followed Karen to another counter.

"Going on a trip?" she asked.

"Something like that."

"How's Eleanor?"

"Fine," she said curtly, making it clear she wasn't in the mood for conversation.

She counted the money for Tabitha, who scooped it into her pocket. She pulled a business card from her purse and slid it across the counter.

"Could you call this number for me?" she said. "It's a ride service."

"Of course," she said.

Tabitha left the card in the store. It was another thing she no longer needed.

She sat on a bench in front of the store, waiting for the car to take her home. She remembered the driver. He was a scruffy, freckled man in his late twenties, a son of the pioneers who'd run cattle here and cut the trees for the railroad. He'd be invisible in most Wyoming towns. He'd do.

She heard the patter of footsteps because she was listening. Tabitha's senses were dull from disease, but the creature that was her now needed them and so they came. If she listened, she could hear; if she looked, she would see. The first day's pain of reforming her eyes was a distant memory. When tired, unfocused, and uncaring, they'd blunt, but when alert, when hunting, she was sensitive as she'd ever been. Her body might betray her, but her senses did not.

David rounded the corner of the grocery at a sprint. He caught sight of Tabitha sitting on the bench and hurried over. The hired car pulled into the parking lot. She stood up.

"Mrs. Anders," he said out of breath. "How are you?"

"I'm fine, David," she said, waving for the car.

"How's Eleanor?" he said.

She looked at him, memorizing his tired, expectant face, knowing it was the last time she'd see it.

"Forget her, David," she said. "She's a cloud."

The car pulled in front of the store and popped the trunk.

"It's my birthday Saturday," he said. "Mrs. Anders, all I want for my birthday is to see your daughter. Can you please get her to come?"

"Don't get your hopes up," she said.

"I miss her," he said miserably. "I want to see her again. It's my birthday. We're having cake and everything. Tell her to come."

"She's gone, David." The driver closed the groceries in the trunk and opened the door for her.

"Then bring her back," he pleaded. "At least for my birthday."

She got in the car and closed the door. David stared at her through the window.

"Home?" the driver asked.

"Home," she said.

CHAPTER THIRTY-THREE

The smell of the white gasoline masked the smell of dirty clothes, tuna cans, garbage, and sick. She sat on the sofa, looking at three cans of it on her coffee table. One was open, the lid beside a box of wood matches.

She felt old. She wore a body close to her actual age and as worn as she was. She wore it like a shroud, feeling the cancer wriggle and kill cells inside her one by one, only to be healed to die again.

Her big plan, the flash of brilliance she had staggering out of Pearce's office, was to disappear in ashes, leave a tragic mystery behind her—Tabitha and Eleanor Anders burned up in flames. It seemed fitting. It was a stupid idea, but it was the only one she had. Like her life with Tabitha, like her dreams of assimilation, the house had been consumed by its own ignorant energies. The question had only been whether she could remain inside while the fire took the house, ending her worries once and for all.

She knew she couldn't do it. Her instinct would kick in and shoot her out a window like a bullet. If there was one thing she knew she was, knew she couldn't change, it was her instinct to survive. She leaned forward and twisted the cap on the gasoline. It was making her dizzy.

The driver had accepted a peck on the cheek for his help getting the groceries to the porch. He'd offered to carry them to the kitchen, but she waited until he left before opening the door and dragging them inside. She ran her tongue down the roof of her mouth and tasted him.

She didn't look forward to the change. Tabitha had been right. Whatever else she was, she was a female. Though she could be male, it was never a comfortable fit. She reminded herself it would be temporary. Just until she figured something else out.

Already the memory of her old shape was fading out of her cells. She could feel it slipping away like a bright but dimming memory. She held it now, but she knew that if she changed into the driver from Tabitha's wrecked and poisoned body, Eleanor would be pushed out and lost to her. She'd need to get another sample from Nebraska to go back.

But there was no going back. Everything was ruined.

She'd need clothes. Nothing in the house would fit. She doubted Dwight's bloody shirt and pants would work. She'd buried them last fall in the yard by the shed. They'd be tatters by now. That meant another excursion. She looked at the gas cans and reconsidered her original plan.

The easiest solution would be to call the driver back, invite him in, take his clothes, and burn his body with the house. She could drive now. Her only firm A of the semester was in driver's education. She could take the car and be to Cheyenne or Pierre before anyone identified the body.

"No," she said aloud in her dead mother's voice. "Be better than that."

She lifted her hand against the rays of evening light seeping through a crack in the curtains, and gazed at her flesh, looking through it like an x-ray. This body was ruined. How had Tabitha endured such pain, such betrayal for so long? Bringing her arm down, she was taken by a terrible and merciful thought. She was glad Tabitha was dead. Grateful she was free of this.

And so should she be.

There was no use in being Tabitha any more. Her last hope to remain in Jamesford was gone. Pearce had refused her simple request to look for a local family to foster Eleanor. There was nothing to be done. The decision was made. For Eleanor's own good, she had to be relocated away from the gossipy meanness of Jamesford.

There was some logic to it, she realized. It was a good idea to get away from here. It was populated with bullies who'd never let her live a peaceful day again. Why did she want to stay here now that Tabitha, her champion, was gone? For the same reason she'd stayed here before, she realized. This was where she was loved, but now it was David that confused her and not Tabitha.

It was over. There was no time. She had the weekend. Monday morning, Pearce would come to take them to Riverton forever. But there was no one to take. Tabitha was gone. Eleanor was gone. All gone.

She stood up and removed her clothes. She let them fall in a clump on the floor. Naked, she went into the kitchen for a bag of chocolate Easter candy. With a mouthful of sugar she ran a warm bath. It would help. She'd be adding mass and that meant she'd be cold—endothermic.

The driver was called Nicholas Parker, and he had acne

scars on his chin and a red mustache. She had no clothes for him, but she couldn't bear Tabitha's cancer another minute. And, she thought, there was David's party. She climbed into the tub.

Eleanor spent Thursday cleaning the house. She didn't think that Pearce would keep her appointment, but just in case, she didn't want to run the risk of losing the few hours she still had. It felt right to clean. She washed Tabitha's sheets, vacuumed every inch, dusted every surface. She even washed the windows where the sun had shown for the last time on her mother.

She took special care in the bathroom. There was a musk there that couldn't be easily identified or explained. Not that she expected visitors, but one never knew. Pearce could drop by any time. It would be her luck that she would now.

If she did, Tabitha was out visiting friends, saying good-bye and wrapping up affairs. If she insisted on waiting, Eleanor would patiently sit with her and wait her out. Eleanor knew patience.

But Stephanie Pearce never materialized on Thursday and Eleanor watched the sunset from her porch, eating a cold PopTart and drinking a glass of iced tea. She watched the high evening clouds turn from white to orange to black, and then disappear against the deep velvet sky. When she went back in the house, she felt complete. It was the feeling she had when she'd put the last details on a long essay or finalized an experiment in science class. It was a sense of accomplishment and conclusion.

She'd come to a peace with Jamesford, Tabitha, and even David. Though she'd been happy here with her mother, all things end. It was not necessarily a bad thing. Tabitha's words after the prom echoed in her thinking: "If you could go back, would you? Taking it all or leaving it all? Would you trade that away?" Again her answer was no. And so she was resigned to her last few hours in Wyoming.

She lost the driver's sample but she wasn't worried. As Eleanor, she could visit Cowboy Bob's unnoticed and get another easily enough.

On Friday, Eleanor shopped. She bought men's Levis, a shirt, a pair of work boots, and a belt, just in case she'd misguessed the pants' size. The woman at the secondhand store raised an eyebrow but didn't pry.

Eleanor put the clothes in a neat pile beside the bathroom and took meat out of the freezer to thaw. She'd cook it all up after David's party and by Sunday morning she'd be gone.

She planted tomatoes on Tabitha's body and was glad she'd decided not to burn the house down. It would be unjust to her memory. Besides, it would rob her of a day if people started to look for her Sunday.

Friday night, she watched a mystery before bed. Twice she caught herself looking for Tabitha to share her suspicions.

Saturday, Eleanor woke up as Eleanor for the last time in her house. She got up, made her bed, and went downstairs to shower before leisurely eating a big breakfast of eggs, bacon, and toast. After she dressed, she brushed her hair and was on the road by ten.

She arrived at the trailer park half an hour later. She walked straight to the Venn's mobile home and up the wooden porch to their door. Before she could knock, she saw the pink invitation taped to the door. She remembered the pink envelope she'd thrown away with the bills and kicked herself. The party was not here. It was at the City Park from ten to one with lunch.

She backtracked through town before crossing the highway and heading to the park. It was nearly eleven thirty when she finally saw the party gazebo. She was dirty and windblown. Her hair was a mess, and she was dust and sweat from head to toe.

"Eleanor!" Wendy said across the grass. Karen watched her from behind a smoking barbecue. Eleanor could smell hamburgers and beef franks but didn't see David.

"Where is everyone?" she asked.

"Oh, they're playing Frisbee. Just the big kids. I wasn't allowed. Now you're here we can play." She pulled Eleanor by the arm.

"I need a bathroom first," she said.

Wendy pointed to a building beside a baseball diamond, and Eleanor dashed inside before anyone else saw her. She heard shouts and laughter coming from the Frisbee game and recognized most of the voices.

Eleanor washed her face with water and towels. She combed her hair with her fingers and straightened her blouse. She put on her headband to tame her hair and show her face. Only when she felt presentable did she go out.

"Eleanor!"

She jumped.

David sprang at her from where he'd been leaning against the fence with Wendy. "Eleanor, you've come!"

He ran to her and threw his arms around her, picking her up and spinning her. Over his shoulder, she caught sight of

Karen surrounded by teenagers at the grill. Everyone was looking at them.

David dropped her on her feet but kept his hands on her. He held her shoulders while he looked at her, as if he were afraid she'd vanish if he blinked or let go for an instant.

"Eleanor, I've missed you."

"I've been distracted," she said, her voice not coming easily.

"I know," he said. "They're sending you to Riverton. It's so unfair."

"You know?"

He nodded. "Small town. How's your mother. Did she tell you I saw her?"

Eleanor looked away. "I'm hungry."

"We have hot dogs and hamagers!" cried Wendy, pulling Eleanor by the hand. David let go and followed them to the gazebo.

Brian, Eric, Jennifer, and Aubrey greeted her warmly. Midge stood beside Henry Creek, who, with Robby Guide, held back and watched her from a back table. Barbara Pennon watched her from the other side no less maliciously.

"Glad you could make it, Eleanor," Mrs. Venn said handing her a plate. "Do you want a cheeseburger or a hot dog?"

"Both," she said.

"Don't eat too much," said Barbara, sidling up beside David. She threaded her arm into the nook of his elbow before he knew she was there. "That's real Oregon Cheese. Very fatty. It'll go right to your hips."

David extricated himself from Barbara, but not before Eleanor took her plate and sat down by Aubrey.

"Where have you been?" she said. "You've gotta have so much homework. What's going on?"

"I had a sick aunt in Shoshone Falls," she said.

"Where?"

"I mean Sioux Falls," she said. She could feel the Indians staring at her. It raised the hair on her neck.

"Hey, Eleanor, are the burgers okay or should we chuck 'em?" It was Brian Weaver.

"If Miss Church didn't make them, they should be fine," she said. He laughed.

"So Sioux Falls," Barbara said. "I thought it was Riverton."

"Her aunt is in Sioux Falls," said Aubrey.

"Oh," said Barbara. "Riverton is next week. Foster family, right? Share a room in a trailer or do you get the couch?"

The group fell silent. Barbara kept her eyes on Eleanor. Eleanor met them.

"What's wrong with living in a trailer?" asked David.

"Nothing. Nothing at all," Barbara said innocently.

"We'll have cake after lunch, and then you kids can play some more," said Mrs. Venn.

"And presents!" shouted Wendy.

"Yes, presents," her mother said.

"Oh," said Eleanor. "Oh no. I didn't get you anything."

"Yes, you did," said David. "You're here. That's all I really wanted."

"It's not much," she said.

"I'll be the judge of that."

"Open mine now, David," said Barbara, handing him a blue box.

"After cake," he said.

"Suit yourself." She sat by Bryce and pouted.

Midge got a soda from the ice chest and sat next to Eleanor.

"Good to see you again, Eleanor," she said quietly. "I was afraid I wouldn't see you again before you left."

"How's Henry?"

"The same," she said.

"I'm sorry," Eleanor said. "Things will be better when I'm gone."

"But I don't want you to go.," There was a tear in her eye.

"Midge?" Eleanor said. "Are you crying?"

The big girl turned away. "You're my friend," she said. "I'll miss you when you go."

"I'll miss you, too," Eleanor said softly, and then she was suddenly engulfed in Midge's arms.

"I'm sorry you have to go to a foster home. I'm sorry your mother's sick. It's all so sad. You're a good person. You deserve better."

Eleanor reached around Midge and hugged her back.

When they broke apart, everyone was watching them.

"This is a birthday, for crying out loud," said Brian. "Not a funeral. Let us eat cake!"

The boys began chanting "Let us eat cake" and everyone picked it up and stomped their feet until Karen lit the candles.

They sang the traditional song and what they lacked in melody and pitch, they made up for in volume. Wendy held her hands over her ears.

David leaned over the cake and took a deep breath.

"Make a wish!" Wendy yelled.

He winked at Eleanor. She blushed. He blew out sixteen red and white candles in a single puff. Everyone applauded.

Midge elbowed Eleanor in the ribs and winked at her. She regretted the headband. She could not hide her crimson checks behind her bangs.

Karen and Aubrey cut cake while Eric took requests for ice cream flavors. The wind had stopped and the air was warm and bright. Eleanor could smell apple blossoms from a distant orchard, the lingering barbecue from town, and the ever-present diesel of the highway. They were all smells of home.

"Vanilla and chocolate ice cream?" commented Barbara on Eleanor's plate. "You must have quite the metabolism."

"I do," she said.

A silver car drove up the curb, over the sidewalk, across the grass, and to the gazebo. Ten feet from the grill, it stopped and honked three short toots. Everyone looked.

"Is there a David Venn here?" a man called, stepping out the car. He smiled broadly and walked up.

"David Venn?" he said to Brian.

"Over there," he said. David stepped up.

"I'm David Venn."

"This, my dear boy, is for you," said the man. He dropped a set of keys into David's hand. "Happy sixteenth birthday from your father overseas," he said.

"What?" said Karen. "There must be some mistake."

"He said you'd say that," the man said. Karen pulled him aside. The teenagers rushed to see the car. David watched them astonished.

"It's a Mercedes," Midge said to Eleanor. "That's a nice car."

David glanced at Eleanor and then his mother talking to the salesman. Then he wandered over to see the car himself.

Eleanor followed slowly but focused her senses on Karen.

"Nine thousand dollars?" she said, almost crying.

"I knocked it down to eight," the man said. "A vet and all."

"Where did he get that kind of money?"

"You're asking the wrong guy."

"He's only sixteen," she argued.

"Lucky kid," he said. Another car pulled up and honked. "That's my ride. Here's my card. If you ever need a quality used car, I'm your guy."

"You've got to take it back," she said. "We don't have eight thousand dollars."

"It's paid for. If you don't like it, sell it," he said. "Come see me. I'll give you a good price."

"You've got to see this, Eleanor," said Aubrey. "It's practically new." She ushered her to the car.

It wasn't new. It was five years old, had twenty thousand miles, and looked as far out of place in a Wyoming country park as a tie on a horse. Barbara glowed in admiration. Everyone congratulated David. "It was pretty cool," they all agreed.

Karen watched the excitement from a distance, chewing her lip. Everyone wanted to be the first to take a ride.

"Can we, Mom?" asked David. "Can we go for a drive?"

"After the party," she said. "We still have cake and other presents."

It was hard for David to concentrate on the other presents and no one seemed to blame him as he ripped through the papers as fast as his mother would let him. Barbara gave him a new Stetson hat. It wasn't cheap. Brian had given him tickets to a concert in Cheyenne in July that caused almost as much jealousy as the silver E320 parked on the grass.

When all the gifts were opened and everyone had had all the cake they wanted, Mrs. Venn relented and let David take three people at a time for short drives around the park.

"Five minutes," she commanded. "And be careful."

David opened the door for Eleanor, but she shook her head. "I'll go later," she said. Barbara was already in the passenger seat anyway. Two more piled in the back seat, and David pulled the car into the lot and then cruised away.

Mrs. Venn watched them go and then set about cleaning the gazebo. Eleanor helped.

"Thanks," she said. "We don't get our twenty dollar deposit back if we leave it dirty."

She watched the car return and shook her head as a new crowd piled in for a ride.

"That's a really nice car," Eleanor said.

"Damn fool thing," she muttered then seemed to realize that Eleanor was right there.

"How's your mother?" she said. "I saw her Thursday. She looked better."

"Thanks, ma'am," Eleanor said, walking away. Mrs. Venn didn't notice she'd ducked the question or that she left.

Finally everyone had had a ride but Eleanor.

"I don't want to," she said. "I've got to get home."

"You didn't give me a birthday present," David said.

"I'm sorry," she said, ashamed.

"For my birthday you have to go for a ride with me," he said. "A long ride. Say, to the top of Wild River Canyon."

David looked to his mother. Her arms were crossed tight against her chest. She looked at Eleanor and said, "Well, I guess it's alright. But it's up to Eleanor. The party's over now anyway. The little-leaguers will be here any second."

"Well, Eleanor?" he asked. "What do you say?"

CHAPTER THIRTY-FOUR

"Your mom wasn't pleased with the car," Eleanor said. David was ecstatic. He drove smoothly out of Jamesford, heading north up the highway. He knew a lot about cars and told Eleanor about the turbo and automotive computer technology. She couldn't share his excitement, but she was glad for him. It was a very nice car. Very nice.

"She's just jealous because it's nicer than hers," David said.

"Why did your father give it to you?" she asked.

"What, don't you think I deserve it?"

"That's not what I meant. It's so expensive."

"It's used. It wasn't so bad," David said defensively.

The canyon road was narrow and winding. It ran through evergreen pine forests that suddenly broke into broad grasslands and crumbling cliffs. It followed a fast-running river swollen with mountain runoff.

"I guess it is a little showy," David said after a while.

"It's nice," Eleanor said. "It's really nice."

"I'll need a car," he said distractedly. "I'll be driving a lot to Riverton."

Eleanor rolled down her window and let in the cool forest air.

"This thing has a great heater," David said and turned knobs on the console. He then rolled down all the windows and let the wind gust through the car while heat blew on their legs. He dug in his backpack and found a sleeved CD. He slid it into the dash and turned it up loud enough so they could hear it over the gale.

"This is the one I made for prom," he said.

David drummed the steering wheel and sang along.

"Angels made these arms and legs, Take me as I am. This is how the world has made me, Love me as I am."

It dazzled her senses. Hot-cold, music-wind, happy-sad. Eleanor closed her eyes and leaned her head out the window and absorbed it all, knowing this moment would be forever cherished.

David leaned over and crooned on Eleanor's shoulder. She laughed and let herself be drawn into the song.

"I'm on the right track, baby. I was born to survive!" she sang.

They let the music and wind speak for them as they drove.

At the top of the canyon was a picnic overlook from where the entire valley could be seen. It was deserted when David pulled the silver car to a stop, and they got out.

"Sure is beautiful," Eleanor said, sitting on a picnic table. "I'm going to miss it."

"You'll only be down in Riverton," David said. "I'll visit you all the time. Every weekend. I promise."

"I don't think I'm going," Eleanor said.

"Barbara said they were taking you Monday."

"She should mind her own business."

"She's not so bad," David said. "Was she right?"

"She's awful," Eleanor said. "But she's not wrong. I'll be gone by Monday."

"By Monday? You mean you might go sooner?"

She nodded.

"You're running away," he said flatly.

She nodded again. "I have to. I have no family."

"Tabitha will be down there. Are you going to leave her?"

"Tabitha doesn't need me anymore. I won't be sent to a foster family."

"It might not be so bad," he said.

"Could you live with people who didn't know you? Who didn't love you?" she said.

David slumped dejectedly. It was his birthday, and she was hurting him.

"I'm sorry," she said. "Let's not talk about it."

"I'll come with you," he said. "I have a car. We can go tonight."

"Don't be stupid, David. I'm not your problem. It's not even funny for you to say that."

"You asked if I could live in a house where no one knows me or loves me? Well, I have. You want to know why my Dad gave me this car? Because he feels guilty about how terrible he is to me all the time. Because he's never there, and when he is, he's nobody you want to know, let alone love. I don't know him. None of us do. He doesn't know us. You know why he's back in Afghanistan? To get away from us. He hates us. He hates me. And I hate him right back."

The bitterness startled Eleanor. David shook in rage.

"David," Eleanor said. "I didn't know."

"I'd hear them fight. For years, I'd hear them fight. They'd say the most horrible things to each other. And you know what I did? I hid under my bed and pretended I was with you. Side by side, we were coyotes eating frogs. It kept me sane. When my dad took a belt to me, I'd tell myself that I'd get away and find you. You were there just outside the house, waiting for me."

Eleanor stared at him. He wiped his nose on his sleeve.

"Eleanor," he said. "I've known you my entire life. I've felt drawn to you from the moment I met you. My mom says I don't know what love is, but she's one to talk. What I feel for you is overpowering. I want to help you. I want to protect you. I can't bear to be away from you. I'll do whatever it takes."

"David, you don't know who I am. What I am," she said.

"Yes, I do," he said. "I know more than you think I do."

Eleanor paused. "Don't believe rumors," she murmured.

"Give me credit, Eleanor. I'm not a dummy. I know who you are. I'd know you anywhere."

Speechless, she could only stare.

"I would go with you," he said. "I owe you that much."

"You owe me nothing. It was your imagination," she said.

"Russell would have hurt me bad. Wendy too, probably."

"I had nothing to do—"

"Don't lie to me!" he shouted. "Not now. Please, not you, not now." His eyes held her in hard command.

"Okay," she said softly.

He looked away. "Look at me boobing away on my birthday. What I must look like."

She scooted beside him and put her arm around his shoulders.

"You're confusing me," she said.

He slid his arm around her waist. "You're freezing," he said.

"I don't feel cold much. Not really. It's genetic."

He took his red school jacket off and draped it around her. She took it gratefully.

"You keep that jacket," he said.

"Thanks." She buried her face in the collar. She loved the smell of it.

"Everything is confused," he said and touched his forehead to hers. "It always has been. Everything except one thing."

"What's that?" she whispered, feeling his warm skin on her face.

"I love you."

He turned his head and their noses touched. He ran his cheek against hers. She inhaled his tears, felt his heat. A sudden vertigo seized her. She was light as a cloud, and when he bent in close to kiss her, she kissed him right back.

Nothing in Eleanor's experience had prepared her for the quickening of that moment. Her skin blazed as if sunburned. Her ears were deafened from the drumming in her chest. Her tongue darted and played with his and savored it. She'd tasted many things, kissed other men, kissed her father, her brother, and family, but nothing had ever been like this. It was chemical. It was electric. It was magical, Pop Rocks, and dreaming. She was drunk.

When they pulled apart, Eleanor had no sense of time. She fell over and rolled on her back laughing wildly like a tickled baby.

David fell beside her. "Oh, wow," he moaned. "Oh, wow." He was out of breath, too.

She couldn't tell how long they lay on their backs staring at the sky before a camper pulled into the overlook and disgorged a pack of pent-up children into their moment.

David turned on his side to face Eleanor.

"Wow," he whispered.

"Wow," she agreed.

Eleanor's body was still tingling when they got back in the car and drove down the canyon.

David watched the road and stole glances at Eleanor on every straight-away. His grin was so broad and constant, Eleanor wondered if his cheeks hurt. Hers certainly did.

When they got in sight of the highway cutoff, Eleanor's heart jumped. A semi roared by, heading north, the direction Eleanor had decided to take the next morning.

"What should I do, David?" she asked.

"It'll all work out," he said, but the words dampened his smile.

"I can't live with strangers," she said. "I can't. It's impossible."

Another truck rumbled past.

"I'll go with you," he said.

"I can't let you do that," she said.

"Let me decide," he said. A car behind them honked for David to pull into traffic.

David glanced in his mirror and pointed the car to Jamesford.

"I need time to think," Eleanor said as the first evening lights of their little town appeared on the horizon. "I need another plan."

"What does Tabitha think?" he said. "They can't just break up a family. Not if she's well."

Eleanor sighed.

"She's not well is she?" he said.

"Take me home," she said.

"It'll be okay," he said, more to himself than to her.

He drove the new, silver car into town and slowly meandered the dirt side roads to Eleanor's house, lengthening the drive as much as he could.

They turned onto Eleanor's block as the last rays of the evening sun faded behind them.

"Oh no," David said.

Startled from her woolgathering, Eleanor looked at her house.

Three police cars were parked in front. An ambulance had its red and blue lights flashing. Stephanie Pearce's Volkswagen was parked in against the curb. The social worker stood on her porch and talked to Sheriff Hannon. Someone had draped a blanket around her shoulders as if she were in shock. The Sheriff consulted a notepad and asked questions. Pearce nodded agreeably.

"Stop the car!" Eleanor yelled.

David slammed on the brakes. The heavy car slid on the crackling gravel and stopped crossways in the road.

"I've got to get out of here," Eleanor shrieked and reached for the door handle.

"Where are you going? It's got to be your mother. Don't you want to see? Where are you going?"

She ripped at her seatbelt and finally found the button release. She tumbled out the open door and into the road.

"Eleanor, what's wrong?"

She scampered behind the car and watched the house. It was too far to hear, even for her excited ears. The message, however, was unmistakable: she had no more time in Jamesford.

As a policeman stretched yellow tape around her fence she saw a medic in white clothes appear at the garden gate. He and another led a steel gurney out from the back yard. On it Eleanor saw a black plastic sack the size and shape of her dead mother.

Eleanor ran.

CHAPTER THIRTY-FIVE

Eleanor hid in a hay barn on the Grizzly's Dude Ranch for two days. She slept in a hollow place under a pyramid of hay bales and made herself wait. Every fiber of her being told her to run. To keep going. To never return. Now. Go now. While she still could. Every fiber, that is, except one. The memory of David's kiss.

Her resolve vanished. She'd come to peace with leaving him. She'd gone to the party thinking that would be her farewell. Perhaps one day, she imagined, they would find each other again, many years from now, and they'd be friends again as before. But after that kiss, after her entire body reacted to the chemistry, she hesitated and considered other options.

Survival was paramount. It would override anything her human mind would concoct. She could still run, could force herself to hide in the forest, find a suitable animal and disappear completely. She might even be able to recall the coyote, but wasn't confident enough to try. What if she couldn't recall it properly? What kind of horrible mutant thing might she become? Would she have the strength and resources to change back?

On the third day, ranchers took a half-dozen bales off her pyramid and loaded them into a pickup truck. She overheard them talking about an overnight ride up the canyon with the "California Group." Eleanor watched them go and then crept out of the barn and across the fence to the tree line. She followed the fence around the ranch until she was behind the guest cabins. It was about noon when she found the right one.

She crept to a cabin and peeked in a window. It was a little two-room hut, not completely unlike her own now-forever-lost home back in Jamesford. One room was a bathroom; the rest was all open. Seeing no one, she pulled off the window screen, slid the window open, and crawled inside.

She went straight for the kitchen. It had a sink and a mini fridge with a single cabinet for dishes and coffee. She'd smelled food inside this cabin and found a box of powdered doughnuts in the pantry. She took these along with a can of coffee, a bag of trail mix, and some chewing gum. She chugged a quart of half-and-half in front of the fridge before inspecting the clothes the tourists left behind. Nothing was suitable. There were men and women's clothes, but they were all very large. She settled for a pair of sandals that could be sized down and a Dodger's cap that smelled like sunscreen. She left the way she came and bolted into the forest.

The plan was desperate and fitting. It would take two changes but both were not so different from herself. Regardless, she'd endure the pain. She had to. This would let her survive and remain.

She followed a seasonal stream up the canyon for several miles until she found a natural dam above a fallen tree. The stump had left a cavity in the bank. The spring runoff had eaten away most of the bottom, but the top still hung over, held together by grass roots.

She took off her clothes and hid her things in the cave. She leaned over the water and looked at her face. She stared at her reflection for a long time, memorizing the face that had been hers but had never been hers.

She listened to the forest to be sure she was alone, and then waded into the stream. The water was frigid but she didn't mind. She lay in the shallows, half submerged, and watched passing clouds through the tree canopy. She ran her tongue over the roof of her mouth and felt the familiar shudder. She closed her eyes and let it happen.

At eight o'clock, David Venn walked alone into his family's trailer park. He kept to the side of the gravel road, walking on the grass in case a car came by, or he needed to run.

He smelled the cooking meals from two dozen mobile homes. He was hungry and felt weak. A neighbor waved to him from the other side. He was a big man in a red apron cooking burgers on a charcoal grill. David waved back and then slid his hands into his jacket pockets.

Two trailers before his, he left the road and walked the backyards. There were no fences between the lots, or rather pads. Though some people had put up plastic slides or dog runs, it was all common property between the back fence and the homes. David found that route unpopulated and private.

He slowed and listened before approaching his trailer. He heard voices within, and placed them in the front room, in the kitchen. He smelled macaroni and cheese and heated frozen fish sticks. He slipped behind the propane tank and waited. When he was sure no one was watching, he snuck to the side of the trailer, pried up the skirt, and slid into the crawl space.

Once out of sight, he unbuttoned his pants and kicked off his sandals. His feet were sore and blistered from the long walk, but the jeans had almost killed him. He put them on wet in the stream, and they'd stretched just enough to pull on, but if he'd had to run in them, he'd probably have cut himself in half.

He wiggled the pants to his knees and then kicked them off entirely. He used his jacket as a pillow, settled down, and tried to rest. Nothing to do until the morning but wait. He was safe here.

He listened to the sounds above him, the scrape of dishes, low conversation, a television turned low.

"So you're not going to talk to anyone anymore, David? That's not very mature." It was Karen talking.

"I've got nothing more to say," he said.

"So is she coming back or not?" Wendy asked.

"No, honey," said Karen. "She did a bad thing."

"No, she didn't!" yelled David. "And she is coming back."

"Then why did she run away?"

"Because she was scared of people like you, Mom," David said bitterly. "Because of shortsighted people like you, who always see the worst and don't wait for explanations. Because she knew her mother was dead, and she knew she'd get the blame, and she knew no one would help her." He was out of breath.

"I'd help her," said Wendy. "She's nice."

"David, it's not worth getting upset over," Karen said. "She's gone."

"If she comes back, what then? Are you going to help her? I sure as hell am."

"David Venn, watch your language."

"She didn't do anything," David said. "She was afraid. Can't you see that?"

"Yes, David, we can all understand that. I'm sure when she's found, the police will get to the bottom of this and everything will be fine. She's just a little confused. She'll get the help she needs."

"So you think she's insane, is that it?" David's voice was shrill again.

Wendy started to cry.

"Now look what you've done. You've made your sister cry. You've scared her."

"I'll call Sheriff Hannon and lock her up. It's illegal to be scared in Jamesford, don't you know?"

"David. You're being unreasonable. You know Eleanor is a troubled girl. Everyone does. How can you be so dense? Remember Halloween?"

"Oh, yes, I remember. Do you? Do you remember when your children were nearly killed by hooded thugs?"

"I meant Eleanor at the truck stop. Those rumors."

"Rumors! That's what I'm talking about. Anyway, let's assume for a second that your vicious slander is correct. Have you asked yourself why she did it?" He paused. "How about to save me and Wendy?"

"You're overreacting. You were never in real danger."

"Arghhhh!" David screamed. From under the trailer, David heard the sound of breaking plates.

"David!" Karen shouted. "Go to your room this instant. I won't have any more of you tonight. You are a trial. I wish your father was here to teach you some respect."

"No," he said. "I'm leaving. I'm going to go to look for her again. Give me my keys."

The sound of the slap was clear and crisp. There was a moment's hesitation and then Wendy howled. But David knew it had not been she who was struck.

After a long time where only Wendy's cries could be heard, David recognized the sound of footsteps going into his room. He expected a slammed door, but it closed gently.

Wendy continued to cry and Karen picked her up and paced the floor with her until she stopped quite a while later.

"It was just a silly fight," Karen told Wendy. "Like Mommy and Daddy used to have. Everything's okay. Just loud."

An hour after that, there was a knock on David's door.

"David, can I come in?"

"It's your house," he said.

Karen stepped inside and closed the door.

"What do you want to have happen, David? Best case scenario."

"Best case?"

"Be realistic," she cautioned. "What do you think we can do?"

"She needs a guardian," he said. "She needs someone to look out for her."

"And you think that's you?"

"I mean a legal guardian. I'd be it if I could. I sure as hell will look out for her if I can."

"Language, David."

"Hell, hell, hell, hell, hell," he said. She sighed, but didn't take the bait.

"It's out of our hands, David," she said. "It's never been in our control. She has social workers looking out for her. They know what's best for her. And now? Well, now, she's got a whole new world of troubles to face. She's . . ."

"If you say 'damaged goods' or anything like it, I swear I'll leave tonight."

She sighed. "I wasn't going to say that," she said softly. "Does she really mean that much to you?" she asked. After a long pause when he didn't respond, she asked, "Does she mean more to you than our family? Than me? More than Wendy?"

"You'll do fine without me," he said.

"So will Eleanor," she said.

"But I won't without her," he said.

"You're young," she said dismissively. "Whatever you think you feel now isn't real. It may feel real, but it fades. It dies. It's nothing to ruin your life over."

"Is that spoken from experience?"

She fell silent.

"Mom. Whatever I told you Eleanor meant to me before, times that by a million. I couldn't leave her if I wanted to, and I don't want to."

"But she's gone," she said. "You have to move on."

"I will move on if I have to. I'll move to find her. It's bigger than me, than you, than Wendy, than even this stupid backwater berg you dragged us to."

"You're so naïve," she said sadly. "It doesn't stay this way."

"It didn't for you, but that doesn't mean it won't for me."

She sighed a long heavy sigh. "Let's see what happens," she

said. "Let's give it time. We'll do what we can, okay? I didn't dislike the girl."

"With friends like you," David said.

"Hey, I said I'd do what I can. Okay? Peace?"

David sighed. "Peace," he said. "Can I have my car keys?"

"We can't afford to replace the dishes you broke. How can we afford gas to cruise all night? Do your homework."

The rest of the night passed without conversation. Wendy wished everyone a goodnight and Karen did the same. David stayed up in his room late at his desk and then fell asleep around midnight. Under the house, in the crawlspace, David made plans for the next day, plans that would satisfy everyone. Well, almost everyone.

CHAPTER THIRTY-SIX

David listened to the classroom murmurs over the click of his boots in the hall. School would let out in fifteen minutes. He'd need to be out of the building before then.

He'd had a good breakfast in the Venn's kitchen, cereal, apples, goldfish crackers, and a half gallon of milk. He'd found pants that fit and a pair of hiking boots that didn't blister his feet. Everything was David's. Everything was stolen except the jacket. That had been given to him.

When he got to the right bank of lockers, he slowed down. He knew the number A202. He made sure he was alone and then pressed his nose to the vent and smelled. He matched her smell like a fingerprint—perfume, lotion, shampoo, phero-mones, and sweat. He took the note from his pocket, glanced up and down the hallway again, and then slid it through the vent.

He was about to exit through the side doors when he heard his name called. He kept walking.

"David Venn," said the voice louder. He stopped and turned. It was Mrs. Hart coming from a side hall.

"Yes, Mrs. Hart?" he said glancing at a wall clock. Ten minutes until bell.

"You've been quiet in class," she said. "Is anything wrong?"

"No, ma'am," he said.

"It's that Anders girl, isn't it?" she said.

"What about her?"

"I know you were friends," she said. "It must have come as quite a blow to learn she was a murderer."

David didn't respond.

"Maybe you should see a counselor," she said. "It was a blow to all of us."

"You never liked her," he said.

"Some people just have a sense, I suppose. You didn't think her strange at all?"

"I don't want to discuss this with you," he said.

"You should see the counselor. Mr. Sullivan is very good."

"Are you sleeping with him, too?" he said.

"What did you say?"

He kept silent. A little late he knew.

"You shouldn't believe murderers, Mr. Venn," she said coldly, her arms held sternly on her hips. "I thought you smarter than that. You looking for another suspension?"

"No, ma'am," he said.

"Watch your smart mouth," she said. "Did you change clothes? I thought you were in blue."

"I had gym class," he said.

"Oh. Well, David, don't let this Eleanor thing ruin you. You're a cute boy, smart, and you have a lot of potential. You can do so much better than her."

The bell rang. The clock was wrong.

"I've got to go," he said and left without another word.

He walked quickly from the school grounds and into a neighborhood of bordering houses, and then headed northeast toward Carter Creek Canyon.

Why did he care what people thought of Eleanor? She was gone. Forever gone. But he had to admit Mrs. Hart was right about one thing: there was murder in the air.

Anyone was capable of killing under the right circumstances. They wouldn't be alive if that ability hadn't been passed along to them. It was all a matter of survival. He could do it. He was on his way to do it. It was survival. It was necessary. It was survival.

He felt the cord in his pocket and hurried to the creek.

He'd waited over an hour before he heard her crashing through the undergrowth. The instructions he'd left were clear but she'd missed the trail anyway and struggled through the bushes. For all her country airs, Barbara Pennon was not a good outdoors-woman.

He'd spent the time planning the aftermath. He didn't know the area well, but he knew that few people came here and those who did usually came on the weekend. Even so, he'd have to hide the body quickly and well. There was a construction site on the other end of the woods a quarter mile away. The foundation was dug. They'd pour concrete in a day or two. He'd go there after dark and bury her.

From what he knew, Barbara's family wouldn't be concerned if she came home late. It would hurt, but most likely she'd be home by eleven o'clock or so. She'd be disheveled, confused, and in need of a shower.

"David. Is that you?" she called.

"Yeah, over here," he said. "You miss the trail?"

"I guess so," she said, breaking into the open. She stood

on the opposite bank of a rushing brook. The noise was the reason for the spot. That and its loneliness.

"Sorry it took me so long. I had to ditch Russell. He thinks he owns me."

"Cross over those stones there," he said, pointing. "Skip the fourth one. It's slippery."

She did as he said and hopped from rock to rock, her heeled shoes nearly dumping her in the stream each time. She waved her handbag at the end of her arm for balance and giggled. He caught her as she lunged over the last one. She tumbled into his arms.

"It's noisy here," she said. "We could make lots of noise and no one would hear."

"Yes, I thought of that." He studied her closely, scrutinized her features and her skin. He touched her blond hair. "Do you dye your hair?"

"No," she giggled. He wasn't so sure. She was blonde, but maybe not this blonde.

"Did you call me into these back woods to look at my hair?" She giggled again.

"I want to kiss you," he said.

"Now you want to kiss me?" she said, playing offended. "Now that Eleanor is a wanted fugitive, you want little ol' me?"

"You won't kiss me?"

"I will," she said. "But what about Eleanor?"

"What?" he said surprised. "What about Eleanor?"

"Is it over between you two?"

"There was never anything to end," he said. She looked at him disbelievingly.

"Whatever," she said. "Sure, I'll kiss you. If it's good, I might even let you kiss me again." She leaned forward and planted her lips on his. She wrapped her arms around his neck and drew him to her. She licked and played in his mouth. He let her. He tasted her and stored the sample for later.

She was frenetic and practiced and he didn't like it. There was no electricity in this kiss, no vertigo, no confusion, no excitement. Had there been, he wouldn't have been able to continue. It was for the sake of that energy that he kissed her now and that he was about to do the thing he'd promised Tabitha he wouldn't do. All this was for that energy, the feeling he didn't understand but couldn't leave.

"How was that?" he asked, pulling away from her. He'd had enough. He took a step toward the creek and watched the water rush by.

"You need practice," she teased. "I can help you with that."

David slid his hand into his jacket pocket. His fingers wrapped around the clothesline cord he took from a drawer in the Venn's trailer.

He'd promised Tabitha. He'd loved her and trusted her. He stared at the water, the creek ever-flowing but never the same from moment to moment. All was change; all was beautiful.

He turned and looked at Barbara. She smiled playfully back and then her smile melted when she saw his befuddled brow. He'd hated her, still couldn't stand her, was jealous of her to his core. But he couldn't do this now. He couldn't kill her without killing himself. He'd made a promise he knew he couldn't keep, but he had no urgent need to break it now. This was unnecessary, foolish, and doomed to fail. He'd be Barbara at sixteen for how long before he'd have to do this again? If he killed Barbara, it was only a matter of time before she was really gone. Her friends and family might see her for a year or two but then she'd have to go or answer questions. It was just postponement. Like Eleanor, she'd have to disappear forever, leaving nothing but riddles, heartache, and loss. She understood loss. She didn't like Barbara, but there were those who did. If she did this terrible thing, how was her selfishness any better than the rest of humanity's? How could she ever feel worthy of loving anyone if she allowed herself to do this now? Tabitha was dead. Eleanor was dead. That was enough.

His mind swirled like sooty smoke. He fell to his knees on the bank and stared in the stones. His mind flashed into focus as he saw his reflection in the water. It was unreal to see David looking up at him, staring at him with his own eyes, loving, sympathetic, caring, and forgiving.

"David?" said Barbara. "You alright?"

He drew in a deep clean breath of mountain air, springtime runoff, and wildflowers. Unclenching his fist, letting go of the cord, he got to his feet.

"Barbara," he said. "I can't do this."

"Don't get ahead of yourself, David. I haven't said you could do anything yet. We're just getting started."

"Go home," he said. "Forget this ever happened."

She stared at him dumbstruck.

"Go," he said.

"You've got a lot of nerve, David Venn," she said staring daggers at him. "Who do you—look out!"

The creek had masked his coming. He heard the rush too late. He turned just as Russell Liddle threw a branch across his head.

Barbara screamed. Russell yelled. David hit the ground.

Before the stars had cleared his vision, Russell was across the stream and on top of him. He pounded David's face with his fists. He heard his nose break under Russell's knuckles and yelled.

His scream melded with Barb's, who pushed Russell off him. She tripped and went down beside him.

Adrenaline surged, fight or flight. David rolled over and squatted on his haunches. His vision sharpened through a clear tunnel. Ancient music played in his muscles. He felt change in his hands and legs, a sudden radical realignment of flesh and bone. A terrible pain he noted but didn't feel. It only fed his feral transformation. He growled an unearthly sound.

Russell kicked Barbara away and picked up the tree branch he'd flattened David with before.

"You've had this coming for a year," he snarled. "No big John from your hooker to save you today. You're going to bleed."

David sprang at him. His legs uncoiled like a lunging snake, his arms outstretched, his hands, boney, tough, curled, and clawed. Russell swung the branch and hit him on the left shoulder as he crashed into him and shoved him on his back.

David rolled over and sprang to his feet, ready for another leap. He looked at his hands. They felt as if on fire. While he watched, two fingernails dropped off. Thick, barbed claws grew from his fingertips, gripping, cutting claws like a cat's. A big ancient cat.

One by one each finger stretched and hardened.

"David run!" Barbara screamed.

He'd given Russell time to stand. He held a six inch hunting knife. His shirt was torn. Blood trickled from his chest where he'd been scratched. The next scratch wouldn't be so kind. With David's new hands, he'd tear Russell's flesh open like a bag of potato chips.

Russell closed on David, wide-stanced, ready to duck, dodge, or lunge. He wouldn't be surprised again.

"Run!"

"Shut up!" Russell yelled at Barbara. "I'll deal with you later."

David tasted copper. His nose bled liberally down his face and dripped from his chin.

His hands felt like they were dipped in acid. He thought about them, let the pain approach through his mental fog, and willed the change to stop. He did. Half his fingers were black tipped claws, the others retreated into fingers. He was not an animal. He was greater than his instinct.

Russell lunged at him blade first, and David spun away. The knife caught the sleeve of the jacket and ripped a three inch tear above his elbow.

"Russell, leave him alone. Nothing happened!" screamed Barbara.

"This ain't wholly about you, you know." He spat and circled David, looking for an opening.

David balled his hands into fists. They were rock hard, but they wouldn't expose any organs if he had to use them against Russell. He felt the claws dig into his palms. The pain threatened to re-trigger the change. He stepped back. Russell took a step closer.

Just then Russell noticed his torn shirt and bleeding chest. "Looks like it's a fair fight after all," he said. "You got a knife, too, huh? Looks like a couple. You won't get another chance to use them, though."

David longed to strike, to unleash the thing within him and taste Russell's blood. And then what? Become him?

Sensing his confusion, Russell lunged again, blade first. David reflexively swatted at the attack, redirecting the trajectory away from chest and neck. Russell caromed to his left, but the knife blade caught David's hand and cut it to the bone.

Russell spun around for another go, but paused when he saw the blood squirting from David's hand in heart-beating rhythm. David cradled his injured finger against his chest and stepped backwards.

Barbara screamed. Russell went ashen. Blood pooled on David's jacket from the unstoppered cut.

He felt the claws grow again. Faster than it started, the bleeding ceased. The flesh knitted. Flames licked at every nerve. Laid bare beneath his retreating reason was a buried, ancient and wild, bestial construct, prehistoric, cruel, angry, and hungry. He knew he had only seconds of control before it'd consume him completely. And then Russell would die.

As if in prayer or explanation he muttered only one word, "Tabitha," before he fled into the forest.

CHAPTER THIRTY-SEVEN

He wandered the forest for hours. He was miles away before he stopped at a spring and drank all he could hold. His hands and limbs had returned to David's; by morning his nose would be fine, sooner if he found food. He was hungry, and though it was probably just in his imagination, he felt cold.

His mind was clear and uncluttered. He let it stay that way and let his feet propel him forward as if entranced. He tried not to think about the damage he'd left for David to clean up. He could do nothing right. He was fighting against the inevitable and only making things worse. He'd sleep before making the final decision. With any luck, he'd find a deer to eat and sample. Another coyote or a fox was too much to hope for, at least at first. He was done with people. It was too hard to be among them. Maybe a thousand miles away and fifty years from now, he'd try again, but not now.

The sun slipped low on the horizon, another stolen sunset in Wyoming from a guest who'd long outstayed his welcome. In tree shadow, he followed the creek to the clearing David had shown Eleanor a lifetime before. He'd sleep there, and in the morning, he'd go.

"Eleanor," David said.

He jumped. David, the real David, sat in the clearing facing the path from the creek. He turned to run.

"Eleanor, don't go," he said.

He hesitated, turned slowly around, and looked at him. He studied that familiar countenance and saw nothing but tenderness. He listened, smelled, and searched for others. There was no one.

"Please, Eleanor," he said reaching out his hand. "Sit with me."

He turned away ashamed. He stared at his boots, blood caked from his wounds. The ruined shoes he would not need in the morning.

"I'm sorry," he said. "I'm a disaster."

"Eleanor, sit by me. I have a blanket. You can be warm."

"I'm a thief," he said. "But I am not a killer. Tabitha died of cancer."

"I never doubted that."

"I've got nowhere to go, no one to be. I've stolen from you, and I'm ashamed."

"My boots? Big deal."

"No, dummy," he cried, spinning to face him. "Look at me. I'm a monster. Look what I can do. Look what I took from you. I took you from you."

"You're not me," he said. "You only look like me. You're Eleanor. I'd know you anywhere now. I think I've seen you look different before, haven't I?"

He nodded.

"You were the trucker that saved Wendy and me on Halloween, weren't you?"

He nodded.

"Russell stabbed you, didn't he? Like he did today."

Again, he nodded.

"At the market. Tabitha. That was you, too. I see it now."

"I'm not human."

"I'm not racist," he said.

He laughed.

"Come sit with me," he said. "I have an overwhelming desire to be beside myself."

He laughed again and reluctantly shuffled over. David lifted his arm and wrapped him in a blanket.

"How'd you know to look for me here?"

"Barbara called to see if I was okay."

"She knows you weren't there then," he said miserably. "I'm a disaster."

"I played it cool," he said. "She was very upset. She wasn't taking in information. Don't worry about it. Tell me what happened. I see the nose job. Where'd you get cut?"

He lifted up his left hand and pointed to his thumb.

"You heal quick," he said.

"One of the perks," he said.

"You were going for Barbara weren't you," he asked.

"I couldn't do it," he said. "It seemed so obvious a solution, but then I thought it out and couldn't do it."

"That's good," he said.

"How long have you known?" he asked.

"Since the day you told me in third grade. I said I believed you. I never doubted."

"But all the research you did."

"What about it?"

"It showed me for the monster I am."

"Stop saying that. A monster would have killed Barbara today. You're no monster."

"What am I then?"

"You're a skinwalker," he said without hesitation. "That's the most accurate description I found."

"It's not a pretty name," he said. "It's the name of a monster."

"I don't think so. I think it's cool. A rose by any other name would still smell as sweet."

"Skunk-cabbage," he said, remembering a book he'd read with Tabitha.

After that, they were quiet for a while and watched the light fade.

"I have to leave," he said finally. "In the morning, after I sleep, I have to leave."

"No you don't," he said.

"I've so totally messed up here. I'll try to come back one day. I'll look different. I'll be an adult this time. You know I'm over fifty?"

"That's a little weird," he said. "You look about sixteen."

He laughed.

"Can you be Eleanor again?" he said finally.

"If I want to go to jail. If I want to get caught."

"Will you trust me?" he asked. "I'll make you a deal. If my plan doesn't work, I'll run off with you and we'll start again somewhere else."

"I don't want that," he said. "You've got a great life here. Even with all the crap, you've got a life. You've got a family. I know what that's worth. I won't take that from you. No way. Even if you think it sucks, you've got one. Be glad."

"Stop telling me what I do and do not have," he said. "I want you to trust me. If you can do that, I might have a solution."

"And if it flops, I'll be captured. Eventually, they'll figure out what I am. Then they'll either kill me, which is the tradition, or maybe, if we believe in Hollywood, I'll be studied like a lab rat for the rest of my life. I can't let that happen."

"I won't let them do that," he promised. "If things go south, I'll get you out. If you don't want me to be with you, fine, but I promise I'll get you out. You'll be no worse off than you are now. Trust me."

"I tried to stay," he said softly. "Look what a mess I made. I need to go."

"You made a mess because you tried to do it alone. You're not alone. Eleanor, I've got to say that it's really weird to look at my own face and call you that, but I know who and what you are, and I want to help."

"I don't want to leave," he said.

"Then don't," he said. "Give me a chance."

"I'm really a girl," he said. "I know that much. I don't know what I really look like, but I know I'm a girl."

"Then we need to get you out of that outfit," he said. "I promise not to look."

He put his head on David's shoulders and sighed. "Tell me your plan," he said.

And he did.

Eleanor's old house was wrapped in police tape. The Mercedes cruised around the block twice to make sure it was empty then parked in a neighboring lot.

David and David got out of the car and crossed the field to the back fence. They helped each other over, and then David found the key hidden under a terra-cotta pot holding a withered, dead tomato plant. He tried not to look at the empty grave, but couldn't help himself. He slid the key in the lock and opened the door.

The place had been tossed by the police searching for who knows what. David found a candle in a drawer and lit it. It was the most light he dared show, and even then he kept it in the kitchen at the back of the house.

"They can't explain the body," David whispered. "Tabitha was seen last week. The body looks to have been buried a month ago."

"See," he said. "A disaster."

He was pleased to see all his food still there. The meat he'd left to thaw had gone bad. He tossed it in a garbage bag, sealed it and threw it out. The smell was unpleasant and too strong.

"Just act dumb," he said. "Let it be a mystery. A ghost story. It's perfect."

"You're just loading more rumors onto me," he said, but threw a plate of ham steaks in the microwave to defrost.

"That's the great thing about it. It's so preposterous that when people realize how stupid it is, it'll suck the life out of all the rumors."

"No, it won't. The Shoshone are on to me."

David paused. "Yeah," he said. "You're not wrong there. But this is the twenty-first century. Even they don't buy it completely."

"It hurts, by the way," he said. "The faster I change, the more it hurts. If I take it slowly, I can do it without howling."

"We wouldn't want that," he said. "I'll run you a bath."

"Cold," he said. "It's exothermic, going down in mass."

"Looks like you've already adopted the role of lab-rat."

"That's not funny," he said, taking off his shirt.

"Sorry. Hey, you ruined my jacket."

"You gave it to me."

"Yes, I did. I'll give you another one."

"You need to wear this one again."

"Yeah," he said.

They met in the kitchen while the tub filled.

"So," David said. "I don't think I can do it myself. You've got to hit me."

"Really?"

"Do it quick."

"And the thumb?"

"Do that quicker still."

"No, don't make me."

"Trust me," he said.

The microwave dinged. David turned and took out the meat. When he turned back, David smashed his fist into his nose and dropped him to the floor, the plate crashed down beside him.

"I'm sorry," he said. "I'm so sorry."

"It's okay," he said. "Give me a towel."

After he did, David left the kitchen and climbed to the loft. He came down in a robe with an armful of clothes.

"I don't want you to be here," he said. "I'll cut your thumb but then you leave. You go to the hospital, get it stitched up. Come back in the morning."

"I don't want to leave you," he said.

"It's your turn to trust me," he said. "I'll be here in the morning. Go work on your mom."

David handed him a knife and put his hand on the kitchen cutting block and turned away.

One swipe of the knife and blood poured onto the floor.

"Now get out of here," he said. "That's deep. It's going to hurt a lot."

"Be here in the morning," he said. "Promise me."

"I promise," he said.

David kissed him on the forehead and left through the back door. Even on the forehead, there'd been an energy. Holding the candle and a box of crackers, he climbed in the tub and gritted his teeth.

CHAPTER THIRTY-EIGHT

The flat, late August plains were hidden behind miles of head-high corn stalks. The little Honda sped along the highway on its newly oiled four cylinders. The windows were rolled down, and David fished through the radio channels for something that wasn't country or didn't yell scriptures over his speakers. He finally plugged in his iPod transmitter and tuned the car to a blank station.

Familiar lyrics began. He turned it up.

"Angels made these arms and legs, take me as I am. This is how the world has made me, love me as I am.'"

"Our song," he said.

Eleanor smiled and sang along.

David's plan was simple, elegant, and relied so heavily on extortion as to make it borderline psychotic. The primary victim of his blackmail was Karen Venn.

David called her from the hospital with eight stitches in the thumb. He'd nearly lost it. Once in the car, he gave her the ultimatum. "Eleanor has returned," he said. "I'm going to run away with her unless you help her."

He looked at with her with his bandaged face and steel

eyes and, as he later recounted to Eleanor, he "pulled at every heartstring" he could find.

In the morning, he'd had no sleep, and Karen called in sick. After Wendy was dropped off at her daycare, the two of them drove to Eleanor's house and knocked on the door.

Eleanor answered. She wore a skirt, the only one she owned, light makeup and clean skin.

"She'll do it," David said.

"I said I'd try," responded Karen.

They got in Karen's van and drove to the Jamesford Social Services Building.

While they waited to see Stephanie Pearce, Sheriff Hannon came through the door. The receptionist had tipped him off. Eleanor heard her make the call from the bathroom on her cell phone.

"Miss Anders, I have a few questions," he said.

"You can talk to me with Stephanie," she said matter-of-factly, but kept glancing at a nearby window.

"I think you should come down to the station," he said.

"Let's try it her way," said Karen. "It might make things easier."

He looked at the three of them and shrugged.

"Okay," he said.

In Stephanie Pearce's cramped office, Eleanor told the story. After the mean Stephanie Pearce told her that the state was going to break up her family and ship them away from their friends and support in Jamesford to Riverton, Eleanor had run away. Her mother apparently told people that she was visiting an aunt. There was no aunt. Pearce knew this from her files. Tabitha thought that she'd come back and so tried to buy time.

Eleanor came home at Easter, hungry and tired. That night, promising Eleanor that everything would work out, she died. Eleanor panicked and buried her mother in the yard. She was scared, lonely, and confused.

She got David's birthday invitation and planned to leave after wishing her best friend a happy sixteenth birthday. She kept low before then so no one would make her go to school and draw out the terrible farewells longer than she could endure.

After David's party, she saw the police at her house and ran away again. She didn't want to live with strangers in Riverton. Miss Pearce was so mean.

David convinced her to come back. Karen Venn had offered to be her guardian until she was eighteen. They could use the extra income. It was a perfect solution.

Karen Venn smiled and agreed, but no one took her to be overly enthusiastic.

That was David's plan. When she was done telling her story of woe and misfortune at the hands of the heartless social worker, she cuddled up to Karen, who did her best to welcome her.

"Tabitha visited me a week ago," she said. "She was very much alive."

Eleanor shook her head. "That's impossible." Looking at the sheriff, she said, "What does this mean?"

His look was skeptical and reserved. He hadn't spoken since he sat down. He cleared his throat before saying, "It's a mystery. I don't know what it means."

"Am I under arrest? Do you really think I would kill my own mother?" She made herself cry. It wasn't hard.

"No," he said. "I need to get an official statement, but

forensics puts the time of death in late April, over a month ago. She died from cancer. It fits with your story."

"What about adoption?" interjected David. "Can she live with us? There's no need to make her life more miserable, is there?"

Pearce's face was red. She'd been painted as a complete villain in Eleanor's tale, and her only defense was that a ghost had visited her begging for mercy.

"It's not my decision," she said. "I'll need to talk to people."

"But you'll recommend it, won't you?" said David. "Please?"

"We'll need to look at your living conditions," she said. "There are many factors—"

"I could live at home," said Eleanor. "My home." She'd gone off script then, and David shot her an ugly look.

"I only need a guardian. I can still live in my house. I've practically lived alone for years," she said. "I do all the cleaning, cooking, banking, everything. You can ask around."

"That's a bit much," she said.

"Why?" said Karen hopefully. She hadn't been pleased with the idea of her son and his girlfriend living under the same roof. "It's a great idea. We're practically neighbors."

"That's a stretch," said Hannon.

"You know I'm self-sufficient," said Eleanor. "You know I can handle it."

"I do think you can handle it," the sheriff said. "But it's not my call."

"You can ask Principal Curtz," Eleanor said, playing every card she had. "I bet he'd back me up. Tell him it was my idea."

And he had.

The case was not concluded, but until it was, Karen was given temporary guardianship over Eleanor. And though the court didn't explicitly approve it, she remained at her old house and slept in the loft.

David had sworn to his mother, on pain of everything that she could think of, to be a gentleman.

"As long as I'm your mother, and you're under eighteen, you two are brother and sister. Do you understand?"

They did, and they promised to behave.

"My life is hard enough," she said, driving back from the police station that night. "Please, don't make it any harder."

"I'll try not to," Eleanor said.

Wendy was ecstatic at having a new sister. Eleanor would sleep over at the Venn's on occasion, taking the couch against Karen's offers of letting her sleep in her bed or making a bed in Wendy's room. In the morning, she'd wake them with a big breakfast of eggs and fresh tomatoes.

When Pearce visited that summer, she'd be pleased to find that Eleanor had completed her classwork and wouldn't be held back a year. She didn't ask to see where Eleanor slept in the little trailer; the whole town knew Eleanor lived alone in the little house on Cedar Street. She cautioned them many times that they were on a limb, that the state was watching them and it wouldn't take much for them to step in and remove Eleanor to another home. She made it clear that except for Karen's offer, there wasn't a parent in Jamesford who'd touch her with a stick, and the Riverton family, after reading about the police search for her and the body in her yard, had also declined to take her. The chances of finding a willing foster family this side of Cheyenne was bleak.

They took the threat to heart, and David and Eleanor were perfect citizens. Whenever they went out together, to a movie or to get an ice cream, they took Wendy along as chaperone.

When Eleanor went to her home, David accompanied her, but did not step inside. They'd give no one the opportunity to gossip.

By August, they felt the town had reluctantly accepted the situation. It helped that there'd been three months without drama. David hadn't pressed charges against Russell, which made the Sheriff both surprised and relieved. A knife attack would make the papers, and without a doubt, Eleanor's name would be brought into it and that would stir up the school lunch poisoning thing again, and the dead woman buried in the yard. The town wouldn't like that. It needed tourists, not the FBI.

Barbara visited David a couple of times during the summer. Eleanor did her best to be polite, but when Barbara pressed her chest into David's arm, Eleanor felt a phantom cord in her hand and went inside. David would follow shortly after, flushed and apologetic.

"It's not me doing it," he said.

"I know, Brother," she said.

"Thanks, Sis."

David accompanied Eleanor on her necessary Nebraska trip. Karen wasn't pleased to have them go on a vacation together, but David promised up and down that they'd behave. Eleanor was going to go regardless, and he might as well go to look after her. Karen didn't understand why, but she sensed the stubborn determination they both possessed to make the trip. In the end, there was nothing to do. She gave them a hundred fifty dollars and made them promise to call her every night. They snuck out quietly at night so no one would see them.

David traded the Mercedes for a little Honda and presented a check for the difference to his mom. When David's father called in July, he would not tell his wife where he'd gotten the money for it. Karen took the call in her bedroom, but Eleanor could hear the conversation over Wendy's cartoons. He was calling from Afghanistan, but when she pressed him about the money, he grew angry and nearly hung up the phone. Karen backed down. Eleanor noted that she did not tell him what David had done with the car.

"The Honda is a better car," David said. "This one I can afford to drive. Even to fix. Much better, don't you think?"

"Much," she said.

They limited themselves to one kiss a week. When the time came, they would catch each other's eye. They'd find a secret place and touch their lips, just a peck, a caress. Just enough to be sure that it was still there, to feel that electrical bolt surge through them again, reaffirming the connection, renewing an unspoken vow.

Eleanor pointed to the road that led to the Batton farm. He slowed to look.

"How far's the house?"

"About a quarter mile up the road," she said. "You can park over there. No one would see you on that side road."

"Is she there? Maybe I should drive up and make sure someone's home."

"Maybe," she said.

"I want to see it anyway."

"Let me get out," she said. "They can't see me."

"They won't see you," he said.

"I can't take the chance."

He stopped the car and let her out.

"Okay," he said. "I'll be back here in five minutes."

"I'll be in the corn," she said.

He drove up the lonely road as Eleanor ducked down the embankment and into the corn rows.

She found a sunny place where a tractor had missed its planting and laid down to watch the clouds. Big, fluffy, white ones floated across the bluest sky she had ever seen. She remembered her mothers, all three of them now. She'd been ready to run for months, ever vigilant for the sound of doom, the voice that would crumble the illusion of her life with the Venns. She'd not been more than a pace away from a door or a window since Karen picked her up that fateful morning. Today she allowed herself to relax and absorb the smell of growing crops.

She wondered how Celeste would look tonight. Had she grown her hair out long? Had she colored it? Had she grown fat or thin? How had the year treated her? It was like the day before Christmas, and she was excited to see what she'd get.

ACKNOWLEDGEMENTS

Eleanor first. Let me thank her for this book. She came to me and stayed with me, and through her strength, I persevered. Together we loved, lost, and learned. I know her. I love her. She is my daughter. To Eleanor I am thankful.

On the other side of the page, let me throw a shout out to Christopher Loke at Jolly Fish Press who embraced me and my story with its weirdness and themes, tragedy and hope. Thanks, Chris, for sharing my vision all the way through.

To my family, eternal thanks. Eleanor could not have lived without my patient wife, distracted sons, supportive mother, and proud father, all of whom fed my imaginings and filled me with the courage to write. Love you guys.

A special thanks to Abby who thought she was just a beta-reader but was in fact a model. I embellished and imagined, created and evolved, but the seed of Eleanor can be found in Abby's smile.

And finally thanks to the great lady who shaped my life and love, but fell to the wicked disease. Lolly, I give you life again in Tabitha, I give you another daughter to love, to nurture and make good. I give you also the battle to fight again, heroically and well. Miss you.

JOHNNY WORTHEN graduated with a BA in English and Master's in American studies from the University of Utah. After a series of businesses and adventures, including running his own bakery, Johnny found himself drawn to the only thing he ever wanted to do—write. And write he does. When he's not pounding on his keyboard or attending writers' conferences, Johnny spends his time with his wife and two boys in Sandy, Utah.